REAPER

ABOUT THE AUTHOR

Janet Edwards lives in England and writes science fiction. As a child, she read everything she could get her hands on, including a huge amount of science fiction and fantasy. She studied Maths at Oxford, and went on to suffer years of writing unbearably complicated technical documents before deciding to write something that was fun for a change. She has a husband, a son, a lot of books, and an aversion to housework.

Visit Janet online at her website www.janetedwards.com to see the current list of her books. You can also make sure you don't miss future books by signing up to get an email alert when there's a new release.

ALSO BY JANET EDWARDS

Set in the Hive Future

PERILOUS: Hive Mind A Prequel Novella

TELEPATH

DEFENDER

Set in the Game Future

REAPER

Set in the 25th century Portal Future

SCAVENGER ALLIANCE

Set in the 28th century Portal Future

The Earth Girl trilogy:-

EARTH GIRL

EARTH STAR

EARTH FLIGHT

Related stories:-

EARTH AND FIRE: An Earth Girl Novella

EARTH AND AIR: An Earth Girl Novella

FRONTIER: An Epsilon Sector Novella

EARTH 2788: The Earth Girl Short Stories

HERA 2781: A Military Short Story

CHAPTER ONE

I first met Nathan when I was riding patrol in the body stacks, driving my four-wheeled buggy past rows of identical, dust-covered, white freezer units. For the last four centuries, the population of Earth had been entering those units, leaving their frozen bodies behind them while their minds started a new life in the virtual worlds of Game. The body stacks kept being extended to make space for more of them, so now the vast underground caverns seemed to stretch on into infinity.

I was startled to see another buggy coming towards me. I'd been working twelve-hour shifts in the body stacks for the last year, arriving at the nearest transport stop at 03:00 hours each day, and collecting the buggy from my shift alternate, Delora. From that moment until I returned the buggy to Delora at 15:00 hours, I'd always been totally alone in these caverns.

When the boredom and the loneliness got too much for me, I'd stop my buggy, wipe the accumulated grime from the transparent viewing window of a freezer unit, and spend a few minutes studying the face of the person inside it. I'd look for clues to their personality, and entertain myself by trying to guess which of the two thousand Game worlds their mind was living on now. Were they the type of person who'd enjoy fighting battles on Medieval, taming one of the wild horses of Meadow, or casting spells on Witchcraft?

I must have seen the faces of thousands of frozen Gamers by now, but this was the first time I'd met another human being in the body stacks with a temperature above freezing point. The boy and I both stopped our buggies by the twin pillars that marked the border between Red sector and Green sector, and gazed at each other in silence.

I saw a boy with straight brown hair who was wearing blue overalls and riding a four-wheeled buggy with green flashes on its black body. He would be seeing a girl with wavy brown hair who was wearing blue overalls and riding a buggy with red flashes. Overalls were the cheapest, most practical clothes available. The shapeless things never fitted anyone properly, but only the glitz crowd bothered about what they looked like in real life. For most kids, the important thing was to decide what they wanted to look like when they joined the Game.

"I'm Nathan," said the boy.

"I'm Jex." My brain recovered from the surprise and started working again. I was riding patrol on Red Sector Block 2, rows 25,000 to 50,000. Nathan must be riding patrol on Green Sector Block 2, rows 25,000 to 50,000. We'd probably just missed meeting each other on the border between our sectors a dozen times before today, and now random chance had finally led to us coming face to face.

"It stinks, doesn't it?" said Nathan.

I didn't need to ask what he was talking about. It was 21 April 2519, and the Leebrook Ashton bill had become law barely three weeks earlier. Kids like us were talking about nothing else, and saying it stank was being overly polite in my opinion.

For nearly four centuries, the law had said that you had to be an eighteen-year-old adult to enter Game. Children with critically serious conditions were exempt from that law, allowed to enter Game early if their lives were at stake, but that was a desperate last resort. Everyone knew that entering Game didn't just freeze your body's age, but had implications for mental development too. Those who entered too young would have problems maturing into adulthood.

The original law about having to be adult to enter Game had existed for good reasons, but the Leebrook Ashton bill had cynically taken advantage of it by increasing the age of becoming adult to nineteen. Now kids like me would be classed as children and have to keep working in the real world for a year longer.

My eighteenth birthday was less than a month away now. I'd expected that to be the day when I'd step into a freezer unit and begin my true life in Game. Now the Leebrook Ashton bill had moved that day a year into the future, and I was spitting furious about it.

I was spitting furious, but I was also well aware our buggies monitored everything we did and said. It was unlikely that any of the supervisors would ever bother checking those records, but I still wasn't going to risk mouthing off about injustice.

I settled for meaningfully pointing at my buggy. Nathan gave it a panicky look. I guessed that he hadn't read the bit in his training manual about the buggies monitoring us.

"You're almost eighteen too?" I asked.

"My eighteenth birthday was two days ago," he said, glancing nervously at the buggies.

Nathan had been even more maddeningly close to entering Game than I was when the Leebrook Ashton bill became law. I pulled a sympathetic face at him, and we reached an unspoken agreement and dismounted from our buggies. We shouldn't be stopping work until our mid-shift break, but society had just stolen a year of our lives so neither of us was feeling very dutiful.

We sat down facing each other, me leaning against a red pillar and him against a green. Technically kids like us shouldn't be riding patrol here, since it was an adult rated job, but those adults who used controlled droids to work from inside Game were needed for more important work than this. It wasn't as if anyone was going to want these bodies again. The bodies of players who might want to defrost in future were all kept in short stay facilities. The freezer units in the body stacks only held the players who'd paid their lifetime subscriptions to Game. They had no need to work ever again, their minds were living an immortal, idyllic existence somewhere in the multi-worlds of the Game, and they'd never want to return to the real world.

They'd never want to return, but maintenance of their bodies was included in the lifetime subscription contract, so control systems monitored the freezer units, and kids like me and Nathan rode patrol checking for problems. Most days you found nothing, but there were occasional oddities that the freezer control systems weren't programmed to detect. In the last month, I'd found tree roots projecting through the ceiling, a stream running along an aisle, and a nest of young rabbits.

Whenever I found a problem, I called my supervisor, an adult called Fraser. He would grudgingly reply from in Game, use a controlled droid to come and inspect the issue himself, and then flag maintenance to take appropriate action. Each call earned him another few credits towards his Game subscriptions. I hoped I'd find as easy a job for myself when I entered Game.

"Do you work for Supervisor Fraser too?" I asked.

Nathan shook his head. "Supervisor Laksha is in charge of Green Sector. She's a mermaid on Game world Aqua."

"Fraser's still deciding where to settle down. He's just changed world to Meadow."

Nathan asked the inevitable question that all kids constantly asked each other. "What Game world do you want to live on?"

"I'll be listing Ganymede as my first choice world on my Game application."

I smiled as I thought of the picture of Ganymede on the wall of my room. It showed a typical image of the shimmering spider-silk houses scattered along Ganymede's beaches, with foaming waves crashing onto the sands, and the glory of Jupiter filling the sky. A girl with silver-coloured, feathery hair, and a delicate trail of sapphire-blue flowers across her forehead, was standing in the foreground. That would be me when I was in Game. That would be Jex when I really started to live.

Nathan raised his eyebrows. "That's a very ambitious choice. Ganymede's a popular Game world, with lots of long term players wanting to move there."

That was what everyone said when I told them my plans. The more officious ones would add a lecture about how I could only list three preferred worlds on my application. If I failed to get accepted by any of those, then I'd be automatically allocated to any random world that would accept me, so it was silly to waste one of my preferences on an impossibly optimistic choice.

I gave Nathan my usual answer, but without the withering tone that I used to the kids who lectured me as if I was a total fool. "My father is going to sponsor my Game application. He's been a Ganymede resident for decades, and is a member of their Admission Committee."

"A member of the Admission Committee sponsoring you!" Nathan gave an impressed whistle. "You're very lucky. My mother calls me every few months from Game, but she's never offered to sponsor me for resident status on her world, and I've never heard from my father at all."

I knew that I was incredibly lucky. There was a strict hierarchy among the players in Game, marked by the colour of the bracelets they wore. Resident or visitor applications from players wearing the gold bracelets of lifetime subscription holders always took precedence over those with the silver bracelets of those still paying annual subscriptions. Players with the bronze bracelet of someone in their first year in Game were always last in the queue, so I wouldn't normally be considered for a world like Ganymede, but the sponsorship of a resident always counted strongly in your favour. The sponsorship of a resident who was also a member of the Admission Committee, combined with my spotless Game record, meant I was almost certain to be accepted.

"I'm in contact with my mother too," I said, "though she calls less often than my father. She's a mermaid like Laksha, but on Coral rather than Aqua."

I didn't mention the fact that my mother had offered to sponsor me for resident status on Coral because I knew she'd never actually do it. I'd learnt as a small child that my mother never kept her promises. When my father said he'd call me next week, he'd do it. When my mother said the same thing, the week would drift on into a month or more before she called, and then she'd act as if we'd spoken only a couple of days ago, expecting me to know all about her newest dress, the party she'd just given, and the latest gossip about her friends.

I understood why she was acting this way. Talking to me

brought back unpleasant memories of the year she'd spent in the real world when I was born, and my mother's method of dealing with anything unpleasant was to try to avoid it. She liked to pretend to herself and her friends that she was the perfect parent, calling her daughter at least once a week, but the reality was that she kept contact with me to a bare minimum.

Understanding why she was acting this way didn't stop her behaviour from upsetting me. Thinking about it was upsetting me now, so I tried to forget about her and focus on my conversation with Nathan. "What Game world do you plan to start on?"

"I'm trying to decide between Venture and Gothic," said Nathan. "I'd have been interested in Flamenco as well, but its first language is Spanish. I'd prefer to start in Game on a world that has English as its first language."

I blinked. If I was being ambitious hoping to start in Game on Ganymede, then Nathan was aiming as low as possible with his choices. Flamenco, Venture, and Gothic were three of the Game worlds that had opened the previous year. Flamenco would have already been flooded with applications from Spanish speaking players wanting to move there, but both Venture and Gothic would be desperately trying to build up their numbers of residents. Any new player with a respectable Game record should automatically be offered resident status by them.

It was horribly rude to criticize someone's choice of Game world, so I tried to make my reply as enthusiastic as I could. "The Game images and descriptions of Venture are very tempting. I may list it as my third preference on my application."

"I prefer to apply to a brand new world rather than one that's centuries old," said Nathan. "Venture and Gothic have all the latest advances in worldscape and creature design. The ghosts of Gothic are especially groundbreaking."

He sounded oddly defensive. I wondered if Nathan's strange choice of worlds was because he had a black mark on his Game record. Even something trivial, like a bad behaviour flag from a childhood dormitory supervisor, could be enough to destroy his chances of getting resident status on an established world.

"I'd never considered starting Game on Gothic," I said.

"Everyone advises new players to start Game in a fully human form to ease the transition from real life, and I didn't think there were any human player forms on Gothic."

Nathan laughed. "All the possible player forms on Gothic are fully human when it's daylight. It's a shapeshifter world like Coral and Aqua, with one key difference. The players of Coral and Aqua shapeshift individually from human to merfolk form whenever they enter the water. On Gothic, there's a mass shapeshift of all players triggered by the moon rising in the sky. That's why Gothic has extra-long nights, twelve hours instead of the standard two hours on most Game worlds, so everyone gets to spend plenty of time in their vampire, skeleton, werewolf or ghost forms."

I frowned. "Surely starting Game as a shapeshifter would be even more confusing than being non-human all the time. My mother was a dryad on Nature for three years before she moved to Coral, and she still found it difficult to adjust to transforming between being a human with legs and a mermaid with a tail."

Nathan sighed. "You're right. Shapeshifting is very disorienting, some players can never adapt to it at all, so it would be wisest for me to start in Game on Venture. I'd still love to be part of the mass shapeshift on Gothic though, and I find the idea of being a werewolf rather tempting."

I laughed. "You'd choose to be a werewolf rather than...?"

I was interrupted by my buggy nagging me. "You are due to commence row 39,118."

Nathan's buggy joined in with the whining a second later, so we reluctantly got back on our feet. "Shall we take our mid-shift break in four rows' time?" asked Nathan. "We could meet here on the border at row 39,122."

I nodded. "Let's do that."

Nathan and I chatted through our thirty minute break on that day, and the following days as well. On the tenth day, we'd just got off our buggies and sat down on the floor to eat our packed lunches when Nathan gave an odd, embarrassed cough.

"I was wondering if we could spend some time together after our shift ends today."

I hesitated. I'd have been happy to meet up with Nathan outside work if all he wanted was casual friendship, but the eager, breathless tone of his voice gave me the idea that he had something much more intimate in mind. Some kids got into relationships with each other before entering Game, but I wasn't planning to be one of them. Nathan would stand no chance of being accepted as a resident of Ganymede, and he wasn't the sort of boy who could dazzle me into abandoning my dreams to join him as a werewolf on Gothic.

I was going to stick to the safely sensible course of action, and save romantic relationships for when I was my true self in Game. I wanted to make that clear to Nathan, but preferably without falling out with him. No phones or other entertainment devices were allowed in the body stacks, so riding the rows of freezer units was hour upon hour of relentless, mind numbing, boredom. Nathan never complained about that, but for me our daily half an hour chat, spent debating the benefits and disadvantages of life on a dozen different Game worlds, was a merciful break in the tedium.

I tried to phrase my refusal as tactfully as possible. "Working twelve hours a day in the body stacks doesn't leave me much free time for socializing."

I was surprised to see what looked like relief on Nathan's face at the rejection. I wondered if I'd read too much into his suggestion of meeting outside work. I'd dropped out of the glitz crowd a year ago, and didn't bother what I wore or looked like any longer, so that seemed the most likely answer.

Nathan started talking about Havoc after that. We were debating whether Havoc or Abyss were the worst worlds in Game, when my buggy started screaming an alarm I'd never heard before. I leapt to my feet and checked the buggy's display screen in panic.

"I've got an unscheduled defrost!"

Nathan's buggy started shrilling as well. "I've got one too," he said. "Another! Three now!"

My screen was showing seven unscheduled defrosts, with more appearing every second. I'd no idea what was happening, but I instinctively jumped onto the seat of my buggy, ordered it to head for the location of my nearest defrost, and then called Supervisor Fraser. He didn't respond. I called again and again, and finally got through.

"I've got defrosts!" I yelled. "What should...?"

I heard a confusion of other voices talking, and broke off my sentence. I'd always been one to one in my previous conversations with Fraser, but this was a conference call. I was patched in with about twenty other hysterical kids.

"Shut up!" Fraser shouted. "Game world Avalon just crashed."

He was drowned out by voices babbling questions. Fraser's words didn't make any sense. I knew it was over three hundred years since a Game world crashed, because we'd all been taught about the Rhapsody disaster in school history lessons. Back then each Game world had only had two servers running it, and a freak simultaneous failure of both Rhapsody's servers had caused it to crash. After that, the number of servers for each Game world had been increased, so now every Game world had four servers running it. It was surely impossible for all four of Avalon's servers to have failed at once.

"I said, shut up!" Fraser shouted again. "We've lost Game world Avalon, and every player who was on that world is going through emergency defrost and waking up. The senior supervisors are sending them all messages over the freezer unit control systems, telling them to lie still in their freezer units and wait calmly until they're restored into Game on a different world."

Oh yah, I thought. Some of those players would have been living in Game for hundreds of years. Now they've suddenly woken up in their old physical bodies, and found themselves trapped in a freezing cold box. They obviously just need to hear a recorded message to be perfectly happy again.

I thought the words, but kept my mouth firmly shut. I daren't risk being sarcastic to any adult, let alone my own supervisor.

"They'll all be hitting their freezer unit panic buttons to send out alarm calls," said Fraser. "Ignore them. Defrosting on emergency cycle puts a huge strain on the human body, so you have to focus on alerts from the medical monitoring system. Anyone got those?"

I studied my display screen. It was flooded with alarm calls, so I hit the filter codes to block everything except medical alerts. "I've got a heart failure case."

"Me too," said a terrified voice that sounded as if its owner couldn't be older than twelve.

"Everyone with a heart failure case has to get there at emergency speed," ordered Fraser. "Find the red syringe in your buggy medical kit, hold the end of the syringe against the bare skin of the person's neck, and press the button."

Other kids were yelling about medical alerts too now, but I ignored their frantic voices. I checked the location of my heart failure case, and ordered my buggy to change direction to go there. As it braked to a halt, and started turning round, I heard muffled screams and a thumping sound.

Freezer units usually had peaceful, steady green lights on their control unit, but the one next to me had lights that were urgently flashing amber. There was someone awake in there, screaming for help and pounding their fists on the lid.

I knew the person in the freezer unit had no chance of escaping by themselves. Every freezer unit in the body stacks had its lid locked shut to stop anyone from nosily opening them and harming the frozen occupant.

I wanted to stop my buggy and check through my alarm calls for the one that had come from that freezer unit. Alarm calls automatically included the unlock code for the freezer lid, so I'd be able to open it and free the unknown player from their prison.

I wanted to do that, but I mustn't. Whoever was inside that freezer unit was well enough to fight to get free. I had to ignore their cries for help and get to the person who was dying of a heart attack.

My buggy had finished turning now and was moving off again. I hit the override button to make it accelerate to emergency speed. The regimented lines of freezer units were a blur on either side of me now, and the buggy engine was whining in protest. I didn't have time to see if the freezer units I was passing had flashing lights on them, and the sound of the buggy engine was too loud for me to hear anything else, but my memory kept replaying the sounds of screaming and pounding fists.

I clung to my speeding buggy for an agonizingly long time, staring at the medical alert message on the screen in front of me, and muttering the unlock code for the freezer unit over and over again. "AKX2281SDV. AKX2281SDV. AKX2281SDV."

The buggy finally braked, coming to a halt so abruptly that I was nearly thrown off my seat. I saw I'd stopped by a freezer unit with lights that were flashing red.

I jumped off my buggy, grabbed the medical kit from the storage locker and found the red syringe inside, then raced across to punch the unlock code into the keypad of the freezer unit. I recited the letters and numbers one last time as I entered them. "AKX2281SDV."

As I finished entering the code, there was a clicking sound from the freezer unit. I grabbed the lid, lifted it, and used the red syringe on the neck of the motionless man inside. I stood there for a moment, looking for any sign of a response, but there was nothing.

Desperate now, I climbed into the freezer unit myself, checked the man's airway, and tried to breathe air into his cold lips. I alternated that with chest compressions for what must have been ten or fifteen minutes, but eventually had to accept that it was useless.

I wearily climbed back out of the freezer unit, and stood looking down at the man. He looked a couple of years older than me, with skin that was darker than mine, closely trimmed black hair, and a hint of a beard. If he'd entered Game at the standard age of eighteen, then he must have defrosted at some point. Women often defrosted to go through one or more pregnancies, but it was far more unusual for a man to return to the real world.

Perhaps this man had needed to be physically present in the real world to do highly specialist, delicate work that a controlled droid couldn't handle. Whatever his reasons for defrosting in the past, the dated clothes he was wearing showed he'd last returned to Game over two hundred years ago. His mind had been exploring the wonders of the Game worlds for more than two centuries, and had now moved on to explore somewhere stranger and far more distant.

I returned to sit on my buggy, and listened to the voices of Fraser and the other kids on the call channel. It was several minutes before I could force myself to speak on the channel and say the single bleak sentence that closed the door on a life.

"My heart failure case is dead."

My voice sounded like it came from a stranger. Fraser didn't say anything in response to my words. There wasn't much that he could say. When a Game world crashed, dumping millions of players' minds back into the real world without warning, their bodies had to be defrosted at dangerous speed to receive the returning consciousness before it was lost to oblivion. There were bound to be some unlucky ones who didn't survive the process.

For the last three centuries, people had only died in real life, while players within Game were immortal. Now there was a corpse in the freezer unit next to me. There'd be other corpses in freezer units scattered through the caverns of the body stacks here and in other parts of the world. Definitely hundreds, and probably thousands of them.

Death had just visited the Game.

CHAPTER TWO

I worked long past the end of my shift that day. Supervisor Fraser announced that the technicians were setting up command sequences and sending them out to all the freezer units that had gone through emergency defrost. Those commands were supposed to order the units to refreeze their occupants and send their minds back into Game on random worlds.

The problem was that the commands didn't work in a lot of cases. Some players had hit their panic buttons so many times that their freezer control system had got hopelessly confused. Other players had injured their hands beating on their freezer unit lids, so the medical monitoring system blocked them from being refrozen.

I drove round my area of Red Sector for hour after hour, manually punching in reset codes on freezer units, and watching until their flashing amber lights turned green in response. I carefully avoided looking through any of the transparent viewing windows of the units. I already had the unshakeable memory of a dead man's face to haunt my dreams. I didn't want to add the faces of living but terrified people.

I glimpsed the distinctive red and white stripes of ambulance buggies several times. The ambulances would be collecting injured players from freezer units, and taking them for medical treatment. Presumably one of the ambulances would be collecting the man who'd died as well.

I saw no sign of Nathan during my travels, but the other

patrol shift had been called into work early to help deal with the crisis, so I did meet my shift alternate, Delora, at one point. She was going in the opposite direction to me, driving a plain brown buggy that must have been borrowed from a central supply store. When she saw me, she gave me a hopeful wave and stopped her buggy, but I kept going. I couldn't face telling Delora about the man who'd died.

When Supervisor Fraser finally said my shift could go home, I went to the nearest transport stop and rode a pod to the accommodation block where I lived. I normally called in at one of the neighbourhood's economy food outlets after work, to get something hot to eat and buy sandwich packs for the next day, but I was too exhausted and shocked to think of eating now. I just went straight back to my room, stripped off my clothes, and collapsed into bed.

It was barely an hour later that my door chime sounded. I was deeply asleep by then, but even if I'd been awake and standing by the door, I still wouldn't have had time to open it before my caller overrode the lock and barged into my room. I opened my eyes to find a gleaming, bronze droid standing over me. It had blue and grey Unilaw markings on its body, and the front of its head displayed the sleek-furred, female leopard face of the adult who was controlling it from within Game.

"You are required to voluntarily attend the nearest United Law facility for questioning," said the droid.

"What?" I sat up. "But... I haven't done anything."

"You may refuse to voluntarily attend, in which case you will be formally charged with murder and arrested."

"What?" I repeated the word, unable to believe this was happening.

"Are you refusing?"

I hastily shook my head. Being questioned by Unilaw was going to look bad enough on my Game record, without being arrested as well. "I'm happy to co-operate voluntarily," I gabbled the words at top speed. "Please let me get dressed."

"You have one minute."

I grabbed the overalls I'd taken off before tumbling into bed, and pulled them on. The droid closed in on me and waved a scanner at the bar code on my left arm.

"Identity verified." The droid clipped the scanner on to the side of its body.

I'd hoped the droid had made a mistake and come to the wrong room, but it clearly hadn't. I felt an instinctive urge to make a run for it, but knew I'd no hope of running away from a tireless metal droid who could track the medical implant chip in my arm. I had to co-operate and have faith in the fact I'd done nothing wrong.

The droid took me by the arm and towed me off along the corridor. I saw a room door open and a boy come out. His face registered alarm as he saw the droid; he took two rapid steps backwards into his room again, and closed the door.

Once we reached the accommodation block's transport stop, the droid released my arm, unclipped something from the side of its body, and used it to gesture at a waiting two-person pod. At first, I assumed it was waving the scanner again, but then I saw that this was a gun. I gasped in shock. I'd seen plenty of images of Game weapons, but never seen a real one before.

"Get into the pod!" snapped the droid.

I hastily climbed into the pod, and the droid got in and sat opposite me. It entered a destination into the pod guidance system, we started moving, and there was a tense, totally silent journey where I couldn't stop myself from staring at the gun. The droid kept juggling it from one bronze hand to another, in such a casual manner that I was terrified the gun would go off by mistake. If that happened, the leopard-faced adult controlling the droid wouldn't be hurt because she was safely in Game, but I could be killed.

I was relieved when the pod finally stopped and the droid ordered me to get out. I found myself on a platform with a vast blue and grey United Law sign on the wall. The droid hustled me through some double doors, along several corridors, then dumped me in a cell and left me. I wanted to pound on the featureless white walls and shout abuse, but forced myself to sit on the rock-hard, narrow bed and wait patiently like a model citizen. Someone would be watching me, studying me, and eventually they'd talk to me. Maybe then I'd find out what was going on. Maybe then they'd find out they'd made a mistake. Maybe then everything would be all right again.

Even as I thought that, I realized I was clinging to false hopes. The brutal truth was that nothing could make things all right after this. Whatever happened now, the fact I'd been dragged in for questioning by Unilaw would remain on my Game record forever. I'd no hope of joining my father as a resident of Ganymede now. I might end up with Nathan as a werewolf on Gothic after all.

I sat there in frozen misery for what seemed like hours before one of the room walls displayed the head and shoulders of three adults in Game. The centre one had a standard male human head, except that it was in the bronze metal of Automaton. On the left was a bird of indeterminate sex, with human eyes but a beaked mouth and a crest of multicoloured feathers. On the right was a bald woman with a distorted face and hooked nose, who was expressing her individuality by choosing extreme ugliness when everyone in Game could be as beautiful as they wished.

Facing three adults at once would have been intimidating even without the prison cell setting. I sprang to my feet and waited in respectful silence.

"Jex," said the bronze man, the tone of his voice making my name into an accusation. "You received a medical alert. Explain why you failed to respond and provide the appropriate medical aid within the statutory three minutes."

Despite my fear of the situation, and anger at the injustice of it, I had an urge to laugh. They'd threatened me with a murder charge over this? Had they pulled in everyone from the body stacks who'd failed to save a defrost from dying of a heart attack? That must be most of the kids on my shift. Didn't these people know anything about the body stacks at all?

"When I got the first defrost alarm, I didn't know what to do," I said. "We're just supposed to patrol and look for maintenance issues."

The bronze man was already scowling impatiently, so I

hurried on as fast as I could. "I called my supervisor. He told us Game world Avalon had crashed, and to focus on medical alerts. I headed for my medical alert location as fast as I could, but getting there within three minutes was utterly impossible."

"Explain why," ordered the woman. Her voice had a hissing, snake-like quality, as unpleasant as the face she'd chosen.

"I went by the quickest route," I said. "I drove my buggy at top speed, and that was faster than I could have run, but it still took a very long time."

The bird glanced off to the side. "Twelve minutes," it said, in clipped, precise tones that could have been either male or female. "Her buggy tracker shows maximum speed and no route deviations."

"Twelve minutes on the shortest route!" The woman spat out the words. "Why were you so far away from your patrol area?"

"I was inside my patrol area, following my designated route, but my area is huge." I tried to explain the sheer scale of the problem. "There are about fifty billion frozen Gamers in the body stacks. I work in Long Stay Area 31, which has about a billion. Red Sector has two hundred million of those. I patrol Red Sector Block 2, which holds ten million freezer units. Those take up a lot of space. 25,000 rows and each row is..."

"Those numbers can't be right." The bronze man cut me off and looked at the bird.

The bird took a while before replying this time. "Her figures are correct."

The woman frowned. "That's a completely unacceptable area for one person to patrol."

She raised a hand. The three images instantly vanished, leaving me with a featureless wall again. I stood there for a moment longer, hesitated, then sat down on the bed again and tried to think things through. If Unilaw officials really had pulled in thousands of kids from the body stacks, they wouldn't have enough active staff to question them, so they'd probably called in retired Unilaw members to help. Adults who'd paid their lifetime subscription wouldn't normally agree to work again, but they'd make an exception in a crisis like this.

I hadn't had a chance to pick up my phone when I was dragged off for questioning, so I'd no way to check the time. I thought I'd been sitting there for about another two hours before the wall changed again. I saw that my three questioners were back, but they'd brought reinforcements with them. Two standard human faces, one male and one female, with bronze metallic insignia on each cheek. These were two of the all-powerful Game Techs who designed and ran the worlds of Game!

I was being questioned by two Game Techs! My vision started blurring and I felt giddy, but I scrambled off the bed and dug my nails into my palms. I couldn't let myself faint.

The bronze man spoke. "How many of you were involved in the bombing?"

"Bombing?" I heard my voice squeak. "What bombing?"

"Don't waste our time with evasion," said the woman. "How many of you were involved with the bombing that destroyed the Avalon server complex?"

"It was a bomb? I didn't know that. My supervisor only told us that Avalon Game world had crashed." I was bewildered. I'd heard of bombings, but there hadn't been any in centuries.

"How could you be unaware of what has been broadcast on every news channel both in and out of Game?" asked the bird. "The Avalon server complex was destroyed by a bomb, and eleven thousand, two hundred, and ninety seven people died during the emergency defrosts."

The number of deaths overwhelmed me. I'd expected hundreds of people to have died during the emergency defrosts. I'd feared the total death toll might be as high as the over two thousand casualties in the Rhapsody disaster. I hadn't allowed for the fact that Avalon was an old and popular Game world with a very high population.

Once I'd absorbed the magnitude of the deaths, the second point hit me. The Avalon server complex had been destroyed by a bomb. I was being questioned by Unilaw about a bombing that had killed over eleven thousand Gamers! This wouldn't just damage my future in Game, it would utterly destroy it.

I fought against my panic and tried to answer the bird's

question. "I assumed there'd been a freak failure of the server complex. I worked to the end of my twelve-hour shift and through half of the next one as well to help deal with the defrosts. When everyone had been sent back into Game on other worlds, my supervisor let the people on my shift leave. I was so exhausted that I went back to my room and fell asleep straight away."

"Sleep," the woman repeated the word as if she barely recognized it. "I'd forgotten about that. It's been such a long time since I needed sleep."

The bird glanced sideways. "The girl's medical chip verifies her story of going directly to her room. There is no record of her accessing any news programmes."

"Unbelievable," muttered the bronze man. He was silent for a moment, and then suddenly threw another question at me. "Why did you want to kill your father?"

"What?" I realized I'd yelled the word. "I'm sorry," I added hastily. "You mean that my father died in the world crash? But he can't have died. It was Avalon that crashed, wasn't it? My supervisor said Avalon crashed." I clung to that thought. "My father can't be dead. He lives on Ganymede, not Avalon."

"Your father was visiting a friend on Avalon when the bomb exploded, and died during emergency defrost," said the bird.

My father was dead! I felt horribly sick, forgot all about the importance of being respectful to adults, and just wailed my distress aloud.

"The man in my block who died? That was my father? I didn't know his body was stored in Red Sector Block 2. The freezer units just have codes. Even when I opened the lid and saw him, I didn't know. I'd never seen his flesh face. I didn't know. I didn't know. I didn't know."

"Quiet!" said the woman.

I put my right hand to my mouth, biting on my forefinger to keep myself quiet.

"Your father died in the Avalon crash," said the bird, "but his body was stored in Long Stay Area 11, Yellow Sector Block 3." Despite its strange, inhuman face and voice, it somehow had an air of sympathy the others were lacking.

I sagged with relief. The idea that I'd looked at my own father's body and not known...

"In my opinion," said the bird, "we're wasting our time interrogating this girl."

"She was flagged twice on our system," said the bronze man. "Once as having a death in her patrol area."

"As did thousands of others," said the bird.

"And again as having a parental death in the crash," the bronze man added. "She has also expressed dissent at the Leebrook Ashton bill. That's a third flag against her."

A recording started playing. I was startled to hear Nathan's voice. "It stinks, doesn't it?"

My own voice replied. "You're almost eighteen too?"

"My eighteenth birthday was two days ago."

"Do you work for Supervisor Fraser too?"

There was a clicking sound as the recording ended.

"The dissent was not expressed by her." For once, the woman seemed to be on my side. "Jex, what is your opinion of the Leebrook Ashton bill?"

"I was disappointed to have to wait another year before I could enter Game, but I understood the reasons for it," I said. "Each year, the Game population and number of Game worlds grows, and so does the amount of maintenance work to be done in the real world."

What I desperately wanted to say at this point was that the billions of adults in Game should be taking on more of that work. I'd no complaint against the adults who'd recently entered Game and were still working. I just felt the ones who'd paid their lifetime subscriptions, and had been living a life of blissful idleness for decades or even centuries, should be contributing something as well.

Given the vast number of lifetime subscription holders in Game, each of them would just need to work for a month or two every century to solve the issue of the increasing amount of maintenance to be done. Of course none of them had considered that answer. Rather than spend a few hours using a controlled droid to do simple jobs like riding patrol in the body stacks, they'd voted to dump the whole burden on kids like me.

I knew that if I said any of those things I'd instantly be charged with the Avalon bombing, so I fought to keep my words and tone of voice totally neutral. "Once adults have paid their lifetime subscription to Game, they've no incentive to spend time working. The school leaving age was already down to ten years old, so it couldn't be reduced any further. That meant the only remaining option was to raise the legal age where children become adult and can enter Game."

The bird had been looking off sideways again, but now its head snapped round to stare at me. I'd no idea why.

The woman made an impatient noise. "You call this three flags against the girl? She was disappointed by the bill, as every child must have been. She failed to save a Gamer due to the appalling size of her patrol area, an administrative matter that must be addressed. Her father died in the server crash, but I can't see how that could benefit her unless he had a fortune in Game credits to bequeath her."

The two Game Techs had been totally silent until now, observing my questioning with unreadable, impassive faces. Now the male Game Tech spoke in a heavily formal voice. "After her father paid his lifetime subscription, he had less than ten credits remaining in his account."

"Then we have nothing against her," said the woman.

She and the bronze man looked at the bird, and its feathers rippled as it shook its head.

"The girl lives and works hundreds of miles from the bombing site. There's no record of her leaving her home area recently or contacting anyone outside it. Release her."

I hadn't realized the bird was the one in charge here, but it had just given an order, and everyone else was hastily nodding in acceptance, even the two Game Techs. That didn't make any sense. A player couldn't be giving orders to Game Techs. The insignia on Game Tech faces showed their hierarchy in a similar way to the bracelets of players, and these two only had bronze insignia, but I knew that silver and gold insignia were very rare indeed, reserved for the highest ranks of Game officials. Even if it was true that these two Game Techs had the lowest possible status, they would still be far more important than mere players.

I was distracted by the door of the room opening. I eagerly turned to look at it, and when I glanced back all the faces had vanished.

The bird had ordered my release, which seemed to mean I was free to go. I walked tentatively towards the door, and out into the corridor. I'd forgotten which way I'd been brought here, so I took several wrong turnings before I found my way back to the transport stop.

I hit the buttons on the wall to summon a single-person pod, and one came rushing up along the rails within a minute. I climbed inside, set the pod guidance system to head for the accommodation block where I lived, and sank back into the seat. My mind was busily rerunning what had happened. The world crash, the screaming alarms, the dead man in the freezer unit, those hostile faces accusing me of murder, and the casual way the bronze man had told me that my father was dead.

My first reaction to the news of my father's death had been an avalanche of grief at his loss. That grief was still there, but I was guiltily aware that it was mixed with selfish fears about my own future.

Nobody could enter Game unless at least one Game world was willing to accept them as a resident, and what world would accept me now? Even Havoc would turn down someone who'd been questioned by Unilaw about a bombing that killed over eleven thousand people.

I'd spent every minute of my life working towards a future that would never happen now. I'd never join the ranks of the immortal Gamers, forever young and beautiful, living their eternal existence of pleasure. The Game self of my dreams, Jex of the silver, feathered hair, had died unborn in the Avalon crash.

I'd only the haziest idea of what would happen to me now. I might be able to hide the fact I was a Game reject until I was nineteen, but those around me would notice when I didn't enter Game on my birthday. The suspicious whispers would start then, and gradually grow louder as the months went by and I still didn't enter Game.

Sooner or later those whispers would turn into open complaints that a Game reject was living and working with respectable kids. I'd be thrown out of my room, lose my job in the body stacks, and have no option other than to go and live among the other Game rejects in accommodation blocks that were scheduled for demolition. You had to have something very serious on your Game record for all worlds to refuse you as a resident. The rumours said that most Game rejects were involved in violent crimes, and their communities were savagely dangerous places.

I covered my face with my hands, comforting myself with the darkness and the warmth of my own breath. We'd been taught to do that in nursery, to calm ourselves when we were frightened. It didn't always work. It wasn't working now.

CHAPTER THREE

When I arrived back at my room, I saw I had less than fifteen minutes before I needed to go back to work. I snatched my phone from where it lay on my bed, set it to play one of the main Game news channels, and listened to a succession of hysterically angry voices while I showered and dressed in clean overalls.

I didn't learn any extra facts from all the outrage and fury. Everyone seemed to believe the same thing as the Unilaw officials who'd interrogated me, that some seventeen or eighteen-year-old kids, bitter about the Leebrook Ashton bill, had planted the bomb to get revenge on the players who'd selfishly voted to keep them working in the real world for an extra year.

I had to admit that was the obvious answer, but making bombs must surely be incredibly difficult and dangerous. Would a group of kids really take so big a risk just to get revenge, or were they actually attempting to force the adults in Game to repeal the Leebrook Ashton bill and do more of the work themselves?

I paused in the act of brushing my hair, and considered that possibility for a moment. I agreed that the system needed changing, but I was utterly opposed to violence as a way of changing it. I thought with fierce, protective anger of the man who'd died in my area of the body stacks. Over eleven thousand others had died the same way. My own father had died that way!

Whatever their motives, the bomber or bombers needed to be caught and stopped from ever doing this again. I hoped that

Unilaw would manage that, but the fact I'd been on their suspect list didn't fill me with confidence.

I was in danger of being late for work and fined half my pay for the day. That seemed a very minor worry now, but I hastily finished brushing my hair into order, and filled my drinking bottle. Since I wasn't allowed to take my phone to work with me, I turned it off and tossed it onto my unmade bed.

As I headed for the door, I automatically reached for the sandwich packs that should have been waiting ready on the shelf. It wasn't until my hand grabbed thin air that I remembered I hadn't bought any sandwich packs yesterday. I wouldn't have time to call in at a food outlet to buy any on my way to work, and I'd rather go hungry than eat the overpriced, revolting sandwiches from the vending machines at transport stops. I snatched a couple of nutrient bars from my emergency store and sprinted out of the door.

I ate my breakfast of one of the nutrient bars on the pod ride, washed down the dryness of it with a few mouthfuls of water from my bottle, and arrived at the body stacks' transport stop closest to my current patrol position with two minutes to spare.

I stepped out of the pod, and saw Delora was already waiting on the platform with the buggy. "All quiet?"

"Finally."

She took my place in the pod, and leant back in the seat with a look of bliss on her face. I watched in envy as the pod whooshed off along the rails. Delora's shift had been off-duty when the bombing and defrosts happened. She hadn't been questioned by Unilaw, so she still had a future as an immortal player in Game, while I would live and die in the real world.

I was dead on my feet from strain and exhaustion, but I climbed onto the buggy, wondering if it was possible to ride it in my sleep. "Jex checking in," I told it, and trundled at standard buggy speed through the entrance to the body stacks.

"You have new instructions," the buggy announced.

I groaned. If I could somehow stay awake, I might manage standard patrol, but nothing that required any thought.

"Your patrol starting point has changed to row 37,500."

That meant backtracking to a point I'd already patrolled, but I was paid to do what the buggy said, not argue with it, so I set off to row 37,500. When I arrived there, I expected to start patrolling the rows of freezer units, but the buggy spoke again.

"Await further orders."

I sat there dutifully awaiting further orders. After a minute or two, Nathan arrived on his buggy, and parked it next to mine. He looked as exhausted as I felt, and clearly hadn't found time to shower or change his crumpled clothes from yesterday.

"Await further orders," his buggy told him.

Nathan dismounted from his buggy, backed away a short distance, and beckoned to me. I hesitated a moment before wearily climbing off my own buggy and following him.

"Did Unilaw pick you up for questioning too?" he whispered.

Nathan seemed to think we were out of range of our eavesdropping buggies. I was less sure about that, but there was little point in worrying about recordings damaging my future when it had already been destroyed.

"Yah. You had someone die then?"

Nathan nodded. There was a short silence. I didn't want to talk about the man who'd died in my patrol area, and I could tell Nathan felt the same way about whoever had died in his.

"Did you get two Game Techs, a bronze man, a woman, and a bird?" I asked.

He nodded again. "The man was from Automaton. The woman confused me for a while, then I worked out she was a bald harpy from Cliffs. I couldn't make sense of the bird at all. I still can't. There are several worlds where players have a bird form, but they all have faces that are far more human than that one."

"Whatever it was, the Game Techs seemed just to be present as observers, while the bird was in charge of the interrogations."

"I agree the Game Techs were there purely as observers," said Nathan, "they didn't say a word during my interrogation, but the bird wasn't in charge of anything. The bird, the man, and the woman all wore Unilaw rank badges on their collars, and those showed the woman was a Unilaw Area Commander, while the bird and the man were only Senior Detectives."

I shrugged. "I don't know anything about Unilaw ranks, I just know that the bird was the one who decided my interrogation was over. From the way the others instantly accepted the decision, the bird was definitely in charge."

"But that doesn't make sense," said Nathan. "If the bird was more important than an Area Commander, why was it wearing the rank badge of a Senior Detective?"

I sighed. "I've no idea, but there's no point in us arguing over who was in charge of interrogating us. All that matters is the interrogations happened. Our Game records will show that we were picked up by Unilaw and questioned about the bombing of the Avalon server."

I dragged my fingers through my hair. I'd accepted the full extent of the disaster now. The Avalon world crash had robbed me of both my father and my future. My mother would react to a situation like this by pretending it hadn't happened, but I preferred to face up to my problems. I did that now, forcing myself to say the grim words that summed up the utter destruction of all my hopes and plans.

"We're both Game rejects now."

There was silence for a few seconds before Nathan spoke with a forced optimism. "Perhaps it won't be that bad."

"It's exactly that bad, Nathan," I said, with the calmness of despair. "No Game world is going to accept either of us."

"We can't apply to enter Game until we're nineteen now," said Nathan. "Unilaw will have caught the real bomber by then. We'll be able to forget all about the Avalon bombing and carry on with our lives."

I winced at his words. "I'll never be able to forget the bombing, Nathan. I was told during my questioning that my father was on Avalon when it crashed. He died during emergency defrost."

Nathan looked appalled. "I'm terribly sorry to hear that."

I couldn't bear to talk about my father any longer, so I hastily changed the subject. "I wouldn't trust Unilaw to catch a mouse, let alone a bomber, but even if they do it won't help us very much. I was listening to some players talking on a Game news channel a few minutes ago. They're utterly irrational with anger about the bombing, and anger like that won't fade in decades or even centuries."

I paused. "Whether the real bomber has been caught or not, the Admission Committees for every Game world will still take one look at the questioning on our records, suspect we were secretly involved as accomplices, and block our applications."

Nathan stared bleakly down at the floor. "That's not fair."

I didn't say anything. I'd learnt as a small child in a dormitory that life wasn't fair. Those who caused trouble often escaped punishment, while their innocent victims got blamed. I'd learnt the lesson again as a medical cadet, when an instructor dropped me from the training programme to cover up her own mistake. The same thing was happening yet again. Whether the bomber was caught or not, the innocent kids working in the body stacks would suffer because of his or her actions.

"Incoming orders," announced the buggies in unison.

Nathan and I hurried back to sit on our buggies. I was expecting Supervisor Fraser's face to appear on the display screen in front of me, but instead I saw a golden-haired, elven stranger.

"I am the senior supervisor for Long Stay Area 31," she said.

I could hear the same words echoed from Nathan's buggy, and we exchanged startled glances.

"We've just had a conference of all senior supervisors worldwide," she continued. "We are aware that all of you worked well past the end of your last shift, and most of you were called in for questioning later. In the aftermath of the Avalon bombing, regular maintenance patrols are a lower priority than being prepared to cope with any further major crisis. You have all been stationed in the centre of your patrol areas to give you the maximum chance of responding successfully to alarms. You will remain at those points for the whole of this shift unless alarms sound."

The woman paused. "You may take the opportunity to rest."

Her image vanished from the screen. I sat there for a moment while my sleep-deprived brain absorbed the information, then I climbed down from the buggy and stretched out thankfully on the floor. It was formed of rock hard, unyielding plastic, but it was still blissful to lie down.

Nathan got off his buggy, frowned, and then selected a spot that was near to me but at a tactful distance. He lay down, tried several positions in an attempt to get comfortable, and then got his bag from his buggy to use as a pillow.

I missed everything that happened in the next six or seven hours, because I was deep in dreamless sleep.

It wasn't an alarm that woke me, or the buggy announcing the end of my shift, but the sound of heavy footsteps. I opened bleary eyes, saw the legs of a droid beside me, and sat up in panic. Now I could see the droid's head wore the face of the bird that had been in charge of my interrogation. It was here to drag me back to that prison cell!

"I'm sorry to wake you," said the bird.

Nathan was sitting up too now, his face showing he was stunned by the bird's words. I was stunned too. Adults didn't apologize to children. We were outside Game. We weren't real people yet.

"I'm here because it's vitally important to hunt down the Avalon bomber," said the bird. "I think you may be able to assist me."

I scrambled to my feet. Nathan literally shook himself, before standing up as well. I still wasn't sure whether I was being arrested or not, but my brain was starting to register some odd things about this droid. It was coloured gold rather than the usual bronze, it had no ownership markings on its chest, and its shape and movements were a more convincing match to a real human being than usual.

The droid's head was especially startling. A normal droid's head was a uniform bronze colour, except for the flat front that displayed the face of the adult controlling it from Game. This droid's head had somehow taken on the colours and contours of the full bird head. It even had a crest of feathers that seemed to ripple as it moved, and a beaked mouth that opened and shut as it spoke.

I couldn't work out whether the droid's head was genuinely changing shape to create those movements, or it was just a holographic illusion. Either way, the uniqueness of this droid proved I'd been right about the bird being someone very important.

"The bombing was a real world crime," said the bird, "so there is a United Law investigation in progress. Since it was a Game server complex that was bombed, there is also an official Game investigation happening in tandem. Finally, since over eleven thousand Gamers died from medical complications arising from emergency defrosts, the players have elected to have their own representative monitoring the progress of both those investigations and reporting back to them. They have asked me to be that player representative."

The bird paused for a moment. Nathan and I waited in respectful silence until it started speaking again.

"My plan was to liaise with the two official investigations while doing some small-scale investigations of my own, but I've hit a problem. I entered Game centuries ago, and I've never defrosted or used a controlled droid to visit the real world. I've been totally immersed in my life in Game, and when I did spare a few minutes to think about the real world, I assumed it was the same as when I left it."

The bird paused again. "This conversation seems horribly one-sided. It would help if one of you would say something occasionally."

I exchanged glances with Nathan and spoke cautiously. "We're finding it hard to tell whether you want us to speak or not. Most adults wear a face that's human to some extent, but it's hard to interpret the expressions on yours, and there aren't any clues in your voice either."

I held my breath, braced for a reprimand, but the bird just nodded. "You have a point. I asked the Game Techs to give me an anonymous appearance and voice to avoid attracting too much attention. That was useful during the interrogations, and there may be times when it's useful again in future, but now isn't one of them."

The droid's head blurred. When it came back into focus, all trace of the bird had vanished. I saw the head of a handsome man, with dark eyes that were filled with laughter, and black, feathered hair that clung closely to his scalp. Nathan and I recognized him instantly and gasped in unison.

"My name is Hawk," said the man, in a voice that held all the expressive tones that the bird voice had been missing. "Am I easier to talk to now?"

CHAPTER FOUR

Hawk the Unvanquished was talking to me, casually smiling at insignificant Jex. When the Game started its first ten year trial, there were fewer than a thousand Founder Players. I wouldn't recognize an image of most of them, only knowing they were Founder Players because of the diamond bracelets they wore, but everyone in both real life and Game would recognize Hawk.

Death Canyon on Ariel was designed to be an impossible obstacle course for pilots flying that world's archaic biplanes, but Hawk made it through, and stunned Game Techs massed to welcome him as he reached the end. Hawk was the champion of the Battle Arena on Medieval for ten years running and retired unbeaten. Hawk led the outgunned and outnumbered army of Ruby in the famous victory over the forces of Sapphire on Civil War.

Those achievements stunned people like me who were interested in the combats and challenges of Game, but it was Hawk's actions in things like the Steppes protest that won the hearts of the wider Game population. Each year on the anniversary of the opening of Game, several new worlds were added. Game world Steppes had problems from the start. Its opening was delayed by last minute technical problems, so it was left out of all that year's publicity about the new worlds, and its treeless plains didn't attract much player interest.

At the end of five years, Steppes still had less than ten thousand residents. The Game Techs decided to shut it down as a failure rather than let it gradually turn into another Havoc or

Abyss. The residents refused all offers of relocation though. They'd grown to love the vast skies of Steppes, and staged a series of protests to try to save their world.

Those protests were failing, ignored by all the major Game news channels, when Hawk arrived on Steppes. He talked a dozen other Founder Players into joining him, and the sight of them in their glittering diamond bracelets drew crowds of reporters. There was an immediate rush of players applying to become residents of Steppes, and the Game Techs decided to upgrade the world rather than abandoning it. They added dazzling night-time auroras and flocks of fire-birds, and Steppes became one of the most popular worlds in Game.

I could think of a dozen more stories that I'd heard about Hawk. He wasn't just a Founder Player but a legend in Game. No wonder the terrified players had chosen him to be their representative.

Hawk stood there, laughing at our stunned faces. "Perhaps I should have stayed as the bird after all. You still aren't talking to me."

He gave us the teasing grin that was so typical of Hawk, and Nathan finally choked out a single word. "Wow."

"You're..." I gulped. "You're my all time hero. You killed the Kraken solo! You..." I broke off, realizing I must sound like a gushing fool.

"That was less impressive than it sounds," said Hawk. "The main problem is wearing down the Kraken so you can reach its weak spot and... Anyway, forget that. I was explaining to you that I'd stupidly assumed the real world had stayed just the same in the last four centuries."

He gave a laugh of self-mockery. "I started controlling this droid about twelve hours ago. The moment I sent it walking out of its storage room at the United Law facility, I could see this world was totally different from the one I'd left behind. The facility corridors were full of controlled droids, but the only people physically present were teenage cadets and a couple of pregnant women."

Hawk gave his characteristic, one-shouldered shrug that I

remembered seeing in dozens of replays of him in Game. "I told myself I should have expected that given everyone enters Game at eighteen now, but a host of trivial physical details keep bothering me."

He turned to point at Nathan's buggy. "Why is there a dark blue apple on that buggy seat?"

"Because I was planning to eat it later," said Nathan.

"I guessed someone was planning to eat it," said Hawk. "What's worrying me is why it's blue?"

Nathan and I exchanged confused looks. "The food outlet had sold out of strawberry apples, and I don't like apple apples, so I bought a blueberry one," said Nathan.

Hawk gave an odd shake of his head as if Nathan's answer had somehow made things worse. "And why don't rooms have any windows?"

"I know that houses in Game have windows," I said, "but buildings in the real world don't. There's no need for them when everywhere has movement-triggered, artificial lighting."

"Yes, but windows aren't just for letting in natural light," said Hawk. "They're to let you admire the views. The small pod things that rush round on railway lines have windows, so why don't the rooms?"

I'd no idea what to say to that. I'd dreamed of having my own house with windows on Ganymede, because I'd have the stunning view of Jupiter in the sky. I'd never considered the idea of having a window in the real world. Even if it had been possible for my room to have a window, which it wasn't because it didn't have an outside wall, the view from it would have just been an area of litter-strewn grass, a couple of broken delivery trolleys, and the wall of the next apartment block.

"The windows in pods are to let you see where you are, so you know if you've reached your destination transport stop or the pod is just pulling in to let an express carriage overtake," said Nathan. "Rooms don't need windows because they don't move."

Hawk still didn't seem entirely happy with our explanations. "There's the odd, faintly green colour of the overhead lighting too."

Nathan and I automatically glanced up at the ceiling. The lights seemed fine to me.

Hawk looked at our uncomprehending faces and sighed. "I told myself that odd physical changes didn't matter. I was reassured to discover the teenage cadets talked using almost identical words and phrases to the ones teenagers used when I entered Game. There was just the odd quirk, like the way they sometimes abbreviated United Law to Unilaw, but otherwise speech seemed to have changed surprisingly little in four centuries."

I frowned. Didn't Hawk realize that there was nothing surprising about kids today using the same words and phrases as they had four centuries ago? We all slavishly copied the speech patterns of the players we saw on the Game news channels and in replays of Game events, particularly famous Founder Players like Hawk, to prepare for when we entered Game ourselves.

"I was fooled into thinking that teenagers' words hadn't changed much so their lives hadn't changed much either," said Hawk, "but then I was invited to sit in on the interviews of older teenage workers from the body stacks."

He pulled a pained face. "I dropped out of the first few interviews within a minute or two because the teenagers were too hysterical with fear to speak. Nathan, you were calmer than most, but usually limited your answers to a simple yes or no. Jex, you were by far the most articulate, and said a lot of things that shocked me, like the point about the school leaving age being down to ten."

There was an oddly vulnerable tone to his voice now. "When I entered Game, teenagers went to school until they were eighteen, and many kept studying for years after that. I'd been aware that the school leaving age had been reduced a couple of times since I entered Game, but I assumed it would still be something like fifteen or sixteen. When I learned that children left school and started work at ten years old, I knew this world bore no resemblance at all to the one I'd left behind, and I'd absolutely no chance of doing my job properly."

The golden droid's hands waved in a gesture of helplessness.

"I can't help hunt down which teenagers planted a bomb when I've no idea what's normal life for teenagers today. I can't judge the progress and decisions of the Game or Unilaw investigations when I don't know the most basic facts about this world. I told the players that I was resigning. I said they needed someone new to Game to do this job, someone who was familiar with the real world as it is now. The players wouldn't accept my resignation though. They aren't willing to trust an unknown new player to represent their interests."

His voice suddenly changed from wistful to briskly businesslike. "I'm stuck with my job, and that means I have to do some rapid learning about what the world is like today. I especially need to learn about how teenagers live and work, so I came here to see you two working."

Hawk had come to see us working and he'd found us asleep on the floor! I flushed with embarrassment and rushed into a hasty explanation. "The senior supervisor said our shift could rest unless there was another emergency. We'd worked long past the end of our last twelve-hour shift, and then Unilaw dragged us in for questioning, and..."

"I understand why you needed sleep," Hawk interrupted me. "You work twelve-hour shifts here?"

"Yah," Nathan and I chorused the word. "We get a half an hour mid-shift break," Nathan added.

Hawk winced. "Working twelve hours a day in Game might be bearable because you'd still have twelve hours a day to enjoy yourselves, but in the real world most of that time must be taken up sleeping."

He turned to look round at the rows of freezer units. "Jex, you said in your interview that you patrol the body stacks looking for maintenance issues. That means riding your buggy along the rows of freezer units, looking for ones showing signs of failure?"

"Yah," I said. "I mean, no. We ride patrol on the buggies, but we aren't checking the freezer units. Those are designed to last at least ten thousand years without maintenance, and have their own control systems monitoring them. Our job is to check for external problems like water damage and potential roof collapses."

Hawk glanced up at the ceiling. "Aren't there more interesting jobs that you could be doing?"

"Most of the interesting work involves signing up for a career path when you're eleven," said Nathan. "You spend the years until you enter Game as a cadet in training, and then work from within Game for another forty years after that."

"You didn't want to make that long a commitment?" asked Hawk.

Nathan was looking defensive now. "I accept there are big advantages in taking the career path route. Cadets have better accommodation and shorter working hours than standard. Once they finish training and enter Game, they get their annual subscriptions paid each year, and their lifetime subscription paid when they complete their forty year term and retire. I didn't try it because there are a hundred kids competing for every space on a cadet training course, and none of the possible careers interested me."

He shrugged. "I've been taking the alternative approach of saving as many credits as I could before I entered Game. My plan was to allow myself a six month holiday and then start work again using a controlled droid. I'd calculated I would be able to pay my annual Game subscription each year and still save enough to pay my lifetime subscription within thirty years."

I'd listened to a lot of kids saying similar things. Their estimates of how long it would take them to pay their lifetime subscriptions varied from a conservative forty years, to a wildly optimistic twenty years. The truth was that it usually took people far longer than they estimated. If you didn't have a career commitment forcing you to work regular hours, then it was easy to give way to the temptation to spend more and more time exploring the delights of Game.

My mother had fallen into that trap, working and saving hard for her first year or two in Game, and then getting sucked into a daily round of parties and socializing. She gradually worked fewer hours each year, until she was barely working enough to cover her annual Game subscription. By the time she'd been in Game for eighty years, she was the only one of her friends still working, the only one still wearing a silver rather than a gold bracelet. The others had paid their lifetime Game subscriptions years or decades earlier.

When her friends started visiting worlds that wouldn't accept anyone in a silver bracelet, my mother was left behind for days or weeks at a time. She was desperate to pay her lifetime subscription quickly, and the fastest way to get the extra credits she needed was to sign up to have a child, but returning to the real world was incredibly hard for her after spending so long enjoying the luxurious life of Game. My mother had hated every minute of the year it took for her to have her eggs harvested, fertilized, implanted, and then go through the process of pregnancy and giving birth.

"What about you, Jex?" Hawk's voice dragged me back to reality.

I hesitated before reluctantly replying. "I signed up for the career path route to becoming a doctor."

"Something went wrong?" There was a sympathetic note in Hawk's voice. "You didn't get a place on the training course?"

I couldn't talk about how I'd been robbed of my future as a doctor now. Not when I'd just been robbed of my future in Game as well. I dodged the question. "I got a place on the course, but not all the medical cadets make it through to the end of training and qualify as doctors. I was dropped from the course a year ago."

"So you've been doing the same as Nathan since then, saving up for your annual and lifetime Game subscriptions?" asked Hawk.

"Yah," I said.

"Women have a big advantage when it comes to saving up for their lifetime Game subscriptions though," said Nathan. "They can use the baby bonus shortcut. Men don't get paid anything for fathering children."

Given I'd just been thinking about the problems my mother had had returning to the real world, I couldn't help glaring at him. "Nathan, fathering a child just involves giving consent for your DNA sample to be used. Are you really claiming a man should get the same bonus payment as the mother who has to spend a year in real life having the baby?"

Nathan took a nervous step backwards. "Point," he acknowledged. "I just meant that you could earn a lot of credits very quickly. Especially if the doctors decide it's safe for you to have twins. Are you rated for twins, Jex?"

"I'm not sharing my medical history with you, Nathan," I said coldly.

Actually, I was twin rated. My mother had a health issue that made the doctors restrict her to having single pregnancies. I'd expected to have inherited the same problem, but was pleasantly surprised when I had my sixteenth birthday assessment. My tests all came back clear, and the doctors were happy to rate me for twins.

I realized I was being unfair to Nathan. He didn't know how much my mother had loathed her time in the real world having a baby, or how it had affected her relationship with me.

"I think I'd like to have children eventually," I added in a friendlier voice, "but not because of the baby bonus. My father was a good parent, calling me every week from Game. I'd like to do the same for my own children one day."

Even as I said the words, a new thought hit me. It would be unfair of me to have children now, because having a Game reject for a mother would be a blight on their future. I was hit by a wave of emotion that was oddly similar to how I'd felt when I heard my father was dead.

Fortunately Hawk didn't ask me any more questions, just wandered across to the nearest freezer unit. He put out a golden hand as if about to clear the grime from the viewing window, but abruptly frowned and moved away again.

"There's something deeply disturbing about this place," he said. "My life in Game has always seemed totally real to me. I'm standing in my castle right now, wearing a virtual visor that shows me the view from this droid's eyes, a microphone that transmits my voice, and a sensor net that makes the droid copy my movements."

I was startled by Hawk's mention of a castle, though I

shouldn't have been. Ordinary players in Game had a house that varied in design depending on the particular world where the player was a resident, but I knew the rules were different for Founder Players. They had diamond bracelets, their own private world of Celestius which no other players were allowed to enter, and castles in the air rather than houses on the ground.

Hawk was still talking. "I'm seeing freezer units that hold the frozen bodies of players, and thinking that somewhere there's a freezer unit holding my own frozen physical body. I could take this droid to that freezer unit, and stand looking down at myself. I could even touch my own body. Which one of me would be real then? The virtual Hawk in Game, the droid I'm controlling, or the frozen body that I left behind four hundred years ago?"

He didn't wait for an answer, just gave a violent shake of his head. "I'd like to leave the body stacks now and see where you live. Could you take me to your rooms?"

I exchanged panic stricken glances with Nathan. The idea of showing our rooms to Hawk was deeply embarrassing, but we couldn't refuse a request from a legendary Founder Player.

"If that's all right," said Hawk.

"Yah." Nathan's voice had an odd, strangled note. "It's just that we'll get into trouble if we leave work before the end of our shift."

"I'll make arrangements with your supervisors," said Hawk. "Moment."

He glanced sideways, as if he was looking at something we couldn't see. There was a long pause and then he nodded. "That's all sorted. Let's go."

Hawk walked away in the direction of the nearest transport stop, moving at the usual rapid, tireless pace of controlled droids. Nathan and I shared another look of despair before getting on our buggies and driving after him.

There was a four-person pod waiting at the transport stop. I didn't bother trying to work out whether Hawk had arrived in it, or summoned it when he was making arrangements with our supervisor. My mind was fully occupied with picturing the state of my room when I left for work, particularly the heap of discarded clothes on my unmade bed. I was desperately trying to work out the crucial point of whether my underwear had been on top of the overalls or hidden underneath them. I had a bad feeling that the underwear was on top.

Hawk paused by the massive black cube of the transport stop vending machine, and studied the slowly scrolling display of its contents and prices. "Sandwiches. Soap. Socks. Sweets. Does this machine really sell all these things?"

"Yah," said Nathan. "Things like overalls and phones too. You can order items that aren't in the basic range as well, but those get delivered to your room."

"Do you buy all your things from these machines then?" asked Hawk.

"Most things except food," I said. "I'd rather eat the vending machine socks than the sandwiches."

Hawk finally lost interest in the vending machine, and we all climbed into the pod. "Where are we going first?" he asked.

I wanted to get the embarrassment over with as quickly as possible. "We can go to my room first. It's in one of the nearest big accommodation blocks."

I punched numbers into the pod guidance system, and it started moving.

"If we're going to meet a lot of people in this accommodation block, then I'd better change back to being the bird," said Hawk. "I don't want to attract a crowd of onlookers."

I glanced at the time display on the pod guidance system. "I doubt if anyone will see us at all. The kids on the same shift as me will all be at work, and those on the alternate shift will be asleep."

"What about the career cadets and anyone who isn't working today?" asked Hawk.

"Cadets have rooms in special class A accommodation blocks, and kids work every day unless they're having medical treatment," I said.

There was total silence for the next few minutes. When our pod stopped, I led the way onto the platform, past the broken double doors that had been stuck open for the last three weeks, and through a maze of corridors to my room. Once I'd punched my combination into the lock, I opened the door and sprinted across to the clothes strewn on the bed. My underwear was, as I'd feared, on top of the overalls, but it just took one lightning movement of my hand to yank the sheet down to cover the whole lot.

I relaxed, turned round, and was filled with embarrassment again as I saw both Nathan and Hawk were looking at the set of Game pictures on my wall. The droid Hawk had a bemused expression on his face as he studied the image of his Game self fighting the Kraken. Nathan was examining the picture next to that, which showed the silver-haired Jex on Ganymede.

Depression overwhelmed me, sweeping away trivial emotions like embarrassment. For the last year, I'd been looking at that image of the future Jex on my wall, dreaming of walking the beaches of Ganymede, fantasizing about spending time with my father and getting to know him better.

Perhaps the fantasies about my father had always been unrealistic. Most people would say he'd more than fulfilled his obligations to me by calling me regularly when I was a child and offering to act as my sponsor when I entered Game. They'd say it was unreasonable of me to hope that he'd spend time with me when I was a player as well. I'd never know the truth now that my father was dead.

The sound of Hawk's voice intruded on my misery. "You work a twelve-hour shift each day, Jex, but you can't afford a better room than this?"

I stared blankly at the Hawk droid for a moment, then realized he'd finally torn himself away from the image of himself fighting the Kraken, and was looking round at the rest of my room. My brain gradually made sense of his question and I forced myself to answer.

"When you're a cadet, all your food and accommodation is provided, so you only get a modest payment in credits. I didn't save much of that, because I expected to have my subscriptions paid for me when I entered Game. When I was dropped in mid-training, I was left with just under a year to save enough credits to pay my first annual subscription to Game, so I had to get the cheapest possible room."

"I'd no idea that teenagers would be so focused on paying Game subscriptions," said Hawk. "Volunteers for the ten year trial period of Game didn't have to pay anything, and we were all credited with lifetime subscriptions when Game opened to the general public. I've plenty of friends who aren't Founder Players, but they all paid their lifetime subscriptions long ago."

He studied the shelf with my store of nutrient bars. "I hope these things aren't all you get to eat."

Nathan seemed to have worked out that I was upset, because he answered that question for me. "We get our meals and sandwich packs from food outlets."

Hawk nodded. "I can hear a strange thumping noise."

"That's the plumbing," I said wearily. "The main circulation pump for this accommodation block is on the other side of my wall. I get an extra discount off my room rent because of the noise."

Hawk turned to look at the Game pictures on my wall again. "You're thinking of starting in Game on Ganymede, Jex?"

"Yah, but that's not possible now."

"Why not?" asked Hawk.

"My father was a resident of Ganymede and was going to sponsor me, but now he's dead and…" Another wave of emotion hit me. I let the words trail off and rubbed moisture from my eyes.

"There are very strong feelings in Game about the deaths in the Avalon world crash," said Hawk. "I'm sure Ganymede will honour your father's memory by offering resident status to his daughter."

I was sure Ganymede would be willing to offer me resident status for my father's sake, right up until the Admission Committee saw my Game record and discovered Unilaw had questioned me about the bombing. After that, they'd never let me set foot on the sands of their beaches. Hawk obviously didn't understand that, and I was in no state to explain it to him.

Hawk turned towards the door. "Thank you for showing me

your room, Jex. It's helped me understand just how much teenagers focus their lives on their futures in Game, and how angry they must have been to have to wait an extra year to start living their dreams. Can we all move on to Nathan's room now?"

Nathan and Hawk headed out of the door. Hawk's words showed he expected me to go with them, but I hesitated. My phone was still lying on my bed, and its message light was flashing. If we ended up going back to the body stacks, and my buggy detected I had a phone with me, then I'd lose my job, but that flashing light might mean my mother had sent me a message about my father's death.

I couldn't walk away from that flashing light. If Hawk took us back to the body stacks, I'd just have to throw this phone away and buy another from a vending machine later. I grabbed the phone, stuffed it into the pocket of my overalls, and chased after Hawk and Nathan.

When we arrived back at the transport stop and stepped into a pod, I hoped I'd have the chance to check my phone messages on the journey, but I was out of luck. Nathan's room turned out to be in another of this cluster of accommodation blocks, so the pod had barely finished accelerating before it was braking again.

I could see a tense, embarrassed expression on Nathan's face as he led us to his room. I wondered if it was because he'd left clothes on display as well, or because his room was hideously untidy. Nathan didn't seem the type of boy to have decorated his room with pictures of semi-naked women.

He opened the door, we went inside, and I blinked in shock. Nathan's room was larger than mine because this was a class C accommodation block. There was a neatly made bed, and one wall with shelves holding obsessively well-organized piles of clothes and possessions. It was the other three walls that stunned me. Every inch of them was covered with pieces of paper, each one holding what seemed to be a hand-drawn image of a player or creature from Game.

I took a step closer to the nearest wall, and saw there were notes written on the papers too. Comments about things like shapeshifting to water form made sense to me, but there were a lot of abbreviations and what I guessed were technical terms as well. I was awed by how much time Nathan must have spent working on these, and then I remembered that the buggies in the body stacks scanned us for forbidden electronic devices like phones, but would ignore simple paper and pencils.

"I see you're aiming to become a Game Tech, Nathan," said Hawk. "Is that another reason you didn't sign up for a career path? You have to be free of other commitments to apply to become a Game Tech?"

"Yah," Nathan said swiftly, using the defensive tones of someone who'd suffered a lot of cruel teasing about his ambition. "I know that the candidates who make it through the application screening phase can have to wait decades or even centuries before they're actually recruited as Game Techs. I'm also well aware that nine out of ten candidates will never be recruited at all, but my dream is to help design new Game worlds one day so..."

He broke off for a moment, clearly struggling with his emotions, then spoke again in a calmer voice. "Official Game policy is to keep everything about world and creature creation totally secret from players to avoid spoiling their Game experience. That means the Game design courses in schools only teach the very basics, but I've been trying to work things out for myself."

Hawk glanced up at the ceiling. "I can see that."

I looked up at the ceiling myself, and was stunned to see that was covered with papers as well. Now I knew why Nathan never complained about the boredom of working in the body stacks. I knew why he was so incredibly knowledgeable about all the different Game worlds. I knew the reason he wanted to start in Game on a brand new world with all the latest advances in worldscape and creature design. All Nathan's oddities made far more sense now.

"Have you put in your Game Tech application yet?" asked Hawk.

"Yah," said Nathan, in a depressed voice. "Candidates enter their applications and take their screening tests a few months before they enter Game. I was called in for mine before the Leebrook Ashton bill increased the age for entering Game. I scored very highly on the technical aptitude test, and the personality assessment test rated me extremely suitable, so I made it through the application screening phase."

Hawk stepped closer to one of the walls, studied a piece of paper, and then moved on to a second and a third. I grabbed my chance to sneak my phone out of my pocket, and furtively checked my messages.

There were two text messages. The first message was the official notification of my father's death. It said that as his next of kin, I would be informed of funeral arrangements in due course.

The other message was from the girl who lived in the room next to mine. There was nothing from my mother. It was foolish of me to have thought there might be. My mother always avoided anything unpleasant, and you couldn't get more unpleasant than my father's death.

I automatically checked the message from my neighbour, expecting it to be about meeting for a meal tomorrow, and was shocked by the words I saw. "Get out of here before the rest of us force you to leave."

I didn't understand how my neighbour knew I'd been questioned about the Avalon bombing, but then I remembered the boy who'd seen me dragged off by the Unilaw droid. He'd have guessed that was connected with the bombing, told all the kids in neighbouring rooms, and the news would have spread rapidly round our accommodation block and beyond.

I didn't know any of the kids in my accommodation block very well – I'd left all my true friends behind when I was dropped from my medical training – so they'd naturally react by ordering me to leave. It wouldn't matter whether they thought I was innocent or guilty. They'd be afraid that just living on the same corridor as me, or saying hello to me in passing, would get them dragged in for questioning by Unilaw as my accomplice.

I bit my lip. Once I got back to my room, I'd have to pack my things and leave. I'd probably find myself jobless within days as well.

"I'm sure you've a very good chance of being recruited as a Game Tech, Nathan," said Hawk. "You must be exceptionally gifted to have worked out so much about Game creatures that you've only seen in replays of Game events."

"Yah, but..."

Nathan broke off his sentence, seemed to hesitate for a second, and then his expression changed to that of someone about to make a desperate gamble. I realized he was going to explain about the problem with our Game records, and appeal to Hawk to help us.

I felt my hands clench in tension. I hated the idea of begging anyone for help, and it was horribly presumptuous of us to make demands on a Founder Player like Hawk, but this was the only hope for both Nathan and me. If Hawk would just put a few words on our Game records, say that we'd been helpful, it would change everything for us.

I listened intently as Nathan started talking, ready to join in with my own plea. "When we were questioned by Unilaw," Nathan began, "that..."

"Moment." Hawk turned his head to look sideways, clearly distracted by something in Game. There was an agonizing wait of three or four minutes before he spoke again. "I've just had a message from the Avalon Survivors Group. They understand me spending time on the hunt for the bomber, they want whoever was responsible caught as fast as possible, but they'd also like me to visit the bomb site on their behalf."

His face twisted in pain. "They shouldn't have had to send me that message. I let myself get too caught up in the interviews and the investigation. I should have realized that my job as player representative isn't just about catching the bomber, but about helping fifty billion distressed players, especially the Avalon survivors, cope with what's happened."

He paused. "I have to go to the bomb site as my first priority now. Thank you for giving me a glimpse of your lives."

Nathan and I exchanged despairing looks. The moment for asking Hawk for help had gone. I saw Nathan turn to face one of his sketches on the wall. I couldn't be sure what it was without moving closer, but judging from Nathan's mournful expression it was probably his planned future self as a werewolf.

"Simple things, like mentioning that a good parent calls their child once a week from Game, have shown me that I know even less about this world than I thought," added Hawk. "Since I can't stay here to learn more from you, I'd like you both to come along and assist me. Would you be willing to do that?"

Nathan and I stared at him in a mixture of disbelief and hope, and eagerly spoke in chorus. "Yah."

"My job means I'll have access to confidential details about both the Unilaw and Game investigations. The Game news channels have all been warned that they mustn't broadcast anything other than official announcements, because the bomber would get that information too, but I don't entirely trust them. I hope both of you understand that everything you see and hear while you're assisting me has to be kept strictly secret."

"Yah," we chorused for the second time.

"That's settled then," said Hawk. "Let's get moving."

He strode off out of the door, and Nathan and I scurried after him. When we arrived back at the transport stop, our original pod had vanished off to carry other passengers, so Hawk called up a new four-person pod, and we climbed in and sat facing him.

The pod started moving. There were no resurrections in the real world like there were in Game. Nothing could bring my father back to me, but I was part of the hunt for the bomber who'd killed him. If that hunt was successful, then Hawk would surely agree to help me and Nathan with comments on our records, and a word of praise from Hawk the Unvanquished would convince the Admission Committee of any world in Game to accept us.

There was still a chance that Jex of the silver, feathered hair would live under the glorious sky of Ganymede.

CHAPTER FIVE

It couldn't have been more than a two minute ride before the pod stopped. I looked at the opening door in surprise. Hawk had mentioned at the end of my interrogation that the bomb site was hundreds of miles away, so I'd expected us to be making a long journey.

Hawk bounced to his feet and lightly stepped out of the pod. His movements were becoming less and less generic and mechanical, and more those of a distinct person. I'd never seen that happen before with a droid. Part of the difference might be because this was an unusual droid, but I was sure most of it was because the incredible Hawk was controlling it.

Nathan and I followed Hawk out onto the platform. I saw we were at an interchange with a major express line, and a sleek, long-distance carriage was waiting for us. Hawk wasn't a kid hoarding as many credits as possible to pay their subscription when they entered Game. He probably had an unlimited budget for his work, so it made sense that we'd transfer from a standard pod to one of the much higher speed long-distance carriages for this journey.

I expected Hawk to lead us into the carriage, but instead he stood utterly motionless with even his facial expression frozen in place. I guessed he'd disabled the droid controls while he did something else in Game. Nathan and I exchanged puzzled glances, and waited silently.

After a few minutes, a delivery trolley whizzed up to me,

braked sharply to a halt, and bleeped plaintively. I realized I was standing on the red square that marked the delivery trolleys' navigation and recharge hub for this interchange, and guiltily stepped aside.

The trolley trundled forward onto the square, stopped, and its green control lights flashed busily for a few seconds as it checked its location and recharged power. The blue light came on to show it was processing further instructions, and it abruptly turned, rolled across to the long-distance carriage, extended its crane-like arm, and loaded three crates in through the door.

We'd obviously been waiting for these crates to be delivered. Did that mean we'd be leaving now? I looked hopefully at Hawk, and saw he'd come back to life again and was watching the delivery trolley roll off to its next job. Judging from the bemused look on his face, delivery trolleys had either been very different back when he entered Game or hadn't existed at all.

Hawk gave an odd shake of his head, turned, and went aboard the carriage. Nathan and I hastily followed, and I saw Nathan purse his lips in a soundless whistle of appreciation. This was a large, luxury carriage. It could comfortably hold twenty people, but we seemed to have it all to ourselves.

We sat down on plush padded seats, with arms that reached round and embraced us as the carriage started to accelerate. I'd never been in a long-distance carriage before, and I didn't like the sensation of being imprisoned. Fortunately, it was only a few minutes before the grasping arms released us. There was a musical chime, and a recorded voice came from overhead speakers.

"We have reached maximum velocity. You are now free to move as you wish. Please return to your seats when the deceleration warning sounds."

"I'm afraid we've got to make a very long journey," said Hawk. "I wanted to use this particular controlled droid during my investigation, because it's an experimental model with a lot of anti-surveillance features. You'll think I'm paranoid about reporters, but I've had a lot of problems with them spying on me in the past, and I don't want them messing up this investigation."

He stood up and went across to open a crate. "The only problem with using this droid was that it was stored in a United Law facility in what used to be called England in my day, while the bomb site was over five hundred miles away."

"This is still called England," I said diffidently.

Hawk laughed. "It's nice to know something hasn't changed. Anyway, we'll be going through a sub-ocean tunnel and deep into the heart of Europe."

He tossed a sealed plastic bag to me, and another to Nathan. "It'll save a lot of pointless explanations if you two are wearing more official looking clothes while you're helping me. There's a shower at the end of the carriage if you want to freshen up. Catch a couple of hours sleep if you want as well. I don't need sleep myself, so try to grab what opportunities you get, and remind me if I forget you have to rest sometimes."

I gestured to Nathan to use the shower first, since my nose was telling me he urgently needed it. He headed off, clutching his plastic bag.

While he was off in the shower, I opened my own plastic bag and inspected the contents. Dark blue, tailored top and trousers, with shoes to match. They reminded me of the uniforms I'd worn as a medical cadet, though these were higher quality so probably intended for adults. The tags showed they were my size, so someone must have checked my medical records. I wondered if Hawk had done that himself, or if he had an assistant in Game, looking up information and ordering things for him.

Nathan took a long time in the shower. He came back wearing his new clothes and with his hair neatly trimmed, looking rather pleased with himself. I headed off and enjoyed a long shower myself. The cubicle had a lot of accessories, and I couldn't resist trying out some of the ones I'd never encountered before.

I had a haircut, a manicure, a body glow, and added a temporary tattoo of blue flowers on my forehead to mimic the way I hoped to look in Game. I dressed in my new clothes, and admired my reflection in the mirror, deciding that I looked even better than I had in my glitz girl days.

I finally realized how long I'd been in the shower, and guiltily headed back out to join the others. They were sitting in the seats again. Hawk had the blank expression that meant he was busy in Game. Nathan was staring at the ceiling and looking bored, but he grinned when he saw me coming.

"Very nice," he said. "I like the flowers."

Hawk's attention returned to us. He gave me a startled look, and then glanced at Nathan. "Much better. I hope you don't mind me saying so, but those baggy things you were wearing were..."

I nodded. "Overalls are cheap and practical, but they aren't much to look at."

"Now I think of it, I should improve my own appearance." Hawk's golden droid body blurred for a second, and then came back into focus apparently wearing clothes similar to ours. "Does that give a better effect?"

"Oh yah," I said, amazed by the transformation.

If you looked closely, you could see the clothes were part of Hawk's droid body, not something he was wearing, but to the casual eye he appeared to be a real man now. I found the effect rather disconcerting. When I was younger, I'd had a lot of fantasies about Hawk, so I felt awkward being so close to what appeared to be his physical presence.

"We're still nearly an hour away from our destination," said Hawk, "so you can have a little doze."

"Erm." Nathan made an apologetic noise.

Hawk looked at him. "What did I forget?"

"Would it be possible for us to have some food to eat?"

Hawk raised his eyes to the ceiling and shook his head. "I ordered clothes. I didn't order food. I knew I was the wrong person for this job. If I can't remember that eating in real life isn't optional then..."

"This is a luxury carriage." I looked round hopefully. "There must be food somewhere."

"A luxury carriage will probably respond to voice commands." Nathan paused before speaking in a self conscious voice. "We wish to eat."

A table promptly appeared from the wall, with a glowing menu displayed on its surface.

"Yah!" cried Nathan.

Hawk laughed, and then spent the next half an hour working in Game. Nathan and I spent the time stuffing ourselves with a three course meal of all the rarest delicacies on offer.

"Warning," announced the overhead speakers, "deceleration will be starting shortly."

Nathan and I sat back in our seats and the table withdrew, taking the remains of my rainbow-coloured dessert with it. The seat arms embraced us in an officious hug, and the carriage braked to a standstill.

I was about to see the site of the bombing that had killed my father. I tensed, and my mind started conjuring up visions of mangled bodies. I knew perfectly well that I was being ridiculous. There'd be no bodies here, the people who'd died in the bombing had all been in freezer units scattered across body stacks in different parts of the world, but I still couldn't help imagining horrors like dismembered limbs.

I fought to block out the gory visions, followed Nathan and Hawk out of the carriage, and was dazzled by bright sunlight. I lifted my right hand to shade my eyes, and saw this was an open air transport stop, surrounded by an area of mostly flat grassland. I thought it looked a bit like a scene from Game world Meadow, but far more boring without the herds of wild horses and the flocks of glitterwings.

I had an odd feeling that something was missing. It took me a moment to work out what was wrong. Every transport stop I'd ever seen had a platform with the red square of a delivery trolley hub next to the massive, black bulk of the vending machine. This platform had a delivery trolley hub but no vending machine.

I forgot about the mystery of the missing vending machine, because a welcoming party of six Unilaw officers was hurrying up to greet us. Our interrogations fresh in our minds, Nathan and I exchanged wary glances, and instinctively moved to a position close behind Hawk.

The Unilaw officers stepped forward and greeted Hawk with

a barrage of compliments. Five of them were the usual Unilaw droids controlled by adults in Game, but I was startled to see a woman who was physically present and very obviously pregnant. She was wearing a silver bracelet on her left arm that was a close imitation of the bracelets players wore in Game. The Leebrook Ashton bill had been carefully worded to make sure that anyone who'd entered Game at eighteen still counted as legally adult if they defrosted. Presumably the bracelet was intended to emphasize that point.

I watched impatiently as everyone fawned over Hawk, thought how idiotic they sounded, and then remembered my own reaction to meeting him. I'd been even worse than these people, gushing about Hawk being my all time hero, and eulogizing about him killing the Kraken.

I comforted myself with the thought that Hawk would have forgotten all about that by now. He had far more pressing things on his mind than a dumb kid wittering on about how wonderful he was.

Hawk took all the hero worship in his stride, acknowledging everyone graciously. Of course he'd had hundreds of years of experience with dealing with adoring fans.

"These are my assistants, Nathan and Jex." Hawk gestured at the two of us. "I'm hoping you'll give us a tour of the bomb site."

Our escorts led the way along a wide concrete path, past a small storage unit, to where the path split into three narrower ones leading in different directions. We followed the path on the left.

"You can see the protective force field of the server complex ahead of us," said one of the droids. "We've got a lot of people going in and out, so we're keeping a gap open."

I looked where the droid was pointing and saw a dome-shaped, opaque shimmer in the air. I'd heard about force fields but never seen one before. I frowned. The bombs must have been placed inside the force field or they wouldn't have damaged the server complex. How had the bomber managed to get through the force field?

It took us less than five minutes to reach the force field. For the first minute or two of the trip, I walked with studied dignity, trying to look as old and official as possible, but then decided I was wasting my time. Nobody was going to pay any attention to me or Nathan when Hawk was around. They might have noticed if I'd thrown all my clothes off and screamed, but I wouldn't have bet Game credits on it.

At close quarters, the force field looked like a strange, glowing curtain. I didn't know what would happen if I touched it, and it seemed a bad idea to try experimenting to find out. I followed our escort through an opening, and grimaced as I saw a zone of devastation.

This area of torn earth and rocks, these shreds of plastic, marked the event that had killed my father and thousands of other people. I felt that I should be saying or doing something as a mark of respect, but nothing like this had happened in hundreds of years so I'd no idea what was appropriate.

"I should have brought flowers," said Hawk, in a shaken voice. "There'd have needed to be thousands of them though. Eleven thousand, two hundred, and ninety seven flowers."

He turned to me. "My condolences, Jex."

I knew it was just a droid standing next to me, but I was deeply aware that the pain in the voice I was hearing was that of the real Hawk in Game. I rubbed the back of my hand across my eyes.

"Thank you," I said. "We have to find out who did this."

The droid hand touched me on the shoulder for the briefest of seconds. "We *will* find out who did this."

There was a moment or two of silence before Nathan spoke in an awkward voice.

"My condolences to you too, Jex."

"Thanks," I muttered.

There was another full minute of silence, and then Hawk walked slowly forward, his head bent as he studied the cratered ground. Our Unilaw escort had been standing still, deferentially watching us, but now they all moved to follow Hawk.

I forced my emotions under control, and made myself look round and take in the details of the bomb site. There were a lot of controlled droids scattered round the cratered area. Most of them had the distinctive blue and grey markings of Unilaw on their chests, but a cluster of a dozen Game droids were standing nearby. I saw that the insignia on the faces of most of the Game Techs controlling them weren't the usual bronze colour, but silver, and then I caught sight of one with gold insignia.

I realized Nathan had gone to join Hawk, so I was standing alone next to a group of intimidatingly high-ranked Game Techs. I hurried to join Hawk as well.

Hawk turned to the Unilaw deputation. "Have you discovered any information about the bomb that was used?"

The pregnant woman replied. "The crater pattern shows there were actually four small devices. They exploded simultaneously, triggered by a timing device. We can't be sure of anything else. There hasn't been a bombing for centuries, so we've no Unilaw staff with experience of bombs, and have to work from information in old texts."

"You could ask Romulus and Remus to help," said Hawk. "They worked in bomb disposal before they entered Game."

The woman looked horrified at the suggestion. "I couldn't possibly trouble two Founder Players. There must be other bomb experts among the players who entered Game in the first century or two."

Hawk gave his one-shouldered shrug. "I'm sure there are plenty who'd claim to be experts, but it could be hard to establish if those claims are true or exaggerated. I know Romulus and Remus are genuine experts, and if I can use a controlled droid to help with this crisis then so can they. I'll get Pendragon to have a word with them."

Hawk knelt to study the ground in more detail. I didn't know if he could make any sense of the oddments of wreckage strewn around us. I certainly couldn't. I didn't even know what a server complex looked like when it was in one piece.

Hawk sighed and stood up again. "I'm not learning much from this. Is it possible for us to see a functioning server complex of identical layout?"

I was startled that Hawk had been thinking the same thing

as me. Everyone turned and walked back to the gap in the force field, and then there was a brief delay as our escorts conferred with a couple of the Game Techs' droids. Apparently only Game Techs and authorized maintenance crews were allowed to visit server complexes. Given the circumstances, the Game Techs were willing to make an exception for Hawk as the player representative, and Nathan and I as his assistants, but they weren't willing to include the Unilaw deputation.

Eventually a four-seater buggy rolled up. The Game Tech droid in the front seat had a face with silver insignia on his cheeks. Hawk sat next to him, Nathan and I climbed into the back seat, and Hawk's fan club watched sadly as we drove off down a path.

"Can you please explain the local geography?" asked Hawk.

Our driver answered the question, using the standard formal speech of Game Techs. "Server complexes are always located in remote areas with low tectonic activity, no extreme weather conditions, and no risk of flooding. For security reasons, each server complex is at a distance from any other structure and protected by a force field. In this particular area, we have a cluster of a dozen server complexes."

I frowned and looked round. There were twelve server complexes in this area. The Avalon server complex was behind us. I could see the force field of another server complex directly ahead of us, which must be our destination. There was what might be another force field over to our right, but it was a long way away.

"So twelve Game worlds are run from this area, and the one nearest the transport stop was bombed?"

I said the words without thinking, and instantly realized that I shouldn't have spoken in front of a Game Tech. I cringed as I waited for a rebuke, but the Game Tech response was emotionless.

"That is correct."

Hawk twisted round in his seat to look back at me, "That's a good point, Jex. It's possible Avalon was targeted for a specific reason, but it could have been randomly chosen because it's close to a transport stop."

There was silence for the next few minutes. Once we arrived at our destination server complex, the Game Tech droid tapped the controls on the buggy, and an opening appeared in the force field ahead of us. The buggy moved inside, and I saw four small grey buildings standing on bare fused rock. The Game Tech parked the buggy by the buildings, and we all climbed down from our seats.

Hawk looked round eagerly. "Fascinating to think this runs one of our Game worlds." He turned to the Game Tech. "You used some sort of security code to get us inside this force field?"

"That is correct."

"The bombs at the Avalon server complex had been planted inside its force field. That means the bomber had got hold of the Avalon force field security code. Who has access to those codes?"

"Only Game Techs and the maintenance crews making weekly inspections."

Hawk walked up to the nearest building and peered at the sign on the door. "This server complex runs Destiny Game world, a world created about the same time as Avalon. I suppose all the worlds run by server complexes in this cluster will date from about the same time."

He turned to look at the Game Tech droid. "How long does the gap in the force field stay open?"

"Two minutes," said the Game Tech. "Maintenance crews take longer than that to do their work, so they have to open the force field again to leave."

"And how often are the force field security codes changed?"

"Err... I'm not sure that..." The calm face displayed on the droid suddenly looked wary, and his formally standardized Game Tech speech pattern faltered.

"Are they ever changed?" demanded Hawk.

"Possibly not," said the Game Tech.

Hawk's voice developed an edge that could cut diamonds. "In the light of the recent bombing, I strongly suggest that all force field security codes are changed immediately."

The Game Tech nodded hastily. "I will arrange for them to be changed."

"Is a record kept when someone requests a security code?"

"I will investigate the possibility of recording such requests in future."

"You do that while my assistants and I take a look around the server complex." Hawk led the way into the nearest building, raised his eyes to the grey ceiling, and began chanting. "One, two, three, four, five…"

Nathan and I exchanged looks of bewilderment.

"…six, seven, eight, nine, ten," Hawk continued, and then abruptly exploded in anger. "Bleeping idiots! The Game Techs run a dozen Game worlds from this area. There are no guards or surveillance cameras, just a maintenance crew riding round on a buggy once a week. The only defence is the force fields, controlled by security codes they never change. They don't even keep a record of who has those codes. Do you believe that?"

He turned to Nathan and me, and we hastily shook our heads. Hawk's ranting didn't seem to be directed at us, but we daren't risk saying a word.

"Perhaps it's understandable that they've grown sloppy after hundreds of years without trouble," said Hawk. "I hope the Unilaw lot can handle this situation better than the Game Techs though or we're all totally in the…"

He broke off and gave us a guilty look. "Sorry if I've been yelling a bit. It's not constructive for me to swear at a Game Tech, but I needed to let off a bit of steam."

"It's all right," I said cautiously. "We don't even know what bleeping means."

"No, of course you wouldn't. I'm four hundred years out of date. More than four hundred years in the case of the swearing, because I learned most of my swear words from Pendragon. He was the eldest of the Founder Players when we entered Game, and it amused him to use swear words that were old fashioned even in his youth. Bleeping is an especial joke of his, because it refers to when they used to bleep out genuine swear words from a recording."

He paused. "Back to work now. There seems surprisingly little in this building."

Nathan and I exchanged furtive glances, and reached a silent agreement. Hawk seemed to have calmed down but we should still tread extremely warily. Hawk was certainly right about there not being very much in this building. There was just a blank screen on the wall, a pedestal holding a small white box, and an even smaller black box at its base. Nothing else.

Nathan peered at the white box. "I think the code on the label means this is the main Destiny world server. Each of the other buildings will hold a backup server that mirrors this one, and any of them could keep the Destiny world running."

He knelt to examine the black box. "This is an emergency power unit. If the normal power supply failed, the emergency power could keep things running for months."

Hawk was staring at the white box. "That little box runs Destiny Game world. Millions of players live there, but that box is so small I could tuck it under my arm and walk away. I'm glad I don't need sleep any longer. If I slept, I'd have nightmares about little white boxes. Somewhere out there is a little white box with me inside it."

He stood there looking round for a moment longer, and finally led us out of the building. We glanced inside the three other buildings, but they were all exactly the same. When we finished and headed back to the buggy, the Game Tech's droid came to meet us, his face still looking wary.

"All force field security codes have now been changed. Future requests for security codes from maintenance teams will need to be authorized by a gold status Game Tech and will be recorded on an audit trail. When a security code is given, it will only be valid for two minutes before being automatically changed."

"Thank you," said Hawk. "As the representative of the player community, I appreciate your rapid response to my concerns."

The Game Tech face cheered up slightly.

"I have another issue that I'd like to discuss with you," added Hawk. "The fact that all four servers supporting a Game world are at the same physical location makes them very vulnerable to a deliberate attack. Is there any way that you can spread out the servers at different locations?"

"The current system was instituted after the Rhapsody disaster," said the Game Tech. "At that time, it was a matter of extreme urgency to provide the quadruple interlinked redundancy that could cope with any conceivable sort of future mechanical breakdown. The simplest and fastest method was to have all four servers at the same physical location. In the light of this bombing, we are already drawing up plans to change the system so each world is supported by servers at multiple locations, however it could take several years to make those changes."

Hawk frowned. "Why would it take so long?"

"Interlinking servers at different locations is more complex," said the Game Tech, "and changing the server configuration of an active Game world could cause the exact problem we are attempting to prevent."

"You mean that making the changes could cause more world crashes?"

"That is correct," said the Game Tech. "The only safe way to make these changes to a Game world is to evacuate the world, shut it down completely, and then bring it back with the new server configuration."

Hawk groaned. "Yes, I can see why going through that process with two thousand Game worlds would take years. I'd now like another look at the bomb site."

We climbed on to the buggy, the Game Tech opened a gap in the force field again to let us out, and we trundled our way back to the Avalon server complex. Hawk made a detailed inspection of the four craters, and Nathan and I dutifully followed him round, looking at every item of twisted wreckage. At one point, Hawk dropped to his knees to touch a white fragment.

"Whether I sleep or not, I'm definitely going to have nightmares about white boxes," he muttered. "Looking at that, and thinking…"

He stood up and went to where the Game Tech was waiting. "What is the current situation of the Avalon population?"

"The first priority was to return them to Game as fast as possible," said the Game Tech. "We were aware that their situation was uncomfortable."

"Yes," said Hawk, "it would have been uncomfortable, thrown out of Game without a second of warning, and trapped in a freezer unit coffin. Eleven thousand, two hundred, and ninety seven people died that way."

The Game Tech winced. "Not only do all Game Techs feel a deep sense of responsibility for those deaths, but many of our own people were caught in the Avalon world crash and several died."

"Yes, I'm sorry." Hawk shook his head. "I'm upset seeing this, but I shouldn't forget it's just as painful for you. You got the population of Avalon back into Game as fast as you could. What happened to them after that?"

"Initially, we loaded them into random under-populated worlds. Once the news broke about the Avalon world crash, all Game worlds responded by offering full visitation rights to Avalon refugees, so they were able to use standard Game world transfer requests to go to other worlds of their choice."

"So the Avalon refugees are still scattered as guests on other worlds?" asked Hawk.

"That is correct."

"Will it be possible for you to restore Game world Avalon?"

"We have already set up one of our reserve server complexes using the central Avalon world structure rolling backup. Running a full world integrity stress test took less than an hour, so we could reopen Avalon at any time and its residents could request Game world transfer home."

The Game Tech hesitated. "Game officials have made no announcement about this, because we are unsure whether the Avalon population will wish us to restore their world or not. We do not wish to cause any offence by making the wrong decision."

The Game Tech face on the droid tried to look impassive, but there was some emotion hidden under the surface. It took me a moment to work out that he was scared. It seemed incredible that one of the self-effacing but all-powerful officials who created and ran the Game could be scared, but these were unique circumstances. There were fifty billion deeply distressed players in Game, and they were looking for an outlet for their anger. One wrong word from one of the Game Techs, and all that pent up fury would find a target.

Hawk looked at the face on the droid, and seemed to see what I'd seen, because he nodded. "It might be best if I handle this in my role of player representative. I can make a broadcast asking the Avalon survivors to vote on whether their world should return or be left to rest in peace. Would you be able to arrange for the voting to open immediately after my announcement?"

"That is correct," said the Game Tech.

"If the Avalon residents want their world back," added Hawk, "then it might make a lot of people, including me, feel happier if you could put armed guards on that new server complex."

"The new Avalon server complex is already being guarded," said the Game Tech.

"Thank you," said Hawk. "I expect the Avalon residents will want some form of memorial to honour their dead, but there's no need to rush a decision on that."

"Whatever memorials are asked for by the population of Avalon will naturally be arranged according to their wishes," said the Game Tech.

"That's settled then," said Hawk.

He went back over to the huddle of Unilaw officers. "You've all been most helpful. I have to go now, but Romulus and Remus have agreed to help analyze the wreckage, and their controlled droids should be with you shortly."

Leaving was a slow process, since all the fans wanted to say a word of admiration and farewell, but we finally made it back to our carriage. Hawk slumped into a seat, Nathan and I sat down as well, and the carriage accelerated briefly, only to start slowing again and stop at the next transport stop.

"I don't know where to go," said Hawk, "but I had to get out of that place before I cracked. Much longer and I'd have either started crying or shouting at someone."

I stared at him, too startled to reply. He was talking like a very vulnerable human being who was overloaded by distress, but surely Hawk couldn't feel like that. Hawk was a glittering, unassailable legend who could cope with anything.

"I've just realized the enormity of what I've taken on here," he said. "I've fought against devastating monsters, I've led armies on Civil War, but that was all literally a game. Hunting down this bomber is real. Over eleven thousand people are already dead. If there's another attack, thousands more people may die, and their deaths would be my fault."

There was a moment of silence.

"I have to leave for a while now," said Hawk.

I was disconcerted. "You're leaving?"

"I'll need to have all my attention in Game while I make the broadcast about the vote for the future of Avalon." Hawk groaned. "I hate giving speeches. I'll be back in... I'll be back after however long this takes."

Hawk finished speaking, and the droid body abruptly changed back to a blank anonymous gold shape and sat inertly in its seat. Nathan went across and waved his hand in front of its head. There was no response.

"He's gone." Nathan stated the obvious.

CHAPTER SIX

Nathan put his finger to his lips, tiptoed to the door, and stepped out of the carriage. Once outside, he turned and beckoned to me. I looked at him in bewilderment, and he beckoned again.

I sighed and followed him out of the carriage. I found myself at a transport stop that was identical to the last one. No, not quite identical. The platform here was completely featureless, without either a vending machine or a delivery trolley hub.

Nathan put his finger to his lips again, and led the way across the platform and out into the surrounding grassland. There were concrete paths similar to those at the last transport stop, but Nathan ignored them, choosing to wade through the waist-high grass until he reached a large rock and sat on it.

I sighed again, and sat next to him on the rock. "Why have we come out here?"

"While we were in the body stacks, our buggies were recording every word we said. Once Hawk arrived, that fancy, anti-surveillance droid of his was probably blocking the buggies from recording us, but he was listening to us himself. Out here in the wilds, we can speak freely at last."

I wasn't sure I wanted to speak freely. I stared round at the countryside, noting the distant glow of a server complex force field over to our right. "Are you sure this rock doesn't have a spy device in it?"

Nathan jumped up and examined the rock. "We could move on a bit further if you think it's suspicious."

"Nathan," I said, in a pitying voice, "I was joking about the rock."

"Oh." He sat down again. "I can't believe what's happened. One minute life was perfectly normal, and then everything was smashed to pieces."

"Yah," I said miserably.

"I know it's even worse for you," said Nathan. "You've lost your father."

"At least I had a proper parent for eighteen years," I said, "while you've never really had a parent at all. I've still got my mother too. At least, I hope I have."

My phone was in my pocket. It was set to silent mode, but I knew I wouldn't have missed it vibrating for an incoming message. I took it out anyway. There was no flashing light.

I put the phone back in my pocket. "Still no message from my mother. That's not a good sign."

"Perhaps she doesn't know that your father is dead," said Nathan. "He wasn't an Avalon resident, so she wouldn't expect him to have been caught up in the world crash."

"I suppose that's possible."

"You could try calling her," said Nathan doubtfully. "I know we're expected to wait for parents to call us, not call them ourselves, but this is a very special case."

I shook my head. "I daren't risk it. I could have called my father in a situation like this, but not my mother. My relationship with her is... Well, it's difficult."

"You'll just have to wait for your mother to call you then." Nathan glanced back at the transport stop. "I wanted to talk to you about Hawk. You know he's incredibly popular in Game."

I gave him a bewildered look. "Of course. That's why the players insisted on Hawk being their representative rather than..."

I let the words trail off as I realized Nathan had said that to lead up to something. "This is about asking Hawk to help us? I'm sure he doesn't understand that the Unilaw questioning has wrecked our futures. If we explain the problem to him, then yah, he might well agree to put something positive on our records and that would solve all our problems."

"He might even agree to sponsor us. Just think what that would mean. With Hawk the Unvanquished sponsoring us, then any Game world would gladly accept us as residents. You could have Ganymede again. I'd have my chance to become a Game Tech one day."

Nathan's face was glowing with joy as he pictured that, but I wasn't going to let myself build up extravagant hopes. I'd fantasized about the future before, and seen those fantasies brutally shattered. There was also the point that this particular fantasy was based on begging Hawk for help. That didn't seem to bother Nathan, but it did bother me.

I shifted uncomfortably on the rock. "We can't ask Hawk to sponsor us. That would make us seem horribly demanding and greedy. We should settle for asking him to put a comment on our records, but we can't do that now. Hawk's under a huge amount of pressure. Over eleven thousand Gamers are dead, he's worried there'll be another bombing and more deaths, and right now he's making a speech to try to reassure fifty billion terrified people."

"I agree," said Nathan. "Asking Hawk for favours two seconds after we've visited the bomb site would be utterly selfish and stupid. We have to wait for the right time to discuss this with him."

He paused. "I really wanted to talk about Hawk for another reason."

"What reason?"

Nathan gave me a wary look. "You're a huge fan of Hawk. You've got a picture of his solo fight with the Kraken on your room wall."

"Yah. I've always thought that Hawk was the most impressive of the Founder Players."

"It's a bit more than thinking he's impressive. When Hawk arrived in the body stacks, you told him that he was your all time hero."

I flushed. "I was overwhelmed to meet Hawk, so I gushed a little, but you were just as bad as me. Your eyes were popping out of your head, and you were gasping 'wow'."

"That's true," said Nathan, "but there's one big difference

between us. However much I admire Hawk, I'm not attracted to men, so I'm not going to start fantasizing about getting into a relationship with him."

"I'm not fantasizing about getting into a relationship with Hawk!" I snapped.

"Really? Ever since Hawk arrived, I've felt as if I was totally invisible, because you're always watching him."

I frowned. That wasn't true, was it?

"And it's not just the way you watch him all the time," said Nathan. "It's... Well, just look at you now!"

I was confused. "What do you mean?"

"The clothes, the hair, the skin, the pretty flowers. Do I have to spell it out? Back in the body stacks, you wore overalls and your hair was a mess. That was good enough when you were with me, but Hawk showed up and you instantly turned yourself into a glitz girl."

I remembered thinking that my new clothes made me look as good as when I'd been part of the glitz crowd. Somehow that made Nathan's comment more rather than less annoying. I launched angrily into my own defence. "I didn't go out and get these clothes, I was given them to wear and I'm wearing them. There were lots of fancy accessories in the shower, so I naturally tried them out. I seem to remember you getting a haircut yourself."

I glared at Nathan. "You're only saying these things because you asked to meet me outside work and I turned you down."

"I'm not discussing this because I'm jealous," said Nathan. "I thought you were an attractive girl even when you were wearing baggy overalls, and I enjoyed chatting to you about all the different worlds and creatures in Game. I had a weak moment when I couldn't resist asking you out, but it was a relief when you turned me down. I knew it would be a huge mistake for me to get into a relationship with you."

I didn't want to get into a relationship with Nathan, but I still felt offended by him saying that. "Why would it be such a huge mistake?"

"Because I want to be a Game Tech."

"I don't understand the appeal of that," I said. "Once players pay their lifetime subscription, they can give up work and spend all their time having fun exploring the worlds of Game. If you become a Game Tech, you'll never stop working."

"If I become a Game Tech, I'll never want to stop working," said Nathan. "You dream of exploring the worlds of Game, Jex, but I dream of creating them. It's not just something I want to do; it's something I *have* to do. I've got a host of ideas inside my head, visions of landscapes and creatures that are asking me to bring them to life."

He paused. "The only problem with becoming a Game Tech is that they aren't allowed to have any ties with players. I know it has to be that way because Game Techs have so much power. The gods of Game mustn't be suspected of having favourites among the players."

The passion in his voice had changed to distress now. "If I'm ever recruited, those Game Tech regulations will apply to me. I'll have to walk away from everyone I ever knew, and never see or speak to those people again. I fell out with my twin brother over this. He said that if being a Game Tech was more important to me than being his brother, if I was going to break off contact with him one day because of my ambitions, then he'd rather we break off contact right away. He hasn't spoken to me in years."

"I didn't know you had a twin brother," I said. "You've never mentioned him before so I assumed you were a singleton child like me."

"Splitting up with my twin was like losing part of my own body. I don't want to go through that again with a girlfriend or wife, so it's best that I stick to casual friendships." Nathan waved a hand in dismissal. "I'm happy to just be your friend, Jex, but I'm worried about what's going on between you and Hawk."

"The real Hawk is in Game," I said. "The two of us are just interacting with a rather fancy droid that he's controlling. Do you seriously think I'm planning to seduce a droid?"

"Of course not," said Nathan, "but I'm concerned that you're getting emotionally involved with Hawk. There was a moment back at the bomb site when something pretty intense was going on between the two of you. Even the Unilaw officials noticed it."

"There wasn't anything 'going on' between us, Nathan. How could you think I was having fantasies about Hawk in the middle of that bomb site? I was upset about my father's death, and Hawk was sympathizing with me."

Nathan sighed. "I expressed myself very badly there. What I was trying to say was that there was a lot of heightened emotion between you two. We're in a very unusual situation here. Hawk's upset about the bombing. You're upset about your father. Hawk may only be represented in the real world by a controlled droid, but you two are starting to connect on a very human level."

"What's wrong with that?"

"There's nothing wrong with it so long as you don't lose track of reality. Hawk's a legendary Founder Player, with hordes of girls throwing themselves at him in Game. He must be very discreet about taking advantage of that, because people don't gossip about him the way they gossip about Caesar. I expect the Game Techs help hush things up. Anyway, I'm worried that you'll start imagining things that can't happen, and end up getting badly hurt."

I knew that Hawk would have had vast numbers of girlfriends. I'd figured it out for myself before Nathan helpfully rubbed my nose in it. "When I was younger, I spent a lot of time fantasizing about Hawk's picture on my wall, but I know the difference between fantasy and reality. I'm fully aware that Hawk would never want to get involved with me, and I wouldn't want to get involved with him either. I'd never agree to be in a relationship with anyone unless we were equal partners, and Hawk and I can never be equal."

I stood up. "We'd better go back to the carriage now. Hawk may be quite a while, so we should get some sleep."

We walked back to the carriage in silence. Once we were inside, I looked up at the ceiling and spoke. "I want to sleep."

A bed appeared from the wall.

"Me too," said Nathan.

Nothing happened.

He sighed. "I want to sleep."

This time he was rewarded with a bed. He lay down on it, while I stood looking at mine with a frown.

"What's the problem?" Nathan asked.

"I don't want to crease my new clothes and I had a thought."

I went across to the crate that had held our outfits, lifted the lid, and laughed.

"What?" Nathan asked again. He rolled off his bed and came over to join me.

"We've got several sets of clothes." I checked the next crate and took out a bag. "Night wear too. They must all be for us, because half of them are my size."

"Must be." Nathan collected a bag for himself. "I doubt that a droid wants to wear them."

I headed off to shower and change into my new luxury night clothes. I was already in bed and half asleep by the time Nathan walked past to get to his own bed.

"Good night," said Nathan.

I grunted an acknowledgement, and drifted off into a dream where I was patrolling the body stacks. Somehow the endless banks of freezer units changed into the beaches of Ganymede, and I became the Jex of the silver, feathered hair. Hawk was with me, his arm round my shoulders, and we were looking up at the glorious spectacle of Jupiter in the sky above us.

"Jex," said Hawk, and his warm lips met mine. "Jex, Nathan," he repeated.

My eyes shot open. I was in reality, not in Game. The golden droid had become Hawk again, and I blushed remembering my dream. Nathan was right that I needed to watch myself. I'd had a crush on the legendary Hawk for years. It would be terribly easy and horribly stupid to let my feelings get out of hand.

"I'm sorry to wake you up," said Hawk, "but I need to discuss some things."

Nathan gave a yawn and sat up. "How did the speech go?"

"I thought I was dreadful, but people seemed happy with it. The votes are already coming in, and it looks like the result will be overwhelmingly in favour of bringing Avalon back. People have varying reasons for that decision. Some just want the chance to pack things from their homes, some want to go back for a visit to pay their respects to the dead, while some are determined to stay permanently." Hawk gave his distinctive, one-shouldered shrug. "That's up to them. Avalon will always bear the mark of the bombing, but..."

He broke off his sentence. "Moment. I've just had another set of messages."

Hawk was glancing sideways, clearly checking his messages in Game. I grabbed the fresh clothes I'd left ready by my bed, sprinted to the shower for privacy, and dressed at lightning speed. When I got back, Nathan had dressed too, and the beds had vanished. Hawk was still concentrating on something we couldn't see, so Nathan and I called up a table and tapped at the menu to order our breakfasts.

We'd almost finished eating by the time Hawk returned his attention to us. "That was the Avalon Survivors Group messaging me about possible memorials. I've replied to them now, and I want to discuss my thoughts about the bombing with you."

Nathan and I hastily put down our knives and forks.

"You can keep eating while we talk," said Hawk.

Nathan picked up his knife and fork again, and started gulping down the last remnants of his breakfast at top speed, but I decided I was already full.

"Given the bombing happened so soon after the Leebrook Ashton bill became law, everyone instantly decided that some disgruntled teenagers were to blame," said Hawk. "I thought that too, but now I've got more information about what happened and I'm starting to question my assumption. How could teenagers make four bombs and get hold of the code for the force field protecting a Game server complex?"

"That's been bothering me too," I said eagerly. "Even if it was a large group of kids working together, I don't understand where they'd get information on making bombs."

Hawk frowned. "In the days before the Game started, there was something called the internet. You could find out a lot of very illegal things using that, including how to make bombs, but first the internet got better policed, and then it was replaced by Game's own information system. That definitely doesn't hold any details of how to make real life bombs."

"I suppose a science cadet might be able to work out how to make explosives," I said doubtfully, "and a technical cadet might be able to make those explosives into bombs, but how would kids get hold of the security code for the Avalon server complex force field?"

"Maintenance teams make regular checks on each server complex," said Hawk. "Perhaps a cadet working on a maintenance team found out the force field code."

Nathan swallowed his last mouthful of breakfast. "That couldn't happen."

"I'm sure the code would only be given to the maintenance team leader," said Hawk, "but a cadet might have seen it being entered and memorized it."

"That couldn't happen," repeated Nathan. "I wanted to know what a server complex was like, so I tried asking a few maintenance cadets. They couldn't answer my questions because they'd never seen one. They told me that cadets aren't allowed on the teams maintaining server complexes. All the work is done by fully qualified maintenance experts using controlled droids to work from Game."

I was thinking something that I wasn't sure I dared to say aloud. Before I could make up my mind whether to risk it or not, Hawk said the words for me.

"The simplest answer is that the bombing was organized by a player in Game who'd done maintenance work on the Avalon server complex. A maintenance expert would probably have the skills to make a bomb too, though I'm less sure how they'd get the explosives."

"But why would a maintenance worker want to crash a Game world?" asked Nathan. "It doesn't make sense when they're in Game themselves."

"There are signs at server complexes that say what Game world it supports," I said. "The bomber could avoid being caught in the world crash."

Nathan shook his head. "A maintenance worker would surely know that a world crash would kill thousands of players."

"Perhaps that was the plan," said Hawk. "Perhaps the bomber hated someone on Avalon enough to try to kill them."

"Why go as far as killing someone?" asked Nathan. "It's easy to avoid anyone you dislike when there are fifty billion players and two thousand Game worlds."

"Avoiding people in Game isn't always as easy as you'd think," said Hawk. "I've been trying and failing to avoid Hercules for four centuries. I admit that we're an unusual case though. It isn't easy to avoid another Founder Player with less than a thousand of us living on Celestius."

"Avoiding people can be a problem for ordinary players too," I said. "Decades ago when my mother lived on Ganymede, she had a boyfriend for a few months. When she broke up with him, he kept following her round and causing trouble between her and her friends. The Game Techs got involved, issued the statutory three warnings for breaches of Game rules, and then permanently banished the offender from Ganymede. Amazingly, that still wasn't the end of it, because the ex-boyfriend kept finding ways to send my mother abusive messages."

"That's terrible," said Nathan. "What did the Game Techs do then?"

"They lost patience and sentenced the ex-boyfriend to spend fifty years on Havoc. He wasn't allowed to send messages to people on other worlds, so he couldn't cause any more trouble for my mother, but the whole thing upset her so much that she ended up moving world to help her forget about it."

I paused for a moment. "I could believe someone as obsessive as my mother's ex-boyfriend might want to kill an enemy on Avalon, but not that they'd crash the whole world to do it. Thousands of people would die, but with millions of players on Avalon there'd only be a tiny chance of their target being among the dead."

"The bomber might have a general grievance against everyone on Avalon," said Hawk, "or might just want to kill random people for no reason. Some people are attracted by the idea of killing another human being."

Nathan looked bewildered. "If a player wanted to kill random people, they could just go and fight duels in the Battle Arena on Medieval."

"Killing another player in the Battle Arena, watching them die in agony, would be enjoyable," said Hawk. "The knowledge that the death wasn't permanent would sour the pleasure though. The winner knows that the loser will be resurrecting back in their home within minutes. Killing someone in real life, knowing they'd died a permanent death, would be far more satisfying."

There was something deeply worrying about the way Hawk said that. Nathan and I gave him matching horrified looks.

"I don't think that way," added Hawk hastily, "but I've met people who did. It's one of the reasons I gave up competing in the Battle Arena."

"Oh." I tried to imagine what it was like to think those things, feel those things, and failed. I decided I should be glad that I couldn't manage it. "I think I'll take the Battle Arena off my top ten list of things to try in Game."

"Unfortunately, even if we're right that a maintenance expert was behind the bombing, that still leaves us with a long list of suspects," said Hawk. "Someone could have made a note of the Avalon force field code years or even centuries ago, and there must be thousands of players who are either current or retired maintenance staff."

"The bomber had to plant the bombs," said Nathan. "It should be possible to narrow down the suspect list by checking which of them were using a controlled droid near the time of the bombing."

Something was nagging at the back of my mind. Something about a vending machine. "Point," I said urgently.

"Yes?" prompted Hawk.

"We're now at the transport stop for a different cluster of server complexes," I said. "Every transport stop I've ever seen before today has had a vending machine on the platform, but this one doesn't."

Nathan gave me a puzzled look. "That's because only the controlled droids of maintenance staff use this transport stop.

Controlled droids aren't going to buy anything from vending machines."

I nodded. "Every transport stop I've ever seen before today had a delivery trolley hub as well, but this one doesn't."

Nathan looked even more confused now. "There's no need for a delivery trolley hub either. Nobody will want to deliver anything to a server complex. The maintenance teams will bring any replacement parts with them."

"Exactly," I said. "The transport stop by the Avalon server complex didn't have a vending machine either, but it *did* have a delivery trolley hub. Delivery trolleys can only travel a limited distance from their navigation and recharge hubs, but the Avalon server complex was very close to the transport stop."

There was a short silence.

"You think the bomber installed a delivery trolley hub at the transport stop, and then used a delivery trolley to plant the bombs?" asked Hawk. "That would be a delivery trolley like the one that brought your clothes?"

"Yah," I said. "Delivery trolleys can interact with the transport system, call pods and ride in them, place deliveries wherever the customer wants. The bomber could just package up the bombs and instruct a delivery trolley to place one at each of four locations at the Avalon server complex."

"But how would the trolley get through the force field?" asked Hawk.

I shrugged. "A delivery trolley couldn't enter security codes itself, but you could attach a device to the trolley. Something that would detect when the delivery trolley arrived at the force field, and transmit the code. You might be able to do it with a phone."

"That's right," said Nathan. "On our last day at school, someone in my class modified a delivery trolley to enter the classroom door code and take in a stench bomb. We never found out who did it."

"If a ten-year-old child could modify a delivery trolley to transmit a code, then a maintenance expert could certainly do it," said Hawk.

He paused to think for a moment. "If we're right about this, then we can't assume the bomber was using a controlled droid at the time of the bombing."

"I expect the bomber was doing something very conspicuously innocent in Game at the time of the bombing," I said gloomily.

"We're going back to the bomb site," Hawk announced, and set the carriage in motion.

CHAPTER SEVEN

As the carriage accelerated, I felt the arms of my seat grab me again. I should have been getting used to them pinning me down by now, but actually I hated it even more. Fortunately I only had to endure the feeling of being a helpless prisoner for a couple of minutes before we were back at the previous transport stop and our seats released us.

We stepped out of the carriage onto the platform, and Hawk walked across to the red square of the delivery trolley hub. "It looks as if this was fitted very recently. There's still grit around the edges where the hole was cut. Why would the bomber go to so much trouble to use a delivery trolley, when it would be easy to plant the bombs using a controlled droid?"

He didn't wait for a reply, just led the way along the path to the gap in the Avalon server complex force field. As we walked through it, Hawk's Unilaw fan club spotted him, and came hurrying over, surprised but delighted by his return.

"I've come to see what progress Romulus and Remus have made," said Hawk.

The crowd backed away again, letting us move on to where two controlled droids were standing next to one of the four deeper areas of crater. The controlled droids bore the markings of Unilaw on their chests, but I recognized their faces as those of Romulus and Remus. The problem was that their Game images always showed the two of them together, so I wasn't sure which of them was which. I thought that Romulus was the one with the shaggy, red hair, and the one with the shorter, green hair was his husband, Remus.

Hawk did a rapid round of hand waving and introductions, which told me I'd got it backwards. Romulus had green hair and Remus had red.

"I appreciate you two agreeing to help me with this," said Hawk. "I didn't think until afterwards that seeing a bomb site might bring back unwelcome memories of your accident."

Romulus frowned. "It raises a few ghosts..."

"... but not entirely bad ones." Remus waved a hand. "You could argue that explosion saved our lives because..."

"... we'd never have entered Game if we hadn't been injured," said Romulus.

"If *I* hadn't been injured," said Remus. "You'd have coped without your arm. I was the one who was dying. No regrets?"

Romulus grinned at him. "I regret every single day of the four centuries that I've had to put up with you."

There was the clashing sound of metal on metal, as Remus gave him a mock slap on the head, and then the two of them turned their attention back to Hawk.

"We're still finding it a bit of a challenge to use the controlled droids," said Romulus, "but investigating the bombing is quite interesting."

"We found enough parts to work out what the bombs were like," said Remus, "and United Law may be able to trace some of the electronic components. The four bombs seem to have been identical except for the fact that one included a timing device that sent a short range signal to trigger all four bombs."

"They're fairly standard bombs," said Romulus. "Not that any bombs are standard now, but this type of bomb was one of the most common ones used for a period of several hundred years. Basic but functional."

"Do you think the bombs were made by a beginner or an expert?" asked Hawk.

Romulus and Remus looked at each other for a moment, exchanging glances that I didn't understand.

"Expert," said Romulus grimly.

Remus nodded. "The explosive was home cooked. The ingredients are easy to get, or used to be easy to get centuries ago, but it's a delicate process. Get it wrong and..." The droid waved its arms in a graphic gesture.

"The devices too," said Romulus. "These were standard bombs, but there were a couple of modifications that help prevent... Well, whoever made this bomb had made a few before and knew the inside tricks."

"Which means we have bad news for you," said Remus.

"I know what you're going to say," said Hawk. "The bombs were made by someone at least a couple of hundred years old. This just confirms what I already suspected for other reasons. One or more teenagers in the real world may have been recruited to help with the bombing, but it was organized by someone in Game."

There was an awkward silence until Hawk spoke again. "I need to look at the points where the four bombs were placed. Were you able to work out their exact positions?"

They both replied at once.

"Within about three inches," said Romulus.

"Within about seven centimetres," said Remus.

They frowned at each other, and then shrugged in unison.

"Either sounds good," said Hawk. "Please show me."

Nathan and I stood watching, while Hawk, Romulus, and Remus did a lot of crawling round craters. Finally, Hawk came back over to us.

"I need to consult a Game Tech about some details."

He turned to look across at the group of Game Tech droids that I'd noticed on our previous visit, made a beckoning gesture, and a droid bearing an image of a Game Tech with silver insignia on her cheeks started walking towards us. Hawk shook his head at her, and pointed his finger at the droid that had a male face with gold insignia shining brightly against dark skin.

The terrifyingly high-ranked Game Tech came over to join us. Hawk waved a hand at Nathan and me in turn. "Nathan and Jex are assisting me with my investigation."

The Game Tech nodded in acknowledgement.

"Romulus and Remus have given me the positions of the four bombs," said Hawk. "If you allow for the small amount of potential error in their measurements, then they form the corners of a perfect square. I can't believe the bombs would have been placed so precisely if a person had planted them, either while physically present or while using a controlled droid."

"I would agree," said the Game Tech. "Player Hawk, your comment seems to indicate you are considering the possibility of the bomber being within Game."

"I am," said Hawk. "Jex noticed something interesting about the transport stop used to access this cluster of server complexes. Are we right in thinking that the transport stops used to access server complexes wouldn't normally have delivery trolley hubs?"

"Moment." It was a few seconds before the Game Tech spoke again. "That is correct."

"The transport stop for this server complex does have a delivery trolley hub," said Hawk, "and it appears to have been recently fitted. We suspect that means a delivery trolley was used to plant the bombs. I'll ask United Law to investigate who fitted that delivery trolley hub, and see if they can try to track down what deliveries were made using it. I believe that's more in their area than yours."

"That is correct," said the Game Tech.

"The next thing is in your area though," said Hawk. "I've got the location of the centre of the perfect square formed by the bomb craters. You must have a physical location of the Avalon server complex stored in Game records. Can you please access it for me?"

A minute later, the Game Tech and Hawk recited a string of numbers in unison.

"Snap," said Hawk.

Nathan and I looked at him in bewilderment.

"It's an archaic word, meaning we have a perfect match," said Hawk. "The delivery trolley was sent to the exact location listed in Game records. It then followed its orders to place each bomb a given distance away from that point in the direction of each of the four buildings."

"The bomber had obtained the physical location listed in Game records for the Avalon server complex." The Game Tech was obviously unhappy about this news.

"Is that location given to visiting maintenance teams?" asked Hawk.

"Maintenance teams should only be told the nearest transport stop to their destination, and which paths to follow on arrival," said the Game Tech. "Moment."

We waited for over ten minutes before the Game Tech spoke in a grim voice. "The physical locations stored on our records are the precise centre of each server complex. That information is definitely not given to maintenance teams. It is held among highly confidential Game design details, so only Game Techs are able to access it, and all requests for that data are recorded on an audit trail."

"So who has requested the physical location of the Avalon server complex?" asked Hawk.

"The sole request on record is the one I just made myself," said the Game Tech, in suicidal tones. "There is evidence that earlier requests were made, but the records of them have been expertly removed from the audit trail."

My brain refused to accept what he was saying. These things couldn't be true, because if they were...

Hawk put the unthinkable into words. "You're telling me that one of your fellow Game Techs was involved in the Avalon bombing?"

"That is correct." The Game Tech wasn't even trying to keep the emotion out of his voice now. "Security on all server complex information is being increased with immediate effect."

"Blocking future access to location information won't help us," said Hawk. "The bomber could have already made a list of the physical locations of every server complex, and we can't change geography."

He was speaking in a harsh, heavily emphasized voice now. "You have to block the bomber's access to the force field codes, or he'll crash another Game world and many more thousands of people will die."

"We are aware of the vital necessity of protecting the force field codes," said the Game Tech. "Special isolation measures are being taken to prevent Game Techs from accessing that information except through authorized channels. To keep authorized access to a minimum, all routine maintenance inspections have been temporarily suspended. Remote diagnostics will be run on all servers daily."

"What happens if those diagnostics show problems with a server?" asked Hawk.

"Maintenance crews will need to investigate any problems reported, but each crew will be accompanied to the server complex by two silver status Game Techs and four armed Unilaw officers. The actual requests for force field codes will need to be authorized by three gold status Game Techs from different departments."

The Game Tech paused. This was a gold status Game Tech, a god of virtual reality, but his rigidly controlled expression had changed to something very human and vulnerable.

"Hawk, I have to appeal to you as an old friend. Please think very hard about the consequences of announcing this development to the Game population. They're already frightened after the bombing. If you tell them that a Game Tech was involved, you'll trigger a mass panic."

"I'm well aware of that," said Hawk grimly. "I'm close to panic myself, imagining all the horrors that a rogue Game Tech could inflict on people in Game. Changing the ground under players' feet to lava. Sending boiling rain down on them. Perhaps even deleting player consciousnesses from Game, so there's nothing but empty shells of bodies left in freezer units."

"There would be billions of players calling for defrost from Game. The system can only handle a limited number of defrosts at one time, and even if it could cope with the volume there'd be no way to house or feed the extra people arriving in the real world."

"Calm down, Kwame," said Hawk. "I'm here representing the players' best interests, and it's definitely not in their best interests for me to terrify them by telling them that a Game Tech was involved in the Avalon bombing. I'm as eager to keep this news secret as you are."

The Game Tech turned to look at me, and then at Nathan. "Jex and Nathan, your discretion on this matter is essential."

My brain was numb with shock. I'd been stunned by the idea that a Game Tech was involved in the Avalon bombing, but it was almost as hard to cope with watching Hawk have this conversation with Kwame. Game Techs were remote, anonymous figures. They never had personal conversations with players.

The whole foundations of my universe were falling apart, but I managed to make myself nod my head. I heard a strangled squeak from Nathan.

"Our discovery has to be shared with the core team that's leading the Unilaw bombing investigation," said Hawk, "but I hope we can depend on them to keep it a closely guarded secret. Will you be able to stop the news spreading through the ranks of Game Techs, Kwame? I'd like to leave the bomber in blissful ignorance of our suspicions."

"Unfortunately," said Kwame, "the new security measures will make it painfully clear to all Game Techs that we suspect one of our own people was involved in the bombing. I believe our best option would be to inform all Game Techs at once, so they can watch for colleagues acting suspiciously."

Hawk sighed. "Very well. All Game Techs will be informed. The core Unilaw investigation team will be informed. The general player population will be left believing that teenagers in the real world carried out the bombing."

"The Game Techs will focus their efforts on making all the security changes necessary to protect the Game worlds and players," said Kwame. "We'll need to protect you in particular, Hawk. As the players' representative, and the most prominent member of the hunt for the bomber, you're a potential target. I'll be watching over your safety myself."

He paused. "With a small team to verify everything I do. I have to be considered a suspect along with everyone else."

"Thank you," said Hawk. "The last four hundred years have been fun and I've still got a few impossible monsters to kill. I've put in a lot of thought on how to defeat the Behemoth, and I'd hate to be deleted from existence before I get the chance to try out my latest tactics."

"I'll do my best to make sure that doesn't happen."

"I have every faith in you." Hawk's smile lasted only a moment before his expression lapsed into one of anxiety again. "I'm tempted to ask you to put armed guards at every server complex."

"In the current situation, we could not refuse that request," said Kwame, "but I doubt that Unilaw could supply the many thousands of armed guards that would be needed."

"There are plenty of players with experience of using Game weapons on worlds like Civil War," said Hawk. "I could ask for volunteers to use controlled droids to..."

He abruptly broke off his sentence and shook his head. "No, we can't possibly risk it. Guards won't be very effective unless they're inside the server complex force fields, and having a group of droids brandishing weapons inside every force field could do far more harm than good. A rogue Game Tech could threaten the players controlling those droids, even torture them, forcing them to damage the servers themselves."

Kwame frowned. "We can assign a team of Game Techs to protect the guards on the new Avalon server complex, but it's impossible to do that for all two thousand worlds in Game. We wouldn't have the spare resources for it at any time, but especially not now. Our people are already going to be working extreme hours to improve Game security and find the identity of the bomber."

"We'd better forget the guard idea then. One final question. Is there any way to change things so people don't defrost if a world crashes? Couldn't you link world servers together, so if one world crashes the others can provide some sort of lifeline for players?"

Kwame assumed the impersonal manner of a Game Tech again "Directly linking worlds would be possible but extremely unwise. There would be a danger of the crashing world bringing down the others that were linked to it."

There was a grim silence after that. I turned to stare round at the bomb site. The Game Techs were the all-powerful ones who created the worlds of Game, but one of them had turned their powers from creation to destruction.

The bombing here had caused the deaths of over eleven thousand people, but we had to worry about other types of attack as well now. A rogue Game Tech could be just as dangerous within Game as outside it. If Hawk's nightmare visions became reality, and a reign of terror started inside Game, then there would be no way for the player population to escape. It was impossible for fifty billion frozen players to return to the real world.

CHAPTER EIGHT

We retreated to our carriage again, and moved on for fifteen minutes before stopping. When I followed Hawk out on to the platform of the new transport stop, I saw we were in the middle of an area of farmland. Hawk didn't say anything, just stood on the platform, apparently watching an autoplough working in a field.

Nathan and I exchanged baffled glances, and waited in silence. It was several minutes before Hawk spoke.

"Back when the players chose me to be their representative, everyone believed some teenagers were responsible for the bombing. My knowledge of the real world and teenage life was four centuries out of date, so I recruited you two to travel with me as my assistants. Now we know a Game Tech was involved in the bombing, I have to rethink my plans."

That sounded as if Hawk had decided he didn't need Nathan and me tagging along on the investigation any longer, and was going to send us back to the body stacks. Bitter disappointment hit me. I knew I should be mentally preparing a speech that would persuade Hawk to help me and Nathan by putting a good comment on our Game records, but I couldn't think of anything except how much I wanted to stay part of the hunt for the bomber.

"I wondered why the bomber went to all the trouble of fitting a delivery trolley hub instead of just using a controlled droid to plant the bombs," continued Hawk. "The answer is that the bomber was a Game Tech and would only have access to official Game droids. If one of those was seen near the Avalon server complex, it could give away the fact that a Game Tech was involved in the bombing, so the bomber decided to use a delivery trolley instead."

Nathan nodded eagerly. "No one pays any attention to ordinary controlled droids, you see them all the time, but every kid notices Unilaw or Game droids."

"Given how carefully Game Techs are selected for their work," said Hawk, "it's hard to believe that more than one of them was involved in the bombing, but we should remember that it's a possibility. There could obviously be any number of players or teenagers involved as well."

I forced myself to overcome my disappointment and speak. "If you're right about the reason for using a delivery trolley to plant the bombs, then there can't be any players involved in this. A player could just sign up for a real world job to get access to an ordinary controlled droid with no distinctive markings."

"Point," acknowledged Hawk. "If there weren't any players involved, that means the Game Tech must be the one who organized the bombing. A Game Tech might conceivably be influenced by a player that was an old friend or lover, but I can't imagine how a random teenager could talk a Game Tech into helping them with a bombing."

"I don't know how a teenager in the real world could even get in contact with a Game Tech," said Nathan.

"Romulus and Remus think the bombs were made by someone at least a couple of centuries old," said Hawk, "so that means our rogue Game Tech must be the one who made them. I can't see there'd be any problem using a controlled droid to make a bomb."

I remembered the Unilaw droid that had sat opposite me in a pod, juggling a gun from one hand to the other. "I can see big advantages in using a controlled droid to make a bomb rather than doing it in person. You don't have to worry so much about making mistakes when you can only blow up a droid rather than yourself."

"Point," said Hawk. "So the bombing was organized by our rogue Game Tech. The fact it was a real world attack was probably a deliberate attempt at misdirection. Everyone was supposed to be busily chasing teenagers in the real world, while the Game Tech quietly controlled events from within Game. We're looking for a Game Tech who has been in Game for at least two or three hundred years and has some knowledge of bombs."

I wasn't sure what was happening now. If Hawk was still discussing details about the bomber with Nathan and me, did that mean he wasn't sending us back to the body stacks after all?

"I think the bomber has to be a high-ranked Game Tech," said Nathan. "Kwame was upset when he told us that only Game Techs could request the location information for a server complex, but then he talked about the records being expertly deleted from the audit trail. The tone of his voice suggested that was even more worrying, as if someone would need high authority to make changes to an audit trail."

"You're right," said Hawk. "Kwame said that future requests for force field codes will need to be authorized by three gold status Game Techs from different departments. That means the Game Techs daren't even trust their highest ranked people any longer."

"A Game Tech being involved in the bombing is terrible news for them," said Nathan.

"It's terrible news for everyone," said Hawk. "Kwame will be making a general announcement to the other Game Techs that one of their own people was involved in the attack. If we're lucky, the bomber will react by doing as little as possible to try to avoid being caught. If we're unlucky, there'll be another attack."

By now I was convinced that Hawk wasn't sending Nathan and me away. "You think there could be another bombing despite all the new security precautions?"

"In theory, the server complexes should be safe behind their force fields now," said Hawk. "It seems unlikely that three unconnected gold status Game Techs would have suddenly been filled with a desire to murder players. My big worry is that the bomber will move on to attack other Game related targets."

My stomach gave a sudden lurch. "Targets like the body stacks. There are fifty different sites around the world, each holding a billion freezer units, and the kids who work there couldn't do anything to stop a bomber."

Hawk winced. "I was thinking of the bomber targeting places

that were important to the running of Game, but you're right. The sheer scale of the body stacks makes them impossible to defend, and a bombing there would have a huge impact on the players. It's not that destroying bodies in freezer units would harm anyone in Game, their minds would still be safe in the system, but it would hit people hard on a deep emotional level. At least, it would hit me hard. I haven't used my physical body in four centuries, I'm not even sure where it's stored now, but I'd hate to think of something bad happening to it."

He paused to rub his forehead, the movement heightening the illusion that he was here with us in person rather than just controlling a droid. "There could be another real world bombing, but there's also the possibility that the next attack happens in Game. The bomber doesn't need to hide the fact they're a Game Tech any longer. They could set the Behemoth loose to rampage through a crowd of partying Gamers, create a volcano in the middle of a music festival, or send a tidal wave ripping across beaches. The players' deaths wouldn't be permanent, but their fear would last for centuries."

I thought what an experience like that would do to my mother. "We have to catch the bomber before any of these things happen."

Hawk nodded. "I won't be able to chase down clues to the bomber's identity within Game, because Game Techs are always hidden behind the scenes of worlds. The only time players see them is when they call for help with something that isn't covered by the automated Game commands, and then it's usually a bronze status Game Tech that appears."

I frowned "Given the situation, the Game Techs should forget the rules and allow you into their areas."

"I don't think that's possible unless they recruit Hawk as a Game Tech," said Nathan. "The special Game Tech areas don't connect with player areas at all. It's like Game Techs live in a whole different dimension of Game."

"I've absolutely no desire to be recruited as a Game Tech," said Hawk hastily, "and I'm sure that any clues in Game Tech areas would involve incomprehensible technical things. It makes far more sense for me to follow the trail in the real world."

He turned to Nathan. "I'll be focusing my efforts in the real world, but the Game investigation team will be sending me reports on their progress. I'll need you to go through those for me and explain any important points."

Nathan looked doubtful. "If you want someone to explain technical details, you should ask a Game Tech for help. I don't know very much, and most of the things that I think I know are self-taught and probably totally wrong."

"I realize that you've limited knowledge," said Hawk. "I'll take you to the United Law facility that's leading their investigation into the bombing. They'll give you comfortable living quarters and all the facilities you need to do some high-speed learning about the technical side of Game. I'll arrange for you to have access to all the Game training texts, and put you in contact with several Game Techs who'll answer your questions."

"Training texts!" Nathan's eyes lit up eagerly for a second, but then he shook his head. "Even if I had all those things, a real Game Tech could do far more to help you."

"I can't use a Game Tech for this, Nathan, because I don't know which of them I can trust." Hawk waved his hands in a despairing gesture. "Our bomber is probably a silver or gold status Game Tech. That means they're in a position of power. They may have already manipulated their way onto the Game investigation team. Even if they haven't managed to join it themselves, they could still offer bribes of promotion and choice assignments to other Game Techs who are on the team."

He paused. "You have to be very careful, Nathan. Always be aware that one of your Game Tech contacts may be helping the bomber, or even *be* the bomber. When you ask them questions, make sure you ask about lots of different things, so you don't give away clues about the direction our investigation is going. Always ask at least two of your Game Tech contacts the same question. If the answers differ, then tell me at once. After seeing your room, I know you've got incredible attention to detail, and will spot any inconsistencies."

Nathan hesitated for a moment before speaking. "Why aren't you asking your friend, Kwame, to do this?"

Hawk groaned. "Kwame grew up centuries ago in a country that insisted on its citizens doing two years of military service. He would never talk to me about what he did during those two years, I got the impression he wanted to forget all about it, but it's quite possible that he picked up some knowledge of bombs. Kwame then entered Game nearly three and a half centuries ago, and we were friends for a couple of decades before he was recruited as a Game Tech. Now he's gold status with a high position on the Game investigation team. Logically speaking, that puts him very high on my suspect list."

I broke in to the conversation. "But Kwame is the one watching your... consciousness data in Game. Surely that means he's in an ideal position to delete it."

"I know," said Hawk. "The me that thinks and feels in Game is nothing but streams of data in a white box in a server complex. Kwame could delete that data from Game, and there'd be nothing left of me but a frozen body with no one at home."

I pictured that and winced.

"That idea terrifies me," said Hawk. "One minute I'm here, the next I'm gone forever. No way to fight back. No chance at all. Perhaps my body could be defrosted, re-educated, and become a person again, but that person wouldn't be me."

He had a strange smile on his face now. "My logic tells me that Kwame should be number one on my suspect list, but my emotions say he's an old friend that I can trust absolutely. I'm betting my life that my emotions are right. Kwame used to defend me in Game battles where death was merely very painful and inconvenient. Now he's defending me from a very permanent death. If I'm wrong about Kwame, and he attacks me, then at least he'll give himself away by doing it."

He pulled a face of self-mockery as he spoke in exaggerated heroic tones. "I will not have been deleted in vain."

"You should consider leaving Game," I said. A few days ago, I would have had a fit at the thought of saying that to a Founder Player. I was pretty worried about saying it even now.

Hawk looked startled. "You know, that option hadn't even occurred to me. I entered the Game over four hundred years ago, and I've never left it for a single day. You're right that I'd be safer back in the real world, but there's a lot more at stake here than just my safety. I can't reassure the other players if I'm not in Game. I can't afford to spend time sleeping and eating. The enemy is way ahead of us already. I need to run faster to catch him, not weigh myself down with chains."

His manner suddenly changed from pensive to decisive. "Nathan, I've explained what I want you to do. Jex, I want you to go with Nathan to the United Law facility. I'll call you whenever I need to discuss problems."

"What?" I shook my head urgently. "There's no point in me going to a United Law facility with Nathan. I'll be able to help you with problems much better if I'm with you."

"If you go to the United Law facility with Nathan, you'll be able to assist him with his research," said Hawk.

I shook my head again. "Asking me to assist Nathan with research into the technical workings of Game is like… like asking a bumble bear to tap dance."

Hawk didn't even smile at my joke. "Perhaps that's true, but you'll be safe at the United Law facility."

"Safe?" I repeated in confusion. "Why do I need to be kept safe? You're the one that's important, not me."

"I'm in danger, Jex. Recruiting you and Nathan to help me has put you both in danger too. You could get hurt just because you're near me, or because the bomber thinks that harming you will discourage me from chasing him. There used to be a phrase for this. I think it was 'collateral damage'."

"You mean the bomber might attack us just to deter you from…" I broke off and started a new sentence. "I'm not going to sit around uselessly at a United Law facility. You recruited Nathan and me because your knowledge was out of date and you needed us to explain how things work these days. You still need me to do that."

Hawk frowned. "I can't deny it would be very helpful having you with me. I'd never have noticed that delivery trolley hub if you hadn't pointed it out. I don't want to drag you into danger though. You have to remember that the bomber has already killed over eleven thousand people and won't hesitate to kill again."

"And you have to remember that one of the people the bomber killed was my father," I said fiercely.

Hawk's droid hands lifted in a very human gesture of surrender. "I can't argue with that. If you're sure you want to take the risk, then you can stay with me on the hunt."

I took a deep breath and nodded. "I'm very sure."

CHAPTER NINE

The carriage was whizzing through a tunnel, heading for the United Law facility. Hawk was busy making a broadcast to the players in Game, so his golden droid sat motionless in one of the seats. Nathan was frantically working on a small, handheld screen.

"This is amazing stuff," he muttered. "I really need about six screens at once, as well as a proper Game Design console."

I glanced at the meaningless complexity displayed on his screen. "Is that a Game training text?"

He nodded, his eager eyes still fixed on the gobbledygook. "I just wish I could run the holo demonstrations."

"Hawk says you'll have everything you need at the United Law facility."

"Yah." Nathan tore his attention away from the training text, and looked directly at me for the first time in thirty minutes. "I hope you'll be all right alone with Hawk."

I glared at him. "Please don't give me a repeat lecture about not falling for Hawk. It annoyed me last time. If you try it again, I could get really angry."

"I thought you were really angry last time," said Nathan.

"I can get far angrier than that. You'd better accept that I make my own decisions, stop worrying about my love life, and concentrate on your own."

Nathan sighed. "I won't have a love life until I get recruited as a Game Tech. Perhaps it's just as well. Everyone says sex in Game is much better than in real life."

"I've never thought of Game Techs having love lives," I said thoughtfully. "They aren't allowed to have relationships with players, but I suppose there's no problem with them having relationships with each other."

"That is correct." Nathan mimicked the formal tones of a Game Tech.

"We're nearly there now," said Hawk's voice.

"Gah." I turned to look at him. The golden droid had returned to being Hawk again, but I didn't know exactly when or how much of the conversation he'd heard. I exchanged agonized looks with Nathan, and the arms of my seat enfolded me lovingly as the carriage started to decelerate.

"I've got the latest information update from Romulus and Remus," said Hawk. "Sadly all the components in the bombs came from basic devices sold by every vending machine. None of them had any identifying marks to give clues to where they were sold or who bought them."

"The bomber is much too clever to leave clues in the bombs," I said bitterly.

The carriage stopped, the doors opened, and I saw this was an indoor transport stop. The blue and grey United Law sign on the wall opposite us was the same as the one at the facility where I'd been questioned, but about twice the size. Hawk gave a barely perceptible sigh as he saw a crowd of controlled droids waiting by the sign. Obviously the Unilaw investigation team included some big Hawk fans.

As I stepped out of the carriage, I got a wider view of the platform, and saw there were four more controlled droids standing apart from the others. They were carrying bulky guns that were clearly designed to have massive firepower. I had a sick moment as I remembered the Unilaw droid that had taken me in for questioning and held me at gun point.

Hawk responded modestly to several compliments, and hurried on to talk about the hunt for the bomber. "Is there any news yet about who fitted the delivery trolley hub?"

One of the controlled droids stepped forward to answer the question. Nathan would probably have been able to work out the rank of the Unilaw official controlling it from the markings on the droid, but I couldn't.

"The hub was fitted a month ago in response to a standard requisition from Game. We asked the Game investigation team to trace the requisition's origin, but they report that all records relating to the request have been deleted."

Nathan groaned. "Of course they've been deleted. If the bomber can delete records from an audit trail, then it would be easy to delete the records of a simple administration request."

"I thought it would be hard for the bomber to get a delivery hub fitted," said Hawk, "but it probably took less than five minutes for our rogue Game Tech to send a standard requisition and delete a few records. Have you made any progress on finding the delivery trolley that used the hub?"

"The delivery system has no record of any delivery to the Avalon server complex," said the Unilaw droid, "but the parcels could have been handed directly to a delivery trolley. We're currently checking the memory information on all delivery trolleys in the area."

I opened my mouth to ask how big an area they were checking, but closed it again. There was no point in me asking for details. I had a low opinion of Unilaw, and felt they were more likely to find a flying pig than the right delivery trolley.

Hawk didn't demand any more details either, just nodded and asked to be shown to Nathan's accommodation. After a brief walk through corridors, where we passed two more sets of armed guards, the three of us were alone again, inspecting an impressive luxury apartment. The living area had lavish, colour coordinated furnishings, but one wall was covered in a mosaic of screens, and there was a complex array of controls beneath them.

"This is wonderful." Nathan hurried up to the wall and began tapping on the controls. Game gobbledygook appeared on one of the other walls, and the contour lines of a hologram monster started forming in midair next to where I was standing.

I was still tense after seeing the armed guards, and reacted by sidestepping rapidly, grabbing a nearby vase to use as a makeshift weapon, and turning defensively to face the monster.

The contours filled in with colour and detail, and I saw it was a werewolf, with worryingly realistic blood dribbling from its jaws.

Hawk laughed at me. "Don't be scared, Jex. Hawk the Unvanquished will slay the beast if it dares to attack you."

I could feel myself blushing. "I was just admiring the ornaments," I said, in my most dignified voice, and faked studying the vase before putting it down again.

A worldscape appeared beside Hawk, and he studied the desert land. "That's Anubis, but I can't see the pyramids."

Nathan tapped a button, and a cluster of pyramids appeared.

"I see you're getting the hang of this well," said Hawk.

I stuck my head into the bedroom and raised my eyebrows at the sight of the palatial bed. "Glitz!"

"That's the first totally unfamiliar word I've heard either of you use," said Hawk. "What does it mean?"

"Glitz means that someone or something in the real world is almost as fancy as in Game," I said. "The word's been around a long time, but no one would be likely to say it within Game."

Nathan stopped messing around with worlds, took a look at the bedroom too, and gave one of his appreciative whistles. "Very nice."

He wandered on into the shower, reappearing after a moment with a puzzled expression. "Why did my shower run a medical scan on me?"

"I've no idea," said Hawk. "Are you feeling ill?"

I burst out laughing, and they both turned to look at me.

"Would you care to explain the joke?" asked Hawk, with a raised eyebrow.

"The only Unilaw staff physically present in the real world will be kids working as cadets, and women taking the option of having babies to reduce their career term by several years. The cadets all have rooms in separate accommodation blocks, so this apartment will be specially designed to care for pregnant women."

Hawk joined me in laughing, while Nathan gave us a wounded look.

I grinned at him. "It's a really luxurious apartment, Nathan, so I don't think you've got too much to complain about."

"Jex and I had better be going," said Hawk. "Nathan, you

should be physically safe here, but the bomber may have found a way to eavesdrop on communications. Remember to set your controls to use a secure, encrypted link whenever you call anyone, especially me. Which reminds me that I asked for…"

He glanced round, went across to a shelf, picked up a fancy looking phone, and handed it to me. "Jex, if you make any calls to Nathan or anyone else connected with the investigation, remember to use this so your conversation is encrypted."

I tucked the phone into a pocket, Hawk and I went back to the transport stop, and headed off in our carriage again. I was relieved to have escaped from the Unilaw facility with its lurking armed guards, but feeling subdued after saying goodbye to Nathan. I was alone with Hawk now. A scruffy girl from the body stacks was keeping company with a Game legend.

The situation hadn't seemed so strange when I was with Nathan. The two of us had managed to chat a bit, and even when we daren't say anything aloud we could still exchange expressive glances, but now…

"You're very quiet, Jex," said Hawk.

"I'm a bit depressed," I said. "There's no way to trace who bought the components used in the bombs. The requisition for the delivery trolley hub came from within Game, and our rogue Game Tech has deleted any clues to who sent it. We don't seem to have any way to make progress now."

"We may still learn something when Unilaw find the delivery trolley that carried the bombs," said Hawk. "The trolley must have a record of who asked for the delivery and how they paid for it."

"I don't believe Unilaw will ever find that delivery trolley."

Hawk gave me a startled look. "Judging from the bitter tone of your voice, you don't like United Law very much."

"I don't like them at all at the moment. Being at that United Law facility, seeing all those armed guards, brought back horrible memories of being dragged out of bed at gun point, locked in a cell, and interrogated."

"Dragged out of bed at gun point?" Hawk repeated my words in a shocked voice. "There was no need for them to treat you that way."

"That's just typical of the way Unilaw officials treat kids." I tried to put my feelings about Unilaw aside and focus on the facts. "The problem with looking for the delivery trolley is that those things roam round all day, delivering orders and taking back things that the customers didn't like or turned out to be the wrong size. At some point during the night, each delivery trolley will call in at its local depot for a few minutes, get checked for damage, and dump the day's delivery information onto the main delivery system."

I paused. "The Unilaw investigation team didn't want to tell you the bad news, but the truth is the delivery trolley that delivered the bombs can't be in active service any longer. If it was, then its information would have been added to the main delivery system by now."

"It isn't in active service any longer," repeated Hawk. "You mean the bomber has somehow disposed of it?"

"Yah," I said. "The bomber wouldn't want that delivery trolley reporting back about a Game droid giving it parcels to deliver to the Avalon server complex. There'd also be the problem of the payment potentially giving clues to the bomber's identity. It would be easy to destroy the trolley after it had done the delivery. The bomber just had to order the trolley to return to collect more parcels, and the poor thing would dutifully come back to be murdered."

I realized that Hawk was giving me an odd look. "Sorry, I know perfectly well that delivery trolleys aren't alive or intelligent, but there's something about the way the lights flash when they're processing instructions that makes it look like they're thinking. I feel sorry for the poor things. Kids are always hijacking them to do things like move furniture, or playing tricks like blocking the depot corridor late at night so there's a whole herd of confused delivery trolleys stuck outside."

"I understand what you mean about the delivery trolleys seeming intelligent," said Hawk. "I thought the same thing when I watched the one delivering crates to our carriage. I'm just surprised that you know so many details about them."

I blushed. "I found out most of those details the hard way. I once borrowed a delivery trolley and attached a lot of painted cardboard to make it look like a dragon. Unfortunately, it decided to head back to its depot in the middle of the night. I had to go chasing after it and drag it back, the trolley kept trying to break free and crashing into walls, and I woke up half the kids in my accommodation block. They kept teasing me about it for years afterwards."

Hawk blinked. "I see," he said, in a confused voice. "Why did... No, never mind that. Getting back to the bombing, wouldn't it have been simpler for the bomber to just blow up the trolley along with the server complex?"

"That would have left a lot of pieces of trolley at the bomb site. Those would have serial numbers that showed the home depot of the delivery trolley, and there'd have been a risk of the memory unit surviving the blast as well."

Hawk nodded. "So Unilaw need to look for the remains of a delivery trolley."

"Yah, but it's a pretty hopeless search," I said. "You can see broken delivery trolleys everywhere you go. If I was the bomber, I wouldn't have taken a glaringly conspicuous Game droid anywhere near the Avalon server complex. I'd have sent the bombs with a delivery trolley from a hundred miles away, waited for the trolley to come back, smashed it, and dumped the remains in the nearest river."

"A hundred miles away?" Hawk's voice rose in disbelief. "How long a distance can these delivery trolleys travel?"

"They can't go far under their own power without recharging, but they can interact with the transport system and call a pod to travel long distances."

Hawk frowned in thought. "The bomber has been incredibly careful not to leave clues. I can't believe they'd risk letting a delivery trolley make a record of them. What if something stopped the delivery trolley from returning to be destroyed? A teenager playing a joke or accidental damage."

"Someone had to give the parcels to the delivery trolley and arrange payment."

"Someone had to attach a phone or something to the delivery trolley to transmit the force field code too," said Hawk.

"Point." I yawned. "I'd forgotten about that. I'm a bit tired."

Hawk shook his head. "I'm useless at remembering you need to eat and sleep. How long is it since you slept properly?"

I tried to work it out, but things were a blur. "I've lost track of time."

"I'll let you get to sleep soon, I promise," said Hawk. "I just need to finish this conversation first. What if the bomber recruited a teenager to deal with the delivery trolley? The bomber could get the teenager to meet their controlled Game droid a long way from the bomb site, and give them the bombs and a device they could fit to the delivery trolley to transmit the force field code. Wouldn't that be a safer way of doing things?"

"Yah. That would avoid the danger of the delivery payment giving clues to the bomber's identity, and nobody would think it odd to see a kid messing about with a delivery trolley, or even dragging a broken one away to be dumped. How would the bomber persuade a kid to help them though?"

"Bribery," said Hawk. "The bomber could offer to pay their lifetime Game subscription. A Game Tech wouldn't need to give them actual credits, just flag their account as paid."

"Point." I thought about it for a moment before shaking my head. "The kid wouldn't take the risk."

"The bomber could make up a story about playing a joke on friends. There haven't been any bombings in centuries, so a teenager would have no reason to suspect the packages contained bombs."

"A kid wouldn't think of bombs, but they'd guess the packages contained something highly illegal. There'd be no reason to ask them to deal with the trolley otherwise, because a prankster could just arrange the delivery themselves. Any respectable kid would stop and think about the risk they'd be taking. Just being brought in for questioning by Unilaw would destroy their chances of getting into a decent Game world, so most of them would turn down the bomber's offer, and the bomber couldn't approach dozens of kids in the hope of finding one who'd agree."

Hawk frowned. "What do you mean? Someone couldn't get into trouble just for being questioned about a crime. You're innocent until proven guilty."

I was tired, I was upset about saying goodbye to Nathan, and seeing those armed droids at the United Law facility had brought back vivid memories of the interrogation that had wrecked my life. The whole lot was piling on top of me, especially the fact that Hawk had been one of those interrogating me, so his naive words hit me on a bitterly sensitive area.

"Maybe that was true four hundred years ago, Hawk, but things don't work like that today. A kid isn't in Game yet, and if you aren't in Game then you don't really exist. Nobody cares about things like fairness and justice for people who don't exist."

"But surely..."

I drowned him out with my angry torrent of words. "A year ago, I was a medical cadet, one of the best in my class, but then I helped our instructor treat a pregnant woman. The instructor made a mistake with the medication, she was about to give the woman an overdose that could harm her babies, so I had to intervene and stop her. The instructor didn't want that incident going on record, so she immediately changed my class grades to be failure level, and dropped me from the medical training programme. There was nothing to stop her doing that, no checks on what she did at all, because no one cared about justice for kids who weren't in Game."

I paused to grab a breath before ranting on. "A year ago, I had my future destroyed because I saved a patient from getting a dangerous overdose. Exactly the same thing just happened to thousands of kids in the body stacks. None of us had done anything except try to save the lives of defrosted players, but Unilaw pulled us all in and interrogated us about the bombing. The fact we were questioned about the Avalon bombing is permanently on our records now. Do you think there's a single Game world that will accept any of us as residents when they see that?"

My fury suddenly burned out into depression. "My dreams of life in Game are wrecked. Nathan's dreams of becoming a Game Tech are wrecked. All the kids Unilaw questioned have had their futures wrecked as well. We're all Game rejects."

I finally realized I'd been yelling at a Founder Player. "I'm sorry," I said hastily. "I know what happened wasn't your fault, it's just the way the world is now."

"Moment." Hawk snapped the word at me with a harsh note in his voice.

There was silence for several minutes. I'd completely lost my head and mouthed off at a Founder Player. I'd destroyed my only chance of ever entering Game, and I'd probably ruined things for Nathan too. I bit my lip. If we were lucky, Hawk would just send us back to the body stacks. If we were unlucky, he'd...

"You were right about the questioning," said Hawk at last. "It was mentioned on both your and Nathan's records, but it isn't any longer. I'm listed as a sponsor for both of you now, and if you ever have a problem getting entry to any Game world, you can tell the Admission Committee to talk to me about it."

I stared at him blankly for a second. Hawk hadn't just sponsored us; he'd got our records cleared! I hadn't known that was possible.

My head struggled to adjust to my new reality, not quite daring to believe it was true. If it was... I had a future again. I'd screeched my anger at Hawk, but he'd still given me back my dreams. The Game Jex would live after all, and walk the beaches of Ganymede with the magnificence of Jupiter overhead.

"Thank you." My voice shook as I said the two hopelessly inadequate words. I remembered myself at fourteen years old, gazing in blind adoration at the images of Hawk on my room wall. I'd thought him the most perfect, the most flawless, the most wonderful hero in Game. I'd been right. No, I'd been wrong, because the real life Hawk was even better than the one I'd imagined.

"I apologize for sitting in on your questioning," said Hawk. "I thought I might learn something useful from it, and I did, but I'd no idea that simply being questioned could harm the future of anyone. Now I understand why most of the teenagers were hysterical with fear."

He paused. "I've asked the Game Techs to remove Unilaw's questioning from the other teenagers' Game records too. It's hugely unjust for innocent people to be excluded from Game worlds because of the bombing."

Hawk was using a controlled droid rather than being

physically present himself, but he still visibly simmered with anger, while I was having a full blown attack of hero worship. I restrained my urge to do a lot of inappropriate things, including a few that probably weren't physically possible with a droid, and there was a pause while we both got our emotions under control.

Eventually Hawk spoke again. "I assume your father tried to help when you were dropped from the training programme, but he didn't have any influence in the medical area."

"I never told him what really happened."

Hawk looked puzzled. "Why not?"

I stared down at my hands. "Because the instructor said she'd throw my friends off the course as well if I caused any trouble. I couldn't put their careers at risk to save my own."

Hawk was silent for a full minute before speaking in an oddly careful voice. "Well, I don't think your instructor should get away with what she did. I'll get an expert to make a discreet check of the course records, looking for evidence that the instructor changed your grades."

I didn't reply because I was finding it difficult to speak.

"I can try to arrange for you to continue your medical training as well," added Hawk. "You could join a class in America, so there'd be no possible problem with your old instructor."

I moistened my lips and managed to speak this time. "No, thank you. It would be difficult for me to go back when I've missed a whole year of training, and... The truth is that the whole idea of becoming a doctor has been soured for me by what happened last year, but I appreciate you offering to help me."

"I understand your decision."

There was yet another long silence. "Anyway," I said at last, "you can see why the bomber wouldn't be able to bribe a respectable kid with a lifetime subscription. Trying to bribe a Game reject wouldn't work either, because someone who can't enter Game would have nothing to gain by having their lifetime subscription paid."

I paused. "Moment!"

I thought frantically while Hawk waited. "You just cleared the questioning from my Game record," I said.

"Yes."

"How did you do that?"

"I threw my weight around as leader of the players' investigation, and got the Game Techs to access your Game record and remove..." Hawk broke off his sentence.

"That's how a Game Tech bribes a kid to do something obviously criminal," I said. "They find a Game reject. Someone with such a serious black mark on their Game record that they'll never be able to enter Game. They offer to clear it. A kid would do anything, anything at all for that."

"Jex, you're brilliant!" said Hawk. "How do we find a black mark on a teenager's Game record after it's been cleared? I'm sure our rogue Game Tech will have wiped any audit trails to cover his tracks."

"Everyone is allocated a Game identity number at birth," I said. "Information about your life, first in the real world and later in Game, goes on the Game record for that identity number."

Hawk nodded.

"But Unilaw must keep its own records on people they question, arrest or charge with crimes," I continued. "A Game Tech shouldn't be able to touch Unilaw records. Compare Game records with Unilaw records, looking for anyone that's had problems with Unilaw that are missing from their Game record."

Hawk grinned. "Totally brilliant! Get some sleep now, while I contact Unilaw and get them comparing records for us. It will be faster if I do that from within Game."

His face abruptly blurred and reverted to an anonymous golden shape. The Hawk in Game had closed down his connection to the controlled droid. Hawk was gone, but I still sat there staring at the discarded droid, my head thinking confused and chaotic thoughts.

Finally, I took out the new phone that Hawk had given me. I was aching with exhaustion now, but I had to make a call before I went to bed. It was only a moment before Nathan's face appeared on my phone screen. I watched his weary expression change to one of pure delight as I told him Hawk had given us back our dreams.

CHAPTER TEN

I woke to a world that smelled strongly of fish. I sat up in confusion, and saw the carriage was stationary with the doors wide open. There was no sign of Hawk's controlled droid, so I went across to look outside. It seemed to be early morning, there were waves rolling in to a pebbled beach, and the fish smell was coming from stacks of empty crates.

I showered, changed into fresh clothes, and caught up with my laundry. After fifteen minutes, I was ready to face the world. There was still no sign of Hawk, so I headed out to search for him.

It wasn't difficult to find Hawk. He was sitting on the beach, throwing stones into the incoming waves, and watching an autoboat towing its nets out at sea. He looked up when I approached, and patted the pebbles by his side.

I sat down. "Where are we?"

"On the south coast of England."

"Why are we back in England, and what are we doing on a beach?"

"I can't think of anything useful to do until Unilaw find a mismatch between records – if they find a mismatch between records at all – so I'm indulging in some nostalgia," said Hawk. "When I was a child, I used to live just along the coast from here. This is the nearest transport stop to it. Apparently, there's nothing left where I used to live, but the autoboats do a bit of fishing from this beach."

"And the fish are transported in crates. That explains the stink around here."

"I didn't know there was one," said Hawk. "This droid precisely replicates sight, hearing, and touch, but it has no sense of smell or taste."

There was silence for a few minutes before he spoke again. "I was an only child. I lived with my parents in a house on the outskirts of a small seaside town. I remember the summers when I was small, the hot days on the beach, and the cries of the gulls soaring overhead. Life was good until I was about thirteen, then somehow things went wrong between me and the other kids. I can't even remember what started that now, but I was targeted by bullies and things got messy. I started skipping school and hiding in my bedroom playing computer games. I lived like that for the next five years."

I wasn't sure what to say, so I kept quiet.

"That was when I signed up for the trial period of Game and was flown to America along with the other volunteers. My body must still be in a freezer unit somewhere over there, but my mind has been wandering the worlds of Game for centuries. I've explored each new world that was added. Vanity, Automaton, Gothic, Ganymede, all two thousand of them. I was so occupied with the Game worlds that I forgot all about the real one. Now I find it isn't here anymore. The world you live in isn't mine, Jex. It's not just the places that have gone, but the whole way of life as well."

He'd been staring out to sea, but now he turned to face me. "Your life must have been so different from mine. It's not just that you left school and started work at ten years old. You've never lived with your parents. You've probably never even lived in a house."

"A house? You mean houses like there are in Game worlds? No, nothing like that. You live in dormitories while you're at school. In theory, each dormitory has an adult supervisor in Game who runs the place. In reality, the oldest kids usually run things, and the supervisor only calls you from Game if you're in trouble."

I winced as painful old memories surfaced. "When you're ten

years old, you leave school and the dormitories, get a job, and pay for your own room in an accommodation block. Having my own room at last, locking the door behind me and finally feeling safe, was the best moment in my life."

Hawk shook his head. "I was so sorry for myself before I entered Game. I thought I had problems and a hard life, but compared to yours… The Game did this, didn't it? The Game and the people like me, the people who were too busy having fun to spare a thought for who was doing the work in real life. Do you compare the childhoods we had with yours and hate us?"

I was startled. "I don't know anything about the way childhood used to be."

"I suppose you wouldn't. Nobody would bother teaching you about it, and you'd be too busy coping with the world you lived in to wonder how it got that way. All your thoughts are focused on planning for the day you'll enter Game."

"That's right." I smiled, rejoicing in the fact I would be entering Game now. "I worked out my Game appearance a year ago. Now I just need to decide on my three surnames."

Hawk laughed. "I don't have any surnames."

I had to laugh too. "Well of course not. We were taught about Game naming conventions as soon as we started school. Founder Players have no surname. First Wave have one surname. The next two centuries of players have two. These days I'll need to have three that make me clearly distinct from all the other people called Jex in the Game. I was planning to use one of my mother's surnames and one of my father's surnames. Now I think I'll use my father's first name, Leigh, as well."

"You said that you planned to have children eventually."

I nodded. "Not for quite a while, but in ten or fifteen years' time."

"And not just because of the baby bonus payments."

Hawk seemed to be quoting something rather than asking a question. Had I said that in front of him? I couldn't remember, but maybe I had.

I nodded again. "Especially now. It's hard to explain this, but my father dying in the Avalon bombing made a difference. I'm a singleton, an only child, like you. My mother defrosted from Game to have a baby because she was desperate to get the credits to pay her lifetime subscription. Now she's paid that, she'll definitely never have another child. My father might have had other children, but now he's dead..."

"Were your parents a couple in Game?" asked Hawk. "I'd never thought about having children, so I'm a bit out of date with how these things work."

"They were never a couple in a romantic sense," I said. "They met on Ganymede. Do you remember me mentioning my mother had problems with an ex-boyfriend when she lived on Ganymede?"

"Yes."

"My mother spends all her time in Game socializing and designing dresses for herself and her friends, but my father is a member of... was a member of both the Ganymede Admission Committee and the Ganymede Residents Assistance Volunteers. He helped my mother get the Game Techs to stop the harassment, and he was one of the few people she kept in touch with after she left Ganymede. When she decided to have a child, she asked him if she could use his DNA, and he agreed."

I paused for a second. "They've been good parents, particularly my father. He always calls... called me every week or two. That made a huge difference when I lived in the dormitories. The bullies always look for easy targets. Most kids are twins, and those usually stick together and defend each other, so the bullies pick on singletons like me. Singleton kids who had no contact at all from their parents had a very bad time. The fact my father was keeping an eye on me from inside Game kept me relatively safe."

I rubbed my eyes with the back of my hand. "I haven't heard from my mother since my father died. It's possible she doesn't know that he's dead. It never occurred to me that he might have been on Avalon during the world crash until I was told in that interrogation room. My mother might still think he's safe and well on Ganymede."

Hawk looked sympathetic. "You should call her and make sure that she knows."

I frowned anxiously. "I should, but I daren't risk it. My mother doesn't like unpleasant things. If I call her and tell her something as awful as the fact my father is dead, I know she'll cut off the call, and I'm worried she might never contact me again."

"I could ask a Game Tech to make sure that she's been notified of your father's death."

I stared at Hawk, startled by his offer. He'd already saved my future in Game, and I didn't like to ask him for yet more help, but I'd lost my father and daren't risk losing my mother too. "That would be very kind of you. My mother is Odele Thorpe Scott Matthys, resident of Game world Coral."

There was a pause before Hawk spoke again. "The Game Tech says that your mother was among those officially informed of your father's death."

I gave a sigh of relief. "That's all right then. It makes sense that my mother hasn't called me or messaged me since then. She's avoiding the issue of my father's death, blanking it out the way she always does with anything bad. I expect she'll wait a couple of months before calling me, and then never mention my father at all."

"That's a very unfair way to treat you," said Hawk.

I shrugged. "It's the way my mother is. It was my father who told me about the harassment problems she had on Ganymede. My mother has never mentioned them at all. When I was a small child, I used to daydream about training to become a great hunter and fighter in Game, and then fighting a duel with my mother's ex-boyfriend and killing him."

Hawk laughed. "Are you still planning to do that?"

"I've realized there's a snag with my daydream. The ex-boyfriend isn't likely to agree to fight a duel with me, and I can't just attack him without getting into a lot of trouble myself. If he ever tries bothering my mother again, it would be far more sensible for me to complain to a Game Tech and get him sentenced to another spell on Havoc. I'd still like to try some of the hunting and fighting though. Perhaps even join one of the battles against the great monsters of Game like the Kraken and the Behemoth."

"I noticed you'd got several battle images on your room wall," said Hawk, "including one of me fighting the Kraken. That's because you've been studying the tactics I used to kill it?"

"Yah," I said, with debatable truth. "Obviously I'd have to train for years before I could think of joining a battle against the Kraken. Anyway, getting back to the subject of having kids, my father's death has somehow made me feel I'd like to have kids myself one day. I want to keep an eye on them, like my father did for me, and give them a helping hand when they start in Game."

There were a few minutes of silence before Hawk spoke. "Things have changed for me too. I knew from the start that investigating the bombing of a Game server complex was going to be a huge challenge, but the situation is turning out to be even worse than I thought."

He paused. "I have a theory about how this hunt will end. This situation is like one of the old legends they use as a basis for some of the Game worlds. If you listen to the silly things they say in Game, then I'm a legendary hero. I'm taking on a Game Tech, one of the gods of the Game who is running amok. I think this hunt will end with me saving the Game, but dying myself."

He turned towards me. "Don't laugh."

I didn't feel like laughing. I could see there was a very real danger that a rogue Game Tech would find a way to delete a player who was hunting him.

"I think I'm going to die," Hawk repeated. "It's strange. I've had four hundred years of fun and fury, I've done so much, but all I can think about are the things I haven't done. One of them..."

He let the words trail off. I waited a moment before speaking.

"One of them is?"

"Jex, I'm four hundred years out of date in some matters. This is one of them. I've never tangled with this area before, and I don't know how... personal... the thing I want to say is these days. It certainly feels personal to me. I don't wish to embarrass you, and you are perfectly free to say no."

I stared at him. Was he really hinting that...? No, he couldn't be.

Hawk blushed, picked up another pebble, and threw it into the waves. "I've never had kids. Now I know I want them. I'd like to be around to keep an eye on them the way you said, but I don't think I will be. I would like to put on record that you have the right to use my DNA to father your children."

I sat there in stunned silence.

He stared out to sea. "Please say no if you don't wish to accept. Even if you do say yes, then you mustn't feel committed in any way. I appreciate you don't intend to have children for years yet. When you do, this would just be there as an option for you. If you care about someone else by then, want to have his children instead of mine, you're free to do that."

"Yah," I said, in a strangled voice.

He turned his head to look at me. "You wish me to put it on record?"

"Yah," I repeated.

We both looked at the sea, the beach, anywhere but at each other. It was a while before I could pull myself together enough to speak again. "How could I say no? Having a Founder Player for a father will give my kids a great start in Game."

I meant to say it in a light, joking voice. I didn't manage it, but Hawk smiled anyway.

"Thanks, Jex. I'm happy knowing you'll be there to watch over them. You think like me, and I was wondering if one day the two of us could..." He stopped. "Moment."

I waited expectantly for a couple of minutes.

"We were right about the bomber recruiting a teenager," said Hawk. "The Unilaw team have found a mismatch between Game and Unilaw records for a boy called Tomath. It's highly unlikely that it's just a random record error, because Tomath lives less than thirty miles from the bomb site."

"Have Unilaw brought Tomath in for questioning yet?"

"No. I've warned them not to do anything that could alarm Tomath. We need to think very carefully before we make our next move. Tomath may not have known what was in the packages when he sent them off in the delivery trolley, but by now he must have realized they were the bombs that destroyed the Avalon server complex. If Unilaw bring him in for questioning, he's not going to admit he was involved in something that killed over eleven thousand people. He'll probably refuse to say anything at all, and even if Unilaw do manage to get him to talk, how much could he tell us?"

"Not much," I said. "The bomber won't have given Tomath any clues to his identity. All Tomath is likely to know is that the bomber is a Game Tech, and we've worked that out for ourselves."

"Tomath's biggest value to us is that he may have a way to contact the bomber," said Hawk, "or the bomber may get in touch with him again to ask him to help with another job. Given all the new security measures protecting Game data, the bomber would surely choose to use Tomath again rather than risk messing around with another teenager's Game record."

Hawk paused and frowned. "I'm not sure how the bomber would persuade Tomath to help him again though. He can't offer Tomath much of an additional bribe now that his record has already been cleared."

"The bomber wouldn't use a bribe but a threat," I said grimly. "Tomath's record has been cleared, but the black mark could be put back again. The bomber might even threaten to pin the whole blame for the bombing on Tomath."

I thought for a moment. "Tell me more about Tomath. Exactly how old is he?"

"A month short of eighteen."

"Where is he living? What class of accommodation block?"

Hawk glanced sideways at something he could see in Game. "Tomath was living in a class B accommodation block but he moved to a room in a class D block three weeks ago. Is that important?"

"Yah," I said. "I'm trying to build up a picture of what Tomath's like, what he's been through, and how he'll be feeling right now. He was living in a class B room, which is the best accommodation you can get unless you're a career cadet. That tells us that Tomath was one of the glitz crowd, spending money on luxuries now rather than concentrating on saving for his future in Game. What did he do to get into trouble, or rather what do Unilaw think he's done?"

Hawk did the glancing sideways thing again. I guessed that he was reading a report in Game.

"It happened the day after the Leebrook Ashton bill became law. Tomath was at a party where a boy was stabbed and nearly died. It sounds like it was a confusing situation, with flashing lights, loud music, and a couple of hundred teenagers packed close together dancing. Nobody saw what happened. The stabbing victim didn't see who stabbed him either, but said he'd had an argument with Tomath earlier."

"So Unilaw brought Tomath in for questioning. Did they have any hard evidence that Tomath had stabbed the boy?"

Hawk shook his head. "Unilaw found the knife in a dish cleansing unit at the party venue. The knife had already been through the cleansing cycle, so any fingerprints and DNA were gone. Unilaw seem convinced Tomath was guilty of attempted murder, but they had no evidence so they ended up releasing him. Tomath moved to the class D accommodation block the next day."

"So Unilaw had no evidence, but they put the fact Tomath was guilty of attempted murder on his record. Typical." I ran my fingers through my hair. "So Tomath was one of the glitz crowd. He spent his money on luxuries and having fun with his friends. He was too young to get into Game before the Leebrook Ashton bill raised the age of entry to nineteen."

I paused. "The glitz crowd held parties the day after the Leebrook Ashton bill became law. Wake parties, where they all wore black and mourned being stuck in the real world for another year."

"You seem to know a lot about the glitz crowd," said Hawk.

"I was one of them for a few years when I was a medical cadet." I smiled as I remembered the friends I'd had back then. Gina, Diane, Bevan, Chen, and the obsessively creative Falcon. "There was a group of six of us, and we had a lot of fun at the parties, especially the fancy dress competitions. Our first effort at fancy dress was when we dressed up as Game monsters. We had a delivery trolley playing the part of a dragon, and laying egg shaped parcels."

"That was the delivery trolley dragon that escaped in the middle of the night?" asked Hawk.

"Yah. After that, we moved on to doing proper re-enactments of Game events. The best one was when we staged a re-enactment of your last two fights in the Battle Arena. Falcon was playing you, I was playing the woman you fought in the semi-final round, and Chen was your opponent in the final. Falcon had us practising the combat sequences for weeks."

My smile faded into nothing. "That was the last event I took part in before I was dropped from the medical course. I couldn't keep in touch with my friends after that. I didn't want to get them in trouble with our instructor, and I couldn't have stayed part of the glitz crowd anyway. I had to work much longer hours and save every credit that I could."

I gave an angry shake of my head, dismissing the irrelevant past. "So, Tomath went to one of the glitz crowd wake parties. All the kids there would have been in a bad mood and having arguments. Someone got stabbed. The victim's medical chip would have sent out an alarm call. Unilaw and the medics arrived, and Unilaw took Tomath in for questioning and decided he was guilty."

"They could be right about that," said Hawk.

"Possibly," I said grudgingly. "When Unilaw released Tomath, he went back to his room. Some of the other kids living in his accommodation block would have belonged to the glitz crowd too, and been at the same party as him. Those kids would know Unilaw thought Tomath was guilty of the stabbing, and want him to leave before he caused any trouble for them."

I shrugged. "Tomath decided to do the smart thing. Grab what possessions he could, and leave fast before the other kids forced him out. He'd want to move far enough away that no one would hear about him being questioned by Unilaw. How far did he move?"

Hawk glanced sideways and blinked in surprise. "Six hundred miles."

"Tomath wasn't taking any chances," I said. "He travelled six hundred miles before looking for a new room. He had to rent one in a class D accommodation block, because getting anything better would involve his Game record being checked. He'd been used to an easy life surrounded by friends. Now he was living among strangers in a comfortless, basic room."

I paused for a moment. "I know what that feels like, because I went through something similar after being dropped from the medical training course. Tomath had bigger problems though. Unilaw had put an accusation of attempted murder on his Game record. No Game world would accept a murderer, so he was a Game reject."

I sighed. "I was nearly in this situation myself. Tomath's life was in ruins. He would have to hide the fact he was a Game reject from the other kids or they'd force him to move again. He'd be limited to getting temporary jobs for a few days at a time, so that no one would bother checking his Game record. He'd know that even worse problems lay ahead. As he got older, people would start asking why he hadn't entered Game."

"But our bomber was looking through kids' Game records," said Hawk. "He was searching for a Game reject living close to the Avalon server complex. He found Tomath and contacted him."

"Yah. Tomath would eagerly agree to do whatever the mysterious Game Tech wanted. He was being offered the answer to all his problems. With a clean record, he could get a better room, a proper job, and enter Game as soon as he was nineteen. Just think how shocked Tomath must have been when he saw the news about the Avalon world crash."

"You've almost got me feeling sorry for Tomath," said Hawk, "but then I remember that he probably stabbed someone and definitely helped the bomber kill eleven thousand, two hundred, and ninety seven people."

"Possibly stabbed someone, and the bomber wouldn't have told Tomath that the packages held bombs."

"Maybe not," said Hawk.

"I expect Tomath is hiding in his room right now, too

terrified to come out. What if another kid goes and talks to him? Tries a bit of blackmail. They've seen something suspicious, and worked out that Tomath helped a Game Tech bomb the Avalon server complex. They're another Game reject, with a black mark on their record that will block them from entering Game. They say that Tomath has to get the Game Tech to help them, or they'll tell their story to Unilaw."

Hawk nodded. "Tomath might co-operate if he thinks it's the only way to stop Unilaw finding out what he's done. What background story would the kid tell Tomath?"

"It should be similar to what happened to Tomath, so he can identify with it. The details will have to be different of course. No glitz crowd. No party. The kid has to be in serious trouble, preferably involving at least one death, but nothing too violent. Perhaps the kid was delivering illegal fertility drugs and a customer died."

Hawk gave me a bewildered look. "Fertility drugs are illegal?"

I couldn't help laughing. Hawk really was incredibly out of date. "Black market ones are. A woman who has twins will get double baby bonus for going through one pregnancy. Since a lot of women have no children, women having more than two children are rewarded with a higher rate baby bonus. If someone has two sets of twins, she gets a huge amount of credits."

Hawk still looked puzzled.

"Some women aren't rated for twins for medical reasons," I continued, "so they just get one embryo implanted. There are drugs that can make an embryo divide into identical twins. In certain circumstances, that can happen naturally, so no one can prove if it was done using illegal drugs. If the pregnancy is successful, then the woman earns a lot of extra credits."

"I see," said Hawk. "So the drugs are illegal because these women are taking a risk by having twins."

"Yah. Sometimes the medical reason for not rating for twins is because there's a danger to the mother; sometimes it's because there's a danger to the babies. Either way, anyone caught supplying illegal fertility drugs faces a minimum charge of endangering human lives, and potentially murder charges as well."

I thought the idea through and nodded. "I'll go and talk to Tomath."

"I'm not sending you to do this, Jex. Remember that Tomath will be desperate to stop a blackmailer from going to Unilaw. He could easily get violent."

I grinned. "Do you really believe that Nathan would be better than me in a fight?"

"I wasn't thinking of sending Nathan either."

"I'll do it," I repeated. "We'll only get one chance to fool Tomath, so we can't mess it up. I know exactly the right things to say. A woman died after taking fertility drugs. Unilaw thought I was involved, and brought me in for questioning. They let me go in the end because they couldn't prove anything, but I've got murder allegations on my Game record that will stop me getting into Game."

Hawk hesitated for a moment. "Since the original Game Company was based in America, English has always been the official language of Game. Those Founder Players who didn't know much English to begin with, all learnt it within their first decade or two in Game, but Tomath is a real life teenager from an area of Europe that didn't speak English in my day. Wouldn't you hit language barriers if you tried to talk to him?"

I shook my head. "Whatever his native language, Tomath will speak English as well. All kids have to learn to speak fluent English, because new players have a limited choice of worlds when they enter Game. They could have to spend decades living on English speaking worlds before they get a chance of becoming a resident of a world that speaks their own language."

Hawk sighed. "All right, I'll let you go and see Tomath and do the talking, but you aren't going alone. I'll find you a bodyguard who knows how to fight and use a gun. He can pretend to be your boyfriend. Would it be plausible for you both to have been involved in delivering the fertility drugs?"

"Yah," I said. "We should start by telling Tomath we were innocent, because any kid would say that, but we want to give him the impression we're actually guilty. That way Tomath will understand us trying to make a deal with him instead of taking our story to Unilaw."

"You have to be very careful when you do this, Jex," said Hawk. "Make sure you don't get hurt, because I don't want anything bad to happen to the potential mother of my possible future offspring."

CHAPTER ELEVEN

"Remember that it's your bodyguard's job to handle any violence, not yours," said Hawk.

I laughed. "You've said that six times now."

"That's because it's very important. I don't want you getting hurt, Jex. Dying in Game is painful, but you wake up safe and well in your home a few minutes later. I'm horribly aware that you're not in Game but in real life, where death isn't just painful but very, very permanent."

"I'll be careful," I said. "Now get back inside the carriage. If anyone comes by and spots the legendary Hawk using a controlled droid, word will spread round the whole neighbourhood and we'll never get away with this."

Hawk went back inside the long-distance carriage, and it started accelerating away, leaving me standing at a deserted transport stop. I stood there for a couple of minutes, thinking through the part I had to play. I wasn't Jex now, but a girl called Emma. I wasn't chasing a bomber, but trying to salvage my Game future.

A group of delivery trolleys came rushing up from a neighbouring storage area. They'd be calling pods in a minute, so I hastily called one myself rather than get stuck waiting a long time. It was only a two stop ride to the apartment block where Emma shared a room with her boyfriend. I walked the length of three corridors to reach a battered door and unlocked it.

I stepped into a room that was shockingly like the one where I genuinely lived. There was the familiar off-white shelving, paper-thin brown carpet, and a plethora of random Game images on the walls. There were even the same patches of rust on the metal frame of the mirror on the wall. The only real difference was this room was larger, and had a double instead of a single bed, because I was supposed to be sharing it with my boyfriend.

I was hit by the thought of what would happen when the hunt for the bomber was over. There'd be no more chasing round after Hawk's controlled droid, no more luxury carriages and fancy meals. After the last few days, it would be hard to go back to my cheap room, basic food, and the stultifying boredom of patrolling the body stacks.

I shook my head. It would be hard going back to my old existence, but I'd cope the way I'd always done, enduring the grimness of life in the real world and dreaming of my future in Game.

I closed the door behind me and started methodically inspecting the contents of the room. The wall shelves held a clutter of cheap personal items, and an assortment of male and female clothes, mostly faded blue overalls like the ones I was wearing now.

I checked the tags on the clothes. I didn't know who'd set up this place for us, but they'd done a good job. The smaller overalls were in my size, and presumably the larger ones would fit my "boyfriend" when he showed up. There was one dress, which was clearly the outfit Emma wore on special occasions. On the bed was a scanty item in black, which looked as if it was intended to please the boyfriend rather than provide any warmth.

I hoped that the fake Game records for Emma and her boyfriend had been set up with as much care as this room. If I managed to talk Tomath into helping us, then the bomber would be studying every detail on those records.

I wandered restlessly round the room again, and then stood looking into the mirror for a while. Our rogue Game Tech could have been spying on Hawk and seen me with him, so I'd removed my flower tattoo and made a few precautionary changes to my appearance using temporary dye and makeup. My brown hair was now blonde, my skin tones were a shade lighter than usual, and I had a different hairstyle. The end result was enough to confuse me when I saw my reflection, so hopefully it would be enough to confuse other people as well.

I combed my hair, gave myself a squirt of cheap perfume, and then sat on a chair, waiting impatiently for my pseudo boyfriend to arrive. Hawk had organized the bodyguard for me at least twelve hours ago. Obviously the man would have to travel to get here, but I'd had to travel a long distance myself. Was my bodyguard coming from halfway round the world, or had he just got lost?

I'd left my new secure phone in the carriage with Hawk, because my old phone was far more suitable for the part of Emma. I couldn't call Nathan to chat on an unsecured link, so I just checked yet again for messages from my mother, and then put the phone away again.

I'd been waiting for about an hour and a half when the door finally opened. A skinny lad in blue overalls came in. He was totally unremarkable, and perfectly believable in the part he was playing. A particularly convincing touch was the fact his black hair was in desperate need of a haircut.

"Hi boyfriend." I grinned at him.

"Hi Emma," he replied. "I'm Michael. I'm told you have to use a fake name for this operation, but I can use my own."

I looked him up and down. "How old are you?"

"Physically? I entered Game three days after my eighteenth birthday. I've spent the last two years in Game, and defrosted to do this job."

Now I understood why I'd had to wait for him to arrive. I'd been assuming my bodyguard was already in real life like me, but he'd had to be defrosted from Game. There'd be a delay while his freezer unit was moved from the body stacks to a medical unit, three or four hours spent defrosting, and then yet more time taken up adjusting to being back in real life and travelling here.

"My physical age can be my age for this operation as well," he continued. "I've been told our cover story is that I was tempted into making some fast credits running errands for a fertility drug supplier. I talked you into helping me, and the first couple of deliveries went smoothly, but we hit disaster the third time. The woman who took the drugs died a few hours later."

I frowned. "Why did she die so quickly?"

"The person making the fertility drugs had made a bad mistake. We've no idea what that mistake was, because we're not medical experts. All we know is that Unilaw caught and charged three of the people involved. Unilaw dragged us in for questioning as well. They couldn't prove anything, so we weren't charged, but the whole thing went on our Game records."

Michael's shoulders sagged in despair. "Life has been a nightmare since then. We lost our jobs in the body stacks, and had to move to class D accommodation. Two weeks later, the kids in our new accommodation block heard about us being questioned by Unilaw. We had to move again, and decided to travel all the way from England into Europe. We've been here for three months now, and we seem to have managed to leave the past behind us this time, but our big problem is that we'll probably be refused entry to Game."

He lifted his head and laughed. "Everyone else was disappointed about the Leebrook Ashton bill, but it was a huge relief for us. We had an extra year before the other kids would start asking why we hadn't entered Game yet. Now we've had another stroke of luck. We see Tomath as our big chance to salvage our futures. We couldn't know about Tomath's record being cleared, but we're sure a Game Tech will be able to do something to help us."

"Very good," I said. "I'm pleased with the way you're entering into the spirit of this."

"You're my girlfriend, Emma, I always try to please you." Michael pointed at the black item of clothing on the bed. "It looks like you try to please me too. I think we had a few fights after we were questioned by Unilaw. You blamed me for getting us into trouble, but now you've forgiven me and we're working together to solve our problems."

"We had a few fights, yah. You think I've forgiven you, but I'm still holding a grudge about you getting me into this mess. I was the one who spotted Tomath acting suspiciously with the delivery trolley. Once I heard about the Avalon crash, I realized Tomath had been involved with the bombing, and came up with the plan to get his Game Tech friend to help us. You understand that I do the talking?"

He nodded. "You understand that I do the fighting?"

"I've been told that several times, yah. Have you got a gun?"

He smiled. "I have two guns and three knives."

I studied him carefully. "I can't see them."

"People aren't supposed to see them."

"You work for Unilaw?"

"That's right," he said. "I chose to take the career cadet approach to paying my lifetime Game subscription, and signed up with Unilaw."

"Sorry to pull you out of Game like this."

"That's not a problem. I volunteered for this. If you don't get hurt then I'm promised a six month holiday when I'm back in Game. If you do get hurt, then I lose my holiday and a Founder Player is going to make the rest of my Game life unbearable, so please let me handle any rough stuff."

I laughed. "Are we ready to go and visit Tomath?"

"I think we are." Michael addressed thin air. "Surveillance, are you ready? What's the situation with Tomath?"

A female voice spoke from a tiny ear piece in my right ear. "We're ready. Tomath left his room briefly an hour ago to buy a stack of sandwich packs. He's back in his room now."

"You're hearing that too?" Michael asked me.

"Yah."

"Let's get moving then. Unless you want to model that little black scrap of clothing on the bed for me." He gave me a mischievous look.

By now I'd decided I liked the boy despite the fact he worked for Unilaw. He wasn't exactly handsome, but he was clearly very bright and had a sense of humour. I laughed at him. "You behave yourself."

He pulled a face of mock innocence at me. "I've no idea what you're complaining about, Emma. I'm your boyfriend. I see you wearing that black lace every night."

We went out of the room, walked along a couple of corridors, and stopped outside a door. I double checked the number on it was right. I was feeling nervous now. That was fine. Emma would feel nervous doing this.

I pressed the doorbell, and heard it ring on the other side of the door. There was a long pause. I rang the bell again, and then a third time. Finally, I gave up on the bell, and tried talking through the door.

"I know you're in there."

There was no response.

I gave a loud sigh. "I know you're standing on the other side of this door. You're listening to me talking, and hoping I'll give up and go away. That's not going to happen. I saw what you did. I found out your name and where you lived. You're very lucky that I was the one who saw you, because most kids would have gone to Unilaw right away. As it happens, I'd rather stay clear of Unilaw because I've had my own problems with them. I'm happy to keep quiet about the whole thing so long as you do me a small favour."

I thought I heard a faint sound on the other side of the door. I waited a minute before speaking again.

"Why don't you open the door and talk to me, Tomath? If you're scared there's a whole mob of Unilaw officers out here, then you're being ridiculous. Unilaw officers wouldn't be standing here arguing with you, they'd just smash the door down and wave guns at you."

I waited a few more seconds. "All right, I'm getting tired of standing out here. Most of the local kids will either be asleep or at work right now. First of all, I'm going to start kicking your door to wake up all the sleeping kids in nearby rooms. Then I'm going to keep screaming the word Avalon at the top of my voice until they all come to see what's going on. Then I'm going to call Unilaw and tell them you were the one who planted the bombs."

I gave the door a kick. There was a sudden scrabbling noise on the other side of it, and a voice called out. "Wait!"

I heard what sounded like furniture being dragged aside, and then the door opened a few inches and Tomath peered out at me. He had lank, greasy, fair hair, and was wearing what must have been an expensive outfit once, but was stained and crumpled now. He gave me a calculating look, and then I saw his pale blue eyes widen as he saw Michael standing next to me. He tried to close the door, but Michael leant on it.

"Yah, there are two of us," he said. "I thought you were more likely to open the door if I kept quiet."

"Shall we go inside to talk," I asked, "or do you want us to discuss the bombing out here in the corridor?"

Tomath stood there frowning for a couple of seconds, and then backed away. We followed him into the room, squeezing past the cupboard that he'd been using to barricade the door.

"I'm Emma," I said, "and this is my boyfriend, Michael."

Tomath spoke in a hostile voice that had only the faintest trace of an accent. "Why did you force your way in here, and why do you keep making wild threats about the Avalon bombing? I know nothing about it."

I gave him a pleading look. "You've got to help us. Michael and I got in trouble with Unilaw over fertility drug smuggling. A woman died. We were totally innocent, but Unilaw put everything on our Game records. We lost our jobs, had to move rooms to a different area, ended up having to move a second time and leave England entirely."

"I've no idea why you're telling me these things," said Tomath.

"Because this is going to stop us getting into Game." I waved my hands in a despairing gesture, and hoped I wasn't overacting my part.

Michael gave a heavy sigh. "You should let me do the talking."

I glared at him. "You keep quiet. It's your fault that we got into this mess."

"I thought you'd forgiven me," he said, in wounded tones.

"You were wrong." I turned back to Tomath. "I know you've got a Game Tech friend who can help us."

I was studying every shifting expression on Tomath's face, and saw his surprise and alarm at my mention of a Game Tech.

"I don't have any Game Tech friends," he said.

"Yah, you do." I reached out a hand in appeal, and Tomath backed away from me. "Please help me."

"Us," said Michael.

I gave him an angry look, and then turned back to Tomath. "We know you planted the bombs. We don't want to have to go and tell Unilaw about it. We'd much rather that you help us get into Game."

I'd built up a mental image of a Tomath that was utterly devastated by what had happened to him. I'd expected him to be terrified by our arrival, not ask too many questions about how we got our knowledge, just eagerly agree to do whatever we wanted. I was disconcerted when he gave me a defiant stare.

"What makes you think I know anything about the Avalon bombing? You said that you saw something. Exactly what did you see?"

"We live a few corridors away from here," I said. "I was coming home from work, walking back from the transport stop, when I saw you with the delivery trolley. I noticed that it didn't look right."

I knew the minute I'd said it that I'd made a mistake. Tomath's face was suspicious now.

"You couldn't have seen that."

I thought fast. The closest transport stop to Tomath's room was on the same line as the transport stop for the Avalon server complex. Hawk and I had guessed that he'd brought the trolley to his room, made the modifications, given it the bombs, and sent it on its way. It only had to go back to the transport stop, get into a freight pod, and after that there'd be no one to see it on its journey. The bomber would have checked the schedule to make sure it didn't run into any maintenance crews at the server complex.

Our guess had been wrong. Tomath had known he was doing something illegal, so he hadn't risked bringing the trolley anywhere near his room, but made the modifications somewhere else. I had to bluff my way out of this, but how? My ear piece was dead silent, which meant surveillance didn't have any helpful ideas.

"You didn't see the trolley when you were coming home from work, Emma," said Michael, his voice making it an accusation. "You've been visiting Ivan again, haven't you?"

"What if I did call in to see Ivan on my way home?" I watched Tomath out of the corner of my eye. He must have worked on the delivery trolley near a different transport stop, but it would surely have been one on the same line. There'd be no point in risking the trolley going to a busy interchange.

I remembered that transport stop where Hawk's carriage had stopped to let me out. We'd chosen it because most of the rooms in that area were empty and being refurbished. That meant there wouldn't be many people around, just delivery trolleys taking items to and from the neighbouring storage area.

I took a desperate gamble. "Ivan's just moved into a newly refurbished room. It's only two stops away, so I thought I'd call in to say hello on my way back from work."

Tomath's expression flickered when I said two stops. My gamble was right. He'd grabbed a delivery trolley at that storage area, and taken it to one of the empty rooms to make the modifications.

"I told you to stay away from Ivan." Michael gripped both my arms and shook me.

I pulled my arms away. "You've no reason to be jealous of Ivan. He's just being friendly, and I lost all my other friends after you dragged me into that fertility drug business."

I turned back to Tomath. "I didn't pay much attention to you and the delivery trolley until I saw the Game droid spying on you. I didn't understand what was going on at the time, but then I heard about the bombing and worked out that you were involved. After that, I just had to ask a few questions to find out your name and room."

I shrugged. "We don't care why your Game Tech friend wanted to blow up a server complex, or why you helped plant the bombs. All we want is for the Game Tech to fix things so we can get into Game. If you arrange that for us, then we'll keep quiet, and everything will be fine."

Tomath's expression had changed to one of acceptance now. He believed that his employer hadn't trusted him and had been spying on his movements.

"All I can do is leave a message," he said, in a defeated voice. "It could be a while before the Game Tech sees it."

"That would be wonderful." I dug a piece of paper out of my pocket. "These are our Game identity numbers. I've put my phone number as well, so the Game Tech can call us. Just get us into Game and I'll be ever so grateful."

"You can believe that," said Michael bitterly. "Emma's grateful to everyone. Ivan, me, you, the entire neighbourhood!"

I whirled round to face him. "Don't talk about me like that!"

Michael grabbed my arm and turned towards the door. "We can discuss this when we get home. Come on!"

The grip he had on my arm was painfully tight, but I decided I'd better delay complaining about it until we were outside. I was shocked when Michael suddenly shoved me forwards so I went sprawling on my hands and knees by the door. I heard the sound of a blow and a loud gasp of pain from behind me, grabbed hold of the cupboard beside me to drag myself to my feet, and turned ready to join in the fight. It was clear that my help wasn't needed though, because Michael was already advancing on a staggering Tomath.

Michael hit Tomath again while he was still off balance, sending him toppling backwards and colliding heavily with the wall. Michael took another rapid step forward, and snatched a knife from Tomath's flailing right hand.

"Did you really believe I was fool enough to let a pathetic creature like you stab us in the back?" Michael gave a contemptuous shake of his head. "You'd better make sure that the Game Tech contacts us, because if we don't hear anything then I'm going to beat you to a pulp before I go and talk to Unilaw."

Michael and I went out into the corridor, and walked back to the room that we were supposed to share. As soon as the door was closed behind us, I turned to Michael.

"You did well stopping Tomath from stabbing us."

"I was just doing my job."

"But I was supposed to do all the talking."

"I thought you needed some help at times. It worked, didn't it?"

"True," I admitted. "I wonder how long we'll have to wait before something happens."

"Maybe hours. Maybe days." Michael gave an oddly one-shouldered shrug, and sat on the edge of the bed. "I'm in no hurry. We can spend the time getting to know each other better."

I gave him a dubious look. Surveillance had this room filled with spy eyes and ears, so he couldn't be suggesting anything too intimate, but I pointedly sat down on a shabby chair in the far corner of the room anyway.

"There's no point in getting to know each other. As soon as this job is over, you'll be going back into Game."

Michael gave me an assessing look. "You must be nearly eighteen though, so you'll be in Game yourself very soon. We could meet up again there."

I wasn't sure if he was serious. It didn't matter whether he was or not. I pointed out the obvious problem with his suggestion. "You're forgetting the Leebrook Ashton bill. I can't enter Game until I'm nineteen now."

He laughed. "A good thing is worth waiting for, and a year isn't all that long. We can exchange Game names now, and you can contact me when you arrive in Game."

I hesitated. I liked the boy, but...

"You clearly aren't interested," said Michael, "so please forget I suggested it. Let's talk about something else instead."

"No," I said. "I think you'll have forgotten all about me by the time I enter Game, but if not... I'll be Jex Thorpe Leigh Grantham, hopefully of Ganymede."

"I'm Michael Dans Lincoln Washington. Call me as soon as you're in Game. In fact, there's no reason why we can't exchange calls before then, and make a few plans for..." He broke off, and gave me an anxious look. "Why are you staring at me like that?"

Michael's one-shouldered shrug had seemed strangely familiar, but I'd been too stupid to figure out why. I couldn't miss the name though. Hawk had been my hero for years, so I knew all the Game trivia about him, including the fact his real life name had been Michael Dans. I'd no idea where he'd got the Lincoln and Washington from, but...

"You're Hawk!"

CHAPTER TWELVE

Hawk hesitated, clearly considering denying everything, and then sighed. "I was being careful to speak like a teenager today, saying yah instead of yes. How did you know I was Hawk?"

"Because of the joke you were playing on me. You thought it was funny to pretend you wanted to contact me when I entered Game, but telling me a Game name that included your real life name gave you away."

I was annoyed about the joke. No, I was far more than just annoyed. I was deeply hurt and disappointed that Hawk had made fun of me like that, but I mustn't lose my temper with him. Even if he looked like an ordinary kid now, he was still a Founder Player. Hawk could mock me all he liked and I just had to accept it meekly.

"That wasn't a joke," said Hawk. "I wanted to meet you as my real self, as Michael, because I thought... Moment."

The skinny kid, who was the real life body of the legendary Hawk, took a phone from his pocket and raised his eyes to the ceiling. "Surveillance, I'm afraid I need some privacy now. Don't worry, I'll turn off the jammer as soon as something starts happening."

He clicked a button on his phone and looked back at me. "If the device in this personal messenger works properly, then I've just jammed all the spy eyes and ears surveillance planted in this room."

"We call those things phones, not personal messengers, these days," I said coldly.

"Ah, the real world has gone back to using the phone word again," said Hawk.

The jamming device in Hawk's phone definitely worked, because the female voice of surveillance started whining away in my ear about their lack of sound and vision.

"Surveillance sounds a little upset," I said.

It was about two minutes before surveillance accepted that Hawk wasn't going to turn off his jamming device and the voice shut up.

"Peace at last," said Hawk. "As I was saying, I wasn't playing a joke on you. I didn't tell you I was defrosting because I wanted to meet you as the real me, as Michael, and I was perfectly serious about exchanging Game names."

My anger was mixed with confusion now. "You weren't making fun of me when you suggested that?"

"Of course I wasn't making fun of you," said Hawk. "Since the first moment I saw you, I've been struck by the way you think through problems, the way that you keep fighting your cause even when you're scared to death, and the way your face burns with anger at injustice. I wanted to tell you how much I liked you, see if you liked me too, but you only knew me as Hawk the Unvanquished."

He brushed a stray strand of black hair away from his eyes. "I've learnt the hard way that it's impossible to build anything good on a foundation of lies. I knew that if I wanted any chance of a relationship with you, then I'd have to stop acting the part of Hawk the Unvanquished, and explain to you about Michael being my real self."

For a moment, I didn't understand what he meant by acting the part of Hawk the Unvanquished and Michael being his real self, but then I remembered how smoothly assured Hawk had always been when he was dealing with his adoring fans. All the times when Hawk had seemed distressed, human and vulnerable, had been when he was alone with me and Nathan, or with old friends like Romulus, Remus, and Kwame.

"You think of Hawk the Unvanquished as your public image rather than your real self?" I asked.

"I think of Hawk the Unvanquished as a public image that's in danger of swallowing my real self whole. I was trying to work out how I could possibly explain to you about Michael. I was scared that you wouldn't understand. I was even more scared that you *would* understand and recoil in disgust, because Hawk is a glossy legend while Michael is just a mess."

He gave that one-shouldered shrug again. "When I decided to defrost from Game, I realized this would give me the chance to solve the whole relationship problem as well. I wouldn't have to explain to you about Michael, because I could show you Michael. I could step free from the public image, and all the complications of being a Founder Player, and meet you as just another teenager."

He paused. "My plan was that if you seemed to like Michael, then I'd suggest we could meet again when you entered Game. If you turned down my suggestion of keeping in contact, I could just quietly fade away without embarrassing either of us. I knew I'd have to give you a fake Game name to contact me, but I could get a Game Tech to make sure any messages for that fake Game name were sent to me."

I was struggling to accept this situation was really happening, let alone work out how I felt about it, so I changed the subject slightly. "I don't understand how you got here so fast. It was less than two hours between me saying goodbye to your droid at the transport stop, and you walking into this room. Just defrosting your body would take a lot longer than that, and you mentioned it was stored in a freezer unit in America."

"My body had already been moved to a medical unit, defrosted, and flown here before I said goodbye to you," said Hawk. "I only had to close the carriage doors, and say I was ready to leave Game. An instant later, I was opening my eyes on a table with a couple of doctors checking me over."

"Didn't it take time for you to adjust to being in a real body again? Surely after four hundred years…"

He laughed. "I spent an hour acclimatizing before I came here. It helped that I've had a lot of experience of adjusting to different Game bodies, swapping between being human to being a ghost, merman, or centaur. Leaving Game was nothing like as shocking an experience as when I entered it."

He was silent for a moment, his distracted expression showing he was thinking back through the centuries. "Both the Game environment and our bodies were pretty primitive back then. I remember how strange it was during the first few weeks. There was no sense of smell at all, and everything you touched felt oddly furry. You kept finding gaps in the world too, where there was nothing but a patch of black mist."

He shook his head. "There have been continuous improvements to Game through the years. Now the experience of being in a Game body matches real life so closely, that waking up was surprisingly easy. Moving around felt quite natural, though there's a sort of dragging, tired feeling about being in a real body. We can eat and drink in Game if we want, though it's not necessary the way it is in real life, so that wasn't too strange either."

He blushed. "The one thing I found hard was... The bodily functions that remove waste products."

I laughed.

"No one has ever felt the need to put that in Game," he said, "and I wouldn't encourage the Game Techs to add it in future."

"Well, I think you made a fantastic adjustment. I'd never have guessed you weren't an ordinary kid just by watching you move around, and you handled Tomath so easily when he tried to stab us."

Hawk pulled a self-deprecating face that was a close echo of one of his Game expressions. "Please don't mention that. For a legendary fighter that was a humiliating exhibition. I was appallingly slow, and it wasn't because I was unfamiliar with a real body. The truth is that I was dreadfully unfit when I was frozen, and I'd just injured a muscle in my shoulder as well."

He rubbed his left shoulder. "That's still sore, so I'm a bit worried about how I'd manage a proper fight. I should be all right with guns. Anything involving genuine muscle power will be difficult, but I'll have to cope because there's no time for me to get into training now."

"I hate to admit it, but Unilaw were probably right after all."

"About what?"

"About Tomath being the one who stabbed the boy at the party. How did you spot that Tomath was going to try to stab us? Did you see his knife?"

"I've spent a lot of time in the Battle Arena," said Hawk. "Plenty of fighters put on a beaten into surrender act just before they try to catch you by surprise with a sneaky tactic. Tomath's expression and voice were those of someone who'd given up, but his muscles were tensing for action. I was ready for him to pull a knife and attack us."

There was a short silence. "Who knows that you've defrosted from Game?" I asked.

"Among the Game Techs, Kwame and his team know. Among the players, Cassandra is dealing with messages for me, keeping up the illusion that I'm still in Game. Other than that, only a couple of doctors and the core members of the Unilaw investigation team know that I'm Hawk. Now you know it too, I'll tell Unilaw to inform Nathan and include him in the operation."

"Why did you decide to defrost anyway? When I suggested it might be safer for you to leave Game, you ruled it out."

"I ruled out leaving Game just for reasons of my personal safety. Leaving Game to track down our rogue Game Tech is different." Hawk grinned at me. His eyes weren't as dark as those of the Game Hawk, but there was something similar in their expression.

"I'm never good at delegating things to others," he said. "I was happy to let Nathan study Game information for me, but that's a very special case. I doubt I'd be able to understand that level of technical information, and on a purely selfish note I don't want to know how the Game Techs design the monsters I fight. It would spoil all my Game fun. I aim to kill the Behemoth solo one day, and if I know the Game design behind it, well, that would be cheating."

I nodded. "I'd feel the same, but Nathan is loving every moment. He thinks it may help him become a Game Tech one day."

Hawk gave me a mischievous look that definitely belonged on his famous Game face. "It'll do far more than that. Nathan's nosing through Game secrets at lightning speed. At the rate he's learning, within a couple of days he'll know so much that the Game Techs can never let him be just an ordinary player."

I blinked. "You mean...?"

Hawk nodded. "Nathan's studying their confidential training texts. He's playing around with actual Game monsters and scenery. They'll have to make him a Game Tech as soon as he enters Game."

"That's wonderful," I said. "Becoming a Game Tech, helping design worlds, is Nathan's dream."

"I was happy to delegate learning Game information to Nathan," said Hawk, "but hunting the bomber and fighting are my job. That's why I decided to defrost. Of course, there was the extra incentive that I'd be able to meet you as my real self."

Hawk seemed to be studying my face. I could feel myself blushing.

"What do you think will happen now?" I asked.

"Tomath said he'd leave a message for the Game Tech. I planted two spy eyes in his room while we were there. Surveillance is watching him like a..."

I grinned. "Like a hawk."

The legendary skinny kid with the unruly black hair matched my grin. "Exactly. I'm sure they'll let us know when he does anything."

"I hope he doesn't take too long. This could get boring."

Hawk had that mischievous look on his face again. "I could suggest a way to entertain ourselves. We're planning to have kids, and there's a double bed here. We could bypass the whole DNA thing."

I stared at him in shock and confusion. "I don't know how relationships worked four centuries ago, but these days you don't tell a girl that you're interested in her and then expect to go to bed with her five minutes later."

Hawk's mischievous expression changed to panic. "I didn't mean it that way."

"As for the DNA thing..." I shook my head. "I've had my contraceptive shots, so I can't get pregnant until they give me my hormone booster."

"I didn't mean the DNA thing either." Hawk groaned. "I was trying to flirt with you, make a light-hearted joke to tell you I found you attractive, and I totally messed it up because I'm Michael again. Whenever Michael tried to talk to a girl, he'd either be too shy to say anything at all, or come out with a horribly crass remark."

"Oh." I thought about that for a moment, and remembered the remark Michael had made about me modelling the black lace for him. I'd known he was flirting back then and laughed. Now I knew Michael was Hawk, it changed everything. I couldn't be sure whether he'd messed up that last attempt at flirtation, or whether I was reacting the wrong way because he was Hawk. It was probably a combination of both things.

"Don't worry, I've got the message," said Hawk. "You aren't attracted to Michael. I thought it meant something that you were willing to exchange Game names with me and agreed I could contact you when you entered Game. I should have known you were just being polite. In Game I'm the mighty Hawk, but here I'm just gawky, incoherent Michael again."

He flopped backwards to lie on the bed. "It's been four hundred bleeping years and nothing's changed. No girl could ever be interested in dating repellent Michael."

Hawk was a legendary hero of Game, but right now he just looked like a deeply depressed teenage boy. I frowned at him before speaking.

"I don't think you're repellent. I'm just bewildered by this situation. I don't understand why you'd be interested in me when you've got hordes of girl fans in Game."

"The hordes of girl fans adore the flawless Hawk the Unvanquished," said Hawk. "There were some moments between us when I let the act slip, stopped being Hawk and was Michael, and there seemed to be a genuine connection between us."

"But everyone is much better looking in Game than in real life, and people say that sex is a lot better in Game too."

"Everyone can be good looking in Game, so it's your personality that matters." Hawk stared gloomily up at the ceiling. "I wouldn't know about the sex, because I never had sex in real life. I hope that jamming device is working properly, because if surveillance heard me say that, then I'll..."

The female voice of surveillance spoke in my ear again. "We're hoping you can still hear us."

"No!" yelped Hawk.

"Tomath was walking round his room," continued surveillance, "he's now using his phone to do something."

Hawk gave a sigh of relief. "For a second, I thought she was going to say a whole mob of Unilaw officers had been listening to my confessions of sexual inexperience."

"Tomath has now put a note on his personal online diary detailing your visit and asking for help," said surveillance.

"Personal online diary?" Hawk turned to me. "Who can see that?"

"In theory your online diary is private," I said, "but everyone's very careful what they put on it. The diary is linked to your Game record, so Unilaw officials and Game Techs can access it."

Hawk nodded. "So now we have to wait until the bomber checks Tomath's online diary."

"If the bomber ever checks it at all. Putting myself in his or her head, I wouldn't care if Tomath had a problem and wanted to contact me. The only time I'd bother with Tomath was when I wanted to order him to do another job."

"Kwame told all the Game Techs that one of their own ranks was involved in the bombing. Our rogue Game Tech will be anxious to know what else we've discovered, and watching Tomath's record for any notes about him being questioned by Unilaw."

"Point," I said. "If our bomber does access Tomath's diary, will Unilaw be able to trace their identity?"

"I doubt it. He or she has covered their tracks very well so far. I expect they'll have a way to check Tomath's diary without leaving any clues, but eventually they'll make a mistake. Game

Techs are used to preparing everything well in advance and being totally in control of a situation. Our bomber will be most vulnerable when forced to respond rapidly to an unexpected event."

"Like us blackmailing Tomath?"

"Yes." Hawk groaned. "I must remember not to say yes but yah, the way all kids do these days, or I'll give myself away."

"If the Game Tech decides to contact us, then we use the same story we told Tomath? Pretend we're desperate and we'll do anything if the Game Tech helps us get into Game."

"Yah."

The voice of surveillance spoke again. "Tomath's personal diary has been accessed."

Hawk sat up, and clicked the button on his phone to stop jamming the eyes and ears in the room. "Surveillance, have you got details of who accessed the diary?"

"The access came from within Game," said surveillance, "but we were unable to obtain any further details since the access lasted for less than one hundredth of a second."

Hawk frowned. "Less than one hundredth of a second? That makes no sense. The bomber couldn't have read Tomath's note in that time."

"The access wasn't done manually by the bomber," said surveillance, in a pitying voice, "but by an automated process."

"Oh, I see." Hawk clicked the jamming button again and pulled a face at me. "Surveillance still seems unhappy with me."

I grinned. "Just a little."

"All Game Techs are computer experts," said Hawk. "It makes sense that our bomber would use an automated process to do things like check Tomath's Game record and diary. Presumably our message has now been sent to the bomber."

I felt a surge of adrenalin, preparing me for instant action.

"The bomber is bound to take a while to decide whether or not to contact us," added Hawk.

I calmed down again. "What if the Game Tech doesn't bother contacting us, just clears our fake records? We won't have learnt anything at all."

"I doubt the bomber would help us without asking for something in return. It's more likely they'd decide to do nothing at all and abandon Tomath to his fate, but they'll be torn between curiosity and caution. I'm hoping that curiosity will win."

There was silence for a while after that. I temporarily abandoned worrying about the bomber, and went back to worrying about purely personal issues.

"You didn't tell me you were defrosting because you wanted to meet me as Michael," I said. "Your idea was to keep pretending to be an ordinary player and wait until I entered Game. I suppose a year doesn't seem that long a time to you, but what were you going to do after that?"

"I planned to mask up."

"Mask up? What does that mean?"

"Founder Players can't go anywhere without attracting huge amounts of attention. Sometimes we get a Game Tech to alter our appearance and give us a fake Game name. Then we can fade into the background and do things without people knowing who we are."

I was puzzled. "But players in Game have an arm bracelet that shows their status. The fact your bracelet is diamond would tell everyone that you're a Founder Player."

Hawk laughed. "We can mask that too; get our bracelets changed from diamond to be gold, silver or bronze like ordinary players. My idea was to mask up, meet you, and see how things progressed. If it looked as if things were working out between us, I'd pick a good moment to tell you who I really was."

"Didn't it occur to you that I might be a bit annoyed about you lying to me?"

Hawk sighed and flopped backwards on to the bed again. "I didn't think this through very well, did I? Apart from anything else, it was utterly stupid of me to think I could hide the fact I was Hawk for weeks or months. The reality was that I couldn't even manage a couple of hours without giving myself away."

"I was totally convinced by your story until you made the mistake of saying your real life name. You looked just like an ordinary kid who'd entered Game at eighteen. How old are you anyway? Physically, I mean. Your real life age is classed as medical information, so it isn't on your open record."

"I told you the exact truth about my age," said Hawk. "I entered Game three days after my eighteenth birthday, which meant I was the youngest of the Founder Players. For legal reasons, the company insisted you had to be over eighteen to enter the Game. If I'd been born four days later, then Hawk would never have existed."

That was a disturbing thought. I couldn't imagine the Game without the charismatic Hawk. There were plenty of other Founder Players, but Hawk was the embodiment of all the Game legends.

"Would you like to know what I thought when I first saw Michael?" I asked.

Hawk leaned on one elbow to get a better view of me. "No one can resist asking to hear that sort of thing. I'll probably regret it."

I closed my eyes for a moment, letting the memory surface. "I thought you needed a haircut. You weren't exactly handsome, but you certainly weren't ugly. You seemed very intelligent."

Hawk tipped his head to one side and back again. "Could be a lot worse. At least you didn't think I had the sex appeal of a decomposing slug."

I laughed. "No, in fact I found you much more attractive than Nathan. You weren't just bright; you had a sense of humour too. When you suggested us meeting up after I entered Game, I only hesitated because I thought you'd have forgotten all about me by then. If you'd asked me for a date in real life instead, I'd have said no because I'm not planning any romantic attachments until I'm in Game, but I'd have been tempted."

Hawk looked ridiculously pleased. "I expect you're just being nice, but thanks anyway."

"I'm not just being nice. If you were truly Michael, I'd happily agree to meet up with you once I was in Game, have a few dates and see if that turned into a relationship between us. The problem is that you're Hawk."

"Stop right there." Hawk sat up and stared at me. "You mean you don't have a problem with me being Michael, you have a problem with me being Hawk? But why? I had the impression you admired Hawk."

I groaned. "I did. I mean, I do. The way I gushed about you being my all time hero when we first met must have made that perfectly obvious. I had a crush on you, had your picture on my wall, had fantasies about you stepping out of the picture and..."

I waved my hands. "That was fine when it was just a fantasy, but there are big problems when it comes to getting involved with you in reality. You're a legendary Founder Player, while I haven't even entered Game yet. Even when I do enter Game, I'll be wearing the bronze bracelet of a player in their first year, and you'll be wearing diamond. There's also the key detail that you're four hundred years older than me."

"Rubbish," said Hawk. "I can't be more than a few weeks older than you."

I sighed. "I meant that you were four hundred years older than me chronologically and emotionally, not physically."

"But that isn't really true. Time spent in Game doesn't touch you the way that real life does. You..."

Hawk broke off his sentence because the voice of surveillance was speaking again. "Can you turn our eyes and ears back on please? Tomath's message on his personal diary has been removed and replaced with instructions to contact you with a location and time."

Hawk grabbed his phone again and clicked the button. "Surveillance, did you get any more information this time?"

"Nothing except that the access was done by the same automated process as before," said surveillance.

"The bomber clearly wants to take control of this situation by sending us to a place of their own choosing," said Hawk.

I had about five seconds to feel sorry for whoever had worked to make every detail of this room so convincing when the bomber would never see it, then my phone buzzed for an incoming call. Hawk nodded at me and I answered the call.

Tomath's face appeared on my phone screen. He gave me a resentful look. "You've got thirty minutes to get to the meeting point." He gabbled a string of numbers before ending the call.

"That location is a new dormitory that will be opening next week," said surveillance. "You've barely got time to reach it using a standard pod, but you could save time by using the high-speed carriage."

"If we're being sent to this location," said Hawk, "we have to assume the bomber already has spy eyes there, and could be watching the nearest transport stops too. We can't risk being seen stepping out of a luxury carriage."

He paused for a moment. "You'd better move the carriage to somewhere close by in case we need it urgently, but Jex and I will do our travelling in a standard pod. Make sure there aren't any Unilaw droids anywhere near the meeting point. I'll try to plant a few spy eyes when I get there, but if I can't then you'll have to wait for us to call you with an update."

"Understood," said surveillance.

Hawk and I hurried out of the door, and started running to the nearest transport stop.

CHAPTER THIRTEEN

Hawk followed me into a two-person pod, and sat opposite me. He clutched the arms of his seat nervously as it started accelerating. "I feel a lot more vulnerable now that I'm back in a human body. Why don't these things have seat safety restraints in case of an accident?"

"Standard pods don't go very fast," I said.

He sniffed the air. "It smells as if someone has been sick in here recently."

I glanced at a suspicious stain on the floor. "I think someone has."

Hawk sighed and clicked the button on his phone. "We can continue our earlier conversation now, though this is the least romantic setting I've ever seen. As I was trying to say, the four hundred year chronological difference between us doesn't matter."

"It matters to me," I said. "So does the vast list of girls you've dated during those four hundred years."

He laughed, and although he looked like a skinny kid, his laughter was pure Hawk. "Would you like to know the truth about me and my past relationships with girls?"

"Yah. No." I waved my hands indecisively. "I know you must have had thousands of relationships in Game, but I don't want to listen to all the gory details. I should though, because hearing it will be good for me, make it absolutely clear that... Yah, tell me about them."

"Thousands of relationships! Me? You're going to be surprised." Hawk was frowning now. "Being here with you, in my old physical body, is amazing. The past is alive again. I'm the real me, Michael, talking to a girl, but she's listening this time instead of ridiculing me. She actually prefers Michael to Hawk the Unvanquished. I can be myself, be open and frank about everything. It's been such a very, very long time since I could do that with anyone."

"Surely you can be yourself with the other Founder Players."

He smiled. "Oh yes, my relationship with other members of the family is very different, but it's also very complicated. Life on Celestius is nothing like the rest of Game. The family established their own rules during the first ten years. There are eight hundred and fifty male Founder Players, and only seventy-nine female, so Michael never stood a chance with any of the women. As for the men... It's not just that there's a lot of long running rivalries, the Founder Players are a strange group of people."

I blinked. "After four hundred years in Game, I suppose..."

"No, no. We were a weird bunch to start with." Hawk's words were spilling out eagerly now, as if they'd been pent up inside him for centuries. "When I was a kid, I played games, but those games were like... Well, with some you saw your character on a screen, and made it move around. With others, it was a bit like controlling a droid from Game, but far more primitive."

He gave a reminiscent smile. "They weren't bad in their way, but then the Game started, and comparing that to old style games was like comparing the sun to the light of a single candle. The Game Company froze your body and took your consciousness into the world of the Game. You weren't a spectator any longer, but genuinely part of events. Obviously there was only one Game world back then."

I tried to imagine Game without the multitude of worlds like Ganymede, Avalon, Coral, and Starlight.

"People were scared to try it," said Hawk. "There were a host of horror stories about what could go wrong. Experts warned of possible tissue damage in freezer units, or data corruption scrambling your brains."

"We studied this in school," I said. "The Founder Players were the brave heroes who led the way and made the Game possible."

Hawk laughed. "Brave heroes. Hah! The truth is that we were a mixture of social misfits, people who were terminally ill, and obsessive gamers. If you couldn't cope with the real world, or if you were dying, or if you couldn't resist the lure of a game that was far more advanced than any other. Those were the ones who entered the Game. Those were your Founder Players."

I didn't know what to say. Everyone knew that some of the Founder Players were a little eccentric, but their illustrious rank entitled them to behave however they wished.

"I belonged to two out of those three categories," said Hawk. "I was an obsessive gamer who had problems coping with real life people. My parents kept saying I should get out more."

He sighed. "I did try that at one point. I gave up my games, joined the real world, even had a girlfriend for three weeks, but then she dumped me in the most appalling way possible. She was the one who said I had the sex appeal of a decomposing slug, but let's give a merciful burial to the rest of the awful details."

He paused. "Funny how much it still hurts remembering what happened back then. I took refuge in my gaming again, and tried to forget that Susanna had ever existed."

I listened, fascinated and unbelieving, trying to fit the boy he was describing together with the legendary Hawk and the competent Michael to make an understandable whole.

"Then the Game Company started advertising for people to sign up and play the trial period of the Game," said Hawk. "They'd made a huge investment and were desperate to prove the horror stories weren't true and the Game was safe. They were offering the chance to play for every hour of every day, physically escaping reality, and they were offering it free! For someone like me, who'd dropped out of school, had no qualifications, no social skills, and no job, it was an irresistible offer."

Hawk shook his head. "When I think of the way you had to start work at ten years old, and care for yourself... I was so immature in comparison. I ignored my parents' objections and contacted the Game Company. They were hesitant because I was under eighteen, but all the candidates had to be flown to America and go through a month of physical and mental tests before entering the Game. That meant I'd just make the legal age limit in time, so they let me be one of the first one thousand players."

I was puzzled. "But there are only nine hundred and twenty-nine Founder Players."

"There were exactly a thousand of us to start with," said Hawk, "and just over a hundred reserve candidates on the waiting list. When the big day came, and we had to sign the documents and step into those freezer units, a lot of us changed their minds. The healthy ones with more to lose. The Game Company pulled in all the reserve candidates as well, but they still ended up well short of their target of a thousand players for the trial."

Hawk pulled a face. "I had a last minute fit of nerves myself, but I was even more scared of the real world than I was of being frozen, so I ended up inside my freezer unit. At the start of Game, everything was chaotic, but then things gradually settled down. Once the ten year trial period was over, and their test subjects were shown to be still rational, or at least as rational as they were to start with, the Game got permission to open commercially. The Game Techs created four new Game worlds, Starlight, Camelot, Ariel, and Elven, and then we got masses of people joining Game."

I nodded. "The ones who call themselves the First Wave."

"That's right. The Game Techs realized the Founder Players would have trouble coping with all the new arrivals, so they revamped the original test world and gave it to us as Celestius. It was our refuge from the torrent of strangers entering the Game, a place where our incompetence at interacting with people, and our little... peculiarities... could be safely hidden from other players."

He paused. "I think the uncomfortable feeling in my throat is because I'm thirsty. Is there anything to drink here?"

"Sorry, this isn't a luxury carriage."

Hawk sighed. "Well, that was when the myths started. The

Founder Players had a special world of our own, we wore special diamond bracelets, so that meant we were special as well. When we ventured out into the other worlds, we found we had a mystique. People looked at us and didn't see the pathetic reality but the illustrious Founder Players of their imagination. Anything strange we did was instantly forgiven. I'd withdrawn from the whole issue of relationships until then, I was just one of a whole mob of rejected excess men on Celestius, but on the other worlds..."

Hawk grinned. "I was a legend, and the girls didn't laugh at a legend."

I forced myself to grin as well, though I knew where this was going and I didn't like it. "You just had to smile and they threw themselves at you?"

He gave a rueful laugh. "Something like that. I'd no idea how to cope with it, so I ran away to spend the next few years hiding on Celestius. By then the major problem with Game was becoming horribly clear. It hadn't been detected during the trial, because any issues were blamed on the unusual nature of the test subjects, but the mass entry to Game made it obvious."

I frowned. "We weren't taught about any major problem in school. What was wrong, and how did the Game Techs fix it?"

"They never found a way to fix it," said Hawk. "You know that people who enter Game as children never develop into proper adulthood?"

"Yah. Everyone knows that you can't progress through adolescence without a real body."

"Well, the Game Company keeps it as quiet as possible, but the adolescence issue is part of a much wider problem. When you enter Game, your body is frozen and kept unchanged, but so is your mind. Your consciousness experiences events in Game, just as you would in the real world, but they don't affect you in the same way. What would change and mature you in the real world, leaves your core characteristics untouched in Game. You can learn new things, you can make new friends and enemies, but your personality stays the same. Kind, spiteful, wise or foolish. Whatever you are when you enter Game, you're stuck with it."

I ran my fingers through my hair, trying to understand what he was saying. "This is because you don't have a real body?"

"I think it's partly that," said Hawk, "and partly that Game stores the basic parameters of your personality. Whatever happens in Game, however much you try to change yourself, you can't. It's like pulling at a piece of elastic. It stretches for a moment, and you think you're getting somewhere, but then it snaps back to its original length."

I shook my head. "Why doesn't anyone talk about this?"

"As I said, the Game Company tries to keep it quiet, and for many people it isn't really a problem. After everything you've had to cope with in the real world, Jex, you've done your growing up, so this issue shouldn't trouble you very much."

"Is this why my mother keeps avoiding unpleasant things?" I asked. "That was her way of dealing with them when she entered Game, so it's impossible for her to change?"

"Probably. As I said, most people aren't affected much. It's been a huge issue for me though, because I entered Game with a lot of problems. Once I understood I could never change while I stayed in Game, I considered leaving to give myself a chance to grow up properly."

He waved his hands. "The problem was that my parents had been killed in an accident during the trial period of Game, and I couldn't face going back to the real world without them. I delayed, and delayed, and every year that passed made it more difficult to think of leaving Game. Finally, I accepted I would never leave. I was forever frozen in time as the socially inept Michael."

"But you aren't socially inept," I said. "I was awed by the way you dealt with your admiring fans."

"That wasn't Michael dealing with them though. When I accepted I could never leave Game, could never change who I was, I came up with my alternative solution. I started acting the part of Hawk the Unvanquished. He was the hero the First Wave newcomers wanted me to be. He was the hero *I* wanted me to be."

He shrugged. "So I adopted my Hawk persona, left Celestius to explore the four new worlds of Game, and went through what the family still refer to as Michael's girl phase. There weren't thousands of them, more like twenty. Only Tasha went anywhere near counting as a relationship though. I thought she genuinely cared for me and I was part of a real couple at last, but she kept trying to talk me into taking her to Celestius."

"But only the Founder Players can enter Celestius," I said.

"At first, we were allowed to take our partners there with us. I didn't want to take Tasha to Celestius though. She only knew me as Hawk the Unvanquished, and I was scared the other Founder Players would tell her about Michael and I'd lose her. We had a dozen arguments about it and eventually…"

This time there was a very long pause before Hawk spoke again. "Well, eventually it sunk into my stupid head that Tasha was only sleeping with me because she wanted to get to Celestius. We had a final huge argument, and she marched off and joined the girls waiting in line for a night in Caesar's castle. He had a constant string of girlfriends back then. Still does, for that matter."

"I'm sorry," I said.

"Some of the other Founder Players were having similar problems," said Hawk. "After a few years of having to step in to deal with the trouble it caused, the Game Techs stopped us taking partners to Celestius, but I was totally disillusioned about the girl thing long before that. Whenever I was with a girl, I was acting the part of the legendary Hawk, hiding the real Michael inside me. There's no way for me to explain how bad that felt. It wasn't just that I could never relax. I felt like a helpless passenger in my own body, watching an imaginary person live my life."

He laughed bitterly. "The last straw was when my real life girlfriend showed up in Game. She'd totally changed her appearance, so I hadn't a clue this was the same Susanna until she told me, and then my Hawk act instantly fell apart. I was totally Michael again, remembering what had happened between us, and terrified she'd say those humiliating things again. I screamed for Game world transfer home to Celestius, and hid in my castle for weeks."

He shuddered. "Obviously Susanna is still in Game. I have

the Game Techs trained to warn me whenever she requests Game world transfer to a world that I'm visiting, so I can run away again."

I blinked. "You're still scared of her after four centuries?"

"I entered Game totally petrified of meeting Susanna again, so I'm still totally petrified. The Game Techs indulge my cowardice over Susanna. I'm one of their pets, you see. A Founder Player who attracts attention by doing heroic things in Game, rather than being a public embarrassment. Most of the time at least. I make a complete fool of myself now and then, but the Game Techs do their best to hush it up, and the player population seems to conspire to keep it quiet as well. I suppose people like having flawless, noble heroes, so they busily polish any dirty marks off the image of the legend."

"Yah," I murmured. I could understand that. Hawk had always been one of my heroes. If anyone had tried to tell me something bad about him, I wouldn't have listened.

Hawk sighed. "Myths seem to develop a life of their own. Anyway, I gave up entertaining adoring girl fans after meeting Susanna. I decided I was better off being alone and myself than constantly acting a part, and moved back to live on Celestius again. When I visited other worlds, I still played my role of Hawk the Unvanquished, but I trained myself to be distantly polite to admirers. I focused on the hunting and trying to beat every impossible challenge in Game. It's been fun on the whole. I've spent four hundred years as an immortal, legendary hero."

He paused. "It's odd to think back on everything that's happened. My parents kept telling me to get out more, and they were killed in that stupid accident." He pulled a sad, wry face. "Maybe if they'd got out less, they'd have entered Game with the First Wave, and still be alive right now."

I kept silent because I'd no idea what to say.

"Some of the female Founder Players changed partner over the years, but they'd met the real Michael so they never looked at me. I never considered trying to have another relationship with a girl until I recruited you and Nathan to help me."

Hawk smiled. "Once you'd got over the initial shock of

meeting me, we started having proper conversations. I risked telling you about my childhood, the problems I'd had with bullies, and how I'd started hiding in my bedroom and playing computer games. You didn't laugh at me. You talked about the time you'd spent living in dormitories, and how wonderful it was to finally have your own room and feel safe. I felt you understood exactly how I'd felt as a boy, and why I acted the way I did. I started wondering if I'd finally met a girl who could accept me for who I really was."

Hawk took a deep breath. "When I decided to defrost for a few days to chase the bomber, I realized I had the chance to meet you as Michael. I knew I'd probably just get rejected again, but I also knew I'd never get another chance like this. If I met a girl in Game, and suggested we both defrost so they could meet Michael, they'd know who he was and be studying him, judging him, comparing him unfavourably to the Game Hawk."

He leaned forward to study me intently. "You were different, Jex, already in real life so I could meet you as a random stranger. I wasn't expecting you to work out who I was. I certainly wasn't expecting you to accept Michael but reject Hawk. There has to be a way to get past that and convince you it's worth us getting to know each other better. There is no four century gap. There is no Hawk. There's just an insecure, eighteen-year-old boy that's been frozen in time."

I shook my head in bewilderment. "You seemed very competent fighting Tomath."

"I find fighting easier than socializing," said Hawk. "You saw Michael's inept attempt at flirting with you. There are other things that I struggle with too. When you've seen more of me, you'll understand what I mean."

"Even if I ignore the legendary Hawk and the four century age gap, you're still a Founder Player and I'm nobody. You live on Celestius and I can't even go there."

"Once you enter Game, I'd be happy to visit Ganymede or any other world you choose," said Hawk. "If things worked out between us, I could move there permanently. Several of the other male Founder Players live outside Celestius with their partners."

"I've heard all about those relationships," I said. "The Game gossip reporters study them relentlessly, looking for signs the Founder Player is getting bored."

"Some of the relationships have worked extremely well for a very long time," said Hawk.

"But the vast majority don't," I said flatly. "The pressure gets too much and things end in a messy break up. The man either goes back to Celestius after that or gets a new partner. In the case of Merlin, *four* new partners."

"Merlin's trying to show the whole of Game he doesn't care about breaking up with Stella," said Hawk. "He's doing his best to make it look as if he dumped her, when she was the one who dumped him and he's devastated about it. Anyway, this isn't about Merlin and Stella, it's about us. I've always wanted a proper relationship with someone who knows and understands the real me. I think you could be that person, and we can take things as quickly or slowly as you like."

He paused. "At least think about it. Tell me what you see as the problems, and we can work out how to avoid them."

I sighed. "There is only one problem, and there's no way to avoid it. I'm not getting involved in a relationship with anyone unless I'm an equal partner. Even if people in Game are unchanging, frozen in time, I..."

I broke off my sentence. "Moment." I buried my face in my hands for a full minute, desperately chasing a train of thought, and then looked up at Hawk again.

"I remember saying exactly the same thing – that I didn't want to be in a relationship unless I was an equal partner – to Nathan. He'd warned me not to get involved with you because..."

"He warned you not to get involved with me!" Hawk almost yelled the words. "When Nathan gets into Game, I'm going to kill him!"

"You can't kill Nathan for three reasons. Firstly, it's wrong to kill people. Secondly, you'll get into trouble. Thirdly, if you're right about Nathan becoming a Game Tech not a player, you'll never have the chance to attack him."

"Point." Hawk frowned in frustration then brightened up

again. "When we've finished this job, I can go over to the United Law facility and beat Nathan up in real life."

"Oh yah," I said, with heavy sarcasm. "The middle of a United Law facility is the ideal place to try beating someone up."

Hawk's frown returned.

"I'm beginning to see what you mean about Michael having a few problems with social interactions," I said. "The only reason Nathan warned me not to get involved with you, was because he thought you wouldn't be interested in me. Nathan has a protective and caring nature, and was worried I'd get hurt."

"Oh." Hawk seemed to calm down a little, but still had a petulant look on his face. "Maybe I won't actually hit Nathan then, just tell him to mind his own business."

"I've already told Nathan to mind his own business. There are times when his caring nature crosses the line into nosiness." I hurried on with my explanation. "My point is that all candidates applying to be Game Techs go through a screening programme. The Game Techs keep the details of that screening secret, but Nathan told us that he scored very highly on the technical aptitude test, and the personality assessment test rated him extremely suitable. Doesn't it make sense that the screening programme is carefully choosing quiet, protective, caring people like Nathan to be Game Techs? People who'll be benevolent, self-effacing guardians of the Game and its players?"

Hawk nodded. "It does, but if that's the case then our rogue Game Tech must have changed drastically over the years to turn into a destructive bomber."

"You've just been telling me that people's fundamental personalities can't change when they're within Game."

"Yes, our bomber must have spent a very long time outside Game to have changed that much. We should get Nathan to check for Game Techs who've spent many years outside Game. Leaving Game must be very unusual behaviour for them, so we might be able to narrow our list of suspects down to..."

"Or there's the other answer," I cut in. "The bomber's personality hasn't changed at all. He never had a caring and protective nature, because he was recruited as a Game Tech before the screening programme started. You described the early days in Game, how different the test world and the players were back then. What about the Game Techs?"

Hawk stared at me, his eyes wide with shock. "You're right. The original Game Techs weren't chosen for anything other than their technical ability with computers."

He scrabbled in his pocket for his phone, and urgently tapped at it. I heard Nathan's voice speaking. He sounded confused.

"I think you've called the wrong person."

"No, I haven't," said Hawk. "I thought you'd been told about me defrosting."

"You're Hawk?" Nathan's voice rose in surprise. "Yah, I've just been told about that, but I was expecting you to look a bit more... a bit better dressed."

Hawk sighed. "Let's skip past the whole disappointing Michael discussion. Can you vouch for me, Jex?"

Hawk propped his phone on the windowsill where we could both see it, and I waved at the tiny image of Nathan. "He really is Hawk."

"Sorry," said Nathan. "It was silly of me to expect..."

Hawk didn't let him finish the sentence. "Nathan, do you have access to any information on the early history of Game?"

"The Game Techs seem to have given me access to all their technical information and the whole history of Game," said Nathan. "It's incredible. Frightening too, because it shows just how worried they are about this situation. They're trusting us because they can't trust each other."

"I need you to check some historical details," said Hawk. "During the ten year trial period, only the players lived inside Game. Once the trial period finished, and Game opened to the public, all the Game Techs entered Game as well. That was the point where the Game Company brought in all the regulations about Game Techs staying discreetly in the background. When did they add the psychological test to the Game Tech recruitment process?"

"Moment." There was a pause before Nathan started

speaking again. "Both things happened at the same time. When the Game opened to the public, the Game Company needed a lot more Game Techs to deal with the rush of players. The new Game Techs were selected for a combination of technical ability and psychological suitability for the work."

"Has the nature of the psychological test changed much over the centuries?" asked Hawk.

"There've been a lot of minor adjustments, but the test is still aimed at recruiting the same type of personality." Nathan hesitated. "You don't look very happy to hear that. Is it bad news?"

"It's very bad news," said Hawk, in a grim voice. "It means that our bomber isn't just a senior Game Tech, but one of the original designers of the Game!"

CHAPTER FOURTEEN

"We can't tell anyone that we suspect the bomber is one of the original Game designers," said Hawk. "The bomber must have an immensely powerful position among the Game Techs. He or she will definitely be able to access the reports from the Game investigation, and possibly even those of the Unilaw investigation as well."

Nathan nodded, his face showing he was still suffering from shock.

"We don't know how the Game Techs would react to an accusation against one of their original Game designers either," I said. "They might hero worship them in the same way that all the players hero worship the Founder Players, and refuse to believe that one of them could be involved in the bombing."

"That's true," said Hawk. "The Game Techs might be less willing to help us if we start making accusations against their heroes. Nathan, do you have any information on the original Game designers?"

"All the details about them will be held on the Game personnel system," said Nathan. "I don't have access to that. I could request it, but..."

"You'd better not risk it," said Hawk. "We have to assume the bomber is monitoring all your requests to the Game investigation."

"I do remember one mention of the original Game designers though," said Nathan. "I skimmed through a whole mass of information about Avalon, including a bit about the design history.

Avalon was the first Game world that the new wave of Game Techs created without any help from the original Game designers."

"And that must be why Avalon was attacked," said Hawk. "The bomber resented new people creating Game worlds enough to still hold a grudge against Avalon centuries later."

He paused. "Do you have any idea how many original Game designers there were, Nathan? Since they were outside Game during the trial period, we just heard disembodied voices talking to us. I don't remember more than a dozen of them, but there would have been a lot more working on the purely technical side of Game. Possibly as many as a couple of hundred."

"There must be a mention of the team sizes in the Game history." It was a minute before Nathan spoke again. "I'm afraid you're underestimating the numbers. There were just over twelve hundred Game Techs back then. They had to create the basic Game before the ten year trial even began, then they were busy working on enhancements and designing new worlds ready for the Game to open to the public."

Hawk groaned. "We can't ask the Game Techs to lock up twelve hundred original Game designers. Jex and I have to go now, Nathan."

"Be careful," said Nathan anxiously.

Hawk ended the call and put his phone back in his pocket. I was sitting in silence, thinking through exactly how dangerous one of the original designers of the Game could be, when Hawk started talking again.

"Jex, I told you what the Founder Players were really like behind all the myths, but there was a detail I didn't mention. Game Techs keep it hushed up, and the family never talk about it to outsiders. We've been together a long time, we don't always like each other, but there's loyalty involved. Anyway, it turns out to be very relevant, so I need to tell you."

He hesitated. "This is surprisingly difficult to say. A couple of Founder Players had even bigger issues than me when they entered Game. Within the first few months, it was clear they were a danger to others."

"They were bullies?"

"This went well beyond bullying. Marcus can be charming sometimes, but has no empathy and isn't limited by feelings of guilt. He seems to regard other people as toys for his amusement. Chiron is less of a problem. He's aware that he's not in control of his own actions, and that confuses and distresses him, so he's eager to be prevented from accidentally harming anyone."

Hawk grimaced. "Once the situation became clear, the family took appropriate measures to keep ourselves safe. We had the situation under control during the ten year trial, but then the Game opened to the public and a whole mob of new players arrived. That didn't cause any difficulties with Chiron, because he'd voluntarily agreed years earlier that he wouldn't leave his castle let alone Celestius. Marcus moved to live on Camelot though, and the First Wave's adoration of Founder Players gave him new opportunities."

I frowned. "Opportunities to do what?"

"Killing people in Game wasn't as bad as it would be in the real world – Game deaths are painful but not permanent, and weirdly enough a couple of the girls seemed quite flattered – but it obviously had to be stopped. So it's kept very quiet, but we have two Founder Players who spend most of their time under house arrest in their castles on Celestius."

I remembered something. "Back when we thought the bomber was a maintenance worker, and were discussing possible motives for crashing Avalon, you said that the bomber might enjoy killing random people. You talked about people you'd met in the Battle Arena, and said a sentence in a very strange voice. 'Killing someone in real life, knowing they'd died a permanent death, would be far more satisfying.' Were you actually quoting one of those two Founder Players?"

"Yes," said Hawk. "I'd met a few people in the Battle Arena who said similar things, but I was on Celestius when I heard those particular words. It was Marcus who said them, and his tone of voice when he said the word 'satisfying' stuck in my mind as especially unpleasant."

He paused. "My theory is the bomber is an original designer of Game with similar tendencies to Marcus. We'll need to attract his interest and keep him talking long enough for Unilaw to track his identity. The best way to do that is..."

Hawk let his words trail off because the pod had started slowing down. I hastily broke in to complete what he was saying.

"The best way is to act the part of someone like the bomber. You'll have to do that, because I'd have no idea what to say."

"Yes, I'll act the part of Marcus. You play my obedient, terrified girlfriend. I just hope the core Unilaw investigation team have followed my instructions about keeping the fact I've defrosted from Game totally secret, not even mentioning it in their own internal reports. If the bomber has found out that I've defrosted, then Tomath being blackmailed will seem a very suspicious coincidence."

I moistened my lips. "You mean that we could be walking straight into a trap?"

Hawk nodded grimly.

The pod had stopped now and the door was opening. Hawk tapped at his phone, slid it back into his pocket, and we both stood up and stepped outside. The bomber could be watching us now, listening to every word we said. I couldn't help looking around the platform for spy eyes, though there was no chance of me seeing the microscopic things.

"We have to go through these doors and take the first corridor on the left," said Hawk.

He strode off rapidly, with me chasing after him. We made the left turn, and I saw heavy double doors with a sign saying "Male Dormitory 87166". The doors were newly painted in the standard yellow used by all dormitories, and awoke grim memories of my childhood. Every time I came back from school, I'd been scared of what would be waiting for me inside my dormitory.

I was scared of what would be waiting for us inside this dormitory too. We could be about to meet the bomber or at least his controlled droid. As I followed Hawk up to the doors I felt a tense, sick feeling of apprehension. When I entered Game, I'd probably be stuck with an unshakeable phobia of yellow double doors.

Hawk led the way inside. I looked round nervously for

droids, but the long room was empty except for the familiar, regimented lines of bunk beds and storage cupboards. Fifty beds against each side wall. One hundred of them in total. The ones nearest the doors would be taken by the bullies, so you had to walk past them every time you entered or left the dormitory.

I shook my head, telling myself that this wasn't my dormitory. I didn't live here. In fact, nobody lived here yet. This dormitory was yet to open, yet to be allocated the adult supervisor who might watch closely to make sure it was a safe and friendly place, or lazily do nothing while a reign of terror was imposed.

I saw Hawk was staring at the beds, and gave him a warning look as he opened his mouth. The bomber would have spy eyes and ears watching us now, and the wrong comment would show Hawk had never seen a dormitory before.

He caught my expression, and hesitated before speaking. "No one here yet. I..."

There was a loud buzzing, and then a recorded announcement came from overhead speakers. "Attention children, your dormitory supervisor is about to address you from Game."

It was the same words, spoken by the same recorded female voice, that I remembered from my childhood. I instinctively moved to stand by the nearest bed, and turned to face the end wall in the approved respectful attitude. Arms at my side, back rigidly straight, and head slightly bowed. Hawk gave me a single startled glance, before moving to stand by another bed and copy my posture.

I thought a face would appear on the end wall – irrationally I half expected it to be the centaur face of the dormitory supervisor from my childhood – but instead the wall changed to pure black. Our caller had disabled vision from his end. That meant the bomber could see us, but we couldn't see him.

"Why should I help you?" The male voice came from the end wall, and was magnified round the room. The perfectly emotionless, silky smooth tones had to mean that a specialized computer process was being used to hide the speaker's true voice, but I thought the original voice was male too.

"Because we would serve you in return," said Hawk.

A long pause. "I have Tomath to serve me."

Hawk smiled. "Tomath is weak. He didn't know he was planting bombs. Now he's found that out, and he's terrified."

"You wouldn't be terrified?"

"I'd be exhilarated." Hawk's smile widened. "Just imagine all those people waking up in their freezer units. How they must have screamed in terror. How they'd fight to escape. How some of them died of fear."

There was a long silence.

"I want to serve you," said Hawk.

There was still no response. I wondered if our rogue Game Tech had gone and we'd lost our only link to him.

"I want the honour of serving you," said Hawk.

The voice finally spoke again. "And the girl?"

Hawk turned to look at me with a face and eyes that were cold as ice. "The girl does what I tell her to do. The girl thinks what I tell her to think. Don't you, Emma?"

I knew he was just acting the part of a killer, but he was so convincing that my voice shook as I replied. "Yah, Michael."

Hawk walked across to me and grabbed a handful of my hair. "You do what I tell you to do. Say it, Emma!"

"I..."

He twisted my hair. It didn't hurt much, but it shocked me enough that I yelled anyway. "I do what you tell me to do," I gabbled.

"You think what I tell you to think."

He twisted my hair again, and the pain triggered an old memory. I was six years old again, I'd tried to protect a friend, and the bullies had turned on me. Where were those older girls now? Had they taken their bullying personalities with them into Game, or had they changed into kinder people in the years between ten and eighteen years old?

There was another, harder yank at my hair. I fought away my old memories, and repeated Hawk's words. "I think what you tell me to think."

"That's good, Emma." Hawk's face came close to me, so I could feel his breath against my cheek. "That's very good."

He let me go, and I hugged my arms defensively round myself. "I'll do whatever you say, Michael. I promise."

Hawk turned to smile at the black area of wall. "I want the honour of being your apprentice. I want to follow in your footsteps and learn from the master."

"If I take an apprentice," said the voice, "he must sacrifice everything else to my service. Do you understand?"

Despite the efforts to hide the speaker's true voice, I caught an overtone to the word "sacrifice" that chilled me.

There was a pause before Hawk answered. "I understand, master."

The blackness on the wall flickered, and a figure was displayed. It wore a featureless cloak, and the face was a skull shrouded in shadows.

"I am the Reaper. The worlds of Game will honour and serve me or be destroyed."

The wall changed to black again, and then two sets of numbers appeared. A location and a time. I tried to memorize them before they vanished and the call ended, but my brain didn't seem to be working properly. It didn't matter. Surveillance would have been monitoring and recording the call.

Hawk turned and stalked out of the double doors. I scurried after him, eager to leave a place where new dark memories had been added to the ones from my childhood. Neither of us spoke until we'd summoned a two-person pod, grubbier but less smelly than the previous one, got inside, and started it moving.

Hawk took out his phone, and tapped at it. "Surveillance, the bomber's call was definitely made in person rather than by an automated process. Did you have time to trace it and get an identity?"

"The call originated from Game, and we obtained an identity number for the caller," replied the female voice of surveillance, "but unfortunately there's a problem."

"What problem?" demanded Hawk impatiently.

"We checked the identity number against our Unilaw records, and it belongs to someone who has not yet entered Game."

"You're sure about that?" I asked.

"Perfectly sure," said surveillance. "The identity number belongs to a seven-year-old child who was in real life school when the call was made. We've dispatched officers to arrest the boy anyway, but..."

"I'd strongly prefer you not to arrest the seven-year-old," said Hawk, in a strained voice.

"If you wish, we can recall the officers," said surveillance.

"I do wish that." Hawk stabbed his phone with his finger to end the call, and turned to me. "I can't believe that Unilaw were going to arrest a seven-year-old child. You were right not to trust their judgement on Tomath, because..."

Hawk suddenly abandoned his sentence and started counting. "One, two, three..."

He reached ten, and I was prepared for him to start swearing, but instead he swung round and hammered a fist against the pod wall. I guessed that this time mere words weren't enough to relieve his pent up stress.

"Our bomber is one of the original Game designers," said Hawk. "He knows how to fake an identity number on a call from Game. He must know hundreds of other ways to dodge security checks as well. We can't assume the server complex force field codes are safe from someone like that. He'll find a way to get the codes and crash more Game worlds."

Hawk turned to face me, the movement bringing him closer to me. My nerves were still jangling, so I instinctively flinched back into my seat.

He frowned. "Are you all right, Jex? I didn't hurt you back in that dormitory, did I?"

"No, I'm just a little wound up by the act back there."

"You were really convincing as a terrified girl."

I didn't want to admit that was because I'd been genuinely terrified, both of the situation and Hawk's behaviour. Four hundred years of playing the role of a Game legend had made him a great actor.

Hawk groaned. "You did brilliantly, but I made a total mess of talking to the bomber. My whole approach to him was wrong.

The bomber isn't another Marcus. He may lack empathy and guilt, but he isn't driven by a desire to cause random death and destruction."

I was still having trouble thinking. I tried to break free from the lingering effects of fear and force my brain into action. "The bomber called himself the Reaper. That sounds pretty death and destruction obsessed."

"Yes, but he didn't respond to me talking about the exhilaration of killing people. I'd lost his interest until I stumbled on the word honour. That was when he started talking to me again, and his last words told us exactly why he bombed the Avalon server complex."

I quoted the bomber's final sentence. "'The worlds of Game will honour and serve me or be destroyed.'"

Hawk leaned back in his seat. "I should have realized that the bomber couldn't have the same problems as Marcus. It wouldn't be possible for a Game Tech to keep a fascination with death and destruction hidden for four centuries, and appropriate action would have been taken to deal with him."

He ran his fingers through his overlong black hair. "The bomber is driven by something entirely different, a massive ego and a desire for power and glory. He wouldn't need to hide that from anyone. The whole population of Game accepts the fact we've got several overblown egos among the Founder Players, so I can imagine the other Game Techs would feel an original designer of Game had a perfect right to be a little egotistical."

I thought that through for a moment. "I think you're right about the bomber wanting power. That's why he brought us to a dormitory to talk to us. He was aiming to bring back echoes of when we were small children living in dormitories, and the all-powerful adult supervisor would address us from Game. I suppose you'll have been immune to that because Michael never lived in a dormitory, but it worked brilliantly on me."

"I'm right about the glory too. The bomber was one of the original designers of Game. When it opened commercially, he would have expected a lot of public recognition, but the Game Company brought in regulations that said he had to stay anonymous. For four long centuries, the bomber has been robbed of all the honour and glory for his achievements."

"He'd be admired by other Game Techs."

"Oh yes." Hawk waved a hand in dismissal. "The other people skulking in the background of Game would admire him, but the vast player population never even knew he existed. The bomber doesn't want to cause death and destruction for its own sake. It's just a way to punish the players for ignoring his achievements."

He paused. "I think the bomber is calling himself the Reaper because he designed the original Game worlds, sowed the seeds that grew into the vast Game universe of today, and now he's going to reap his harvest."

"Why would he wait four centuries to do this?"

Hawk shrugged. "I don't know. Something must have happened to make him particularly angry. Whatever that was, the Reaper has started his bid for power and glory, and he isn't going to stop. I expect he'll crash at least one more Game world to demonstrate that none of our precautions work against him. After that, he'll speak to the whole population of Game in the same way that he spoke to us in that dormitory. They have to honour and serve him, or he'll wreak havoc across the worlds of Game."

I opened my mouth to ask why the Reaper would want billions of people quaking in fear of him, but closed it again. The bullies who'd ruled my childhood dormitory had enjoyed terrorizing smaller girls. The Reaper was just aiming to do the same thing on a vastly bigger scale.

Hawk's voice took on a note of despair. "And there's nothing we can do to stop him. Surveillance will watch the meeting point the Reaper gave us, they may ambush his controlled droid, but I'm sure the Reaper will be able to fake his identity number when he controls a droid from Game. We'll be left with no clue to his real identity except that he has an inflated idea of his own importance, and I expect a lot of the original Game designers have ego problems."

I was bewildered. "Aren't we going to meet the Reaper

ourselves? I thought you were trying to be recruited as his apprentice."

"That was my plan, but I can't go through with it now," said Hawk. "You heard what the Reaper said. His apprentice has to sacrifice everything to his service. It's perfectly obvious what he meant. My stupid act practically offered you up as a victim. The Reaper wants me to take you to the meeting point, so he can prove his power over me by making me kill you."

I hadn't realized that. No, I had realized it, but part of me had been frantically blanking out the knowledge. That was why I'd been finding it so hard to think since the Reaper said the word 'sacrifice'. My brain had shut down in self defence, because once I started thinking, once I accepted that we had to do whatever the Reaper demanded if we were to have any chance of catching him, there was only one thing I could say.

I took a deep breath. "We have to catch the Reaper, Hawk. We have to do whatever it takes to achieve that. It's just a matter of statistics. Over eleven thousand people died in the Avalon world crash. If the Reaper crashes another world, then thousands more will die. I'm just one person so..."

I thought my voice sounded unnaturally calm about it. Part of my head was unnaturally calm as well; the part that was telling itself this wasn't real, just a bad dream. Another part of my head wasn't calm at all. It was screaming that it didn't want to die a heroic, self sacrificing death.

Hawk rubbed his forehead. "I'm not murdering you, Jex. I've committed my fair share of sins, but I'm not going to kill anyone, and especially not you. I fought for years in the Battle Arena on Medieval, and when I accepted my prizes I was covered in the blood of my opponents, but the deaths and the blood weren't real. Killing you would... Moment!"

I knew we'd both had exactly the same thought. We didn't need me to die. We just needed to convince the Reaper that Hawk had killed me.

Hawk grabbed for his phone again. "Surveillance, we have to stage a fake murder for the Reaper. We've a very long way to go and barely two hours to get there. We'll transfer to the long-distance carriage to gain time, and somewhere along the way you have to help us set things up so Jex can look convincingly dead. I've no idea how we do that, but..."

I snatched the phone from Hawk's hand and spoke rapidly into it myself. "The glitz crowd hold fancy dress competitions where the entrants dress up as people from Game and re-enact Game events. A year ago, a group led by a medical cadet called Falcon Rodriguez won the England area championship. They staged a re-enactment of Hawk's last fight in the Battle Arena, using fake blood, trick knives, and holo effects."

I paused to breathe. "I'll contact Falcon Rodriguez and get him to meet us at the medical cadet accommodation transport stop. I'll tell him to bring all his equipment for faking injuries, because I need his help to stage a murder to..."

I broke off for a second. It wouldn't be a good idea to tell Falcon we were trying to catch the Avalon bomber, because he was notoriously bad at keeping secrets. "Well, I'll have to think of a good reason why I'm faking my own murder."

CHAPTER FIFTEEN

We were back in our familiar luxury carriage. In one of the seats sat a golden droid. That had been Hawk's alter ego, and now Hawk was the skinny, dark haired boy sitting facing me. There was something disturbingly surreal about seeing the pair of them together.

It was even more surreal to have Falcon Rodriguez here with us. Falcon didn't seem to have changed at all since the last time I'd seen him. I'd told him a paper-thin story about a plan to make my old instructor confess to altering my grades. Fortunately, Falcon hadn't paid any attention to my reasons for faking my own murder, focussing in on what, for him, was the only important point. We were about to put on a performance, and any performance organized by Falcon Rodriguez had to be absolutely perfect.

Falcon smoothed a final dab of makeup over the fake skin on my neck, stepped back, studied the result, and nodded. "Done."

"It itches," I complained, moving my right hand towards my neck.

Falcon slapped my hand away. "Don't scratch the fake skin or you'll disturb the blood packs underneath, and you..."

He turned to point at Hawk. "I want a proper knife flourish from you when you cut Jex's throat, not those pathetic slicing gestures that you were doing in rehearsal. Remember that when the trick knife cuts Jex's throat, releasing the fake blood to cover her in gore, it will also trigger the injection of the drug to knock her unconscious and slow her breathing. You should wait for two seconds to give the drug time to work, and then let her go so she slumps dramatically to the floor."

"I'm still not sure that it's a good idea to inject Jex with that drug," said Hawk.

The perfectionist Falcon waved a dismissive hand. "Jex said it was vital for her to be a convincing corpse."

"Yah, but I don't want you making a mistake and turning her into a genuine corpse."

"I never make mistakes," said Falcon.

Hawk closed his eyes for a moment, before speaking in a strained voice. "If you've finished work, then we can drop you off at the next transport stop."

"I'm staying to watch the performance," said Falcon.

Hawk leaned across to adjust the carriage guidance system. "That isn't possible in this case."

Falcon frowned. "You're just being difficult."

"No, he isn't," I said. "Thank you for the help, Falcon. I'm very grateful, but this is one performance where you'll have to settle for watching the replays later."

He gave me one of his wide range of sulky looks. "I'm not leaving."

"If you stay, our instructor will recognize you, and that will ruin my whole plan to make her confess."

He folded his arms. "The instructor will probably recognize you too. I told you that hair dye isn't much of a disguise. You should let me use flesh coloured wax to make your nose look a different shape."

"My appearance is all part of my plan," I said. "You aren't, so you have to go."

"But..."

I interrupted him. "Falcon, do you remember that you wanted me to play the Founder Player, Venus, in our Battle Arena event? Do you remember how I said I wanted to play a combat role instead? Do you remember how you twirled a sword around, said that girls were useless in fights, and I lost my temper?"

Falcon was looking wary now. "Yah, Jex."

"Do you want me to lose my temper now?"

"No, Jex."

I smiled. "Then you'll do what you're told, and leave quietly at the next transport stop. Please give my best wishes to everyone, particularly Gina. Tell them that I'm sorry I vanished a year ago, but I was in trouble and I didn't want to get them in trouble too. I hope it will be safe for me to get in touch with them soon."

A couple of minutes later, Falcon carried his equipment cases out of the door. "Now don't forget to send me the replays, Jex."

"I won't," I said.

Hawk waited until the carriage was moving at express speed again, and then gave a heartfelt groan.

"We should have told Falcon the truth about us trying to catch the Avalon bomber. If he knew I was Hawk the Unvanquished, then maybe he'd have believed me when I said no sensible fighter makes fancy flourishes with a knife when cutting someone's throat."

My neck was itching unmercifully again. I gripped the arms of my seat to keep my hands safely still. "Whatever you told Falcon, it wouldn't have made the slightest difference. He has tunnel vision when it comes to public performances. We don't exist as people. We are mere actors carrying out his orders."

"Are you sure we can trust Falcon's drug arrangement? I keep remembering that your instructor nearly gave someone an overdose."

I sighed. "I hate to say this, but Falcon's right when he says he never makes mistakes. He wasn't just top of our class in medical training; he won a major medical scholarship, and was a far better doctor than our instructor. The maddening thing about it was that he never seemed to do any work."

"I wish I could cut his throat instead of yours. What did you do to him when you lost your temper?"

I grinned. "Falcon was holding a sword while he was sneering at me, so I grabbed another sword, attacked him, defeated him in a duel, and threatened to cut his ears off unless he gave me a combat role. That's why we ended up re-enacting both your semi-final and final fights in the Battle Arena."

Hawk laughed. "How could you be friends with someone that dreadful?"

"Falcon was always a bit single minded, but things didn't get really out of hand until he went along to a glitz crowd party when he was thirteen. He discovered their Game re-enactment events, and dragged a group of us into helping him stage an event himself. I've always pictured Falcon having a great future organizing festivals and events in Game."

"If he does, then I'll make sure to avoid everything he organizes."

Hawk tapped at the screen on the wall next to him, and the image of a Unilaw droid appeared. The face of the adult controlling it was a woman with startlingly bright blue eyebrows.

"Surveillance, as before I'll try to plant some spy eyes when we get to our destination," said Hawk. "I'm sure the Reaper won't just call us this time. He'll come to meet us using a controlled droid. If we go through with acting out the staged murder, I'll hopefully leave with the Reaper's controlled droid, while Jex remains as the unconscious corpse."

"Understood," said the woman.

Hawk turned to look at me. "Jex, the Reaper may be watching the meeting point even after his droid leaves, so everything has to happen just as it would if you were really dead."

He paused for a second. "Which would be what exactly?"

"The medical chip in my arm would send an alarm signal saying I'd been killed," I said. "Medical would report my death, and then Unilaw controlled droids would respond and collect the body."

Hawk nodded. "So Unilaw droids have to come and collect your body, after which they can ship you to the same facility as Nathan. They'd better have a medical team waiting there in case you need treating for after effects of the drug."

"Michael would obviously be a suspect for his girlfriend's murder," I said. "Unilaw would be chasing after him, tracking his medical chip. I can see you've got a bar code on your left arm. Do you have a medical chip as well?"

"Fortunately, yes," said Hawk. "We didn't have either of those things four hundred years ago, but the doctors gave me a bar code and injected a medical chip into my arm when I defrosted. Unilaw controlled droids should start hunting me just the way they would a real murderer."

"Understood," repeated the woman.

"But what if they catch you?" I asked anxiously.

"I'm assuming the Reaper will have a way to prevent Unilaw from tracking my medical chip," said Hawk. "After all, he's been prepared for everything else so far."

I hated the idea of Hawk heading off on his own under the orders of the Reaper, but I had to accept it. If I was supposed to be dead, then I couldn't go with him. "You must be careful."

He smiled. "Don't worry. I won't be playing this part for long. The next thing the Reaper asks me to do will probably be far more drastic than just killing one girl, and then my act will fall apart. If we're lucky, we'll have the clues we need to catch him by then."

I hoped we'd be lucky and catch the Reaper, but if we did then the hunt would be over, Hawk would go back into Game and I'd go back to my job in the body stacks. I felt a sharp stab of regret at the thought. Now Hawk had cleared my record, I'd enter Game myself a year from now. He'd suggested we could meet up then and...

I stopped and gave myself a mental slap. I'd made my decision, and told Hawk that I couldn't get involved with him. That was the right thing to do, the rational thing to do, and I mustn't start wavering about it now. For a few short hours, Hawk had been Michael, just another kid like me. We'd briefly been on equal terms, with no age gap and no power differential, but once we were in Game there'd be a huge gulf between us again. I'd be a clueless newcomer, while Hawk was a living legend.

Hawk had finished talking to surveillance, and turned off the screen. Now he swivelled round in his chair to face me again.

"It's strange really. The Game Techs keep watch over the

players, and know everything about us. They create our worlds, police our behaviour, and record our triumphs and misdemeanours. Every Game Tech must know all about me, including every hideously embarrassing moment that I'd like to forget myself, but I know nothing about how they live. Game Techs appear to perform tasks with perfect, anonymous, professionalism, then vanish back to their own secret areas of Game."

Hawk frowned. "Whatever goes on in their closed society, the original Game designers are likely to be hero worshipped and virtually untouchable. It won't be enough for us to identify the Reaper. We'll need to give the Game Techs absolute proof of his guilt."

"Game Techs have bronze, silver, or gold insignia on their faces, depending on their status," I said. "Players have bracelets. Bronze for newcomers, silver for those still on annual subscriptions, gold for those who've paid lifetime subscriptions, and diamond for Founder Players."

"You're thinking the original Game Techs might have diamond insignia?"

I nodded.

"I've never heard of anyone seeing a Game Tech with diamond insignia, but one of the original Game designers wouldn't be sent to run trivial errands for players."

Hawk took out his phone and dumped it on an empty seat. "We'd better leave our phones here. If the Reaper's droid checked them, our whole background story would fall apart."

I abandoned my phone too, and we sat in silence for the next couple of minutes. We'd be stopping soon, moving into an ordinary pod, and then meeting the Reaper and faking my death. These were the last few minutes of us being alone as two kids.

"Michael," I said.

He looked up, startled by the tense sound of my voice, and brushed the tangled black hair out of his eyes.

I was probably burning bright red with embarrassment, especially with the fairer skin of my blonde disguise, but if I chickened out now then I'd always regret it. "We can't have a relationship in Game, it would never work, but I would like a kiss."

He looked uncertain. "This isn't just charitable kindness to poor, unattractive Michael?"

"No," I said. "I don't offer kisses unless I genuinely want to kiss someone. Of course, you have to want it too."

He grinned and his dark eyes seemed to light up with excitement. "I do," he said. "I really do."

We both stood up and moved towards each other. It was a clumsy kiss, but that somehow made it even more special. It told me that Michael wasn't hiding behind his Hawk persona, but kissing me as his real self.

CHAPTER SIXTEEN

The meeting point turned out to be a dusty, featureless room. Someone had lived here once, you could see the marks where the bed had been, and there was a scattering of beads in one corner from a broken necklace. Everything else was gone now. All the furnishings had been ripped out from the rooms in this corridor, ready for a refurbishment in a few months' time. Even the doors had been wrenched from some rooms. Ours still had one, but it was open, waiting for our visitor.

I stood inside the room, arms hugging myself for reassurance, using the body language of a frightened girl. I wasn't acting; I was truly petrified at the idea of Falcon's drug knocking me out. I hated the idea of being unconscious in this situation, totally helpless, unable to defend myself or even run, but Falcon was right that it would make me seem far more authentically dead. If the Reaper decided to test me with a kick or an extra prod with the knife, there'd be no betraying cry or movement.

Hawk was wandering restlessly round the room. "No instructions here. We wait."

I knew that Hawk hadn't just been searching for instructions from the Reaper, but also planting some of the spy eyes he'd brought with him. The surveillance team would be watching us now, but if anything went wrong then they had no one in range to help us. It was too big a risk to have Unilaw controlled droids lurking around what should be a deserted area.

"Michael," I appealed hesitantly. "I don't like this."

He grabbed my arm, pulling me close, holding me his prisoner.

"We wait! Understand me, Emma?"

I gave a shaky nod. It shouldn't be long now, I thought. Travelling in the express long-distance carriage had gained us a lot of time, but we'd had to divert off our route to collect Falcon, so we'd arrived with barely five minutes to spare.

There was a movement in the doorway. A droid was standing there, its markings showing it belonged to Game, but its bronze head had no facial display to show who was controlling it.

I instinctively tried to back away, but Hawk tightened his hold on my arm, yanking me back and forcing me to stand still. He'd said how unfit his body had been when it was frozen, complained about his lack of muscles, but his grip was still bruising me.

The droid approached us. I didn't dare to speak, and Hawk just bowed his head respectfully.

"I am the Reaper," said the droid. Its voice wasn't computer generated, but it was being enhanced with deep, echoing tones that removed any hint of humanity.

The droid began to circle us, like a hunter circling his prey. Hawk turned on the spot to keep facing it, dragging me round with him, and I gave a terrified squeak of protest. He covered my mouth with one hand to silence me, while the other kept hold of my arm.

I had my eyes fixed on the droid. I couldn't see any weapons, but I was sure it would have at least one. A gun, or more likely a bomb, to dispose of us if we were judged useless. The Reaper was only controlling the droid, he wasn't physically present. He could blow up the droid and the two of us with it, and not be harmed himself.

"Are you ready to pay the price for your apprenticeship?" asked the droid.

"I'm ready, master," said Hawk.

The droid was still circling us, and Hawk kept spinning me round to face it. I was feeling giddy from the motion when the droid finally stopped moving and Hawk stopped too.

"It is time," said the droid.

Hawk laughed, loosening his grip on me for a moment, and I caught a glimpse of a terrifying smile on his face. I shivered, wondering if he was copying the smile of the Founder Player, Marcus. Hawk's act was so convincing, that part of me wondered if this was genuine, if his mind had been stretched too thin by four hundred years of immortal glory and finally shattered.

Hawk drew his knife. I started shaking, and broke my mouth free from his hand. "Please. Michael. Don't you love me? Don't…"

His hand smothered me again, and he forced me down to my knees. He was behind me now. I couldn't see him, only the anonymous droid standing watching me.

"Of course I love you," said Hawk. "That's why I'm giving you this great honour, Emma. The honour of buying my apprenticeship to the Reaper."

He pulled my head back against him, and his mouth came down to kiss my forehead gently. "I love you. Always."

Out of the corner of my eye, I saw the knife in his right hand as it flashed down to cut my throat.

CHAPTER SEVENTEEN

"I'm all right on my own from here," I said.

The Unilaw officer guiding me through the maze-like corridors of the United Law facility stopped, took a wary look at my face, and hastily hurried off rather than trying arguing with me.

It was just as well. My respect for adults in general, and the forces of the law in particular, had worn thin since the Avalon world crash, and I was barely controlling my anger. I'd just recovered consciousness on the medical table to find half a dozen Unilaw officers gathered round me, all busily removing the remains of the blood and fake skin. My clothes appeared to be undisturbed, but I still felt my privacy had been violated. They could have waited the extra few minutes until I was properly awake before messing around with me!

I continued down the corridor and pressed the doorbell at the side of Nathan's apartment door. When he opened it, he gestured at my bloodstained clothes.

"Hawk does an impressive murder. When he cut your throat, there was blood spurting everywhere."

I wasn't interested in his spectator's view of my death. I walked forward, and Nathan dodged aside to let me in.

"You were a good victim too," he added. "You looked totally terrified."

"That's because I *was* totally terrified," I said. "I was sure the Reaper's droid was carrying a bomb. I thought that if we did anything to make the Reaper suspicious then he'd blow us up."

The apartment living area looked very different to the last time I'd seen it. Most of the furniture had been shoved aside to leave a central space clear for a holo worldscape that included creepy stone buildings adorned with gargoyles, and ramshackle thatched cottages. I guessed it was Game world Gothic, and it confirmed my opinion that I'd never want to live there.

Three of the room walls were dotted with pieces of paper, several showing mysterious diagrams, but most just covered with notes in Nathan's obsessively neat handwriting. I turned to the fourth wall, with its mosaic of screens, and my attention was caught by a screen showing an image of me and Michael in the dormitory. At this moment, when I was acutely aware of Hawk as a physically vulnerable human being rather than the glittering immortal Gamer, I could only think of him as Michael.

Nathan noticed me looking at the screen. "Would you like me to replay the murder for you?"

"No, I wouldn't!" I snapped. "What's happening? Where's Michael?"

Nathan looked evasive. "Bit of a problem there. We don't know."

I turned to glare at him. "Why not? Unilaw should be tracking him by now."

"Unilaw were ready to track his medical chip but..."

"But?" I spat out the word.

"After Michael sacrificed you, the Reaper ordered him to cut the chip out of his arm."

I stared at him. "Michael really did that?"

Nathan nodded. "I couldn't watch. The murder was fake, your blood was fake, but Hawk cutting into his arm was real."

I couldn't help picturing Michael digging into his own flesh with a knife. Medical chips were injected deep into the muscle of your arm. Getting one in there was easy but cutting one out... "Has Michael activated any of the spy eyes he's carrying?"

"Not yet," said Nathan. "He probably doesn't think it's safe."

There was a long silence.

"Try not to worry," said Nathan awkwardly. "I'm sure Hawk will be fine. Think of all the things he's done in Game."

"This isn't Hawk!" I screamed at him. "This is Michael!" I found myself echoing Hawk's favourite centuries old swear word. "This isn't the bleeping Game, this is real life!"

Nathan cowered.

"I should have known this would happen," I ranted. "I warned Michael that Unilaw would track his medical chip. He said the Reaper would have a plan to deal with that. I assumed the Reaper would have a way to disable the medical chip, not order Michael to..."

I broke off, ran into the bedroom, blundered through it to the shower, and locked myself in.

"Your contraceptive treatment is still active," the shower told me in a comforting female voice. "You should attend the medical centre for your hormone boost in preparation for egg harvesting and fertilization."

I threw up. Fortunately showers are equipped to deal with that problem, especially showers designed to care for pregnant women.

I must have been in the shower for about a quarter of an hour, when I heard Nathan's tentative voice calling from outside. "Are you all right in there, Jex?"

"Yah."

"A delivery trolley brought clothes for you. I've put them on a chair just outside the shower door."

"Thanks."

"I'll go back in the other room then."

I'd been sitting on the shower floor, but now I forced myself to get up. I washed off the fake blood, got rid of the dye and makeup from my hair and my skin so I looked myself again, got the clothes from outside and dressed. Finally, I threw the old overalls I'd been wearing into a garbage chute. I was in the habit of being as frugal as possible, but it would be impossible to get all the blood out of them.

When I went back into the living area, I saw Nathan was staring at his mosaic of screens. He dragged his attention away from the multitude of flashing images and turned to look at me.

"I'm not being callous, Jex. I told you that I couldn't watch what happened, but Hawk will be fine once he's had medical treatment."

I didn't reply, just dragged a chair over to sit next to Nathan, and gestured at the screens. "What is all this stuff?"

"I'm following the chase for the Reaper, studying Game training texts, and reading things about the history of Game."

"All at once?"

"Yah." Nathan frowned. "The more I learn, the more I realize how lethal a rogue Game Tech could be, particularly one who'd worked on the original design phase of Game. We've got to catch the Reaper before..." He broke off. "Hawk!"

Nathan pointed in excitement to one of his displays. It had zoomed in on a map, and a dot was flashing.

"Has he activated a spy eye?" I asked.

Nathan shook his head. "Since we lost Hawk, Unilaw have been using facial recognition software on all their surveillance camera images to watch for him. There were a couple of false alarms earlier, you can imagine how many black-haired boys are wandering around in blue overalls, but that flashing dot has just changed from amber to green. That means it's been confirmed as Hawk."

"Where is he?"

"He's just got into a pod at a main transport interchange. Unilaw are tracking the pod itself now. Look, you can see the green dot is moving." Nathan grinned. "I've managed to get a live feed of the information coming in for the Unilaw team leader. It's amazing what people will do when I use the magic words, 'Hawk says.'"

Nathan leaned forward to tap his controls. "With luck I can..." A new display appeared, this one showing a skinny kid in blue overalls getting into a one-person pod. The clip only lasted a couple of seconds but it was definitely Michael.

"The Reaper's controlled Game droid doesn't seem to be with Michael."

"That droid's been deactivated," said Nathan.

"Did the Reaper use another fake identity number to control it?"

Nathan pulled a face. "Yah. This time the identity number belonged to a six-month-old baby."

"Let's hope Unilaw doesn't arrest the baby," I said bitterly.

"It's lucky that the Reaper didn't use the identity number of an adult in Game, because they'd have been blamed for the bombing."

"The Reaper couldn't use the identity number of someone in Game. If the Game data integrity system spotted two different people using the same identity number, then all sorts of alarms would start screaming."

Nathan paused. "I've been trying to work out how the Reaper is managing to use fake identity numbers to do things. It's a lot harder than you might think, because identity numbers are controlled by the Game security system. I think the Reaper must have helped design that security system and left himself a back door."

"What's a back door?"

"If the Reaper helped design the security system, he could leave himself a weak spot. His own secret way into the system. A back door."

I thought about that. "I don't know nearly as much about these things as you do, but the Reaper being able to mess around with the Game security system sounds bad to me."

"It's incredibly bad."

"Can we find out who designed the Game security system?"

"The Game Techs have given me access to a mass of Game information, but nothing about the security system. They'd want to keep that secret from..."

Nathan was interrupted by a soft buzzing noise. He turned to look at one of his displays. "Unilaw Reception say they have an incoming call for you, Jex. It's player Odele Thorpe Scott Matthys, resident of Coral."

"Agh. That's my mother." I buried my face in my hands. Why did my mother have to call me at a moment like this? I couldn't face discussing my father's death with her right now. Not when Michael was in danger and might die too. I couldn't explain about that to my mother. I couldn't even explain what I was doing at a United Law facility.

I looked up sharply. "How could my mother know I'm here? She should be calling my phone, and I left that back in the long-distance carriage. Nathan, accept the call!"

CHAPTER EIGHTEEN

An image of my mother appeared on the screen in front of me. Her long, sea-green hair cascaded round her perfect face. Her eyes were a dark emerald colour, and there was a hint of mermaid scales around her hair line. In my earliest childhood memories, she'd been a dryad on Nature. Her hair had been the reddish-brown of autumn leaves then, and floated around her head like a halo, but her eyes had always been exactly the same green.

"Happy birthday, Jex," she said.

I glanced at another of Nathan's screens to check the date. "It's not my birthday until tomorrow, Mother."

"Well, that's close enough. I'm sorry I didn't contact you about your father, but it would have been a difficult conversation."

I opened my mouth to reply, but she lifted a delicate webbed hand to stop me.

"Let's forget all about it." She hurried on, sweeping the issue of my father's death aside. "Your boyfriend just called me. You hadn't told me you had a boyfriend. You should tell your mother about these things."

She waved a reproachful finger at me. "I don't understand why you're at a United Law facility, or why your boyfriend was calling me. He insisted it was vitally important that I give you a phone number and ask you to call him to talk privately, but you mustn't do that if you have any doubts about him."

She hesitated before speaking again in an anxious voice. "I know there are some people who appear charming to begin with but then become frightening. If this boy is one of those people, he may try to manipulate you with emotional blackmail and threats to make you stay in a relationship with him. He's probably involved me to add extra pressure, he may get your friends to talk to you as well, but you mustn't give in."

I was stunned. This was the first time my mother had ever referred to what she'd gone through with her ex-boyfriend on Ganymede. She hated to think about unpleasant memories, let alone talk about them, but she was doing it now because she was worried about this situation. From her viewpoint, it must look as if a strange boy was trying to force me to contact him, and I'd been driven into taking refuge at a United Law facility.

I'd never been sure that my mother had any real feelings for me, but now I knew that she did. She was afraid I might be in danger, so she'd forced herself to mention a dreadful time and give me a warning.

"There's no need to worry about me, Mother," I said. "I've just accidentally lost contact with my boyfriend and I want to talk to him very much."

My mother gave me the number, and then hastily vanished back to her sea world of gentle beaches and coral reefs. Of course she'd be eager to end this call, but she'd hopefully call me again soon. Next time she'd be able to talk to me without mentioning my father's death or unpleasant memories.

"Hawk must want us to call him using a secure, encrypted link," said Nathan.

He had our outgoing call active in seconds. Michael's weary face appeared on the screen. He looked exhausted and strained, but he was alive.

"Jex! It's really good to see you in one piece. Hello Nathan." Michael gave a heavy sigh, took something from a carton and bit into it. It looked like one of those awful sandwiches you got from vending machines.

"It's good to see you too," I said. "Surveillance spotted you entering a pod. Why haven't you activated a spy eye?"

"I didn't want anyone hearing this conversation but you two," he said, "so I bought a phone from a vending machine. I'm sorry about involving your mother, Jex. She didn't seem very happy about me contacting her, but I didn't dare to call the Unilaw facility or anyone connected to the investigation on an unsecured link. This was the only way I could think of to get my new phone number to you."

"Don't worry about that," I said. "I think it's helped the situation between my mother and me. More urgently, Nathan has had an idea. He thinks that the Reaper helped design the Game security system and has left himself a back door into the system. That's a way..."

"I know what it is," interrupted Michael. "That explains how the Reaper plans to... Well, never mind that now. I need to ask the Game investigation team for help. My problem is that I need a team of Game Techs with very high authority, but I have to make sure the Reaper isn't one of them. How can I do that? Asking them to exclude the original Game designers could alarm the Reaper."

"Remember that we worked out why the Reaper attacked Avalon," said Nathan, "It was the first Game world to be created without the involvement of any of the original Game designers. You could ask for a team of Game Techs who worked on the design of Avalon. If the Reaper heard about that, he shouldn't be alarmed but confused, thinking that you're following some misleading clue about the Avalon bombing."

Michael's tired face managed a grin. "Well done, Nathan! Avalon's designers should have very senior ranks by now."

He abruptly ended the call, but within a minute another image appeared on the screen, showing the interior of a standard one-person pod with Michael lounging on a seat. I noticed a rough bandage was bound round the top of his left arm. It was heavily stained with blood, but he could still move the arm because he used his left hand to drop half a sandwich back into its carton before speaking.

"Surveillance, can you see and hear me?"

The voice of surveillance echoed slightly. "We can see and hear you, Hawk. We've been tracking your pod's progress through the transport system, but we couldn't see you until you activated the spy eye." There was a note of reproach as she said the last few words.

"It was too risky for me to activate a spy eye earlier," said Michael. "A lot has been happening. I need you to get a team of Game Techs to help us. They should all be members of the original Avalon design team."

There was a pause before surveillance replied. "We've made the request to the Game investigation team."

"Patch the Game Techs into the spy eye channel as soon as they're ready. Jex and Nathan, are you in channel too?"

Nathan tapped the screen. "We're here."

"Good."

Michael retrieved his sandwich. He had time to finish eating it and have a drink before there was a new female voice on the channel.

"This is the leader of your requested Game Tech team."

"Welcome," said Michael. "I know I don't look like it at the moment, but Unilaw can vouch for the fact that I'm Hawk. I called for defrost and managed to get recruited by our bomber. Now, how large is your team, did you all work on the design of Avalon, and are you somewhere safe from eavesdroppers?"

"Twelve, correct, and correct," said the Game Tech. "Is Avalon likely to be attacked again, and should we evacuate its population?"

"That shouldn't be necessary," said Michael. "The one absolutely vital thing is that your rogue Game Tech doesn't find out what I tell you or what we're doing. He's trying to blow up another server complex. Our new precautions prevent him from using a delivery trolley to plant the bombs, so he's sending me to plant them myself."

He gestured casually at the floor in front of him. "I've got four bombs with me. I've been told the transport stop for the target server complex, and the code to let me into the storage unit there to get a buggy. I've been told the paths to follow to get to the server complex. I'm supposed to be there, waiting outside the force field, in…"

Michael glanced at the time on the pod guidance display. "In exactly forty-seven minutes. At that point, the bomber is supposed to send me the security code for the force field. Once I've used the security code, I've got two minutes to enter, plant the bombs, and get out before the force field closes again. The bombs are timed to explode fifteen minutes after that."

"You don't intend to plant the bombs?" The voice of the Game Tech leader had lost the standard calm, polite manner, and sounded close to panic.

Michael grinned. "I'm not playing along with the bomber that far. I'll drop off the bombs somewhere on the way to the server complex."

"The new security arrangements require three gold status Game Techs from different departments to authorize requests for force field security codes," said the Game Tech leader, in a despairing voice. "If the bomber can still obtain them, then he must have multiple gold status co-conspirators among our ranks."

"I believe there's only one Game Tech involved in this," said Michael, "but he may have a way to get past the security checks. I need your team watching for him to access the force field security code. I believe the access should be recorded on an audit trail?"

"That is correct," said the Game Tech leader.

"I expect the bomber will try to delete the record of his access from the audit trail as soon as he's got his security code. Will you be able to copy the information before he can delete it?"

"That is correct."

"Then we should be able to get the bomber's true identity number. Once you've proved who he is, then immediately call whoever you need to arrest him. We won't need to hide what we're doing after that."

I tapped the screen to let me speak. "Michael."

"Yes, Jex?"

"The Reaper might have put a spy eye on your buggy so he can watch you planting the bombs. If he sees you stop and abandon the bombs on the way to the server complex..."

Michael groaned. "You're right, Jex. I'll have to take the

bombs with me as far as the force field. When the Reaper sends me the force field code, I won't use it, just dump the bombs and drive my buggy away. With the protective force field still active, the bombs won't be able to damage the server complex when they explode."

I gnawed anxiously at my bottom lip. "I strongly suggest you drive away at top speed after you dump the bombs."

Michael laughed. "I certainly will. I don't want my head blown off."

He turned off the spy eye. Nathan and I sat in silence after that, watching a screen display the green dot that marked Michael's position on a map of the transport system. After a while, Nathan leaned forward to get a closer look at the dot. "Has the pod stopped?"

"Yah. Michael must be getting out now, and collecting the buggy. We won't hear anything more from him until..."

We both turned to check the time.

"Sixteen minutes to go," said Nathan.

We watched the minutes and the seconds tick away. I was bracing myself for something to happen at the end of those sixteen endless minutes, and jumped nervously when I heard the voice of surveillance speak before that.

"Two minutes."

The Game Tech leader replied. "We're ready."

Sixty slow seconds later, surveillance gave another time check.

"One minute."

I started counting seconds. I'd got to eighty-one before anything happened.

"We can see an authorized request for a force field security code," reported the Game Tech leader. "Second authorization received. Third authorization received. Copying audit trail and checking identity numbers of..." She broke off.

An image from a spy eye appeared on the screen in front of me. Judging from the way the picture was jolting around, Michael had stuck the spy eye to the buggy control panel ahead of him, and was driving along the path at top speed.

"I've dumped the bombs," he gasped. "Any luck identifying the bomber?"

"That is correct," said the Game Tech leader, in tragic, mourning tones.

"One of the original Game designers?" asked Michael sympathetically.

"That is correct." The Game Tech leader didn't ask how he'd known that. She was too traumatized to care. "All three authorizations came from the same person, but they had different department numbers."

"The bomber has a back door into the Game security system," said Michael. "He must have been using that to change his department number between the authorizations. You're taking steps to arrest him?"

"That is correct."

"It's awful for them," murmured Nathan. "The Reaper was one of the first guardians of Game. Knowing he betrayed the trust the players have in us, deliberately killing those under our care, is..."

I noticed the betraying shift, as Nathan changed from referring to the Game Techs as 'them', and said that significant 'us' and 'our'. I turned my head to look at him, saw his expression, and hastily faced away again. A moment of pain like that deserved privacy.

"I assume you've worked out what server complex I was supposed to destroy," said Michael. "What Game world was the bomber attacking this time?"

"Your target was Celestius," said the Game Tech.

Michael flinched. "The Reaper sent me to bomb Celestius! My own world. My own family."

"That is correct." The Game Tech paused. "I regret to inform you that we have failed to apprehend the bomber."

"Why? What went...?"

Michael's voice was drowned out by a loud explosion, and the screen went black.

CHAPTER NINETEEN

I sat next to where Michael lay on a medical examination table, and watched the controlled droid of a doctor working on him.

"It's just a few bruises," said Michael.

It had taken seventeen minutes for a medical team to reach Michael. For seventeen minutes, I'd thought he was dead. During that endless time I'd discovered something. My head had decided to do the sensible thing, and refuse to get involved with Michael. My emotions weren't sensible, and were already involved with him.

"Bruises, mild concussion, and an arm wound." The doctor cautiously manipulated Michael's right hand and wrist.

Michael winced in pain.

"And a sprained wrist," said the doctor.

"All right, bruises, a bump on the head, a small hole in my left arm, and a sprained right wrist." Michael sounded irritated.

"A big hole in your left arm," said the doctor.

"It took a few attempts for me to find the medical chip and cut it out." Michael winced again as the doctor did some repair work on his arm. "I need to get back into Game now."

I bit my lip. Michael couldn't leave, couldn't turn back into Hawk the Unvanquished, before I had the chance to talk to him privately. I had to tell him I'd changed my mind. No, not exactly changed my mind. I still believed that any relationship with him would end with me being badly hurt in the future, but there was a new factor to consider. Not getting involved with Michael would mean me being badly hurt right now. I wasn't sure exactly where that left us, but I didn't want him vanishing back into Game before I had time to work it out.

"I've given you accelerated healing injections," said the doctor, "but the treatment will need twelve hours to complete before you can be frozen."

"I can't wait around for twelve hours. I need to…"

I didn't let Michael finish his sentence. "The doctor is right. It's incredibly dangerous to freeze someone who has an open wound. You have to let your arm heal properly before you enter Game."

"But I've got fifty billion players waiting for me to…"

I cut him off again. "They'll have to keep waiting for another twelve hours. If you insist on being frozen with that open wound, the resulting tissue damage will mean you have to be defrosted in a few days' time to have your arm amputated. Would you like me to talk you through the details of the amputation process?"

"No, I wouldn't!" said Michael. "All right, I'll wait. It's probably just as well that you didn't finish your medical training, Jex. Your bedside manner is terrifying."

"Effective though." The doctor gave me an approving nod. "Long term players are always impossible when they get real life injuries. They think it's like Game, where they can go home and be healed within a few minutes."

Michael sat up. "What about you, Jex? Were you hurt much when I cut your throat? The way the blood sprayed everywhere was terrifying, and I couldn't see you breathing at all. It wasn't until I saw you on my phone display that I was sure I wasn't a murderer."

"You should have known the blood was all fake, and the lack of breathing was only because I'd been injected with that drug. I just had a few bruises, and I was treated for those hours ago. Everything is healed now. Look!" I rolled up my sleeves and displayed my arms. "Not a mark on me."

"It's the state of your neck that's been worrying me. I thought I'd cut too deeply with the knife and…" Michael slid off the table and moved to give my neck a close inspection. "All right, your jugular vein seems intact. Let's go and get a status report from Nathan."

"I'd recommend food and sleep as well," said the doctor.

"And a shower," I added.

Michael paused on his way to the door, and sniffed himself suspiciously. "Do I...?"

I laughed. "A bit. Mind you, I'd sweat a lot as well if I was carrying bombs around."

"We don't sweat in Game," said Michael. "We don't get tired physically in quite the same way either, though doing too much can get very wearing mentally. I've been having a difficult time since the Avalon bombing."

We went out into the corridor. "There's something I need to say." I took a deep breath. "I changed my mind. About us."

Michael gave me a startled look. "About us having a relationship?"

"Yah. I don't want us rushing into anything, or..." I broke off my sentence. There was no need for me to worry about us rushing into anything. Not when Michael was going back into Game and I was stuck in the real world until I was nineteen.

"I promise not to rush anything," said Michael.

He turned to face me, hesitated, and then shook his head. "No, I just promised I wouldn't rush things, and I desperately need a shower, but... I'm glad, Jex. I'm really glad."

We stood there for a couple of minutes, just looking at each other, before a pregnant woman came walking along the corridor. We hastily dodged aside to let her pass, and then headed for Nathan's room. As soon as we were inside the door, Michael turned to Nathan.

"How bad do I smell?"

I laughed at Nathan's stunned expression.

"On second thoughts," said Michael, "don't answer that. Jex has already told me I stink."

He walked on into the main living area, and blinked as he saw the furniture crammed into corners and the holo worldscape dominating the centre of the room. "Is it possible to remove Game world Gothic so we can sit down?"

Nathan had been staring at me, mouthing a question with raised eyebrows, but now he hurried across to sit at his mosaic of screens. He tapped at the control bank, and the sinister landscape of Gothic vanished.

Michael grabbed a large, cushioned chair, attempted to drag it into the centre of the room, and gave a yelp of pain. I spoke in a withering voice.

"Michael, you have extensive muscle damage in your left arm and a sprained right wrist. Do I really need to explain why it's a stupid idea for you to try moving heavy furniture?"

There was an appalled gulp from the direction of Nathan. Michael turned to give him a reassuring smile. "Don't worry. That's just Jex's way of showing how much she cares about me."

I didn't see how Nathan reacted to that, because I was busy towing two chairs into the centre of the room. I sat in one of them, Michael slumped down into the other with a sigh of relief, and Nathan swung round in his seat to face us.

"Have the Game Techs caught the Reaper yet?" asked Michael.

"No," said Nathan. "The Game Techs tracked his location to backstage on Game world Witchcraft."

"What's backstage mean?" I asked.

"It's a Game Tech term for their special hidden areas on Game worlds," said Nathan. "A team of Game Techs went to Witchcraft to arrest the Reaper, but he vanished."

Michael was a fraction of a second ahead of me in asking the obvious question. "How did he vanish?"

"The Game Techs are still trying to work that out," said Nathan. "When they confronted the Reaper, he disappeared. They assumed he'd used a standard Game teleport or world transfer, but their attempts to track a new location for his identity number keep failing. It's as if the Reaper has left Game entirely."

"He can't have left Game," I said. "If he'd somehow managed to put himself through emergency defrost, we'd know about it. After the Avalon bombing, any unscheduled defrost in the body stacks would instantly be reported to Unilaw."

Nathan nodded. "It's more likely that the Reaper's found a way to stop his location from being tracked."

Michael sighed. "If the Game Techs can't find the Reaper, have they at least given us some information about him?"

Nathan nodded again. "The Reaper's real name is Harper. He was the original creative director of the Game. That means he was the person who decided the base concept for each of the first few Game worlds."

I frowned. "The base concept? You mean things like deciding Automaton would be centred on robots, and Coral would have merfolk?"

"Yah," said Nathan. "The Game Techs are clearly devastated that Harper was the bomber. My impression is that they have a few troublesome Founder Game Techs, but Harper was considered to be perfectly reasonable. He just had a few ego problems and a grievance about the Game Company's policy of anonymity for Game Techs."

"I can understand Harper having a grievance about that," said Michael. "He was the one who decided the concepts for the original Game worlds. He'd think of them as his own personal creations. When Game opened to the public, and people rushed in to explore his worlds, he'd feel entitled to fame and respect. Instead, he was robbed of recognition for his creations and forced to remain in the shadows."

Michael shook his head. "Then there was another blow. People were flooding into Game, and more worlds were urgently needed. New designers were brought in, and allowed to supplant Harper's position by designing worlds as well."

"It makes sense that Harper attacked Avalon because it was the first world that wasn't his creation," said Nathan, "but why would he want to attack Celestius? Harper would have been involved in both its original design and the project where it was revamped to become the Celestius we know today."

"Yes, Harper would have been the one who decided the basic concept of Celestius, with its castles in the air," said Michael. "He didn't want to attack Celestius itself, but the Founder Players who live there. For four centuries, Harper has watched all the praise and hero worship that should have been his being heaped on Founder Players like me. Harper built the Game, while we just played around in it, but we got the fame and honour instead of him. You can understand why he'd feel cheated by that and hate all Founder Players."

"Umm, maybe," said Nathan nervously.

"All that anger and resentment has been burning in Harper for centuries," said Michael, "so what triggered him into taking action now?"

"For four centuries, the Game has been growing steadily in size," said Nathan. "Last year, the Game company held a major review of potential problem areas. Everyone knows that review flagged the increasing amount of work needing to be done in the real world, so the Leebrook Ashton bill was passed. There was also a big reorganization of the Game Tech hierarchy, and Harper was deeply unhappy about the effect on his position."

"Harper felt he'd never been given the recognition he deserved," I murmured, "and then his position in the Game Tech hierarchy was threatened. He decided that he was never going to be famous and loved for creating Game worlds, so he'd be famous and feared for destroying them."

"Harper began by crashing Avalon to shock the whole of Game," said Michael. "That was supposed to be blamed on a resentful teenager, but it would be followed by crashing Celestius. Harper would kill a lot of the Founder Players who'd stolen his glory, demonstrate that both Unilaw and the Game Techs were powerless against him, and then make some sort of announcement to the population of Game."

He paused. "Harper successfully crashed Avalon, but then his plan started going wrong. We worked out that a Game Tech was responsible for the bombing, which meant all the security systems were improved, and then Jex and I contacted Tomath. A couple of blackmailers were an unpredictable threat to Harper's carefully prepared plan, so he decided to eliminate both of us. First he got me to murder Jex, and then he lied to me about when the bombs would explode. Harper didn't time them to explode fifteen minutes after I'd planted them, but when I'd still be inside the force field. I was really lucky that I didn't use the force field code, just dumped the bombs and drove away."

I couldn't help picturing what would have happened if the bombs had exploded just a few seconds earlier. Michael wouldn't just have minor injuries, he'd be…

A buzzing sound interrupted my thoughts. Nathan turned in his chair and tapped rapidly at his bank of controls. "A report just came in."

"Have the Game Techs caught the Reaper?" asked Michael.

"No, this report is from Unilaw," said Nathan. "Tomath's been killed in an explosion."

CHAPTER TWENTY

"Tomath's been killed in an explosion!" Michael and I repeated in unison. "When did that happen?" Michael continued solo.

"At about the same time as your bombs exploded," said Nathan. "The Unilaw team were focusing their attention on you at the time, so there was a delay investigating."

"The Reaper planned to kill Michael and me," I said. "He must have decided to make a clean sweep of things and kill Tomath as well."

"Yah," said Nathan. "A delivery trolley took a parcel to Tomath's room. The packaging said it contained a new luxury model phone, but it was really a bomb. When Tomath opened it there was a massive explosion. Fortunately, the kids in the closest rooms were at work at the time, so only Tomath was killed."

Michael sighed. "Given how many people were killed in the Avalon crash, I don't have much sympathy for Tomath. He might not have realized he was planting bombs beforehand, but he did once they'd exploded. If he'd gone to Unilaw back then, and told them what he knew, he'd still be alive."

Michael was silent for a moment. "Do we expect any more drastic things to happen in the next ten minutes?"

"No," said Nathan.

"Then I'll go and shower. Hopefully that will stop Jex wrinkling her nose whenever I get close to her. Could you find me fresh clothes and something decent to eat? I had a sandwich earlier but it tasted awful."

"That's because the sandwiches from vending machines are packed with preservatives," I said. "Those don't just taste bad, but can attack your stomach lining and..."

Michael hastily interrupted me. "Please, Jex, don't tell me what horrors that sandwich may have done to my stomach. I'm already having gory visions of someone amputating my arm."

Michael wandered off through the bedroom and into the shower. Nathan glanced after him, and then gave me a worried look.

"You told a Founder Player he stank?"

"I hinted that Michael could use a shower."

"And you said he was being stupid when he tried to move that chair."

"It wasn't an intelligent thing to do, was it?"

Nathan frowned. "I heard Hawk kept annoying surveillance by jamming their spy eyes. What's been going on between you two?"

I could feel myself blushing. "Nothing lurid. We just wanted some privacy while we discussed plans for the future."

I wasn't going to mention the kiss. It wasn't Nathan's business. In fact, none of what had happened between me and Michael was Nathan's business.

Nathan shook his head. "You told me that nothing could happen between you and Hawk."

"It wasn't happening between me and Hawk. It was happening between me and Michael." I waved a finger at Nathan. "And don't start giving me dire warnings about Michael going back into Game and becoming Hawk the Unvanquished again. I know all that. I know things can't possibly work between us, but..."

I let the words trail off, and waved my hands in a gesture of helpless despair.

"I wasn't going to give you any dire warnings," said Nathan. "When we talked about this before, I was worried that you'd fall for Hawk, he wouldn't be interested, and you'd get hurt. Things are different now. The way you were acting when you got back here after the fake murder told me you were deeply involved with Hawk, but he keeps throwing glowing looks in your direction as well. If you've got as far as discussing plans for the future, then he's obviously serious about making things work between you, so I don't see there's a problem."

"There's going to be nothing but problems," I said grimly. "It'll be a year before I can enter Game. A year for Hawk the Unvanquished to forget all about me. Even if he doesn't, there'll be a four hundred year age difference, and a huge power gulf between us. Every news channel in Game will be watching us and waiting for our relationship to fall apart."

"You're sometimes a bit pessimistic, Jex."

"I'm not pessimistic. I've just had a lot of experience of things going horribly wrong. Now, you organize the clothes for Michael, while I order food and drinks for us."

Fifteen minutes later, I'd arranged a table of food in the middle of the room, and a delivery trolley had brought a set of clothes. Nathan took those through into the bedroom, and a few minutes later Michael appeared.

I stared at him, confused by his appearance. It wasn't just that he was wearing respectable clothes. He'd had a haircut as well.

"What do you think?" he asked, looking at me.

"I was getting used to your floppy hair, but I admit this looks better."

"I felt I probably needed a haircut after four hundred years. You wouldn't believe what that shower said to me."

"I would," said Nathan gloomily. "I really would."

I laughed. "When I showered earlier, it told me to have my hormone boost in preparation for egg harvesting and fertilization."

Michael choked. "Even in my worst days, I could have phrased that more romantically." He looked at the table. "I see we've got blueberry apples."

I nodded. "They're my favourite. You should try one."

Michael picked up an apple, and took a cautious bite. "This does taste rather good," he admitted. "It isn't going to do anything dreadful to my stomach lining?"

"Blueberry apples are highly nutritious," I said.

We spent the next few minutes loading food onto plates and

eating. Nathan and I finished our meal well ahead of Michael, because of his habit of cautiously inspecting each new item and taking nervous sample bites. I frowned as I watched him trying to decide if he should risk a piece of cake.

"I know it isn't necessary to eat and drink in Game," I said, "but people enjoy having picnics and banquets, so you must have met all these foods before. Is the problem that they taste different in Game?"

"No," said Michael. "People on Celestius tend to stick to the foods we knew and liked before we entered Game."

"You don't spend all your time on Celestius though," said Nathan.

"No, but if I go to an event where there's food involved, people make sure there's plenty of my favourite…"

Michael was interrupted by another buzzing sound from Nathan's bank of controls. Nathan scurried across to tap at them. Michael and I watched hopefully, but got restless when he didn't say anything for a full minute.

"Is that a report from the Game Tech investigation?" I asked.

"Yah." Nathan was still staring at his screens.

"Judging from the expression on your face, it isn't good news," said Michael.

"It isn't," said Nathan. "The Game Techs couldn't track Harper's location using his identity number, so they tried the alternative method of looking for his constream. That's the stream of data in Game which… Well, it's a bit hard to describe, but you can think of it as Harper's consciousness in Game."

"I've never found a good way to describe it either," said Michael. "I like to think of myself as a person, not a lot of data floating around in a computer."

"Everyone's constream has its designated position in the Game system," said Nathan. "When the Game Techs checked the designated position for Harper's constream, they found it had been deleted."

I shook my head. "I can't believe that Harper would just delete himself from existence."

"Harper hasn't deleted himself," said Nathan. "I've explained to you before that Game Techs can enter areas of Game that players can't reach. Game Tech constreams are also held in completely different data storage areas from those of players. When a player is recruited as a Game Tech, an automated process is used to transfer the new recruit's constream from player data storage to Game Tech data storage."

He paused. "When Harper vanished, it was because he'd run that automated process in reverse."

I tried to work out what that meant. Michael got there faster than me. "You mean that Harper has changed himself from a Game Tech into an ordinary player?"

"Yah," said Nathan. "Harper's recreated himself as a player, but he's changed both his name and his identity number. The Game Techs can't find any clues to what player name he's using now, what he looks like, or where he went."

Michael's eyes widened in alarm. "Could he have gone to Celestius?"

"That's the one world in Game where Harper definitely can't be," said Nathan. "The system only allows entry to Celestius for those on the list of Founder Players."

"Could Harper have added himself to that list?" I asked.

"There are under a thousand Founder Players," said Nathan. "It was easy for the Game Techs to check that no new ones have suddenly appeared. You can't have two players with the same identity number, so Harper can't have duplicated an existing Founder Player."

I had an extremely nasty thought. "Is it possible that Harper has deleted one of the Founder Players from Game and replaced them?"

"No," said Nathan. "This automated process is used to transfer a single constream between the player and Game Tech data storage. It couldn't have affected any other players."

"So, the Reaper has created a new player identity for himself," I said. "We know he isn't a Founder Player, but other than that..."

Michael groaned. "There are fifty billion players in Game, and any one of them could be the Reaper."

CHAPTER TWENTY-ONE

There was a long silence before Nathan spoke. "I'm sorry. After all you two went through…"

Michael literally shook himself. "No. We mustn't let ourselves think of this as a failure. When this investigation started, no one could think of anything more useful to do than randomly arresting kids from the body stacks."

I frowned as I remembered the Unilaw droid that had broken into my room and held me at gunpoint.

"Think how far we've come since then," said Michael. "We've found out which Game Tech was the Reaper, and that means we can trust the rest of them. It's a huge relief to know I can enter Game again without worrying that the Game Techs guarding my back might delete me."

"Are we sure that the Reaper was the only Game Tech involved in the bombing?" I asked.

"The Reaper was planning to make himself the ruler of Game," said Michael. "I can't believe he'd be willing to share his throne with another Game Tech. It's not just his ego that would stop him involving a rival, but his caution too. Another Game Tech would be a potential threat. We know the Reaper reacts to threats by eliminating them, and he'd be well aware that he couldn't eliminate another Game Tech as easily as a teenager."

"Yah," I said thoughtfully. "The Reaper would stick to recruiting convenient tools that he could dispose of easily when their usefulness was at an end."

"The Reaper had centuries to prepare for this," said Michael. "It's not surprising that he'd have an escape route ready to use if things went wrong, but transferring to being a player must severely limit his actions. He won't be able to use any special Game Tech abilities now, will he, Nathan?"

"Definitely not. The systems and tools that Game Techs use are accessed from their backstage areas of Game. It's impossible for the Reaper to reach those now that he's an ordinary player. When players ask to move location within Game, they can only go to player areas. When Game Techs move location, they can either go to player areas or backstage."

"The Reaper just has to get a job in the real world to have access to a controlled droid though," I said. "That means he'll still be able to make bombs. He shouldn't be able to get hold of the force field codes for the server complexes now, but he could attack other vulnerable places."

"If the Reaper arranges another bombing," said Michael, "we'll get clues to his new identity. He won't be able to bribe any teenagers by clearing their records now, or play around with identity numbers to hide who is controlling a droid."

"Point," I acknowledged, "but I'd still feel happier if we had a way to catch him before there's another bombing. Do the Game Techs know which frozen body belongs to the Reaper?"

"Yah," said Nathan. "It's under guard now, but guarding the Reaper's frozen body doesn't stop him doing things in Game."

"Of course not," I said, "but can't the Game Techs run checks to find what player owns that body?"

Nathan sighed. "They've already gone through their records, but no player is listed as owning the Reaper's body. He's probably set up his new identity without any information on a physical body. That's not going to attract attention, because a lot of players don't have a body any longer."

"What? No physical body?" I shook my head. "How could that happen?"

"When someone critically ill enters Game, their body may not survive the freezing process," said Nathan. "You end up with an orphaned mind in Game with no body in the real world. After four centuries of rushing people into Game before they die, there must be hundreds of thousands of players in that situation."

I could see that was better than letting someone die in real life, and logically the person in Game was just as real whether they had a body in a freezer unit or not. Still, I found it disturbing to think of people not having a physical body at all. Presumably they'd be told about their situation, perhaps they'd even be asked if they wanted their body buried or cremated. I wondered if they ever thought of themselves as ghosts haunting Game.

Michael abandoned the remains of his meal and stood up. "I need to report back to Game now, and then we should all get some sleep. Is it possible to get more beds in here, or do we have to share? If so, I'm first in line to share with Jex."

I threw an apple core at him. "We agreed not to rush things!"

Nathan coughed pointedly. "I'll, um, see what I can arrange about beds."

Michael wandered over to the mosaic of screens and tapped at the controls. The four screens at the centre of the mosaic merged together to form a single, larger screen, and a woman appeared on it. She was wearing a purple sari trimmed with gold, and had diamonds sparkling on her dark forehead. I knew she was in Game, because she was too lovely to be a real human being. Besides, I recognized her even before Michael greeted her with a grin.

"Cassandra, it's me."

This was Cassandra, who people called the Dream Weaver. Everyone agreed she was the loveliest of the female Founder Players. Not because of her looks – anyone could choose to be beautiful in Game – but because of her smile. People said it was the most fascinating smile of any woman in Game, and eulogized about the Mona Lisa and Helen of Troy. Cassandra was smiling at Michael now.

"Not quite Hawk the Unvanquished," she said.

He pulled a face of self-deprecation. "No, Michael's back."

She laughed. "Michael looks better than I remember him in the old days. Did someone pin you down and forcibly cut your hair?"

"They have machines that cut your hair now," said Michael. "I tried one out while I was showering. I was worried it would cut my ears off, but it didn't."

He turned to gesture at me and Nathan. "Cassandra, you know all about me defrosting to help Jex and Nathan chase the bomber. Jex, Nathan, this is Cassandra. She's been helping me hide the fact I'd left Game."

Cassandra nodded. "Hello Jex. Hello Nathan."

Nathan was staring in awe at Cassandra. He blushed and mumbled a greeting. I was a bit tongue tied too. It wasn't just that I was being introduced to Cassandra the Dream Weaver. Michael was smiling at her in a way that meant she was very special to him. I felt horribly jealous.

"So..." said Michael, or Hawk. "What's happening in Game, Cassandra?"

She sighed. "The player population is getting upset. It's been a long time since you gave them an update."

"Unavoidable. If people saw me as Michael, they'd lose all confidence in my ability to save them from a rat, let alone a bomber. Besides, I've been very busy."

"But you're coming back to Game to make a broadcast now?" she asked.

"I'm afraid I won't be in Game and ready to make a broadcast for about another twelve hours."

"Twelve hours!" Cassandra took a deep breath. "I don't think I can keep people calm for that long. They're losing faith in the Game Techs, Unilaw, and even you."

"I could give you an update to pass on to them."

She looked doubtful. "It would have to be something good."

Michael thought for a moment. "It should be safe to let people know that I'm not in Game now. Let's go for the sympathy vote. Tell people that I defrosted to chase the bomber in real life. Say that I've been wounded, and I need to heal up before returning to Game or I'll have to have my arm amputated. I'll be back in Game and making an important broadcast in twelve hours' time."

Cassandra's eyes widened with concern. "You've been wounded? Are you all right?"

"I'll be fine," said Michael. "Absolutely fine, so long as I let my arm heal before they freeze me."

"The players should respond to that," said Cassandra. "Heroic Hawk chasing the bomber in the real world, struggling on despite his wounds, willing to die permanently to save his fellow players."

Michael laughed. "I'm sure you'll make a great speech. There's one more thing I need to tell you."

His expression abruptly changed to be deadly serious. "This is for your ears only, Cassandra. Tell your husband if you wish, but no one else. I'll tell the player population about it eventually, but I'll need to break the news to the family first."

She looked alarmed. "What's happened?"

"The bomber tried to blow up another server complex. Jex helped me get recruited as his assistant. She acted the role of human sacrifice, and was even willing to die genuinely if necessary. That meant I found out about the bombing and was able to stop it, but... The bomber's target was Celestius."

Cassandra's famous smile vanished. She no longer looked assured and immortal, but like an ordinary woman.

"Thank you for stopping the bombing," she said, her eyes going from Michael, to me, and to Nathan in turn. "I would have died."

I wasn't jealous of her any longer. I'd just been reminded of the fact that she'd been married to Thor for more than three hundred years, and anyway Michael had told me that none of the female Founder Players had ever been interested in him.

I hastily tried to reassure Cassandra. "There were millions of players on Avalon when it crashed, so over eleven thousand people died in emergency defrost. With less than a thousand people on Celestius, a world crash might not cause any deaths at all."

She lifted a graceful hand to stop me. "You don't understand, Jex. People entering Game now are still young and healthy, but the Founder Players were very different. A third of us entered the Game because we were terminally ill. My body was very weak indeed. Even a planned defrost would be extremely dangerous for me. An unscheduled, high-speed defrost would certainly have killed me and many of the rest of the family as well."

"Oh," I murmured, thinking of how the players would have reacted to the deaths of hundreds of their legendary Founder Players. It would have been far worse than the panic after the Avalon deaths.

Cassandra made a visible effort to pull herself together. "I'll give your message to the player population, Hawk. I'll leave you to tell the family about... the other news."

The call ended, and Michael turned to Nathan. "Beds?"

"Beds?" asked Nathan blankly.

The tension in Michael's face was replaced with amusement. "The flat things you sleep on. I thought I was the one who was four hundred years out of date on things like food and sleep."

"Oh yah," said Nathan. "Beds. Sorry."

"Don't be. I needed a moment of humour. I've been going through a whole series of living nightmares in the last few hours. Thinking I'd really killed Jex. Carrying round bombs. Finding out I'd been sent to destroy my own home, my own family. Seeing Cassandra's face just now made everything pile on top of me. We came so close to losing the whole Sisterhood, and that's..."

Michael broke off and brushed his face with his hand. "I mustn't rip myself apart over things that didn't happen. I don't know how I'm going to tell the family about the attack on Celestius though. I can't lie to them, not about something like this, and if Cassandra takes it that hard then some of the others will be totally hysterical."

He shook his head. "People seem to think Hawk is an invulnerable legend, but I have limits. Here in the real world, being Michael again, that's even more true. A funny moment is just what I needed to relax. Please, let's forget human sacrifices, bombs, the Reaper, everything, and think about silly things for a while."

Nathan gave him a thoughtful look. "If you want to think about silly things, then just remember that shower."

Nathan tugged three chairs into a line, went over to the wall, and worked on a control panel. The chairs shuffled closer together and merged to form a small bed.

"That's one bed," he said cheerfully. "Now the one in the bedroom is extra large to give pregnant women plenty of comfortable space. At least, that's what it told me."

I giggled. "Your bed talked to you?"

"Oh yah," said Nathan. "The shower and the bed are both worried about my hormones, so they talk to me a lot."

Michael and I followed him into the bedroom. "I think I can..." Nathan adjusted a control panel at the side of the bed.

"Are you sure you wish to make that change?" asked the bed.

"Yes, I'm sure," said Nathan.

"During pregnancy a larger sleeping area..."

"Just shut up and make the change," said Nathan.

The bed split down the middle and the two sides moved smoothly apart, but it still wasn't happy about the new arrangement. "If you wish to restore default sleeping accommodation then..."

"I don't!"

Nathan waited a moment, in case the bed tried to mutiny, but it stayed silently in two halves.

"I think the bed's sulking," said Michael, with a grin. "I feel a bit like sulking too. If we'd been stuck with that large bed, and it came down to a fight over which of us was going to share it with Jex, I was pretty sure I'd beat you, Nathan."

"I'm not so sure," said Nathan, looking at Michael with concern. "Do you realize you're swaying from side to side?"

I could see what he meant. Michael had seemed perfectly normal while he was getting the news report from Nathan. He'd looked tired while talking to Cassandra. Now he was clearly about to drop from exhaustion combined with the aftermath of stress.

"It doesn't matter who would win now," said Michael gloomily. "You've blown both our chances by finding us three beds. I know what Jex is going to say."

I grinned and said it. "You two sleep in the bedroom. I'm sleeping next door."

I went out of the bedroom, and was startled to find Michael following me and shutting the door firmly behind him. I gave him a reproving look. "I said you two were sleeping in the bedroom. You promised not to rush things between us, and frankly you're in no state to rush things anyway."

"I know," he said. "I just need to talk to you about something in private."

"Yah?"

"In the morning, I have to go back into Game. I've arranged for two freezer units to be brought here where Unilaw can keep them safely under guard."

I frowned. "Why do you want two freezer units?"

"I don't think the Reaper will risk another bombing. I think the chase is moving away from the real world and into Game. Will you come there with me, Jex?"

I had to replay his words in my head to make sure I hadn't somehow misheard them. "You want me to enter Game now? I'd love to, but I have to wait until I'm nineteen."

Michael shook his head. "If I say I want to take my assistants into Game to help me catch the bomber, nobody is going to start arguing about the Leebrook Ashton bill. It's best that Nathan stays working here in real life for a little longer, he wouldn't be allowed access to Game design information as a player in Game, but you can come with me."

Michael looked expectantly at me, but I was still too stunned to speak.

"You can stay here with Nathan if you prefer that," added Michael. "I promised I wouldn't rush things between us. You can think about it and tell me your decision in the morning."

He didn't wait for an answer, just turned, went back into the bedroom, and closed the door. I heard a muffled female voice through the door, which had to be a bed giving advice on suitable hormone therapy, and gave a shaky laugh.

I cleared away the remains of the food, lay down on my own bed, and stared up at the ceiling. I had to choose between bypassing the Leebrook Ashton bill and entering Game right away, or waiting in the real world for another year. It wasn't a hard decision to make. All my life, I'd been dreaming of entering Game, and now I had the chance to go there with Michael.

The fact that Michael would enter Game and become Hawk was going to complicate things, the fact we were going there to chase the bomber would complicate things even more, but there was no way that I was going to be left behind.

Tomorrow would be my eighteenth birthday. I'd always dreamed of entering Game on that day. The Leebrook Ashton bill had snatched that dream away, but Michael had handed it back to me. Tomorrow, the Jex of the silver, feathered hair would come to life.

CHAPTER TWENTY-TWO

"Are you nearly finished?" asked Nathan.

"Nearly." I frowned at the screen in front of me. "I didn't expect Game Registration to take this long. I'd set up my appearance and basic facts ages ago. I knew I still had to do the final personal details section, but I wasn't expecting all the movement sequencing as well. I must have looked really silly doing the arm waving and jumping up and down."

"The movement sequencing is very important. It means you'll move in Game like yourself, rather than using standard automated movements."

I remembered something. "Michael mentioned he'd injured a shoulder muscle just before he entered Game. It must have affected his movement sequencing, which is why Hawk always does that one-shouldered shrug. Anyway, I'm just finishing my answers to the, erm..."

Nathan grinned. "Sexual preference details?"

"Erm... yah. When we were taught about Game Registration in school, they didn't mention these questions."

"We were nine years old at the time," said Nathan.

"Point, but it says my answers will go on my open record for anyone to see."

"Having players' sexual preferences stated on their open record avoids a lot of unfortunate misunderstandings."

"Assuming people are honest about them. Which I doubt very much."

Nathan laughed at me. "Are you hiding a dark secret, Jex?"

I ignored him. "Just a couple more questions now."

I entered my last two answers and lifted a hesitant finger. "I'm done. I think I'm done. I hope I haven't made any mistakes. Perhaps I should go through and check my answers again."

"Just carry on and complete your registration," said Nathan. "It doesn't matter if you've made a mistake, because you can always ask a Game Tech to correct it later."

I took a deep breath, confirmed my registration, and a wild surge of emotion hit me. Jex of the silver, feathered hair was real now. She was in Game, still sleeping, waiting for me to wake her, waiting for me to become her.

"I'm registered with Game," I said, my voice shaking.

"Congratulations," said Nathan.

"I'm sorry you aren't doing this too. It's not fair."

He shook his head. "Working here with Game texts, learning all about Game design, is an incredible opportunity. It has to improve my chances of eventually being recruited as a Game Tech."

I thought Nathan would be recruited as soon as he entered Game. The Game Techs surely wouldn't want to leave him running round as a player for even a few days when he knew so many Game secrets.

I daren't say that, because I mustn't risk raising any false hopes. I just smiled and stood up. We went out of Nathan's apartment, and headed down the corridor to an anonymous, white room. I expected to find Michael waiting for me, but there was only a doctor's medical droid standing next to two freezer units.

I'd spent the last year riding patrol in the body stacks. Red Sector Block 2 had held ten million freezer units just like the ones in front of me. Now I was going inside one myself. I'd been dreaming of this moment all my life, but I still felt a last minute shiver of apprehension.

I remembered Michael saying he'd had last minute doubts about entering Game for the ten year trial, and a lot of the other volunteers had backed out entirely. I could understand that. If I was uneasy about stepping into a freezer unit now, people must have been terrified back then. Four hundred years ago, no one knew if the Game was safe or not. No one knew if the primitive freezer units would work, or if they'd destroy the minds and bodies they were supposed to preserve.

"Nervous?" asked a voice from behind me.

Michael had arrived. I turned round to face him. At this instant, he was still Michael, but this was probably the last time I'd ever see him like that. The doctor was waiting expectantly, and the last few seconds were ticking away for me and Michael.

"A bit nervous," I said.

Michael nodded. "I'll stay with you while you start the freezing process, and then catch up with you in Game. Cassandra has been talking to the Ganymede Admission Committee. They've rushed through accepting you as a resident, so you should be waking up in your new house there."

He went across to the nearer freezer unit, and stood by the open lid. We had an audience of a doctor and Nathan watching us, which ruled out any dramatic last words or kisses. I went over to the freezer unit, clambered awkwardly inside, and sat down.

The doctor checked the freezer unit controls, and started going through the final checklist before freezing me. "No metal items in your pockets, Jex?"

"They're empty." I tugged them inside out to prove it.

"You aren't wearing any jewellery?"

"No jewellery."

The doctor waved a scanner at me anyway. Medical rules stated that multiple checks had to be made on these things, because body contact with metal objects could cause horrendous damage during the freezing process.

The doctor's droid head finally nodded approval. "Please lie back and relax."

I lay down, and shuffled to get comfortable. Michael and Nathan moved to stand, side by side, next to my freezer unit. Michael was smiling down at me. Nathan looked understandably wistful.

"Goodbye." I aimed the word at Nathan, but it was really for

Michael. I'd be able to call Nathan and talk to him from within Game, but Michael was vanishing forever.

What would happen when Michael was the glittering legendary Hawk again? Would he still be interested in me, or had everything that happened between us just been a brief aberration? Part of a strange, vulnerable time when he'd returned to being the boy from four hundred years ago? Once he was a Founder Player again, Hawk might get caught up in his old life, and forget that he'd ever shared a clumsy kiss with a girl from the body stacks.

The transparent lid was closed on top of me, and my vision grew hazy as the gases were pumped in. During my training as a medical cadet, I'd learned about every step of the freezing process, but it was still weird to have it happening to me.

I'd constantly imagined my first entry into Game, playing it through a thousand times, but none of them had been like this. I'd expected to be frozen in a medical unit, and for my freezer unit to be transferred to a short stay storage area until I was past the period of defrosting to work or to have babies.

I'd never expected to enter Game from a freezer unit in a United Law facility. I'd never expected a Founder Player to be standing next to me in his physical body, smiling at me as the gases took effect and my eyelids drooped and closed.

CHAPTER TWENTY-THREE

People spoke of strange experiences as they made the transition into Game. While some felt nothing at all, a few were aware of a chilling blackness, while others had curious and very vivid dreams. In my case, I was alone on a vast, grey, featureless plain. There was no one in sight, but I could hear the faint whispering of voices.

I stood on the plain, unable to move, for about thirty seconds, and then suddenly I was in a room in Game. I could tell from the design of the room, the shape of the doorways, and the mauve mistiness of the air that this was a house on Ganymede. I was arriving at my new home there as Hawk had promised.

For the next second or two, I still couldn't move, but then I was stepping forward. It was almost like moving in real life, except for a feeling of lightness and well being. I felt as if I would be able to run endlessly and never tire.

I gasped in exhilaration, and was instantly struck by the smell and taste of the air. I'd studied a host of images of Ganymede, but hadn't known that the air here would have its own scent, a distinctive mixture of flowers, spices, and salt. For a second, it confused me, but then I accepted it as part of the uniqueness of Ganymede.

I looked down at myself, and saw I was wearing the blue and silver sleeveless dress I'd chosen for my entry to Game. I lifted my left arm and studied it. The bar code had gone, and instead, spiralling up my forearm, there was a bronze bracelet. Soft, apparently part of my skin, but shining brightly. I ran the fingers of my right hand over it with a smile, and indulged myself by just looking at it for a few minutes. The bracelet summed up everything. After all the years of dreaming and planning, I was really here in Game.

There was an ornate wooden chair standing next to me. I reached out to feel the cool solidness of wood, the smooth polished surface, and the intricate grooves of the pattern carved into it. I was used to the battered plastic furniture in my old room, and now I had furniture modelled on real life antiques. I found myself laughing in an odd mixture of delight and bewilderment.

A soft, automated voice spoke from the air above me.

"Player Jex Thorpe Leigh Grantham, resident of Ganymede, you have a player requesting Game world transfer into your home. Do you accept the Game world transfer request from player Hawk, resident of Celestius?"

"Yah," I said.

I waited, but nothing happened.

The voice spoke again. "Response not recognized. Do you accept the Game world transfer request?"

I realized I needed to use the formal Game commands I'd been taught in school. "Game command. Accept Game world transfer request."

There was a delay of about a minute, and then Hawk appeared next to me, motionless and blank eyed. I stared at him, worried that something was wrong, and then worked out he was still in Game world transfer from his home on Celestius. The process only lasted a second longer. I could tell the instant he truly arrived, because his handsome face filled with life. He took a deep breath, exhaled, and turned to smile at me.

"It feels good to be back in Game." His smile widened as he inspected me. "I like the hair."

I blushed guiltily at Hawk's words. "I planned my Game appearance a long time ago. I like feathered hair. I wasn't copying yours."

"I know." He walked round me, studying me from all sides. "This suits you. The essence of your own face is still there. Many people make the mistake of losing their original selves entirely. I did that with Hawk, making him everything that Michael wasn't. Cassandra was much wiser; her Game face was just a more perfect version of her own younger self."

He shrugged one shoulder in his distinctive way. "It took me decades to understand the full importance of rooting your Game appearance in reality. Game is just a fantasy, a living dream. Your Game persona is a thin layer of illusion, masking your true self that was shaped by experiences in the real world. You have to hold on to that true self, or you'll stop being a person at all, and a vital part of that is seeing something of your real face when you look in the mirror. By the time I had the sense to appreciate that, it was rather too late to change my face to look more like Michael."

I shook my head. "I think there's more of Michael's face in Hawk than you realize. Michael's got black hair too. His eyes aren't as dark as Hawk's, but there's a lot of resemblance in the facial shape and expressions."

Hawk sighed. "I hate it that I can't properly savour this moment with you, but I need to have a quick conference with Kwame, catch up on Game news with Cassandra, and then make a broadcast to the players. Do you mind if I do that here?"

"Of course not. You do what you need to do. I'll wander round the room and get used to being my real self at last."

I looked round the room as I spoke, and had a breathless moment as I saw that translucent drapes were drawn across what had to be a large window. I only needed to draw back those drapes and I'd see the sky that I'd dreamed of for so long. I made an instinctive movement towards them, and then stopped. No, let the drapes stay closed for now. My dreams of entering Game hadn't been of looking at Ganymede's sky through a window, but standing outside and looking up at the magnificence of Jupiter overhead.

"Perhaps after your broadcast, we could go outside together, admire the sky, walk on the beach, and..." I broke off, because I was assuming too much. I had to remember I was talking to Hawk now, not Michael.

"The first time that you look up at Jupiter is unforgettable," Hawk said. "I'd love to share that with you."

While Hawk had been studying me, I'd been absorbing his appearance too. I'd seen a host of Game images of Hawk and thought they were realistic. I'd seen a controlled droid walking bearing his image, and thought that was stunningly accurate too. Now I could see that both those things had just been pale reflections of the original.

Hawk's face was constantly changing expression, each feathered hair on his head lifted and shifted delicately with every step he took, and the exuberant movements of his body were filled with personality. His clothes, layers of glittering black gauze worn over the top of silver chain mail, were totally different to the neat blue tailored outfit portrayed by the droid, and as his left sleeve shifted I caught a glimpse of the dazzling diamond bracelet that marked him out as a Founder Player.

"Game command. Request Game Tech assistance," said Hawk.

Kwame appeared, looking even more startlingly different than Hawk. Previously, I'd only seen Kwame as a standard Game droid with a mask-like image of a face. Now he was fully human and was wearing a Game Tech uniform, the badge golden to match the golden insignia on his face.

"I'd like a similar console setup to the one I use at home," said Hawk. "Please put it over in the corner out of the way. I shouldn't clutter up Jex's new house."

Hawk pointed to a corner of the room, and it suddenly had a set of screens hanging in thin air, with a carefully placed chair in front of them. I was startled to see these weren't modern screens, but dreamlike, surreal representations of ancient computer equipment from four centuries ago.

I frowned. The diamond bracelet on Hawk's arm was a symbol of the status gap between us, and these screens were an uncomfortable reminder of the difference in our ages.

"Thank you," said Hawk. "Now we need to discuss the details of my broadcast. I feel we still can't tell the general player population that a Game Tech was involved in the bombing. In fact, I think we'll need to keep that secret permanently, because destroying the players' trust in Game Techs would leave them living in fear."

Kwame nodded. "The Game Techs strongly agree with you on this point."

"I haven't even told Cassandra that the bomber was a Game Tech," said Hawk. "I hate lying to her, but I also know just how much the truth would scare her. It was frightening enough for me, thinking about how a Game Tech could turn the ground beneath my feet into molten lava, but I had the option to leave Game. Cassandra is trapped here, because she'll die if she tries to defrost."

I stood there watching Hawk talk. Half of my mind was listening to his words, while the rest of it was still absorbing the multiple differences between being in the real world and being in Game. I'd found Hawk's clothes confusing at first. The flimsy, multi-layered black robe, shot through with glittering threads, had seemed curiously impractical for Hawk the Unvanquished. Now I realized that it could be shrugged off in a second to leave him free for action in the silver chain mail.

I was fascinated by that chain mail. As Hawk moved, the robe drifted to reveal shimmering areas of intertwined silver links that clung tightly to him, as flexible as a second skin. I couldn't help wondering whether the chain mail felt hard or soft. I was tempted to reach out and...

"Jex," said Hawk.

I jumped guiltily, thinking for a second I'd not just thought about the action, but actually touched him.

"I'd like your opinion of this too. I can't tell the player population the full truth, but I need to say something to boost their confidence. We've made progress. Harper is far less dangerous as a player than he was as a Game Tech. The situation has improved, and I need to find a way to convey that improvement to the players."

Hawk paused. "I'm thinking of telling people that Tomath was the one organizing the bombings. He's now dead in the real world, but we're still searching for his accomplice, the Reaper, who helped with minor jobs."

I blinked. "You're planning to reverse the truth, claim that Tomath was the bomber and the Reaper just helped out with minor jobs? Isn't that likely to annoy the Reaper?"

Hawk grinned. "I'm hoping it won't just annoy the Reaper, but make him so furiously angry that he can't resist attacking me."

I chose my words carefully. "I'm not sure that's a good idea. The Reaper may have changed himself from a Game Tech to a player, but he'll still be dangerous."

"The Reaper has hidden himself among fifty billion players," said Hawk. "We seem to have no way to track him down, so the only way forward is to provoke him into doing something that gives away his new identity."

"Yah," I said doubtfully, then remembered I was a player in Game now and should speak properly. "I mean, yes," I hastily corrected myself, "but using yourself as bait to lure him out is asking for trouble."

"The Reaper shouldn't be able to bomb server complexes any longer, so he can't crash the Game world that I'm visiting. He can't get through the security at the United Law facility to harm my freezer unit either. If there's no way for him to attack me in the real world, he'll have to attack me in Game, and I'm a legendary fighter."

I groaned. "I still think this is a bad idea."

Hawk waved both hands, palms upwards. "Cassandra told us that the players are getting hysterical. I have to tell them something reassuring. They'll be a lot happier if I say that the bomber is dead, and we just have to tidy up the loose end of finding his accomplice in Game."

"Exactly what are you planning to tell the players about Tomath?" asked Kwame. "It would be unwise to add further fuel to the existing anger against teenagers in the real world."

"There was a point when Jex, Nathan, and I thought that the bomber might be a player in Game who was a current or past member of a server complex maintenance team," said Hawk. "I can use that idea now."

"This version of events seems highly preferable to publicizing the truth," said Kwame.

"I'll just give a bare outline of the story in this broadcast," said Hawk. "We can tell people more details later, when we've had time to think through any flaws in the story and come up with a convincing motive for Tomath attacking Game worlds."

He moved across to the screens. "I need to talk to Cassandra now."

Kwame nodded. "Please request the assistance of a Game Tech when you are ready to make the broadcast."

Kwame vanished into thin air. I pictured him reappearing in a mysterious backstage area of Ganymede, accessible only to the Game Techs. I found myself imagining those areas as being like the dream I'd had entering Game. Grey and featureless places.

Hawk sat down at his screens, waved a hand, and Cassandra appeared beside him. Not the full Cassandra, just an image of her head and upper body, floating in midair.

"I've prepared a condensed version of the main Game news stories for you," she said.

Text started rolling down one of the screens, and Hawk leaned forward to study it. "What's the general Game mood now?"

"The players are deeply worried about the situation, sympathetic to their hero Hawk, eagerly anticipating what you have to say."

Hawk concentrated on the text floating past his eyes for a moment longer, and then his face suddenly changed. "I don't believe this! One, two, three..."

When he finished counting to ten, he started swearing, using archaic words that no longer carried much meaning. After a few seconds, he got control back, and looked first at me and then at the image of Cassandra.

"Sorry about the language."

I laughed. "I didn't understand most of it. These days everyone tends to say wrecked, or shout about Behemoth's backside, or something more..." I coughed.

Cassandra smiled. "The Sisterhood of Celestius should make you wash your mouth out with soap, Hawk, but I understand your reaction. I'm as appalled as you by what's been happening."

Hawk stood up. "I know you told me people were hysterical, but how could they behave like this?"

"The situation exploded after you defrosted," Cassandra said.

"I made an appeal for calm, but was ignored. You couldn't do anything from outside Game, and I couldn't drag you back here when you were in the middle of chasing the bomber."

I'd no idea what was going on, but I could hardly interrupt an intense conversation between two legends of the Game and demand explanations. Things would surely become clear soon.

"This is my fault," said Hawk. "I told you to announce I'd defrosted to chase the bomber in real life. The population of Game would have taken that as confirmation real life teenagers were responsible for the bombings."

"The situation was already out of control before that," said Cassandra, "and anyway you aren't responsible for the actions of other players."

Hawk ignored her. "Game command. Request Game Tech assistance. Kwame, get back here right now!"

Kwame appeared and gave him a reproving look. "You wish the assistance of an appropriate Game Tech?"

"I wish to strangle someone," said Hawk. "I've just discovered why you said it would be unwise to add further fuel to the existing anger against teenagers in the real world. How did the Game Techs let things get this bad? Witch hunts in Game!"

I blinked. What did Hawk mean by witch hunts?

"Emotions ran very high at the Avalon memorial service," said Kwame. "Every player in Game was watching it, and unfortunate things were said by survivors who were mourning their dead friends and lovers."

"Fifty billion frightened and angry people, Hawk," said Cassandra. "They felt the investigations weren't achieving anything, and the calls for revenge at the Avalon memorial service made some of them decide to take action themselves. Since the bombing was in the real world..."

"So this was just like the panic mass arrest of kids from the body stacks," Hawk's voice was icy with anger. "If you can't get the real bomber, then pick a random target for your rage. Attack the new players who've recently entered the Game."

He shook his head. "Simple logic should tell everyone that those new players must have entered Game before the Leebrook

Ashton bill raised the age for entering Game to nineteen. That means they were in Game themselves when the bombing happened, but logic doesn't matter here. The new players have come from the real world, they symbolize the place that hurt you, so hurl your accusations, insults and stones at them anyway!"

I understood what this was about now. People were being attacked. People who'd recently entered Game. People like me!

CHAPTER TWENTY-FOUR

Hawk glared at Kwame. "Why didn't the Game Techs stop this?"

"We did everything we could," said Kwame. "Initially, only a few new players were being targeted, and we allocated them Game Tech bodyguards. After the speeches at the Avalon memorial, events suddenly escalated."

He waved one hand in a gesture of helplessness. "Every player wearing a bronze bracelet was suffering abuse or worse. Official announcements condemning the behaviour and threatening punishments for the guilty parties had little effect. It was impossible to allocate Game Techs to guard every player wearing a bronze bracelet, especially when our top priority had to be making changes vital to the safety of Game."

"Why didn't you just change all the bronze bracelets into silver?" demanded Hawk.

"That solution was considered. The sole reason players wear a bronze bracelet for their first year in Game is to let other players know they are new to Game and may need assistance. We decided against changing the bracelets. We were concerned it would just increase the problem by making those wearing silver bracelets into targets as well."

Kwame paused. "I assure you that all those wearing bronze bracelets are now safe from harm."

"Safe, yes," said Hawk. "With a choice of being kept under voluntary house arrest for their own protection, or moving to live on a prison world with their fellow social outcasts."

"Indigo is a very beautiful Game world," said Kwame. "These people have the chance to visit a world that would not normally be open to players until the next Game Anniversary, and the Game Techs patrolling there are not prison warders but ensuring their safety."

"Indigo may be positively idyllic," said Hawk, "but it doesn't change the fact that the new players have been driven into hiding there by an angry mob. I've learned a lot about the lives kids lead these days. They spend the first ten years of their lives living in dormitories. If they're lucky, they'll get a call from a parent in Game every week or two which gives them limited protection, but many are totally ignored and an easy target for bullying older children."

"It is unfortunate that..."

Kwame's attempt to speak was drowned out as Hawk ranted on. "At ten years old, they have to leave school, find a place to live, and slave away working twelve-hour shifts every day. It's a harsh existence, and the only thing that keeps them going is their dreams of Game. They spend years planning their Game future, saving every credit they can towards their Game subscription. The new players in Game, the ones wearing bronze bracelets now, must have thought themselves so lucky. They'd just made it into Game before the Leebrook Ashton bill sentenced them to another year of drudgery. They had a few weeks or months in their longed for new homes, were living their dream at last, but now..."

Hawk shook his head. "One minute they had welcoming neighbours and people who were becoming new friends, the next everyone turned against them and they had to go into hiding on Indigo. Do you think they'll ever want to go back to their dream worlds after this? Do you think they'll want to live next door to the people who spat insults and threw stones at them? And what about Jex? She risked her life to keep the players in Game safe. It's obscene to think of those same players attacking her."

Kwame kept warily quiet, and I was too shocked to speak. What Hawk had said about the refugees on Indigo was perfectly true. Their dream worlds would be forever soured for them, the mere mention of their names conjuring up horrible memories. I didn't want to feel that way about Ganymede. I'd spent so many years picturing my idyllic future here. It mustn't become a place like my old dormitory, remembered with a shudder of relief that I'd escaped it. I mustn't risk going out of my house, not even for a second.

I rubbed my hand across my eyes. There'd been the intense strain of the last few days, the nervous high of waking up in Game, and now this hammer blow. I was feeling overwhelmed by it all.

"We can inform all Ganymede residents that Jex is here by your personal recommendation, Hawk," said Cassandra.

"No, we can't," said Hawk. "When we arranged for Jex to be given resident status on Ganymede, we swore the members of the Admission Committee to secrecy about her connection to me."

I frowned. Hawk hadn't told me that particular detail.

"Admission Committee members see lots of confidential information on players' applications for residence," Hawk continued. "They're used to keeping secrets, but we can't expect the whole population of Ganymede to be that discreet. If we tell them that Jex is here by my recommendation, the story will be on every Game news channel within minutes, and the Reaper will see it. There's no point in stopping people throwing rocks at Jex if it means inviting the Reaper to come to Ganymede and do something far worse."

"The protective measures you requested for Player Jex have already been put into place," said Kwame. "It would also be possible to change her bracelet from bronze to silver. Making that change for a single player would have no negative consequences."

"Protecting Jex isn't enough." Hawk turned to face Cassandra. "Do you remember lecturing me centuries ago, Cassandra? I'd been whining about how I'd been bullied as a boy in real life, and you told me that I had the chance to do something about that now. You said that the Founder Players had been given a powerful position in Game, and I could use that power to help people who were suffering from bullying or other injustice. That hit home. I've tried to have Hawk help people whenever possible, and we need to help all the new players now."

"I totally agree," said Cassandra. "The player population wouldn't listen to the Game Techs, they wouldn't listen to me, but they may listen to you, Hawk. There's now less than five minutes to go before your broadcast."

Hawk hesitated. "I can think of one thing I could say to help the new players, but I'm worried it might cause other problems. No, now I stop to think about it, I've already caused those problems."

He slapped his forehead with his right hand. "It was a mistake to tell people that I'd defrosted. It was an even worse mistake to tell them I'd been wounded. I should think harder before I open my big mouth."

"You have four minutes to think hard before you open your big mouth," said Cassandra calmly. "Are you broadcasting from Jex's home, or coming back to Celestius?"

"I don't think I should broadcast at all," said Hawk. "I need to discuss something with Jex. Can we delay this an hour?"

"Do I really need to answer that?" asked Cassandra.

Hawk groaned. "I'll broadcast from here. Kwame, can you make it look like I'm on Celestius?"

One wall of the room turned brilliant white, and then showed an image of a marble tower.

"Three minutes," said Cassandra.

Hawk went to stand in front of the tower. Suddenly it wasn't just an image, the tower seemed to be physically present, appearing through the floor of the room and continuing up through the ceiling. There was an elegant balcony encircling the tower, and Hawk was standing on it.

"Game broadcast channel is now open," said Kwame. "We're running Cassandra's pre-recorded introduction."

"Two minutes," said Cassandra.

"I hate making broadcasts. I hate it. I always hate it," complained Hawk. "Why me? Why do you people always pick on me? Why can't you let me stick to killing monsters?"

I stared at him, drawn out of my personal misery for a

moment by the shock of seeing Hawk totally lose his calm assurance.

Cassandra smiled at me. "Hawk always gets last minute nerves before making a broadcast. One minute."

Hawk buried his face in his hands for thirty seconds, then smoothed his feathered hair into place, and shook his robe into position. He took a deep breath.

"Three, two, one." Cassandra gave a nod.

Hawk looked perfectly calm and relaxed now. "Hello, everyone. I apologize that you haven't had an update from me for a while. Cassandra has already told you that I'd defrosted to chase the bomber. I can now tell you that there were actually two people involved in the Avalon world crash. The bomber had an accomplice helping him with the simpler, menial jobs."

Hawk paused for a second. "The bomber was a lifetime subscription holder who'd been in Game for over three centuries. He'd originally done work involving explosives, before moving to work on a server complex maintenance team, so he was able to use his old knowledge to crash Avalon. The accomplice was another lifetime subscription holder, who was hiding his true identity behind the ludicrous name of the Reaper."

I blinked. Hawk was obviously determined to make the Reaper as angry as possible.

"When I got close to catching the bomber in Game," said Hawk, "he defrosted to hide in the real world, and gave himself a new identity as a man called Tomath. I defrosted too, returning to the real world for the first time in four centuries to chase him down."

Hawk gave a rueful laugh. "Maybe I shouldn't have run off and defrosted like that, but I had two teenagers assisting me in the real world. The plan for hunting down the bomber involved one of them taking huge risks. I felt I couldn't stay safely in Game while that was happening, so I went along to help."

I was still shocked after hearing about the witch hunts. Now I had something new to worry about. I hadn't expected Hawk to mention me or Nathan in this broadcast. How would that affect my situation?

"The plan was that we'd get ourselves recruited to help with the next bombing," said Hawk. "I doubt that we could have fooled Tomath into recruiting us, but fortunately his accomplice, the Reaper, is far less intelligent, suffering from massive ego problems and delusions of being the rightful ruler of Game."

I pictured how the Reaper would feel listening to this broadcast, and choked.

"Not so fortunately, the Reaper's twisted fantasies meant I had to act a part I hated and do dreadful things to please him." Hawk grimaced. "I thought for a while that I'd killed my own assistant, not a Game death but a real death, and I've never felt so devastated in my whole life."

Cassandra's image had been watching Hawk, but now I saw her head turn sharply to look at me instead. Hawk had said the experience of being in a Game body matched real life very closely these days. He was right. I could feel myself growing hot with embarrassment at the curiosity in Cassandra's eyes. I forced myself to concentrate on what Hawk was saying.

"Well, the plan worked. The Reaper recruited me, and sent me off to collect the bombs from Tomath and plant them at a server complex." Hawk spoke in a voice of self-mockery. "You should have seen me back then. Imagine my nerves in case I dropped a bomb. Imagine my joy when I was finally able to dump them. I was just running away when the bomber decided to blow them up and get rid of me."

He paused. "I survived, but the bomber was less lucky. He didn't know that I'd planted one of his own bombs in his room. When he detonated the bombs I was carrying, the bomb in his room exploded too. Tomath was killed, and I'm not crying about that."

He was silent for a moment before speaking again. "I'm back in Game now and hunting Tomath's accomplice. The Reaper isn't nearly as dangerous as Tomath was, but he still has to be dealt with as soon as possible."

Hawk's expression hardened into something cold and grim. "I've one final point to make. Everyone has been understandably distressed and angry about the deaths during the Avalon world crash. Some people have been venting their anger in exactly the wrong direction, attacking the players wearing bronze bracelets. Let me say this one more time to make it absolutely clear. Tomath was a lifetime subscription holder wearing a gold bracelet. The Reaper *is* a lifetime subscription holder wearing a gold bracelet."

Hawk's voice carried an open threat now. "Spread the word that new players in bronze bracelets are to be treated with every respect from now on. One of my assistants nearly died while helping me trap the bomber and make you safe. She's in Game right now, and she's wearing a bronze bracelet. My other assistant will be entering Game soon as well, and he too will be wearing a bronze bracelet. If anyone tries insulting or harming either of them, they'll find themselves in combat with Hawk the Unvanquished!"

Now I understood why Hawk had been talking about me and Nathan in his broadcast. He was using us to make life safe again for all the new players.

"I should have a lot more information for you in my next broadcast," said Hawk, in a friendlier voice, "but that's all for now."

Hawk stood there for a few seconds longer, then the marble tower disappeared and my room returned to normal.

"We're done," said Cassandra.

Hawk stretched his arms out wide, then let them fall to his side with a sigh. "I hate giving speeches. How did it go? Big audience?"

"That is correct," said Kwame. "Estimated at over forty-eight billion."

"What were the other couple of billion doing?" Hawk asked, in mock complaint. "Initial reactions?"

The image of Cassandra showed her holding an elegant hand mirror, and reading the text flowing down it. "I'm scanning the main Game forums now. There's a whole torrent of comments coming in. People are pleased. Feeling a lot safer now. They liked the personal adventure element. Everyone is taking note of the point that both Tomath and the Reaper were lifetime subscription holders. I'm seeing rapid changes of attitude to players in bronze bracelets, and some guilt about the way they've been treated. There's a lot of speculation about your mysterious assistant who nearly died, and jokes about the danger of having to fight Hawk the Unvanquished. People are definitely taking that threat seriously."

"Good," said Hawk. "I want them to take it seriously. I want everyone who's been harassing the new players to picture Hawk appearing in front of them, brandishing a two-handed sword."

Cassandra's smile hovered on the brink of laughter, and I could see why it fascinated people. "I'm afraid people want to watch the replays of you chasing the bomber."

"Replays?" Hawk choked. "What replays? This happened in real life, not Game. It wasn't automatically recorded to be played back for an audience, and I certainly don't want the whole of Game watching surveillance footage of the mighty Michael!"

"I'm sure the Game Techs could modify the images to enhance Michael's appearance a little," said Cassandra.

"A little? They'd have to enhance it an awful lot." Hawk literally cringed at the idea. "I couldn't say in the broadcast that the bomber's second attack was targeting Celestius. It wouldn't have been fair to let the family hear the news from a general broadcast, especially when they might be away from Celestius so outsiders could see their reaction. I have to tell the family first and then include it in my next broadcast."

Kwame frowned. "Is it wise to make that information public?"

Hawk gave him a frosty look. "I'm not keeping it from my family. They have a right to know they may be in specific danger. I hope and believe that we're safe from more bombings, and the Celestius server complex is now under constant Unilaw guard like Avalon, but the Reaper is in Game and might attack Founder Players."

"But..." Kwame began.

"Whether Hawk chooses to make a general announcement or not," interrupted Cassandra, "I will definitely inform the family. Under these circumstances, many of the Sisterhood may wish to stay in safety in Celestius. Few of us are skilled in fighting, or take the pain of Game deaths lightly, and there could be other unpleasantness as well."

Kwame sighed. "Very well. I agree the Founder Players should be informed of the attempt against Celestius, but does the whole population of Game have to know?"

Hawk shrugged. "You should know that Caesar and Blades can't keep secrets. Once they hear about this, the rest of Game will know it within five minutes. Is the Amphitheatre free at the moment?"

"It has been kept free in case it was required for your broadcast," said Kwame.

"Then I'm calling a family meeting," said Hawk. "Cassandra, can you tell everyone that we're meeting at the Amphitheatre in two hours' time, so I can tell them news of the utmost importance."

"I can get them there sooner than that if you want," said Cassandra.

"No, I need the two hours for something else." Hawk smiled at me. "Jex and I are going outside so she can get her first view of Ganymede's sky."

Cassandra had just said there was a lot of speculation on Game forums about Hawk's mysterious assistant who'd nearly died. The second people saw me with Hawk, they'd guess I was that assistant. Images of me would be shown on every news channel, and there'd be a storm of gossip about my relationship to Hawk. I wasn't ready to cope with that. There was the problem of the Reaper too. I seized on that excuse to delay things.

"If you want to hide your connection to me from the Reaper, then it's a bad idea for us to be seen together. I'd rather wait a few days to make sure that the problems for new players are over before going outside anyway. There's no rush to see the sky."

"Oh yes there is," said Hawk. "You've been looking forward to seeing Ganymede's sky for years, Jex, and you aren't going to wait any longer. Since you're a potential target for the Reaper, the Game Techs have taken special measures to protect you, including putting your house on its own private beach. That means you don't have to worry about hostile neighbours, and if a wandering shell collector does happen to stumble on this beach then..."

He shook off his black robe, revealing the shimmering chain mail underneath, and raised his right hand. "Durendal!" he ordered.

Durendal, the great blade that Hawk had wielded to slay the Kraken, flew out of the sheath strapped across his back. The sword hovered in midair above him, Hawk took hold of its hilt, and his dark eyes laughed at me.

"No one will dare to harm you, Jex. Not when you have a legendary warrior guarding you."

CHAPTER TWENTY-FIVE

I lay on the fine sand of Ganymede's shoreline, gazing up through the misty air at the vastness of Jupiter filling the sky. Its swirling storms glowed with multicoloured light, in an ever-changing kaleidoscope of patterns. Jupiter was both terrifyingly menacing and stunningly beautiful.

"I've seen hundreds of images of Ganymede's sky, but actually lying here and looking up at Jupiter is overwhelming. It's like I'm not just seeing it, but physically feeling its presence."

Hawk was standing next to me, watching my expression and smiling. He was still holding his sword, Durendal, the naked blade gleaming red as it reflected the light of Jupiter.

"Ganymede is one of the worlds that players either love or hate," he said. "It all depends on whether you find the massive bulk of Jupiter hovering over your head glorious or horrifying. Some people take one look at the sky and instantly decide to leave. Others want to stay forever."

He paused. "Do you find Jupiter glorious or horrifying, Jex?"

"This will sound silly," I said, "but I don't know. When I look up at Jupiter, I'm not sure if I'm trembling with delight or with fear, and somehow the contradiction adds to the fascination."

"Yes!" Hawk made a flourishing gesture with Durendal that would have impressed even Falcon, before sheathing the sword and lying down on the sand beside me. "I understand exactly what you're saying. When I look up at Jupiter, I feel the same mixture of joy and panic that I feel going into battle against a vast Game creature like the Kraken."

He gave a joyous laugh. "I suspected you would feel that too. The first time I saw you, when you were being questioned at that Unilaw facility, you grabbed my attention. All the other kids, even Nathan, were tongue tied with fear, but you kept arguing your cause. I could see from your face that you were just as scared as the others, but in you the fear was blended with anger in the distinctive mix that makes a true fighter."

I turned my head towards him, and found myself gazing straight into his intent, dark eyes. He smiled, but I could feel myself growing hot with embarrassment, so I hastily stared upwards at Jupiter again.

"I've always had an anger problem," I said. "I've fought against it all my life, tried to train myself to keep my temper under control, but it's still got me into trouble several times over the years. Back when I was six years old, I lost my temper with the dormitory bullies, flew at them in anger, and got a blow to my forehead that put me in hospital for two days. Look!"

I pointed out the faint white line just below my hairline, and Hawk propped himself up on one elbow as he turned to examine it. "You chose to keep the real life scar on your Game face?"

"Yah. I mean, yes. Every time I look in the mirror, I see the scar, and tell myself it's better to think things through than blindly lose my temper."

"Does that work?"

I was intensely aware of his face being close to mine, and wondered if he was planning to kiss me. "You should know that it doesn't. Remember how I screamed at you about the black mark on my record that had destroyed my Game future? Remember how I lost my temper with Falcon and threatened to cut his ears off? When I was arrested and questioned about the bombing, I was lucky that I was too scared to lose my temper."

"I hope you aren't angry with me about what I said in my broadcast," said Hawk. "I knew I should have discussed it with both you and Nathan first, but there wasn't time."

His face moved away from mine, and he lay back on the sand

again. I was both relieved and disappointed. It occurred to me that I had the same contradictory feelings about Hawk as I did about Jupiter.

"I understood exactly why you mentioned us," I said. "The whole of Game was watching that broadcast, so you had the perfect opportunity to change people's attitudes to the new players. It worked. Now everyone's feeling guilty about how the new players have been treated, so it should be safe for the refugees to leave Indigo. A lot of them won't want to go back to their old homes, but decide to make a new start elsewhere in Game, and hopefully the guilt reaction will mean they're near the top of the queue for resident status on worlds instead of last in line."

I paused to laugh. "I've just realized that I haven't looked at my own new house yet. When I stepped outside, the sight of Jupiter was so mesmerizing that I just rushed to the beach and lay down to look at the sky."

I stood up and turned to look at my house. It was how I'd always pictured it, a graceful seashell shape, woven in mauve and white spider silk, with a pink flowered creeper climbing up one side.

I spent a full minute admiring the house before I turned again to look at the view along the bay. The sea glittered in ever-shifting shades of red and mauve, with a fringe of white foam where waves were hitting the beach. The sand was white too, but with a hint of delicate pink. I noticed another house further along the beach, frowned, and pointed at it.

"I thought you said this was a private beach, so why is there another house here?"

Hawk stood up too, his face flushed with embarrassment. "That house is mine. Founder Players have castles on Celestius, but we're allowed to have ordinary houses on three other worlds as well. I wouldn't want to force my company on you, so I wouldn't live in that house except at your invitation, but I need to have a house here so I can reach this place quickly. The Game Techs have set this beach up as a restricted destination, so only residents can request teleport or world transfer here."

"That's another protective measure because I might be a target for the Reaper?"

"Yes. It's not totally impossible for someone to walk here, but it would take them a long time."

I shook my head. "Are these precautions really necessary?"

"Definitely. My plan is to do everything I can to anger the Reaper, and then parade myself around Game in the hope that he can't resist attacking me. The Game Techs will be watching and waiting for that to happen. When the Reaper attacks, they'll just need a minute or two to work out his new identity number, and after that the Reaper is doomed. Whether I kill him in the fight and he resurrects, or I take him prisoner, or he manages to kill me, it will make no difference. The Game Techs will be able to track him anywhere he goes, and arrange to teleport him into a Game prison."

Hawk paused. "The one big flaw in my plan is that the Reaper knows I've had four centuries of combat experience. Game Techs do test fights against Game creatures, but nothing to compare with the scale of fighting I've done. Basic common sense should tell the Reaper that attacking me will end in him getting captured, put on trial, and probably sentenced to be expelled from Game and executed in real life."

"You're right. If the Reaper has any sense at all, he won't attack you."

"My big worry is that I'll goad him into going for an alternative target instead, someone that he should be able to kill fast enough to escape before the Game Techs get his identity. If all the other Founder Players take refuge in Celestius, then the Reaper's obvious choice of an alternative target is you."

I shook my head again. "I'm not important enough for the Reaper to risk attacking me."

"Do you remember how I opened my big mouth and let the whole Game population know that Hawk had defrosted to chase the bomber and been wounded?"

"Yes."

"I was tired and in pain, so I didn't think through the consequences of saying that. It told the Reaper that Michael had really been Hawk, and since Hawk wouldn't casually cut a girl's throat in real life that meant Emma's murder had been faked."

Hawk groaned. "Thanks to my stupidity, the Reaper knows that two people fooled him with a fake murder. Two people wrecked his plan to crash Celestius and kill hundreds of Founder Players. Two people drove him into giving up his Game Tech powers and becoming an ordinary player."

He paused. "When we visited the bomb site, I kept introducing you and Nathan to people. The Reaper will have seen reports about that. He might even have had a controlled droid there himself, wearing a false face with bronze or silver status insignia, so he could enjoy viewing the havoc he'd caused in safe anonymity."

I thought of all the droids at the bomb site, imagined one of them being controlled by the Reaper, and pictured him watching Hawk, Nathan, and me. "Ugh."

"The Reaper will have worked out that if Michael was me, then Emma must have been my assistant, Jex. He'll hate you nearly as much as he hates me."

I imagined the Reaper searching for me, finding me, and coming to inflict the most painful Game death he could on me. I sat down on the sand again, reached out my hand to pick up a tiny shell, intricately patterned in ivory and mauve, and stared fixedly at it so that Hawk wouldn't see the fear in my face.

"So I'm supposed to stay hiding alone on this beach?"

"I'd prefer us to either be here together, or travelling together, most of the time," said Hawk. "If the Reaper tries attacking us, then I can defend you. The problem is that I'll sometimes need to go to places where you can't accompany me. Family meetings are traditionally held in the Amphitheatre rather than on Celestius itself, but they're strictly private."

He sat next to me. "When I have to be away, then I want this beach to be a safe hiding place where the Reaper can't find you."

I didn't like Hawk's assumption that I was a poor defenceless creature that had to be hidden away from the Reaper. My fear changed into anger, and I dropped my shell back on to the sand and turned to look Hawk in the eyes. "Would it really be such a bad thing if the Reaper found me?"

Hawk gave me a disbelieving look. "Of course it would be a bad thing. If the Reaper attacked you, there'd be no way for you to escape. Game is designed to prevent players from using Game teleport or world transfer commands to leave a combat area. If people losing a fight could just run away in the middle, then all the Game duels and fights with monsters would just be a farce."

"I know. Once the Reaper attacked me, I couldn't use a Game command to leave the combat area, but neither could he. I'd just need to stay alive for the minute or two it took the Game Techs to get his identity."

"A minute is a very long time in a fight, Jex. An experienced fighter can kill a novice in a few seconds. The Reaper would kill you and escape before the Game Techs had a chance to find out his identity. You'd die pointlessly, and a player's first Game death is always a traumatic experience."

"A Game death would hurt, but it wouldn't be permanent," I said, trying to convince myself as much as Hawk.

"I'm the one playing bait to bring the Reaper out of hiding, not you," said Hawk flatly. "Game is designed to mirror the experiences of real life as closely as possible, so your Game death would be excruciatingly painful. Believe me, I know this only too well, because I've died a lot of times over the centuries."

"Stop and think about this for a moment."

"I don't need to think about it. You're an easy target. I'm not."

"Which is exactly why my plan is better than yours. The Reaper isn't likely to risk attacking you, but he could be tempted to attack me. We just need to arrange for me to be out in public somewhere with Game Techs watching me, and have someone give away the fact I'm your assistant."

I paused. "There'll be reports on all the Game news channels within minutes. The Reaper will see them and have to make a snap decision on whether he grabs his chance to attack me. If he believes the news has leaked accidentally, he'll think I'll be a quick, easy kill."

"He'll be right too."

"Not if Hawk the Unvanquished gives me combat lessons."

Hawk actually stopped to consider that for a moment. "I'm sure I could train you to be a lethal sword fighter, but that would take months or years rather than weeks. However, I've just thought of a crucial point. You couldn't use Game commands to run away from your fight, but I could use them to join it."

"So I'd just have to stay alive and fighting the Reaper long enough for you to arrive and help me kill him. How long would that take?"

"Game world transfer involves extra delays while the system checks things like visitation rights," said Hawk, "so we'd have to set things up for me to be on the same world as you and use Game teleport to join you. I'd still take almost a full minute to go through the transition process though."

He frowned. "Given the circumstances, we might be able to talk the Game Techs into giving you enhanced armour to help you stay alive in the fight until I join you. We can discuss this with Kwame after my family meeting. Let's get back to enjoying the view of Jupiter for now."

We lay back on the sand again. I stared at the ever-changing storms of Jupiter, and tried to work out if I was pleased or terrified that Hawk was taking my suggestion of playing bait for the Reaper seriously now. At the moment, terrified seemed to be winning. A few minutes ago, I'd been explaining to Hawk how my anger had got me into trouble in the past. Now it had driven me into volunteering for something that I probably wouldn't be able to handle.

"Did you know that I originally planned to call myself Hercules," said Hawk, "but someone else grabbed the name?"

I grinned with relief at the change of subject. "Let me guess. Would that happen to have been the Founder Player called Hercules?"

"Yes. We had to do a month of tests before we entered the Game. Hercules is a malicious person who likes making other people miserable, and he spent the entire month targeting me. We went through Game registration in alphabetical order, so he was ahead of me picking his Game name, and grabbed Hercules because he knew I wanted it. That left me with only a couple of minutes to choose myself a new name. The Game Company had been encouraging us to choose names out of old legends, preferably Greek or Roman, but my mind went a complete blank and I couldn't think of any of them. I decided to call myself Hawk as a temporary solution, but ended up keeping it."

He laughed. "Hercules stole my name, and I've spent four hundred years beating him up in duels to punish him for it. He's refusing to fight me anymore. These days he just sends me messages saying 'Let's save time, Hawk. You win.'"

"I don't blame Hercules for refusing to fight you," I said. "Hawk the Unvanquished is bound to defeat him every time."

Hawk rolled on his side to face me, and put his arm round me. The links of his chain mail armour were surprisingly warm and soft against the bare skin of my arm. I was hit by a tense feeling that wasn't panic but was its very close relative.

This wasn't Hawk as Michael. This was Hawk as I'd seen him receiving the champion's crown of the Battle Arena on Medieval, this was the Hawk who was the General of the army of Ruby on Civil War, this was the glittering hero who could take his pick of the twenty-five billion women in Game and couldn't possibly be interested in me.

The glittering hero couldn't possibly be interested in me, but his hand was gently pulling me close to him. His lips pressed against mine, and I felt a dizzying mixture of fear and delight. Getting involved with Hawk was foolish, dangerous, and an utterly irresistible prospect.

Hawk drew away again. "Jex," he murmured, "I know I promised I wouldn't rush things, but..."

He broke off because an automated voice was speaking from the air above us. "Player Hawk, resident of Celestius, you have an emergency priority incoming call from United Law facility 814. Do you accept the call?"

"Why?" Hawk tipped back his head and yelled his frustration up at Jupiter. "Why now? Couldn't you have waited five more bleeping minutes before...? Oh, all right. Game command. Accept call."

Nathan's head and shoulders appeared, hovering in midair

in front of us. I saw his eyebrows fly up in speculation as he saw us lying on the sand with Hawk's arm round me. "I'm sorry to interrupt you," he said.

I hastily shuffled further away from Hawk, and felt his arm holding me back for a second before he groaned and let me go.

"I'm sorry you interrupted us too, Nathan," said Hawk. "I don't suppose it can wait until later?"

"Erm, not really. The Game investigation has asked me to tell you some very important news."

"And it can't be good news, or they'd have told me themselves," said Hawk wearily. "What's happened now?"

"The Game Techs have been checking up on Harper's recent actions," said Nathan. "You know that Game items, especially weapons, have different abilities added to them. To put it very simply, a sword has the ability to cut a player. A club has the ability to cause blunt trauma."

"I know." Hawk sat up. "There were errors making weapons a few times, where the wrong ability got added to something. Hercules got hold of a dagger that didn't stab you, but hit you like a massive club. He nearly got me in that fight, but I managed to... Anyway, I understand what you mean."

"Well, all the standard items are made by an automated process," said Nathan, "but Game Techs also have a process that lets them make individual enhanced items with any of a huge list of useful abilities. Every item that's made that way is recorded on an audit trail, but there was no record of anything ever being made by Harper."

I sat up too. "He must have made some items in four centuries. If there are no records left at all, then he must have deleted them to hide something."

"Exactly," said Nathan, "but this time Harper missed something. He didn't know that Kwame's team had set up an automated process to make copies of key audit trails at random intervals. The Game Techs have been going through those old copies, and found one that shows Harper made some enhanced items a couple of days ago."

"What sort of enhanced items?" asked Hawk.

"One was a tracking item. The Game Techs use those to track the location of problem players as they move through Game. There was a weapon too. The audit trail was copied at the instant the weapon was completed, so it's impossible to tell if Harper made any other items after that."

I didn't like the sound of this. I didn't like it at all. "Harper made these items a couple of days ago. By then, all the Game Techs had been told that one of their own people was involved in the bombing. Harper was getting worried, so he made himself these enhanced items in case he had to use his escape route and become a player. He'll have either found a way to take the items with him during his escape, or hidden them somewhere so he could collect them when he was a player."

Hawk nodded. "We have to assume that Harper has all the items he made with him right now. I suppose the weapon has an exceptionally nasty ability."

"Yah," said Nathan, in a despairing voice.

"Since you can't make yourself say what that ability is," said Hawk. "I'm guessing that means it's the worst thing imaginable. Harper's got a weapon that can erase a player's mind from the Game."

CHAPTER TWENTY-SIX

"I'm afraid you're right," said Nathan miserably. "Harper made himself a deletion weapon."

"What?" I shook my head in disbelief. "How is something like that possible? Why would the Game Techs have a process that can make weapons to delete players?"

"Deletion weapons are designed to work on Game creatures not players," said Nathan. "When players lose a fight in a hunting zone, the zone is supposed to reset automatically after the last player in the combat area dies, and that reset dispels the monster. However, there's sometimes a glitch when a major monster kills multiple players simultaneously. The zone reset fails to happen, the monster stays active in the hunting zone, and any spectators are stuck there unable to leave. The simplest way to sort out the situation is to send in a Game Tech with a deletion weapon."

He sighed. "One scratch from a deletion weapon is enough to deal with even the Behemoth. Unfortunately, it's relatively easy to modify a deletion weapon so it works on players as well as Game creatures."

"Is it possible to track the location of this weapon?" I asked, without much hope.

"Only a few very significant items, like the Monarch's Crown on Civil War, or Excalibur on Camelot, are designed so their location can be tracked within Game," said Nathan.

I assumed that meant no. Hawk had buried his face in his hands. Now he looked up again, and shouted at the top of his voice.

"Game command. Request Game Tech assistance. Kwame! Now!"

A moment later, Kwame appeared in front of us. "Requesting the presence of a specific Game Tech by name is a severe breach of protocol."

Hawk stood up and glared at him. "One of your Game Techs crashed Avalon, killed eleven thousand players, and is running amok in Game right now with a deletion weapon. Do you seriously want me to waste time discussing this situation with a random, bronze status Game Tech?"

"Point," said Kwame. "However, using the phrase 'appropriate Game Tech assistance' would communicate the fact that your request was connected to the Reaper situation, and I would respond in my current role as crisis co-ordinator."

Hawk didn't bother to reply to that. "The Reaper has an item that lets him track players in Game, and it's painfully obvious that he'll have been using it to track me. He'll have watched me appear in Game on Celestius. He'll have seen me use Game world transfer to come to Jex's house here on Ganymede. He'll know I'm on this beach right now. He could appear right in front of us at any moment."

I pictured that happening, the Reaper appearing in front of us, and the combat that would follow. Hawk was a legend in Game, with four centuries of fighting experience, but it would only take one scratch from a deletion weapon and he'd be gone forever. I was glad that I was still sitting down, so I could force my hands deep into the sand to make sure they didn't tremble.

"Only residents can teleport to this beach," said Kwame.

"You just appeared here and you aren't a resident. Game Techs can use teleport to appear anywhere in Game. They can even enter houses without the owner's permission if a player's safety is thought to be at risk. Are you totally sure that the Reaper hasn't made himself an enhanced item that will let him do the same thing?"

Kwame frowned. "We are confident that the Reaper cannot bypass the integral Game design measures controlling access to Game Tech areas and Celestius. Given the Reaper played a key part in the original design of the Game, it is hard to rule out the possibility of him having an enhanced item that gives him access to other areas."

"Even if he can't teleport here, the Reaper could get here by walking, and I'll need to leave Jex alone soon to go to my family meeting."

"I will arrange for a team of Game Techs to watch the house, the beach, and all approach routes," said Kwame.

Hawk rubbed his forehead in the gesture that he only used when under extreme stress. "There's also the problem of what I say at the meeting. How can I explain to my family that the Reaper's got hold of a deletion weapon without admitting he's a rogue Game Tech?"

Kwame started speaking but Hawk lifted a hand to stop him. "Don't try suggesting that we keep the existence of this weapon secret. I'm not letting my family roam round Game worlds in the belief that the worst the Reaper can do is inflict a Game death on them. Not even Hercules deserves to be wiped out of existence with a single slash of a sword or stab of a knife."

Nathan coughed nervously. "I watched your broadcast, Hawk. You said that the bomber was the dangerous one, he'd been in Game for over three centuries, and had worked on server complex maintenance teams."

"Oh yes." Hawk winced. "I told the whole of Game that the dangerous bomber was dead, and the Reaper was just a harmless errand boy with an ego problem."

"I've been reading about what happened after the Rhapsody world crash three centuries ago," said Nathan. "There was a massive effort to increase the number of servers for each Game world from two to four. To speed the process up, the maintenance staff were given temporary access to Game Tech systems."

"Point," said Kwame. "The maintenance staff were only given very limited system access to allow them to run tests on the new server configurations, but we could claim that the bomber was accidentally given access to the tools for creating enhanced Game items."

Hawk nodded. "So I have to tell people that the bomber was

the one who created the enhanced items. When he decided to defrost from Game, he gave them to the Reaper for safekeeping."

He paused. "All right. Kwame, Nathan, I'll talk to you later."

Kwame vanished into thin air.

Hawk waited a bare second before speaking again in a pointed voice. "Goodbye for now, Nathan."

"Oh. Right. Goodbye." Nathan's image vanished as well.

I was still being distracted by nightmare visions of Hawk fighting the cloaked figure of the Reaper. The pair of them circled each other, swords clashing, and then the Reaper's blade caught Hawk's finger. It was the tiniest of cuts, but it was enough. The Reaper pulled down the hood of his cloak, and his skull face laughed as Hawk faded away and vanished.

The sound of Hawk's voice brought me back to reality. "We have to forget the idea of you playing bait for the Reaper, Jex. It's far too dangerous. I'll draw the Reaper out of hiding myself."

"No," I said sharply. "If playing bait is too dangerous for me, then it's too dangerous for you too. The Reaper would only need to scratch you once to delete you from the Game. There'd be nothing left of you but an empty shell of a body in a freezer unit."

Hawk gave his characteristic one-shouldered shrug. "I should be able to hold out long enough for the Game Techs to get the Reaper's identity before he deletes me. If I can kill him before he deletes me that would be even better."

He laughed, but I didn't find it funny. I remembered what Hawk had said back on another beach in the real world, about how a hero versus a god doesn't usually end well for the hero.

Hawk turned grim again. "I'm sorry, Jex. I hate saying this, but you have to defrost from Game. Right now."

"What?" I shook my head. "I'm not defrosting."

"This beach isn't a safe hiding place any longer. The Reaper could come here, erase you from Game, and I…"

Hawk broke off for a second before speaking again. "I couldn't cope with that, Jex. You have to defrost from Game and stay safely in a United Law facility while I deal with the Reaper."

"I'm not going to sit uselessly in a United Law facility, waiting to hear if you've got yourself murdered. The Reaper will probably do the sensible thing and stay safely in hiding. The situation could drag on for years, decades even."

"It won't," said Hawk. "I'll play target. Lure him out. We'll get him."

"No!" I folded my arms. "I refuse to leave Game. If the Reaper knows that I'm on Ganymede, then I can change my Game appearance and hide on a different world."

As I said the words, I realized that would only work if I stayed away from Hawk, left the hunt for the Reaper, gave up Ganymede, and abandoned Jex of the silver, feathered hair to give myself a new name and appearance. What would I be left with after that? Perhaps I'd be better off leaving Game after all. At least then I could be with Nathan, talk to Hawk in Game, and stay part of the hunt for the Reaper.

"It's too late for you to try hiding from the Reaper," said Hawk. "He's been tracking me. He'll have found out your identity number by now, so he can track you anywhere you go in Game."

He paused. "You have to defrost, Jex. As soon as I've dealt with the Reaper, you'll be able to re-enter Game. The Leebrook Ashton bill specifically states that anyone who has entered Game counts as legally adult, so you won't have to wait until you're nineteen. You can stay at the United Law facility with Nathan until..."

A musical chime interrupted him, and Hawk groaned. "I need to get to the Founder Players' meeting and break the news to them about the attack on Celestius. I'll escort you to your home now, and the Game Techs will stand guard over you until I'm back. We'll finish this conversation then."

I didn't want to go back to my house, but Hawk wouldn't leave until I did, and I couldn't make him late for this meeting. It was going to be agonizingly hard for him to tell the other Founder Players, his family, about the intended bombing of Celestius.

We walked back towards my house. I'd been looking forward to living in a house of my own ever since I was a small child. I couldn't let the Reaper snatch it away from me and force me out of Game. There was Hawk too. The gulf between the two of us was too wide already, and it would grow wider with every day we were apart.

"I'll stay in the house while you go to the meeting," I said, as we went inside, "and then we'll discuss how best to handle this situation. You wanted us to see if things could work between us. Me running away and defrosting, while you stay here risking your life as bait for the Reaper, isn't the way to start a relationship."

Hawk went across to sit at the screens in the corner. "There's no need to discuss this situation. You have to leave Game, Jex. If you won't call for defrost yourself, then I'll have to do it for you." He waved a hand at the screens.

All my pent up fury at this situation abruptly focused on Hawk. "Whether I defrost or not is my decision! No one can force me to leave Game if I don't want to go. I've already paid my first annual subscription."

"What's happened?" asked Cassandra's voice. "Who's trying to force you to leave Game, Jex?"

I gave a startled look at the screens, saw her image had appeared on one of them, and felt myself flush in embarrassment.

"Jex has to leave Game until I've caught the Reaper," said Hawk. "The Game Techs have discovered the Reaper has a deletion weapon. It can erase a player from Game, destroying their mind, and I'm afraid he'll use it on Jex."

"It could be years before you catch the Reaper," I said fiercely. "You may never catch him at all. I'm not going to hide in a United Law facility in real life until I die of old age."

"You have to leave Game, Jex," said Hawk. "I understand you'll hate me for making you defrost, but I'd rather you were alive and hating me forever than have you left as a mindless frozen body in a freezer unit."

Cassandra gave us a worried look. "I must go to the meeting now, Hawk. Everyone's already at the Amphitheatre waiting for us." Her image disappeared.

"I have to go too," said Hawk. "I'm sorry, Jex, but... Game command. Request Game world transfer to the Amphitheatre."

He vanished.

CHAPTER TWENTY-SEVEN

I drew back the drapes covering the great expanse of window in the downstairs room of my house, and stood there for a long time, staring out at the incandescent beauty of Jupiter. My anger had an edge of depression now. Jupiter was even more magnificent than in my dreams, but I'd always pictured my father being here with me on Ganymede, and I could only share its beaches with his memory now.

I blinked away moisture from my eyes, turned my back on the window, and tried to comfort myself with the fact that I was far more hopeful about my relationship with my mother now. I thought back through that last conversation with her. She'd forced herself to speak about a dreadful past experience because she was worried about me. I couldn't ask her to visit me on Ganymede, it held too many bad memories for her, but perhaps she'd invite me to visit her on Coral one day.

I walked up a spiralling corridor to another room full of clothes and other fripperies. Depression had beaten my anger into submission now. It had been stupid of Hawk to order me to defrost from Game rather than let me make my own decision, but it would be equally stupid of me to react by stubbornly insisting on staying in Game whatever the consequences.

The harsh truth was that if I stayed in Game I wouldn't be a help but a liability. A team of Game Techs would have to guard me day and night, and I wouldn't dare to go anywhere near Hawk in case he got himself deleted trying to defend me from the Reaper.

I let out my breath in a long sigh of defeat. I loved my new house, but I had to leave it and go back to the real world. I'd have to spend endless days and nights at a Unilaw facility, waiting for the Reaper to attack Hawk, and knowing there was no guarantee that Hawk would win that fight. The Reaper wouldn't just be armed with a weapon that could erase Hawk from existence, but could have other items that gave him extra advantages as well.

I sighed, picked up a hand mirror, tapped the glass, and sent a message to Nathan asking him to call me on a secure line. There was only a moment's delay before his face appeared in the mirror. The scene behind him showed that he was sitting at the bank of screens in his apartment.

"Hi Jex." He whistled in appreciation. "You look really glitz."

I saw the expression on Nathan's face, instinctively glanced downwards at myself, and belatedly realized the dress I was wearing had a hint of transparency in certain areas. The effect wasn't blatant, just a little suggestive, and I had more important things to worry about right now.

"Hawk wants me to defrost and join you at the United Law facility," I said bluntly. "He's worried that the Reaper will be tracking both of us by now, and may attack me with his deletion weapon."

Nathan's face twisted in sympathy. "I'm worried about that too, Jex. I understand how much you'd hate leaving Game, but it's your safest option."

"I know that."

"This isn't a bad place to be," Nathan added. "I'm having a great time."

"You're having a great time playing with Game training texts. I'm not interested in that technical stuff." I waved my free hand in dismissal. "Forget that for now. I called you because you mentioned the Reaper could have made other enhanced items as well as the tracking item and deletion weapon. He can't have anything that makes him stronger or faster than other players, can he? If he does, then Hawk won't stand a chance."

"The Reaper can't possibly have superhuman strength, or speed, or anything else," said Nathan. "All players have exactly the same basic abilities. The sole individual variation is the fitness factor, whether you've been training hard or not, and that has only a small effect on things like your strength."

He paused for a moment. "I'm perfectly sure about this, because the Game Techs wanted to give Hawk temporary superhuman abilities to help him defeat the Reaper. Unfortunately, that's impossible without redesigning the whole player area of Game."

"That's a shame."

"Yah, though making Hawk superhuman would have set a dangerous precedent."

"Who cares about that?"

"The Game Techs do," said Nathan. "If Hawk was given superhuman abilities to defeat the Reaper, then half the fighters in Game would start demanding them for trivial reasons."

I shrugged. "Since it's impossible to give Hawk superhuman abilities, it doesn't matter. Can the Game Techs give Hawk enhanced armour to help him?"

"Armour only reduces the amount of injury from an attack. It couldn't stop Hawk from being deleted."

I groaned. "At least the Reaper's totally limited to using the enhanced items he's got already. He can't enter the backstage areas of Game, so he can't reach the Game Tech systems to..."

I let my words trail off as a thought nagged at me. I started my sentence again. "The Reaper can't enter the backstage areas of Game unless he changes back into a Game Tech."

Nathan gave me a puzzled frown. "I don't know why you're looking so worried. You've just said the Reaper can't reach the Game Tech systems, so he can't change himself back."

"I accept the Reaper can't change himself back," I said urgently, "but he could get the Game Techs to do it for him. He just has to fool them into recruiting him as a new Game Tech!"

"Point." Nathan had a look of agony on his face. "The Reaper could have set up his new identity with the Game record of a perfect candidate for Game Tech, added himself to recruitment lists, and... I'll warn the Game investigation team that they must stop all recruitment of new Game Techs until the Reaper is caught. If he got back into the Game Tech areas, he could use his back door into the security system again and do anything he wanted."

I knew what this meant for him. "I'm sorry, Nathan."

"Members of the Game investigation team have been hinting I'd be recruited," he said mournfully. "It even sounded as if they were considering giving me an exemption from the Leebrook Ashton age rule, the same way they did with you, so I could enter Game and become a Game Tech right away. The Reaper has ruined everything though. I suppose I should have known it was too good to be true. I need to talk to people now so…"

I nodded. "Bye Nathan."

I ended the call, and went back down the spiralling corridor to sit by the vast window, with its panorama of Ganymede's beach and sky. Eventually a disembodied voice spoke to me.

"Player Jex Thorpe Leigh Grantham, resident of Ganymede, you have a player requesting Game world transfer into your home. Do you accept the Game world transfer request from player Hawk, resident of Celestius?"

I stood up. "Game command. Accept Game world transfer request."

Hawk appeared, dressed in a silver cloak emblazoned with a hawk in flight, and wearing a silver circlet on his black, feathered hair. He saw my stunned expression and blushed.

"Official family meeting. Formal dress required. Coat of arms and crown compulsory. Personally, I think it's silly dressing up like this, but some of the family are romantics. The rest of us go along with it as harmless fun."

"Is the meeting over now?" I asked.

Hawk's look of embarrassment changed to one of utter weariness. "No, we're just taking a break to give people time to recover from shock. Initially, the family took the news that the bombs were intended for the Celestius server complex fairly well, but then they started thinking through what could have happened. A third of us dead. The whole Sisterhood wiped out. Avalon can rebuild, but we could never have brought back Celestius without…"

He broke off before finishing the sentence, and shook his head. "I was thinking things through too, and was hit by just how close Celestius came to disaster. If the two of us hadn't tracked down Tomath. If we hadn't fooled the Reaper with that fake murder. If the Reaper had planted the bombs himself using a controlled droid instead of getting me to do it."

I reached out a hand to touch his arm. "Celestius is safe, Hawk."

He was under attack by nightmare visions, and barely aware of me. "There would have been another set of bomb craters, my whole family would have been dead or broken, and it would have been my fault."

This time I gave his arm a shake. "Celestius is safe," I repeated.

Hawk's eyes focused on me this time. His face was still twisted in pain, but he was back in reality. "First I terrified the family with the news of the bombing, and then I made things worse by telling them the Reaper has a weapon that can delete players from Game. Perhaps I was wrong to pile all these horrors onto them, but they need to know that they're specific targets. They've got the right to be given an idea of relative risks, and consider their best options for staying safe."

He'd moved on from picturing nightmares, only to start beating himself over the head with misplaced guilt feelings. I tried distracting him.

"I talked to Nathan. We realized the Reaper might have set things up to get himself recruited as a Game Tech again."

There was alarm in Hawk's face now. "We'd better..."

I interrupted him. "Nathan's already warning the Game Techs that they have to stop all recruitment until the Reaper is caught. Obviously, Nathan knew what that meant for him."

"Poor Nathan. Had the Game Techs said anything about recruiting him?"

"He said they'd been hinting about it."

We sat in silence after that until the disembodied voice spoke again. "Player Hawk, resident of Celestius, you are being offered a Game world transfer to the Amphitheatre by player Cassandra, resident of Celestius. Do you accept the Game world transfer offer?"

"The meeting must be reconvening," said Hawk. "I hope they don't ask me too many awkward questions. When people have known you for centuries, it's easy for them to spot when you're lying."

"Player Jex Thorpe Leigh Grantham, resident of Ganymede," said the disembodied voice, "you are being offered a Game world transfer to the Amphitheatre by player Cassandra, resident of Celestius. Do you accept the Game world transfer offer?"

"What?" I gasped. "Why me? You said that your family meetings were strictly private."

"Cassandra wants you present as a witness," said Hawk. "You helped stop the bombing, so the family may have specific questions for you."

The disembodied voice nagged us. "Response not recognized. Do you accept the Game world transfer offer?"

"Game command. Accept Game world transfer offer," said Hawk, and he vanished.

I gulped. I was about to face the massed Founder Players of Celestius in the famous Amphitheatre of Game. "Game command. Accept Game world transfer offer."

CHAPTER TWENTY-EIGHT

The Amphitheatre was used for the most important meetings in Game. I'd often seen images of it when I watched Game news channels. Its design was based on the old Roman amphitheatres, with an oval, flat area that was surrounded by banks of seating. There was no countryside or city around it. The Amphitheatre was made of glowing marble, and hung alone in the blackness of space, lit by a host of bright stars hanging above it.

The Game Techs adjusted the size of the Amphitheatre according to the number of seats needed. Sometimes it was vast, holding hundreds of thousands of people. Sometimes it was tiny, with just a few dozen players present. Now it was scaled to hold the Founder Players of the Game, fewer than a thousand people.

I stood in the centre of the Amphitheatre, watching the legendary ones arriving by Game world transfer. They were all dressed in either silver or gold, their cloaks bore individual emblems, and their crowns varied from simple circlets to large and ornate creations.

"Jex." The word seemed to echo round me.

That was Hawk's voice. I turned towards the sound, and saw him beckoning me to a line of seats at one end of the central area. I went and sat down next to him. We were the only ones sitting here, so I assumed these seats were reserved for witnesses.

"We'll sit here until we're called to answer questions," said Hawk. "Have you been in the Amphitheatre before?"

I gave him a look of disbelief, and he slapped his forehead with the palm of his right hand.

"No, that was a stupid question. You can tell the pressure is getting to me. Well, when you stand up, everything you say is automatically broadcast for the whole audience to hear." He grinned. "That can be embarrassing if you do it by accident."

The Amphitheatre seats were almost full now. Mostly with people wearing silver, but there was a thin scattering of gold among them. I studied them for a moment, spotting the familiar faces of my childhood heroes, and worked out the colour system.

"The female Founder Players wear gold, and the male ones silver?"

Hawk nodded. "The Sisterhood wear gold."

"The Sisterhood," I repeated. "Am I right in thinking the female Founder Players act as an organized group?"

"Of course they do. They're outnumbered ten to one by men. At the beginning of the ten year trial period of Game, they had terrible problems. Obviously not with me." He made a gesture indicating innocence. "I was a nice, shy boy."

I frowned. "The Game Techs didn't keep order in the Game back then?"

"Well, they did their best, but remember that they were outside the Game during the ten year trial, and they'd no real penalties they could impose on anyone. Game development had got behind schedule. The Game Techs' top priority had been getting things like player senses working properly, but even there they'd had to cut corners by leaving out the sense of smell. The world construction was in a much worse state, still riddled with major problems like trees flickering in and out of existence, and there were vast, blank areas where the scenery hadn't been added at all. With so many other things to worry about, it wasn't surprising that the Game Techs hadn't even got as far as thinking of things like Game prisons."

He sighed. "Once a few of the leading male troublemakers realized they could get away with almost any behaviour, the situation started spiralling out of control. Not that it was always the men to blame, some of the women were stirring up trouble as well, but..."

He let that sentence trail off, and hurried on with another. "Anyway, the women got together, formed the Sisterhood, and called in all their husbands and friends to help them try to impose a system of law and order. I had to decide if I wanted to stand idly by watching innocent people being randomly attacked, or volunteer to join the Sisterhood's efforts. I ended up as one of Cassandra's bodyguards, so Hawk the Unvanquished was right in the middle of the action, killing people."

I stared at him. "You weren't really killing other Founder Players?"

"Only when necessary to defend Cassandra, or rescue someone else from trouble. I remember thinking it was like the plot of one of the old style games I'd been playing, where I was fighting to restore order in a war torn land, except this was a game where things like pain were too horribly real."

"But what were the Game Techs doing during this?"

"Throwing fits and threatening to defrost the lot of us," said Hawk, "but we knew they couldn't do that. Abandoning the trial would have sent the Game Company straight into bankruptcy."

He shrugged. "Eventually, things calmed down, and Cassandra and Pendragon organized a series of meetings. The whole family discussed what rules we should impose, and agreed on punishments for misbehaviour. Mostly involving guilty parties being confined to their castles for appropriate lengths of time. We adjusted the rules over the next couple of years, and got everything reasonably settled by the end of the trial period. Celestius has been run according to those initial rules ever since."

"What are these rules?"

"Given our unique circumstances on Celestius, we needed a few special rules to stop troublemakers disrupting relationships, but the rest are almost identical to the rules in the rest of Game. In fact, the Game Techs based most of the Game rules on ours. A big stabilizing factor in Celestius was bringing in a system where each of the female players acts as sister to some of the men. I was lucky that Cassandra was grateful enough for my help to agree to be my sister. She was married to Pendragon for the first few decades in Game, but then they split up and I optimistically suggested Cassandra and I could be more than brother and sister."

"Since she's been married to Thor for over three centuries, I'm assuming Cassandra said no."

"Cassandra said a painfully polite no." Hawk winced at the memory. "She explained that she was very fond of me, but her feelings towards me were motherly, if not grandmotherly. She said that was because of the real life age difference, I was eighteen and she was seventy-three, but we all knew we were living in Game permanently by then so I thought age didn't matter. I assumed it was really because I'd been so ghastly as Michael."

I laughed. "Michael isn't as bad as you think."

"No, he's much worse," said Hawk. "Now I can see Cassandra's point about age. As I told you before, experiences in the dreamlike existence of Game don't change your personality. Cassandra had lived for seventy-three years in the real world, buried a husband and a daughter, and suffered a long terminal illness. She's a wise and compassionate woman, while I'm an eighteen-year-old boy with emotional problems. She knows all about my Hawk act, and the fact that you only have to scratch the surface of the legendary hero to find Michael underneath."

I was about to reply, when I saw Cassandra had moved to stand in the centre of the Amphitheatre. When she spoke, her voice was broadcast across it.

"We are all present once more, except for our two brothers who are indisposed."

I didn't understand her words for a moment – no one was ever ill in Game – but then I remembered there were two Founder Players under house arrest.

"This meeting is now in session," she continued. "Hawk mentioned some surveillance footage to me, so I've requested it from the Game Techs."

"Oh no." Hawk made a whimpering noise.

"It's all right," I whispered. "The Game Techs will have edited out anything awkward."

"They won't have edited out Michael!"

A flat screen appeared in midair at the far end of the Amphitheatre. There was a pause while a few people changed seats to get a better view, then the screen started showing heavily edited surveillance footage of Michael and Emma talking to Tomath.

"If I suddenly vanish," whispered Hawk, "I've suffered a Game death from embarrassment and I'll be back after I resurrect on Celestius."

"You don't look any worse than I do," I whispered back.

The Founder Players didn't seem interested in our looks, just in what was happening. The scenes with Tomath were followed by Michael and Emma at the dormitory, receiving the call from the Reaper. Hawk cringed as he watched Michael yanking at Emma's hair. I felt like cringing too, because my Emma persona looked scared senseless through the whole thing.

When that sequence ended, a male voice called out from the audience. "You still aren't very good with girls, are you, Hawk?"

"This isn't a time for jokes, Hercules," said Cassandra.

"I'll kill him," muttered Hawk.

It was the murder scene next. When I saw my "death", I could see why it had scared Michael so much. Falcon had clearly got even better at faking injuries since winning the area championship. My throat seemed to have been cut to the bone, and there was blood everywhere.

We then had Michael cutting the medical chip out of his arm with a knife. I turned my head away and watched the audience during that bit. Some of them seemed to be avoiding looking at the images as well.

Finally, there was a few seconds of Michael on the buggy, and getting blown up by the bombs. The screen went blank, and there was a long silence before Cassandra spoke again.

"Hawk, can you stand please?"

He stood up with a barely audible sigh.

"Let's go over the current situation again," she said. "I think a lot of people were too shocked to take in all the details the first time you explained them. The bomber is dead, but his accomplice, the Reaper, is still in Game?"

"Yes."

"You don't know anything about the Reaper, except that he's male and a lifetime subscription holder?"

"That's right."

"You told us that the Reaper has a deletion weapon. This could remove a player from the Game, without allowing their consciousness to return to their real life body. In effect, permanently killing them, although the physical body would remain in the body stacks."

"Yes," said Hawk. "There's a danger the Reaper will attack someone with this deletion weapon to take revenge for Tomath's death."

"You believe that the Reaper is likely to direct his attacks primarily at you and Jex, because you prevented the Celestius bombing and killed Tomath, but any Founder Player is a potential target?"

"Unfortunately, yes," said Hawk. "The Reaper sees himself as the rightful ruler of Game, and bitterly resents the fame of the Founder Players."

Cassandra nodded. "Then we have two main issues to discuss. Is Celestius safe now, and are we as individuals safe when we leave it? Game command. Request Game Tech assistance."

Kwame appeared before Cassandra had even finished saying the words. He'd obviously been waiting to be called.

"Is Celestius safe?" asked Cassandra.

Kwame's face was calm and controlled, but his body language looked nervous to me. "Maintenance crews no longer have any access at all to the Game Tech systems. Extensive changes have been made to protect force field codes. Any request for a code must now be confirmed by multiple gold status Game Techs. Once a force field code has been supplied to a maintenance crew, it will automatically change within two minutes."

I admired the way that each individual sentence was true, but the total implied something that wasn't.

"The main Celestius server complex is now under constant

guard by armed Unilaw officers," said Kwame. "While you were all in the Amphitheatre earlier, we took the opportunity to adjust the Celestius server configuration to include servers at two different secret locations. All three server complexes would have to fail for Celestius to be harmed."

I blinked. I remembered a Game Tech explaining they'd need to shut down a Game world to reconfigure its servers, so Celestius must have briefly vanished from Game. I could see why the Game Techs had grabbed their chance to do that furtively. Players wouldn't react well to the suggestion of shutting down their Game world at any time, but it could trigger blind fury in these circumstances.

I wondered what the Game Techs had done with the two Founder Players under house arrest while they shut down Celestius. Presumably there'd have been some time taken up running tests as well. Had Marcus and Chiron spent a confusing hour or two in a Game prison?

The silver-cloaked figure of Atlas stood up in the audience, and called out in a bitter voice. "Very nice, but why didn't you do these things centuries ago? If Hawk and... what's her name, Jex, hadn't stopped the bomber, my wife would be dead!"

"I understand and share your anger," said Cassandra. "We will return to that point later, but for now we need to focus on the issue of our future safety. Hawk, do you believe the new arrangements are secure?"

"I can't think of any weaknesses," said Hawk.

"So Celestius should be safe," said Cassandra, "and the Reaper will not be able to reach us while we remain there. The problem is what happens when we go to other worlds. Are we even safe here in the Amphitheatre?"

"At this moment," said Kwame, "Amphitheatre access is routed via Celestius. Manual intervention by Game Techs was required to bring Jex here."

"So the main danger to us will be if we leave Celestius to visit other worlds?" asked Cassandra.

"That is correct," said Kwame.

"I'm hoping the Reaper realizes he may only get one chance

to attack someone," said Hawk, "and that he saves his anger for me, but I'd still advise the rest of the family to stay on Celestius."

Merlin rose to his feet, his skin shimmering with the glitter effect that marked residents of Starlight. "I've just come here from Starlight. Stella had finally agreed to meet me and talk things over. We were going to try to ignore all the gossips and make things work again, but this changes the situation. If I go back to live with Stella on Starlight, will I be putting her life at risk as well as my own?"

"I'm afraid so. You shouldn't assume that you'd be safe even within Stella's house. As I said, the Reaper's preferred targets are going to be myself and Jex. My plan is to wander round the worlds outside Celestius, parading myself as a target until the Reaper attacks me."

"Won't he guess it's a trap and just stay in hiding?" asked Fleur.

"I'll just have to be so tempting that the Reaper can't resist trying to kill me permanently," said Hawk.

"If Hawk needs to be irresistible, we'll all be stuck on Celestius for centuries," called Hercules.

"And what of Jex?" asked Cassandra.

"She wanted to play being target as well," said Hawk, "but she hasn't my combat experience so that would be suicidally dangerous. I've told the Game Techs that Jex will be defrosting immediately after this meeting for her own protection. She can remain safely under guard at a real world United Law facility until we've caught the Reaper."

Fury hit me. I'd reluctantly accepted I should leave Game, but Hawk hadn't bothered to ask my decision. He'd just told the Game Techs I was defrosting. I jumped up and shouted in outrage.

"Hey! I'm not a criminal. You can't just tell the Game Techs to throw me out of..."

I broke off, realizing my shouts were being broadcast around the Amphitheatre, echoing like thunder, and all the Founder Players were staring at me. I gulped, hesitated, and sat down again.

"Jex risked a real life death to save Celestius," said Cassandra. "It hardly seems fair to reward her for that by forcibly removing her from Game and imprisoning her in a United Law facility."

"Of course it isn't fair," said Hawk. "It wouldn't be fair if the Reaper erases her mind from Game either."

Cassandra looked at Kwame. "Game Tech?"

"Player Hawk had not made it clear that the defrost request was being made without player Jex's consent," said Kwame. "There is no precedent for removing a player in good standing from Game against their will."

"This meeting is now in temporary recess," said Cassandra. "I request the Sisterhood to accept my Game world transfer offer to my castle on Celestius."

She vanished. The rest of the golden cloaks rapidly disappeared from the Amphitheatre as well until only silver were left.

Hawk turned to Kwame. "If you haven't got a precedent, you'll have to create one."

Kwame shook his head. "The Game Techs must be wary of setting precedents. They will inevitably be cited by other players making similar requests."

Hercules promptly stood up in the audience. "If we can request that Game Techs throw people out of Game, I want Hawk thrown out."

Hawk glared at him. "I challenge! Name the time and place!"

"I'm not fighting you again," said Hercules. "You've killed me about two hundred times already."

"Chicken." Hawk turned back to Kwame. "You have to make Jex defrost, or she could be murdered right under your nose."

I sat listening to the argument and wondering what to do. After all the fuss, it would be embarrassing to interrupt and explain that I'd been angry at Hawk ordering me around but I'd already decided I should leave Game. I glowered in Hawk's direction. This situation was all his fault.

Someone sat down next to me. I turned my head, startled, and saw a heavily muscled giant of a man, with blond hair and a taste for clothes made out of leather. Hercules had come to talk to me.

"Hello, Jex." He stared down at my legs.

"Hi, Hercules," I said warily.

"Emma looked nice, but you look even nicer."

He lifted his head a little, and focused his eyes on my neckline. I wished I'd changed clothes before coming to the Amphitheatre. I felt the ideal costume for sitting next to Hercules would be heavy plate armour.

"Everyone looks a lot better in Game," said Hercules. "Especially Hawk. Didn't you think Michael was repulsive?"

I felt like insulting Hawk myself, but I didn't appreciate hearing Hercules doing it. "No. In fact, I couldn't see why Michael had such a complex about his appearance, but now it makes far more sense to me. You had a whole month to undermine his confidence before entering Game."

Hercules laughed. "You're giving me far too much credit. Someone else had undermined Michael's confidence before I even met him. I just had to complete the good work."

If I'd had a knife with me at that moment, there'd have been Game news channel headlines about me stabbing a Founder Player.

Hawk spotted Hercules sitting next to me, abandoned his argument with Kwame, and came to stand pointedly looming over the two of us. Hercules smiled smugly up at him, before turning his attention back to me.

"Perhaps we could get together some time, Jex. I'd like to get to know you a lot better."

I gave him my most insincere smile. "That's very kind of you, but the answer's no."

"Don't tell me you're Hawk's exclusive property."

"I'm a free agent," I said, "but I know perfectly well that you're only asking me out to try and provoke Hawk into hitting you in front of a Game Tech. I suppose your plan is that the Game Tech will be forced to intervene, and then you can enjoy Hawk getting lectured on Game rules section 3 in front of all the other Founder Players."

Hercules grinned at me. "You're a smart girl. I can understand why Hawk loves you. Always."

He stood up, waved cheerfully at Hawk, and headed back to the main Amphitheatre seats.

Hawk stood there scowling for a moment longer, before sitting down beside me again. "Perhaps I could arrange for the Reaper to delete Hercules from Game."

I laughed. "Why did Hercules quote what you said to me when we faked you cutting my throat? Surely he knows that was just part of the act."

Hawk stared up at the stars overhead. "Hercules has been studying me for four centuries, working out every weakness he can attack. He knows I wouldn't have said those words unless they were true."

"What?" I stared at him, shocked and disbelieving. "We've only known each other for a few days, and a lot of that time you were just controlling a droid from within Game."

"I know it's far too soon to make declarations," said Hawk. "I only said that I loved you because of the situation. I was Michael again. I was going off with the Reaper, and there was a fair chance I'd die. I was in real life, so it wouldn't be a temporary Game death, but very permanent. I wanted those words to be the last thing I said to you, even if you thought I was just acting."

I couldn't cope with discussing this right now. I was too annoyed by Hawk trying to force me to defrost. I was too aware of the host of male Founder Players still lounging in their seats and watching us. I changed the subject instead.

"Why do you and Hercules have this long running, childish feud? If it's because he stole your name, you should forget it. Hawk suits you much better."

"I was irritated about the name, but then we entered Game and I decided I preferred being called Hawk. The situation improved between me and Hercules, because he was too busy chasing after Fleur to spend time tormenting me, and we were actually allies during the big period of fighting. The problems started up again when the First Wave arrived in Game. Hercules liked showing off to them, but I was much better than him at fighting the big monsters, so the new players admired me more than him. When they started calling me Hawk the Unvanquished, Hercules bitterly resented them not giving him a title too, and started playing malicious tricks on me. Then Fleur dumped him, Hercules blamed me for their split, and our feud became very, very, serious."

I didn't like the sound of that. "You and Fleur were...?"

"Fleur would have laughed in my face if I'd tried approaching her. What happened was Hercules rigged a booby trap at their castle, and invited me over in the hope I'd walk into it. Unfortunately, Fleur came home unexpectedly. She walked into the trap instead of me, a huge cannonball landed on her head, and she got Game killed. When she resurrected, she was coldly furious, and dumped Hercules on the spot."

I shook my head in disbelief. "I'm not surprised Fleur dumped him, but why did Hercules blame you for what happened? It sounds like it was entirely his own fault."

Hawk sighed. "Hercules wasn't going to blame himself, was he? Fleur never forgave him for killing her. She'd suffered years of pain in real life, entered Game to escape it, and..."

Hawk broke off and stared at the centre of the Amphitheatre. All seventy-nine female Founder Players had appeared there, in thirteen neat rows of six golden-cloaked figures, with Cassandra standing at the front.

"Oh no," muttered Hawk. "They're in war formation. Please don't let them be after me."

"Game Tech," said Cassandra, in a voice of ice.

Kwame stepped forward to face her, looking utterly terrified.

"When we entered Game, many Founder Players were warned a normal defrost would be dangerous for them due to their ill health," said Cassandra. "Is it true that an emergency, high-speed defrost would be fatal for the people given that warning?"

"That is correct," said Kwame.

"So all of those would have died if the bombing of Celestius had succeeded?"

"That is correct."

"That includes the entire Sisterhood?" Cassandra stared at him in accusation.

He nodded.

She was out for her pound of flesh. "I'd like your verbal answer for the record. That includes the entire Sisterhood?"

"That is correct."

I was feeling sorry for Kwame by now. After all, none of this was his personal fault. Cassandra still hadn't finished though.

"Will all male players who received that warning please stand?"

Many of the silver-cloaked figures around the Amphitheatre stood up. I was somehow startled to see Caesar was among them.

"All of those Founder Players currently standing would have died." Cassandra threw the accusation at Kwame.

"That is correct."

"In the light of that, the Sisterhood of Celestius wish to make a request."

Kwame seemed to be holding his breath as he waited for her to continue.

"We wish to offer Founder Player status to Jex," said Cassandra.

CHAPTER TWENTY-NINE

Reality blurred and fell apart, so I totally missed the conversation for the next few minutes. When I finally got my brain working again, there was a debate going on about precedents. I glanced at Hawk. He was listening intently with a worried expression on his face.

"The Game Techs must be wary of setting precedents. They will inevitably be cited by other players making similar requests." Kwame said the same words he'd said earlier. I guessed that he was quoting from the Game Tech regulations.

"In this case, we would hope there could be no similar requests. Or," asked Cassandra acidly, "do you expect Celestius to face destruction on a daily basis?"

"Point," said Kwame. "It's just that I have to pin this down exactly. You know what happened when we allowed you to bring partners to Celestius, and giving someone Founder Player status is far more drastic."

I noticed that Kwame had stopped using formal Game Tech speech patterns. He was losing his grip on this situation too.

"So," he continued carefully, "you're speaking on behalf of the Founder Players of Celestius? They're requesting that Jex be given Founder Player status in recognition of her key role in preventing the bombing of the Celestius server?"

"I speak on behalf of the Sisterhood of Celestius," said Cassandra, "however I'm sure the entire family will agree that it's unfair that Jex should be forced to leave Game when she saved our lives. She may not be safe anywhere else in Game, but she would be safe on Celestius."

"This isn't a temporary measure?" asked Kwame. "You don't want Jex's Founder Player status to be removed when the situation becomes safer?"

"Founder Player status has always been permanent," said Cassandra. "We didn't want to set a precedent for removing it when our brothers became... ill, and we don't want to set one now."

She gestured around the Amphitheatre. "All of us were given Founder Player status as a reward for risking our lives by joining the Game for the ten year trial. Without us, there would be no Game today. Jex would be given Founder Player status as a reward for risking her life to stop the bombing. Without her, there would be no Celestius today."

Kwame brightened up and went into formal Game Tech mode again. "That is correct. We do have an existing precedent for this. May I withdraw and confer with other Game Techs while you take a formal vote of all the Founder Players?"

"The Sisterhood have already voted on this matter, and are unanimously in favour," said Cassandra, in a meaningful voice, "but I will take a formal vote of the rest of the family as well. Does anyone have any questions to ask before that formal vote is taken?"

Kwame vanished into thin air. There seemed to be a lot of urgent conversations going on in the audience. I wasn't sure if that meant the male Founder Players were against me being given Founder Player status, or just startled by the suggestion.

Hawk shook his head. "I can't believe this is happening."

I frowned at him. "You don't seem very happy at the idea of me becoming a Founder Player."

"Of course I'm happy. It means you can stay in Game and be safe on Celestius. It's just that on other worlds people see what we choose to let them see, and the Founder Players are glittering legends. Here on Celestius, all the masks that we hide behind are gone, and we're our real selves."

He groaned. "I've plenty of friends here, but I've got enemies too, particularly among the single men. They'll be eager to cause trouble between us, by telling you all my faults and describing every mistake I've made in the last four centuries. I can see Hercules is starting his attack already."

I turned my attention back to the Amphitheatre, and saw Hercules was standing up in the audience.

"We've never had anyone join us before, so can you clarify the rules regarding Jex?" he asked.

Cassandra nodded. "Jex would naturally be a member of the Sisterhood, and have our full support against any attempts to disrupt her chosen relationships. As always, the sole condition applies that her chosen relationships should not impinge on a prior, publicly declared relationship of any other sister."

"Jex has told me she's a free agent," said Hercules, "so I'd like to make it clear I'm interested in a relationship with her."

I heard Hawk muttering at my side. "I'll kill him. Very slowly and painfully. Over, and over, and over again."

Cassandra sighed. "This isn't the time or place for making relationship offers, Hercules. Does anyone else have questions, or are we ready to vote?"

There was silence.

"Very well," Cassandra said. "Please stand if in favour of the invitation to Jex."

There was a ripple of silver around the area as male Founder Players stood. Hawk sighed and stood up with them. After a moment, they all sat down again.

"Against?" asked Cassandra.

They all remained seated.

I gripped the cool marble arms of my seat. "This can't be happening," I murmured. "This really can't be happening."

"The Founder Players of Celestius have voted unanimously in favour," said Cassandra. "Player Jex Thorpe Leigh Grantham, resident of Ganymede, is to be given Founder Player status as a reward for risking her life in the real world to stop the bombing of the Celestius server complex. Without her actions, there would be no Celestius today."

She turned to smile at me. "Welcome player Jex, resident of Celestius."

I glanced hesitantly at Hawk. "What do I do now?" I whispered. "Ask for a Game Tech to…"

"You don't need to do anything." He pointed at my left arm.

I looked down and saw the bracelet on my forearm was sparkling diamond.

CHAPTER THIRTY

I'd been a Founder Player living on Celestius for nearly two weeks now. Hawk had been away for most of that time, wandering hopefully round other Game worlds, braced ready for the Reaper to attack him. In fact, Hawk was supposed to be away right now, but instead he was standing opposite me on the balcony of the highest tower of my castle.

He gave me an anxious look. "I don't understand why you aren't shouting at me."

A pair of winged horses flew by the balcony, and started playing hide and seek in the drifting white clouds below us. I made the mistake of looking down at them, and caught a glimpse of an emerald green coastline a dizzying distance below the clouds. I'd always thought that Celestius having castles in the air was a charming idea, but castles on the ground seemed far more appealing at the moment.

I forced my attention back to Hawk. "Do you want me to be shouting at you?"

"It would make a lot more sense to me. I can see it was unreasonable of me to come dashing back to Celestius to interrogate you about why you'd been visiting Merlin's castle, and I've seen you lose your temper before. Like when you were telling me about having your Game future wrecked by Unilaw questioning."

"I shouldn't have screamed at you about the Unilaw questioning," I said. "It wasn't just unfair when I knew you weren't the one who'd decided to bring all the kids from the body stacks in for questioning, but incredibly dangerous as well. You could have reacted by sending me and Nathan back to the body stacks. Instead, you got both our records cleared, and those of all the other kids as well. I was so grateful for that. I'm still grateful for that. I admire the way that your own experiences of bullying have made you try to help others."

Hawk was still looking worried. "And you lost your temper again when I tried to force you to defrost from Game."

I stabbed a forefinger at him. "You deserved to get yelled at that time. You don't make my decisions for me."

Hawk lifted both hands in surrender. "I knew I'd no right to force you out of Game. I was just terrified that the Reaper would delete you from existence."

He paused. "Anyway, what's worrying me is that both those times you lost your temper over things you really cared about. If you're staying so calm about me doing something that could totally mess up our relationship, then maybe that means it isn't important to you."

"It's not that I don't care about our relationship," I said. "It's that I understand why you behaved that way. Before I became a Founder Player, I was feeling horribly insecure about our relationship. Now you're feeling just as insecure."

"I didn't believe the message from Hercules," said Hawk. "I guessed he was just saying you were dumping me for Merlin to cause trouble between us, but then Lancelot called me and he said that..."

I lifted a hand to stop him. "Let's forget all about what Hercules, Lancelot, or anyone else told you. I hope that if you hear any more gossip about me, then you'll try to trust me rather than panicking."

"I'll do my best."

The two winged horses stopped playing hide and seek, and came skimming across to hover, feathered wings beating like those of hummingbirds, next to our balcony. Hawk moved to sit on the parapet and leaned out to stroke them.

"Would you please stop doing that?" I said, in a tense voice.

Hawk pulled his hand back and gave me a confused look. "I thought you liked the winged horses."

"I love the winged horses. I'm just worried about you sitting on the parapet and leaning out over a sheer drop."

He was obviously even more confused now. "You were sitting on this parapet with me a few days ago."

"Yes, but two hours ago I nearly plummeted to my death, and I'm still feeling a bit nervous about heights."

Hawk frowned. "You fell off this balcony?"

"I didn't fall off this balcony. I went for a ride on a winged horse, so I could admire the sight of my castle floating above the clouds. I was having a wonderful time until I reached out to try to stroke a passing bird and fell off my horse."

I shuddered as I remembered that dreadful moment. "The ground was rushing towards me, and I was panicking too much to think. I was about to be hit in the face by a mountain, and achieve fame as the first person foolish enough to suffer a Game death by falling off a winged horse on Celestius, when I finally had the sense to scream a Game command and teleport home to my castle."

"You wouldn't have been the first," said Hawk. "Caesar killed himself falling off a winged horse the day after the Game Techs introduced them to Celestius. No one would have thought you especially foolish anyway. We've all made glorious fools of ourselves many times in the last four centuries. Hercules killed Fleur with that booby trap, Uther sank his own castle, even Cassandra has had her embarrassing moments."

"How do you sink a castle?" I asked.

Hawk gave me a joyous grin. "Uther overloaded it. He wanted his towers to be bigger than anyone else's towers. When the Game Techs made the requested changes, the castle plummeted from the sky, landed in mid-ocean, and sank underwater. I'll show you the replay of it later. It's hilarious."

I laughed. "Didn't the Game Techs realize that would happen?"

"Well, they claimed they didn't, but we had our suspicions they sank the castle deliberately. Uther had been annoying them for years, constantly asking them to make adjustments to his castle. They're quite happy to make occasional changes, and they're expecting you to want quite a lot done to this place because it's new, but Uther was hassling them every few hours."

"I think my castle is perfect the way it is." I made a sweeping gesture to indicate the delicate towers around us. "I love all the flowering creepers growing up the walls, and the way the roofs of the spires are woven in spider silk like the houses on Ganymede."

Hawk stood up. "If you're feeling uncomfortably high up here, why don't we ride a winged horse down to the surface of Celestius? We could visit a private beach of mine."

I shuddered again. "I'm not ready to get back on a winged horse yet."

"I was thinking that we could both ride on the same horse. I could hold on to you very tightly so you couldn't possibly fall off."

There was something odd about his voice when he made the suggestion. I looked at him suspiciously. "That sounds like it could get a bit intimate."

"Not really."

I narrowed my eyes. "So if Hercules suggests taking me for a horse ride, I can happily accept?"

"All right," Hawk admitted. "Celestius is the only place with winged horses. I've never been on the right terms with any of the women here to try it myself, but I gather that sharing a horse is regarded as one of the erm... fringe benefits of having a relationship with another Founder Player rather than an outsider. Apparently, the wing movements... Don't laugh like that."

It was at least two minutes before I finally managed to stop giggling.

"So," said Hawk, "you can fulfil my wildest erotic fantasies by flying on a winged horse with me, or we could just ask for a Game teleport to the beach."

I grinned. "Difficult decision. Very difficult."

He sighed. "Game command. Request group teleport to Hawk private beach."

A minute later, I was standing on a beach. This was very

different from the beaches on Ganymede. There were grey and white pebbles worn smooth by the sea. There were gulls circling over the blue-green of the ocean, their high-pitched cries cutting through the background sound of wind and waves. The sea breeze was chilly and held a strong tang of salt mixed with a faintly unpleasant smell of seaweed.

After two weeks of the ornate loveliness of the scenery in Game, this place seemed remarkably ordinary to be Hawk's private beach. When we started walking along, the pebbles bruised my toes through my dainty shoes.

That reminded me of something. It took me a moment to track down the memory. "We sat on a beach like this in the real world, when we were talking about… about children. This place isn't based on that beach, but one from further along the same coastline, isn't it? It's the beach from your childhood."

Hawk smiled. "Yes, this is where I played as a child. I asked for it to be copied, so I could come here, forget about Hawk, and remember who I really was. The beach just ends in grassland though, there's no road and no house. I felt that copying the house, the furniture, and my old room, would be where sentimentality crossed the line into being morbid."

I nodded, and looked across at the grassland. "Can we walk over there for a bit? I need tougher shoes to cope with these pebbles, and I don't want to teleport back to my castle just to change my shoes."

Hawk took my arm as we walked across to the long, wiry grass. There were just a few scattered flowers in pink and blue, instead of the mass of colours you'd expect in Game. They seemed all the prettier for being scarce.

"So what have you been doing since I last saw you?" Hawk asked.

"I've mostly been adjusting to living in Game instead of real life. That's been much harder than I expected. It isn't one big thing, but a whole host of little differences. Like the way the days are so long and the nights are so short."

"Celestius has the standard Game day and night length," said Hawk. "There's no need for nights to be more than a couple of hours long when people don't sleep in Game. If someone particularly enjoys night skies, they can go somewhere like Starlight or Harvest Moon."

"That's another thing," I said. "Why does Celestius have three identical moons in different colours?"

Hawk grinned. "Because of a programming error."

"What?"

"It was a mistake that crept in when the Game Techs revamped the original Game world and made it into Celestius. It was a while before they had time to fix the error, and by then we'd got fond of our moons and wanted to keep them. Celestius has had a triple moon ever since."

I laughed. "As Hercules helpfully told you, I visited Merlin's castle. The poor man had been messaging me every day to ask for updates on the hunt for the Reaper. He's terrified that he's going to lose his last chance of salvaging his relationship with Stella. He's been calling her every few hours, but that isn't the same as visiting in person. Anyway, I ended up going over to Merlin's castle and talking to both of them. I told them that they just have to wait patiently."

"They could have a very long wait," said Hawk gloomily. "I've done everything I can to tempt the Reaper to attack me. I even agreed to let the Game Techs release that surveillance footage of the awful Michael."

I shook my head. "There's nothing awful about Michael, and anyway the Game Techs enhanced those images beautifully, so we look almost like our Game selves."

"I still look like Michael to me, and I hate everyone in Game watching replays of me murdering you. I thought it would make the Reaper so furious to have the whole population of Game watching us trick him, that he'd be bound to attack me, but it's achieved nothing. I'm starting to worry that the Reaper will never attack me."

Hawk looked deeply frustrated at this idea, but I secretly hoped it was true. These days, I was only too well aware that behind Hawk the Unvanquished was a very vulnerable Michael, and that every incredible victory over one of the challenges of Game had been hard earned by many failures and a lot of temporary Game deaths. If the Reaper attacked Hawk, then there would be no second chances, because death would be real and permanent.

"I visited Cassandra's castle as well," I said, "and I've been calling a lot of people including Nathan and my old friends from my medical cadet days."

"How did your old friends react to you becoming a Founder Player?" asked Hawk.

"Diane, Bevan, and Chen were a bit tongue tied. Gina seemed to cope a lot better. We did a lot of talking about what happened when I was thrown off the medical course. The instructor told the rest of my class that I'd been lying to them about my grades for years. Gina didn't believe that, but she couldn't do anything about it."

Hawk slapped himself on the side of the head. "I forgot to contact my expert. If there's any evidence of your instructor changing the records, she should have found it by now."

"It doesn't matter any longer. Gina told me that when the news broke about me becoming a Founder Player, the instructor instantly quit her job. Silly of her. Even if we'd found enough evidence to get her fired from her post, she'd have been paid a proportion of the cost of her lifetime Game subscription. Quitting means she's broken her contract, so she gets nothing at all."

"She was probably afraid that you'd make a public statement about what happened and turn the whole of Game against her. There'd be no way for her to defend herself, because no one would listen to the word of an unknown doctor against a Founder Player."

I gave a startled laugh. "I remember the instructor telling me that no one would listen to the word of an unknown medical cadet against a doctor. Anyway, she's dealt out her own punishment, so I'm forgetting about her now."

"What did the insufferably smug Falcon think of you becoming a Founder Player?"

"Falcon didn't even mention it. He was too busy talking about the replays of the fake murder, and complaining about you not flourishing the knife enough."

Hawk groaned.

"I don't think I mentioned before that Falcon's mother is a big fan of yours. She named her twins Falcon and Eagle in your honour, but Gina always uses her second name because she thinks Eagle is a silly name for a girl."

Hawk gave me a wary look. "I get the impression that you're especially close to Gina. I hadn't realized she was Falcon's twin sister."

"Don't worry about that. Gina finds Falcon just as maddening as the rest of us." I paused. "I've had several calls from my mother too. She used to avoid calling me because I was a reminder of the unpleasant time she spent in the real world when I was born. Now I'm a Founder Player, I seem to make her think of more pleasant things, because she's calling me every day."

"Are you happy about that?"

"Mostly. It was difficult finding things we could talk about to start with, but then Cassandra said she was going to arrange a big party for me to be formally introduced to all the Founder Players. My mother is helping me plan what to wear. Will you be able take time off from playing bait for the Reaper, and be my partner at the party?"

"Definitely. I..."

An automated voice spoke from somewhere above us. "Player Hawk, resident of Celestius, you have an incoming call from player Hercules, resident of Celestius. Do you accept the call?"

I saw Hawk hesitating, and shook my head at him. "You can't seriously be considering talking to Hercules."

He pulled a face of despair. "I never know what to do in these situations. I can beat Hercules in a physical fight, but I'm no good at his warped mind games. If I accept his call, then I know he'll say something that makes me have one of my immature Michael moments. If I reject the call, then I know he'll start sending messages to other people about me, and that will end up causing trouble too."

"Do you accept the call?" repeated the voice.

Hawk sighed. "Game command. Reject call."

"Call rejected," acknowledged the voice.

"It's totally irresponsible of Hercules to cause you problems while you're trying to trap the Reaper," I said.

"Hercules saw the surveillance footage. He heard me tell you that I love you. He blames me for him losing Fleur, so he can't resist trying to get his revenge by messing up my chances with you."

"I don't understand how you can be so heroic about the big things like chasing the Reaper, but go into a blind panic over Hercules playing childish tricks."

"It's easy to be heroic about battling the Reaper," said Hawk. "It's much harder to cope with Hercules sticking verbal pins in me. I'm scared that he'll keep hitting my weak points, making me show you the worst side of Michael, and eventually you'll get so sick of me that you go off with someone else."

The automated voice spoke again. "Player Jex, resident of Celestius, you have an incoming call from player Hercules, resident of Celestius. Do you accept the call?"

"I knew it," said Hawk bitterly. "I wouldn't talk to him, so now he's calling you to tell you something poisonous about me."

"Hercules can't tell me anything at all because I'm not listening to him. Game command. Reject call."

"Call rejected," responded the automated voice.

"He'll call you again," said Hawk.

"If Hercules keeps bothering me, I'll get a Game Tech to block all calls from him. You should do that too."

"It won't work. Nothing ever does. Hercules will find a way to get a message to you that starts an argument between us."

I frowned. "When we were in the Amphitheatre, you mentioned Celestius had special rules to stop troublemakers from disrupting relationships. After Cassandra suggested making me a Founder Player, I was too dazed to follow the situation closely, but I remember her saying something about me being under the protection of the Sisterhood as well. Hercules is deliberately trying to cause trouble between us. Surely that isn't allowed."

"Yes, Celestius has rules to stop troublemakers disrupting relationships, and the Sisterhood are very strict about enforcing them, but those rules don't apply to us because... Jex, if we have this conversation, then I'm scared I'll say the wrong thing and we'll have another fight about you making your own decisions."

"What's the problem here? Talk to me, Hawk. Tell me why the rules don't apply to us. I need to understand what's going on."

He let his head sag forward for a second as if in defeat. "The rules don't apply to us because you've publicly stated you're a free agent. That means Hercules can use any tactics he wants to compete with me for your attention."

"What?"

Hawk flushed. "I'm not complaining about that, Jex. I accept that I'd no right to order you to leave Game. I accept that I've no right to push you into a relationship with me. I've been avoiding even discussing this because I knew..."

I interrupted him. "Wait a minute. Back in the Amphitheatre, Hercules came to sit next to me, and asked if I was your exclusive property. He knew I was angry at you for trying to make me defrost, used the word property to make me even more annoyed, and I made the mistake of saying I was a free agent. When Cassandra suggested making me a Founder Player, Hercules grabbed his chance to repeat that in front of everyone. Am I right that he was deliberately setting up a situation where he'd be free to try to split us up?"

"Yes." Hawk was watching me very intently. "Hercules is an expert at manipulating people."

"I resent being manipulated. I'm beginning to understand why you keep challenging Hercules to duels."

"If he hadn't used the word property to upset you, what would you have said to him about us?"

I stared across at the sea to avoid looking at Hawk. "I'm not sure. A girl in a bronze bracelet could hardly stake a claim to having a relationship with a Founder Player, so I was leaving it to you to tell people about us."

"You aren't wearing a bronze bracelet any longer," said

Hawk. "On Celestius, the woman is the one who makes any public declarations about the changes in her relationship status. She can decide to be exclusive with one person, or several, or free to any approaches."

I risked turning my head to look at him. His expression was one of tense excitement as he waited for me to reply.

"I'd like to stop Hercules causing trouble between us," I said carefully, "but I don't want us to be rushed into anything drastic before we're ready. If I told people we were in an exclusive relationship, what exactly would that imply?"

Hawk was grinning at me now. "Exclusive is a statement that you currently aren't open to receiving other relationship offers. What it means beyond that is your decision."

"If I announced we were exclusive, you wouldn't start assuming anything? We could still gradually work things out between us in our own time? You'd be happy with that?"

Hawk nodded. "I've been waiting four hundred years to have a proper relationship, so we can take all the time you want."

"How do I make the announcement?"

"You call Cassandra, and she'll message all the Founder Players about it."

I laughed, not because the situation was funny, but because it was so surreal. I thought back to the day I'd been sleeping, exhausted, on the ground next to my buggy in the body stacks. When Hawk the Unvanquished's controlled droid appeared, I'd hardly dared to speak to him, but now I was publicly announcing I was in a relationship with him. Unbelievable.

"It's a shame that I need to keep going off to other worlds, trying to tempt the Reaper out of hiding," said Hawk. "If we're entering into an exclusive relationship, then we should be spending more time together."

I wanted to suggest I could go with him, but Hawk would have enough problems defending himself from the Reaper without having to defend me as well. I had to do the sensible thing and stay on Celestius where there was no way for the Reaper to reach me.

And that was the moment that I realized there'd been a flaw

in our logic. Perhaps I wasn't safe on Celestius, perhaps no one was safe on Celestius, because there was a way that the Reaper could have reached here after all.

I fought to keep my voice sounding calm and relaxed. "I'd like to go home and call Cassandra before Hercules causes any more trouble. Do you think you can stay on Celestius for a day or two at least? We should celebrate the start of our official relationship."

"I don't see any reason why I can't stay on Celestius for a couple of days. It's becoming painfully clear that the Reaper isn't in a hurry to murder me."

"I'll call you later then. Game command. Request teleport home."

Hawk and the beach vanished, there was the usual blurry minute of transition, and then I was standing in the great hall of my castle. I hurried towards the nearest mirror and tapped it, but I ordered it to call Nathan not Cassandra.

CHAPTER THIRTY-ONE

"Hi Jex." Nathan's face smiled out of the mirror in front of me. "I was hoping you'd…"

I didn't let him finish the sentence. "I've thought of something terrifying. Are you sure that no other players can eavesdrop on this conversation?"

"Are you alone in your castle?"

"Yes."

"Then it's impossible for other players to spy on you."

"Good. Can you get Kwame to join me here?"

Nathan frowned. "It's against protocol for a player to request a particular Game Tech by name."

"Whether it's against protocol or not, we urgently need to discuss this with a Game Tech, and that Game Tech has to be Kwame because of his specific knowledge."

"Oh. Right then."

Nathan turned away from me to do something. I waited impatiently for a minute, and then Kwame appeared next to me.

"You requested the presence of an appropriate Game Tech," he said.

"Yes. We need an urgent conference about the Reaper."

"Is player Hawk joining us?" asked Kwame.

"No, he isn't," I said grimly. "Hawk has to be excluded from this. Please follow my logic and tell me if it's right or wrong. The Reaper used an automated process to change himself from a Game Tech into a player with a new identity."

"That is correct," said Kwame.

Nathan listened in anxious silence as I continued talking. "We believe the Reaper envied the Founder Players because they got the public accolades that he was denied."

"That is correct," repeated Kwame.

"Therefore, when the Reaper gave himself a new player identity, he'd ideally wish it to be that of a Founder Player."

Kwame hesitated, clearly considering saying something, but settled for the standard reply. "That is correct."

"There aren't any new player names on the list of Founder Players, and the automated process used by the Reaper couldn't have deleted or replaced an existing Founder Player." This time, I didn't give Kwame the chance to say anything, I just swept on. "What about a Founder Player who wasn't in Game at the time?"

Kwame stared at me for a second before speaking. "Moment."

Nathan looked appalled. "The Reaper changed himself into a player just after the bombs exploded. Hawk wasn't in the Game then. You think that the Reaper has replaced Hawk?"

"I don't want to be right," I wailed.

We endured at least two full minutes of agony before Kwame spoke again. "Unfortunately, it would have been possible for the Reaper to take Hawk's place in Game during his absence."

"If the Reaper did take his place," I asked tensely, "what would have happened to the real Hawk when he entered Game?"

"His stream of consciousness would have been unable to enter its designated position in the Game system," said Kwame. "His mind would not have survived."

There was a long silence.

"Could that really have happened?" asked Nathan. "Do we have the real Hawk in Game, or do we have the Reaper pretending to be Hawk? The Reaper will have been watching the Founder Players for centuries, so he'd know how to act the part of Hawk."

"There've been a few times lately when I thought Hawk was behaving oddly," I said miserably. "He got in a ridiculous panic over me visiting Merlin, when he should know perfectly well that Merlin is only interested in Stella."

"Player Jex, you must be aware that player Hawk has grown deeply attached to you," said Kwame. "The constant stress of the Reaper situation would explain his overreaction to a perceived threat to your relationship."

In other circumstances, I might have blushed, but I was far too worried to be embarrassed. "Yes, but was that Hawk over-reacting due to stress, or the Reaper misjudging the part he was playing? Is there a way of examining Hawk's consciousness stream to see who he is? Can you see what he's thinking?"

"No," said Kwame. "Constreams are variable format data, changing their structure from instant to instant, which makes it impossible to access and interpret the data in any particular segment."

I didn't understand any of that except the word no. That was enough. "Hawk's told me that people can't change their fundamental personality while they're in Game. He said it was because Game stores the basic parameters of your personality."

"That is a gross over-simplification of a complex issue," said Kwame.

"But something like that happens," I said. "Can you check the parameters of Hawk's personality before he left Game against those when he re-entered? See if the numbers are the same?"

"Describing the personality characteristics as either parameters or numbers is seriously misleading," said Kwame, "but we can attempt a comparison. This may take a little time."

Kwame vanished. I stood there, still staring tensely at the spot where he'd been.

"My impression is that personality characteristics are a sort of cross between a fluid, multi-dimensional shape and a set of equations," said Nathan.

He was just an image in a mirror, so I couldn't strangle him. I had to settle for glaring at him. "Shut up, Nathan."

"I'm worried about Hawk too," he said. "I just thought it would help if I explained what Kwame is trying to compare."

"Well, it doesn't."

We waited in silence until eventually Kwame reappeared. "There are noticeable mismatches between the two sets of personality characteristics."

I felt my hands clench into fists. "So the Reaper has taken Hawk's place?"

"Not necessarily," said Kwame. "Hawk's personality could have changed during his time outside Game. You wouldn't usually expect significant shifts in just a few days, but Hawk went through a series of dramatic and deeply emotional events."

I tried to relax my hands, but my fingers didn't seem to want to move.

Nathan groaned. "So, how do we work out whether Hawk is acting oddly because he's scared he'll lose Jex, or whether it's because he's really the Reaper?"

"I'll ask him to fight something," I said. "That will soon tell us if he's the real Hawk or not."

"The Reaper will have taken part in test combats against many Game creatures over the centuries," said Kwame. "He would be reasonably convincing in a fight."

"I'm sure the Reaper could beat most standard Game creatures," I said, "but Hawk is the only person in Game to have ever defeated the Kraken solo."

"You intend to ask Hawk to fight the Kraken?" Kwame thought for a moment. "If the Reaper is masquerading as Hawk, he could still defeat the Kraken using his deletion weapon."

"I've watched the replays of Hawk fighting the Kraken dozens of times," I said. "It took him twenty minutes of combat to wear the creature down and go for the death blow. What would happen if the Reaper used his deletion weapon? Would the Kraken drop dead at the first scratch?"

"That is correct," said Kwame.

"Then that wouldn't look a very convincing fight. The Reaper would either have to make an excuse not to fight the Kraken at all, or fight using an ordinary weapon for a while before grabbing a plausible time to use the deletion one. How long do you think he could last solo against the Kraken? Two minutes, possibly three or even five, but definitely not twenty."

Kwame nodded. "It should certainly be possible for a team of watching Game Techs to determine if a victory against the Kraken was legitimate or achieved with the aid of a deletion weapon."

"I'll call Hawk right away then." I was desperate to get this over with, so I'd know whether Hawk was alive or dead.

"Player Jex," said Kwame, "you must be very careful. If the Reaper has replaced Hawk, then he could use his deletion weapon to erase your mind from the Game."

"If the Reaper has replaced Hawk, then he has the chance of spending eternity as an adored Founder Player. He won't want to give himself away by murdering me."

"That is correct," said Kwame. "However, if the Reaper realizes you suspect him, then he may feel he has nothing to lose by killing you."

Nathan was frowning. "There's one big problem with your plan. Hawk could be his real self and still refuse to fight the Kraken. If I had a girlfriend, and she suddenly called me and demanded I fight a hulking great Game monster, I know I'd refuse."

I considered this. "Point. I'll ask Hawk to give me a hunting lesson. There's no reason for either Hawk or the Reaper to refuse to do that. Then I'll gradually work up to asking him to fight the Kraken."

"And what if he does fight the Kraken and loses?" asked Nathan. "Just because the real Hawk managed to kill it once, that doesn't mean he'll manage it every time."

"The real Hawk would be doing his very best to win," I said. "Hawk the Unvanquished wouldn't want me to remember the day I agreed to be in an exclusive relationship with him as the day I watched him defeated by the Kraken."

CHAPTER THIRTY-TWO

Hawk and I were wearing matching outfits in silver chain mail that was surprisingly light and supple to wear. We were in one of the hunting zones of Celestius, wading through knee deep grass, with scattered trees around us.

"You look nervous about this hunting trip," said Hawk.

I was far more than just nervous. I was sick with tension. I was afraid I'd flinch away from Hawk and make him suspicious. I was totally terrified of discovering Hawk really was the Reaper. Fortunately, if I appeared nervous, there was a good explanation for it.

"You're a legendary warrior. I've never been in a genuine fight before. I'm going to make a complete fool of myself."

I looked warily round at the trees, wondering what might be hiding under cover. I couldn't see anything more dangerous than a bush with nasty looking thorns, but we were here so I could fight something. Logically, that meant there was something around to fight.

Hawk stopped by a large rock, and sat down on it. "Forget whether you're likely to make a fool of yourself or not, because there's a far more important question. Are you sure that you want to try hunting? You mustn't feel under pressure to fight Game monsters because I do it. I like tackling challenges, so I do the warrior thing. Sometimes I get hurt, and that can be very painful. I don't enjoy pain one bit, but I've learned to handle it. Many people can't."

He paused for a moment. "Take Fleur for example. She spent years suffering pain in real life and entered Game to escape it. Her only Game death was when Hercules killed her, and I've told you how she reacted to that. She thinks that hunting, deliberately risking being hurt for no real purpose, is silly. She's right. I'd understand if you decide to go back to your castle right now."

I listened to what Hawk was saying, but I knew I couldn't run away back to my castle. Hunting in general might have no real purpose, but this hunting trip definitely did. It was worth suffering some pain to find out if I was in a relationship with Hawk the Unvanquished or Hawk the Reaper.

The big danger was that I wouldn't just get hurt but killed, because that would bring this trip to an abrupt end. The experience of being in Game mirrored real life as exactly as possible. Hawk had repeatedly warned me that a Game death was very painful and the first Game death was especially traumatic.

If I was killed hunting, I knew the real Hawk would be worried and insist on me taking a long break to recover, while the Reaper would know it was hardest to imitate Hawk when he was fighting and would grab the excuse to abandon the hunt. I'd be left in an agony of suspense, still unsure if this was the real Hawk or if he'd been lost to data oblivion.

Hawk, or the Reaper, gave me an earnest look. "What I'm trying to say is that my feelings for you don't depend on whether or not you want to hunt. It might be fun to battle lethal monsters together, but there are plenty of other experiences we could share in Game."

He gave a strangely anxious laugh. "But I'm assuming far too much here. I've admitted that I love you, but you haven't given me a hint of how much you care about me."

"Don't be silly. The fact I've agreed that we should enter into an exclusive relationship is a very big hint that I have deep feelings for you. Whether I decide I'd like to do more hunting in future or not, going on a hunting trip with you today is important to me. I've spent years watching the replays of your famous Game combats. Today is a special day for us, so I want to bring the past and future together by having my first hunting lesson with you, and then…"

I broke off and gave him a pleading look. "After I've done

some hunting myself, can I watch Hawk the Unvanquished fight something?"

He looked eager rather than reluctant. The ridiculously pleased expression on his face reminded me of the way Michael had looked back in the real world when I told him I'd have been tempted to have a date with him. I'd been grimly resigned until now, braced to find out that Hawk was gone and the Reaper was wearing his image. Weirdly, the fact it was such an awful idea, made me feel it had to be true.

Now I was far more hopeful. The Reaper had known Hawk for four hundred years, so of course he would be able to imitate him, but that expression belonged to Michael not Hawk. I couldn't bet the lives of everyone on Celestius on a fleeting facial expression, I needed much better evidence, but still...

"You'll let me show off?" Hawk asked with a grin. "You'll let Hawk the Unvanquished demonstrate his big weapon for you?"

I was puzzled by the sound of his voice when he said that. "Am I missing something in what you just said?"

He laughed. "In my day, that would have been a suggestive remark."

I was almost convinced. This was Hawk making the old joke about him being centuries out of date. On the other hand, the Reaper was an original Game designer, so he must be even older than Hawk. He'd know all about the past as well.

I managed a smile. "I'll not only let you show off. I insist on it. Promise you'll give me my own private demonstration of Hawk wielding his mighty weapon."

He made a choking noise.

"What?" I asked.

"Innuendoes," he whimpered. "I know you didn't mean what that implied but... Be very careful you don't say anything like that to Hercules, or any of the rest of the family. It's like the jokes about men wanting big towers on their castles."

I blinked. "It means that? But why? A tower sort of makes sense, but a sword doesn't."

"It's not worth worrying about the psychology behind it," said Hawk. "You just don't want to give people the wrong idea."

He stood up. "Now, if you get serious about hunting, fighting, or any heavily physical activities in Game, you'll find there's a lot of training involved. Today, we'll just let you try fighting something easy and get a feel of the experience. That avoids you being bored by weeks or months of preparation, just to find you hate the whole thing at the end of it."

He smiled at me. "The downside is that you won't have a clue what you're doing. You'll be hopeless, but don't worry about it. If you find you enjoy the challenge of this, then I'll help you train, and I promise you'll end up a good hunter and fighter. You're intelligent and you think fast, which are the two key things you need. Everything else is achieved by pure hard work."

"Do I get a weapon now?" I asked.

Hawk had Durendal in its sheath on his back, a one-handed broadsword at his left side, a slender rapier at his right side, and dagger sheaths on both forearms. The man was a walking weapon store, while I was totally unarmed. Given my worries about him being the Reaper, this was unnerving, though I knew having a weapon wouldn't help me if it came to fighting him. I was a total novice, and would stand no chance of winning against an experienced fighter.

Hawk drew the broadsword and handed it to me.

"No shield?" I asked.

"There's a lot of skill involved in using a shield properly in combat. For your first lesson, it's best if you concentrate your attention on using your sword."

I frowned down at the broadsword. "If I'm not using a shield, wouldn't I be better off with a two-handed sword like Durendal?"

"Absolutely not. A two-handed sword is one of the heaviest weapons in Game, the blade is massive, and when you get it moving fast there's a lot of momentum involved. I don't want you cutting your own head off, so you're starting with a weapon that's much lighter and easier to control."

I looked around at the waving grasses. "What am I supposed to fight?"

"Over there." Hawk pointed. "It's dozing in the shade of that tree."

I squinted into the sun, and saw a barely visible, black furry object lying among thick grass. "It's a bear. No yellow stripes, so it isn't a bumble bear."

Hawk laughed. "I'm not insulting you by sending you up against a bumble bear. They're so fat they move at a snail's pace, and they keep falling over their own feet. If you lie down and refuse to defend yourself, a bumble bear might manage to scratch you a little, but it's really far more dangerous fighting a tree trunk. You're here to fight a battle bear. Those are plain black, except for the white markings on the ears and chest."

"I see." I stared across at the battle bear. "It seems a shame to wake it up when it's happily dozing in the sunshine."

"The bear isn't happy," said Hawk. "It isn't sad either. It isn't thinking or feeling anything at all, because its every movement is directly controlled by the Game system. At the beginning of Game, every creature was like that, but once the First Wave settled successfully into Game people worked out that we had immortality here. The whole population of Earth was trying to move in at once, the Game needed more worlds fast, and the Game creatures were given their own artificial intelligence."

I listened uneasily as he continued.

"Using autonomous artificial intelligence meant the Game system no longer had to run each creature's movements directly. A.A.I. meant we were able to have masses of butterflies and bees, flocks of seagulls, and shoals of fish, each with their own tiny consciousness stream in Game."

I didn't say a word. I was starting to feel sick.

Hawk laughed. "But then the Game Techs got a few surprises. The wildlife was set up to have natural lives, including eating, breeding, and having a limited lifespan. First came the simple problems, like creatures breeding too fast, so the Game Techs hastily added automatic population limits by making fertility dependent on the number of a particular species that was already around. Then came the real shock of Game creatures starting to evolve. They couldn't change their appearance but they could change their behaviour."

I finally spoke. I knew I'd be safer keeping my mouth shut,

but it was my life, and my decision what risks I should take. We were inside a hunting zone. Kwame had a team of Game Techs watching every move we made, and had locked down every normal way out except through Game death and resurrection. If the Reaper killed me, then they would have him trapped, and could deal with him once and for all.

"I didn't realize you knew so much technical stuff," I said. "You're sounding like Nathan."

"I only know these things because I lived through several decades where Celestius suffered from one A.A.I. problem after another. It wasn't just that the dangerous creatures in the hunting zones developed better attack tactics and became far more lethal. Previously harmless wildlife in ordinary areas of Game started to become a threat too. There were the hummingbirds that evolved to have a taste for blood instead of nectar. There were the bees that started attacking in swarms and stinging people to death. I'm not even going to hint at why we don't have ravens on Celestius any longer."

Hawk gave his one-shouldered shrug. "The Game Techs went back to using direct system control on all the dangerous creatures in hunting zones. Outside the hunting zones, they kept putting extra limitations on the A.A.I. wildlife to stop them evolving, and removed a few species that persistently caused trouble. In the end, they got everything working smoothly. Anyway, my point is that you don't have to worry about being unkind to the bear because it has no thoughts or feelings."

I wasn't sure what to think. The Reaper would have been one of the Game Techs making those changes to the wildlife. Hawk was only a player, but I could believe that a hunter paid very close attention to changes in the creatures he fought.

"Go and fight your bear now," Hawk ordered. "I'll be right here, watching your back."

He sat down on the rock again, and relaxed, seeming amused. I looked at my sword, took a deep breath, and started walking forward.

"Don't take your eyes off the bear for a single second," Hawk warned me. "When it spots you, it'll charge."

I watched the patch of fur in the grass, hardly daring to blink as I took a few more paces forward. The bear seemed to go straight from sleeping to ferocious attack, leaping up and bounding straight at me at startling speed. I gripped my sword tightly, and swung it at the beast, while dodging sideways. I was aiming for the bear's throat, but it reared upwards at the last second, so I struck its chest instead.

The bear landed heavily on the ground beside me. It was up again an instant later, advancing on me again, and I could see where my blade had left a red gash across the white-furred chest. I took two rapid steps backwards, and then stabbed with my sword. I missed the neck again, but this time the blade went deeper into the chest, and was yanked out of my hands as the bear recoiled. I grabbed desperately for the sword hilt, trying to retrieve it, but the bear was on me again, its front paws knocking me over backwards.

I lay helpless on the ground, the bear poised over me, and there was an instant when time seemed to stop. I was aware of a mass of sensations. The tearing pain from claws raking my left shoulder. The rancid stench of the bear's breath. The sight of the bear's white tufted ears folding backwards to flatten themselves against the side of its head. The furious, red eyes looking into mine, as it drew back and bared its teeth for the kill.

I was braced for my first Game death, when there was a flash of steel. The bear went limp and collapsed on top of me.

"You did well," said Hawk, strolling over to stand next to me.

I lay there, half buried under the crushing weight of the dead bear, and totally bewildered. "How did you kill it? You weren't anywhere near us."

"A throwing dagger." He pointed at the blade buried in the bear's forehead. "Battle bears have a vulnerable point there. When it reared back, it gave me a beautiful clear shot."

Hawk lifted the bear carcass up while I crawled out. I was feeling giddy from shock, and there was a burning pain in my left shoulder, but my arm still seemed to be working. "Thanks."

"I promised to watch your back. The bear scratched the left side of your neck a little. Did its claws get through the chain mail as well?"

"Yes." I stood up, and loosened the fastenings of my armour to expose my shoulder. Twisting my neck round awkwardly, I could just see where blood oozed from a set of claw marks.

"Maybe I should wear plate armour another time," I said.

"I find you take less damage from each hit with plate armour, but you get hit far more because you're slower at dodging. You'll have to make your own decision on what armour to use, but I like chain mail as a compromise between weight and protection. Wearing leather can work well too, but the way Hercules has all the gaps to show off his rippling muscles is ridiculous. It's no wonder that I can always kill him in a fight."

Hawk leaned close to examine my neck and shoulder. "There are two ways to deal with injuries in hunting zones. One way is to teleport back to your home where you'll get automatic accelerated healing. The other way is to just put a bandage on it and keep hunting."

I couldn't go back to my castle until I knew if this was Hawk or the Reaper. "I'll try the bandage. I'm here to get the real hunting experience."

Hawk went back to the rock that he'd been sitting on, tapped the side of it, and an opening appeared. I gave a startled gasp, and he laughed.

"The large rocks contain emergency medical supplies. It's no real advantage in a hunt. It just saves us from having to carry bandage packs."

Hawk took out a thin, flat, beige object, and brought it back to me. "You just choose a bandage the right size and shape, and press it down over the wound like this."

I frowned as he applied the bandage. "It looks like an outdated, adhesive bandage."

"The Game Techs haven't bothered changing the appearance of bandages for a century or two."

Hawk stepped back, and I studied my shoulder. My wound was still throbbing, but the bandage seemed to be keeping the bleeding under control.

"If you stayed in the hunting ground for a day or two," said Hawk, "you'd probably find that wound got infected, but you should be all right for a few hours. Battle bears don't have poisonous bites or stings. If you get hurt by something that does, you need to head straight home to heal up."

I nodded.

Hawk retrieved my sword, cleaned the blade on the grass, and returned it to the sheath at his side. "So what did you think of hunting?"

"I've never felt so aware of everything that was happening around me," I said. "It was like all my senses were heightened. I was pretty useless at the fighting though. You literally had to save my neck."

"It was your first fight, Jex, and a battle bear is quite a nasty opponent. I wouldn't have let the fight go on as long as I did without intervening if I hadn't been impressed by how well you were doing. I hadn't taken the training you did for the re-enactment fights very seriously, but you've obviously learned something from it."

Hawk looked up at the sky with a reminiscent smile. "You did far better than I did in my first fight in Game. I was as smug as your friend, Falcon, as I headed into the hunting zone. I was an obsessive gamer, an expert on combat in a dozen of the old style games, and convinced I could handle anything in this one too."

He laughed. "In the games I'd played, it was easy for a new player to kill small creatures with a few random waves of a sword, and I expected that approach to work here too. I found a lesser mountain lion, charged, waved my sword, and got a huge shock when the lion didn't drop dead. Game was designed to mimic reality as closely as possible. In this case, the reality of a person using a sword to fight a dangerous creature. Waving my sword around randomly was useless, and when the lion clawed me it really hurt!"

"It does," I agreed.

"I ended up dying horribly, and it was unbelievably painful. All of us who were obsessive gamers had similar experiences, and some sensibly decided to concentrate on different things after that, like socializing with the other players. They said there was no point in fighting monsters if you didn't gain any treasure, or flashy weapons and armour that other people didn't have. I was stubborn, and found the idea of socializing even more frightening than being eaten by lions, so I started learning to use a sword properly."

He grinned, and moved his eyebrows up and down suggestively. "Now would you like to fight another battle bear, or shall I demonstrate my skill with a large weapon?"

"I'd like the demonstration."

Hawk did the routine of holding up his right hand and summoning Durendal by name.

"Why do you summon Durendal like that," I asked. "You just drew the one-handed sword from its sheath."

Hawk spoke in heroic tones. "Because this is no ordinary blade. This is Durendal, and it was bathed in the life blood of the Kraken!"

He dropped the dramatic act and returned to using his normal voice. "Because you carry the sheath for a two-handed sword on your back. Drawing the sword in a hurry is tricky, and several people sliced their own necks doing it, so the Game Techs put the voice command thing in to stop them whining."

I gurgled with laughter.

"Durendal is just a standard, two-handed sword. I requested a customized hand grip, but other than that it's no different from the weapons any beginner in Game can have."

He paused. "Now what would you like me to fight for you? How about a tyrannosaurus rex?"

I forced an eager smile. "I'd love to watch you fighting the Kraken."

"The Kraken!" Hawk stared at me. "You're joking, aren't you?"

"You know I had an image of your solo fight with the Kraken on the wall of my room back in real life," I said. "Actually being in Game and watching you fight it would be an incredible experience."

Hawk scratched his right ear, looking nervous. "All the chasing round after the Reaper has made me miss a lot of training sessions, so I'm not at peak fitness. I need every tiny advantage I can get to stand a chance of killing the Kraken. You're sure you don't want to settle for me killing a dinosaur?"

I listened uneasily to his excuses. "If you could at least try to fight the Kraken, it would make today perfect for me."

Hawk sighed. "You're a hard woman to please, Jex." He looked around the grassy landscape. "I think the sea is this way."

He led the way, and I followed unhappily. Hawk had been saying exactly what Nathan had said earlier. Hawk the Unvanquished didn't really win every fight. If he lost to the Kraken within the first few minutes, that might mean he was the Reaper, or it might just mean that he hadn't been lucky this time. I needed a definite answer here, both for the safety of Celestius and for my own peace of mind.

We reached a small cliff top, and stopped to look down at the waves crashing in on a rocky shore. Hawk's face took on a grim expression. "Game command. Creature request. Named opponent. Kraken."

The shoreline below us changed. The rocks at the edge of the sea turned from grey to black, and then tripled in size. The beach itself turned to a flat expanse of shale.

"Jex, you should stay on this cliff top outside the combat area," said Hawk. "The Kraken anchors itself to the rocks when it's fighting, to prevent it being dragged onto the land. It won't come anywhere near you."

I nodded.

He took a deep breath. "Wish me luck."

"I do," I said. "I really do."

I surrendered to my emotions, and reached up to give Hawk a brief kiss on the lips. He grinned at me in response, and then turned to walk along a narrow path down to the beach. As he arrived, something large surfaced in the sea, with great, green, saucer-like eyes. The Kraken had awakened and was studying its opponent.

Hawk adjusted his grip on Durendal to hold it firmly with both hands, and then shouted out to sea.

"Lord of the waves, I challenge you!"

The Kraken responded by moving slowly in towards the

shore. Two huge tentacles wrapped themselves round the larger rocks, while its bulbous body moved into the shallow water, and the six remaining tentacles readied themselves to attack.

Hawk was moving now, a tiny figure compared to the bulk of the Kraken. He darted in amongst the tentacles, weaving to and fro between them, slashing at them with the two-handed sword before jumping back to safety. I'd watched the replays of him doing this dozens of times, but it was very different standing here on the cliff top, with the sound of the Kraken's piercing screeches in my ears, and the sea wind blowing the cold, salt spray into my eyes.

This was no replay, there was no guaranteed outcome, and I could see what a deadly dance this was. One mistake, one slip, one error of judgement, and the Kraken would have Hawk in its grasp. I was counting seconds now. With each one that went by, it was more likely that it was genuinely Hawk fighting on that beach.

My count reached one minute, and then two. I could see the Kraken's tentacles were bleeding in a dozen places, oozing thick greenish-black blood onto the beach. That was good because the blood loss would weaken and slow the Kraken. That was bad because the Kraken's blood could seep through gaps in a player's armour and burn their skin.

The silver clad figure on the beach was working doubly hard now, dodging both the attacking tentacles and the toxic pools of blood that had collected among the rocks. I was still counting seconds. After Hawk defeated the Kraken solo, all the best hunters in Game had studied the replays and tried to match the feat themselves. Many of them had died in seconds, a few dozen had made it to the three minute mark, but no one had lasted longer than five.

When my count reached three minutes, I was almost certain it was Hawk on that beach. In another two minutes, I'd be absolutely sure. I was chanting the seconds aloud now, my words barely audible above the Kraken's cries, but I broke off as I saw Hawk stumble on a loose rock. He staggered, fell, rolled sideways to escape one lashing tentacle, only to have another beating down at him.

I held my breath, thinking he'd lost the fight at that point, but Hawk lay on his back, stabbing upwards with Durendal, and cut deep into the threatening tentacle. As it recoiled, he rolled sideways again to miss a cascade of lethal blood, and was back on his feet an instant later.

I'd lost track of the seconds now, but I didn't care about the time any longer. I couldn't believe that anyone but Hawk could have come that close to disaster in a combat with the Kraken and managed to recover. I was jubilant now, cheering every time Hawk inflicted another wound on the Kraken, yelling encouragement that he couldn't possibly hear.

The battle continued for what seemed like an endless time. I could see that Hawk was tiring, each thrust of Durendal was visibly more difficult, but the Kraken was weakening too. Then the pattern of the combat changed. Hawk was feigning attacking moves but not following them through.

I'd seen this before in the replays of his last fight with the Kraken. The long attrition fight had achieved its purpose, the movements of the Kraken's tentacles were far slower now, and Hawk was waiting for the right moment to take the huge gamble of committing himself to the final attack.

That moment came as a tentacle swung low across the rocks. Hawk didn't dodge this time, but leapt forward to land on the suckered skin. He stabbed down at it with Durendal, and the tentacle drew back in pain, carrying him upwards to the vast bulk of the Kraken's head. Poised there precariously, Hawk raised his sword and thrust it dagger like into the nearest eye of the Kraken. Not into the centre, but diagonally into the corner, where the massive blade could reach the Kraken's brain.

The Kraken reeled backwards, screeching and tentacles flailing, sending Hawk crashing down on to the beach. He lay there motionless, as the Kraken's tentacles folded in like a dead spider and it sank under the waves.

I ran down the path to the beach, screaming Hawk's name, and saw him lift his head. He struggled to his feet, and I threw myself at him.

"Hawk, you're alive!"

CHAPTER THIRTY-THREE

"It was a stupid idea," said Hawk, lounging in a chair and grinning at me. "When the Reaper changed himself into a player, he didn't know that I'd defrosted. He wouldn't have tried to take my place in Game when he thought I was still there myself."

I adjusted the single shoulder strap of my ankle length, silk dress, which glittered silver with hints of blue. I was getting ready for Cassandra's promised party to welcome me to Celestius and formally present me to the family.

For the last ten days, Cassandra had only been making the vaguest of comments about this party, saying it took a very long time to organize these things properly. Yesterday, I'd called her to say I was in an exclusive relationship with Hawk. Strangely enough, she'd immediately told me that everything was ready for the party to happen this evening. Of course Cassandra was a close friend of Hawk.

"The Reaper could easily have discovered you'd left Game," I said. "He'd have been watching your every move because you were leading the players' investigation. He could have got suspicious because you'd stopped making broadcasts, or spotted a clue in one of the reports. After that, he just had to try tracking your identity number to confirm that you weren't in Game any longer."

I still wasn't sure if I was happy with my dress. Cassandra and Hawk had said that I should wear whatever I liked, but Celestius would probably have its own unique traditions for party clothes, and I wanted to fit in with the other Founder Players.

"All right," said Hawk, "it was perfectly reasonable for you to be worried the Reaper might have taken my place, but you only needed to ask me a few questions to prove I was me."

I wove a strand of sapphires through my feathered hair, and studied the effect in a wall mirror. "Asked you what exactly? What question could I ask where I was totally sure that you knew the answer, but the Reaper didn't? A question where there was no chance of him guessing the right answer? If you thought that I was the Reaper, what would you ask me?"

Hawk considered this. "Point."

I pinned a sapphire flower to the strap of my dress. "Is this neckline too revealing?"

"Not in my opinion."

I frowned at my reflection. This dress was supposed to cling to me, but was it clinging too much? I reminded myself that my mother thought it was perfect for me, and she was an expert on clothes.

"Anyway, it was definitely worth killing the Kraken." Hawk had a sickeningly smug look on his face. "The way you ran down to that beach and threw yourself at me was unforgettable."

I sighed. This must be about the hundredth time that Hawk had said that.

"I'm not saying that it couldn't have been even better," he added. "You'd probably have taken things a lot further if you hadn't known a whole team of Game Techs were spying on us, and I'd have been in a better state to enjoy it if I hadn't just been knocked senseless by a tentacle, but it was still a glorious moment."

I sighed again. "I was a little relieved that's all. There's no need to keep gloating about it."

"I've been watching the replays," said Hawk happily. "I've seen the look on your face. You love me. You've met Michael, but you still love me. That's amazing."

I was tempted to throw a cushion at him, but I was in a good mood. Not quite as odiously cheerful a mood as Hawk was in, but still a pretty good mood. We'd made no progress on finding the Reaper, but we'd proved he wasn't Hawk, and that was enough for me right now.

"I'm ready," I said.

Hawk bounced to his feet and put his arm round me. "Game command. Request group teleport to the Grand Ballroom."

There was the usual moment of disorientation as we swapped location, and then I took in my surroundings and blinked. "I thought the Grand Ballroom would be a grand room."

"Originally it was," said Hawk, "but the Game Techs have given Celestius a whole series of improvements over the centuries. Somewhere along the way, the Grand Ballroom lost its roof, and turned into a dancing lawn surrounded by formal flowerbeds. After all, there was no need for a roof when we can ask the Game Techs to make the weather warm and dry. Since then, a whole series of extra garden areas have been added until it's a bit of a maze."

"I see what you mean."

We were standing at the top of a flight of steps, which led down to a huge flat area of grass. Around it were a random scattering of tables and chairs, while a host of paths led off into the surrounding gardens. I could glimpse marbled columns, fountains, and statues dotted among the trees and flowerbeds. In the far distance, the evening sunlight glittered on the surface of a lake.

There were a lot of Founder Players sitting in the seats around the edge of the dancing lawn. As Hawk took my arm, and we started walking down the steps, they all turned their heads to look in our direction. I instinctively tensed and stopped moving.

"Relax," said Hawk. "Everything should be very peaceful at the start. We'll just be exploring the gardens and chatting to a few people."

I forced myself to carry on walking down the steps at his side. "What happens later?"

"At sunset, there'll be fireworks. After that, Cassandra will formally present you to the family. The dancing will start when the triple moons rise, and carry on all night."

"The night on Celestius is only two hours long."

"Normally it's only two hours long," said Hawk, "but on party nights the sun doesn't rise until we're ready to go home.

Our record party night was forty-five hours long, but that was because Fleur finally agreed to marry Helios about seventeen hours into the party. Everyone thought it would be a wonderful idea to carry straight on with holding the wedding. Well, everyone except Hercules, and I threw him in the lake."

We reached the lush green grass of the dancing lawn. I looked anxiously round at the Founder Players, studying their clothes, and was stunned by the assortment of styles. The women wore outfits ranging from tasteful white cascading drapes to garish metallic clothes that flashed in different colours. There were some men in highly functional armour, others in luxurious silks and velvets, and a few wearing the kilts that were popular on worlds like Highland and Jacobite.

Hawk laughed at the stunned expression on my face. "I told you there was no need to worry about your clothes. Everyone wears whatever they like at these parties. I stick to wearing chain mail and carrying Durendal, because I prefer to be armed when I'm near Hercules."

He paused. "Actually, when I look at the family in their party gear, I can see the point of the formal dress code for our meetings at the Amphitheatre."

Cassandra walked across the grass to join us. She was wearing a sari that had strands of gold running through its deep red material, and her long dark hair was tumbling loose around her shoulders.

"Jex, welcome to your first party on Celestius. Your dress is beautiful."

"Thank you," I said. "My mother helped me choose it. She'll be delighted to hear that you liked it."

"We're expecting all but one of the family to be here to meet you," added Cassandra.

"All but one?" Hawk raised an eyebrow. "Does that mean Marcus is having one of his sociable spells?"

Cassandra nodded, turned towards me, and spoke rapidly in confidential tones. "Chiron is consistently troubled to an extent that he can't be permitted to leave his castle, but he's always pleased to have visitors. Marcus goes through a cycle of behaviour.

He locks himself away for a long time, not answering calls or accepting any visitors, but then there'll be a period where he wants to talk to people and is willing to control his behaviour. During those times, we try to include him in family gatherings."

She raised her voice back to normal speech levels. "Jex, I'd suggest you meet Marcus relatively early in the evening, since he may become in urgent need of a rest at any time. I'm sure Hawk will be there to... introduce you."

"Oh yes," said Hawk. "I'll be around to give Jex any... introductions she needs. I assume you're arranging the usual rota of people to keep an eye on Marcus. I'm sorry I can't help this time."

"Of course I expect you to stay at Jex's side this evening," said Cassandra. "Thor, Pendragon, and Ulysses will be keeping an eye on Marcus."

She smiled at me, then walked away to join the bulky, blond-haired, figure of Thor. I turned to Hawk, and caught him looking round with a harried expression.

"What's the matter? Marcus isn't that bad is he? Surely I'll be safe with Hawk the Unvanquished guarding me."

Hawk rubbed his forehead. "I'm not worried about physical attacks, from Marcus or anyone else. I'm just concerned what the family may say to you."

We walked on across the grass, and followed one of the paths into the gardens. The heavy, sweet scent of lavender hit me, and I saw that miniature, purple flowered hedges lined the path. Insects flew busily between the flowers, and a hummingbird swooped low past my shoulder.

"You mean that you're worried what Hercules may say to me," I said, "but you shouldn't be. Cassandra's messaged all the Founder Players to tell them I'm in an exclusive relationship with you. If Hercules starts telling me malicious things about you, I just have to tell Cassandra that he's trying to cause trouble between us, and the wrath of the Sisterhood would descend on him."

"That's true." Hawk looked more cheerful now.

"What would the Sisterhood do to Hercules anyway?"

"Put him on trial for breaching the rules of Celestius. If he was found guilty, then he'd be punished by a suitable period of being confined to his castle. Hercules would normally have the option of leaving Celestius to live on another Game world until his sentence was completed, but that won't be possible given the current situation with the Reaper."

I was puzzled. "Surely someone under house arrest can't just change world and live freely again."

"These punishments aren't proper house arrests," said Hawk. "The guilty party is just warned to stay in their castle."

"So what happens if Hercules ignores the warning and leaves his castle? Things aren't the way they were during the ten year trial period of Game. The Sisterhood can't send a mob of their friends and husbands over to kill him."

Hawk didn't say a word. He had an expression of exaggerated innocence on his face.

I stared at him in disbelief. "I can't believe the Game Techs would let that happen."

Hawk led me into a flower covered arbour and we sat down on a wooden seat. "The Game Techs accept that there has to be a system of keeping order on Celestius. They don't like us killing people, but things very rarely go that far these days."

"Can't the Game Techs enforce the house arrests themselves?"

"According to Game Tech regulations, they can only impose house arrest on players in cases like Chiron and Marcus. Other Game worlds remove resident status from troublemakers, which usually makes them behave better on their next world, though stubborn cases end up somewhere like Havoc or in Game prison. The Game Techs don't want to set the precedent of removing Celestius resident status from a Founder Player, or throwing one of us in Game prison, so they put up with us dealing with our problems ourselves."

He laughed. "The Game Techs do use the odd minor sanction themselves from time to time, like when Poseidon woke up and found his castle was infested with ants, but…"

He broke off his sentence as two people looked into the

arbour. I tensed, but Hawk's smile reassured me that they were his friends not his enemies.

"Jex, meet Artemis and her husband, Sword."

They said a few words of welcome to me, and then Artemis turned to Hawk. "I heard you'd been fighting the Kraken again. I thought you said that fighting it once was more than enough."

"I did," said Hawk, "but I had to kill it again to impress Jex."

I blushed.

"You had to kill the Kraken to get Jex to agree to having an exclusive relationship with you!" Sword glanced at Artemis. "I'm deeply thankful you didn't insist on anything quite that dramatic from me."

"So you should be," Artemis teased him. "You wouldn't last thirty seconds against the Kraken."

"Actually, it was fun fighting it again," said Hawk. "I'm getting nowhere tracking down the Reaper, so I could vent my frustration on the Kraken."

There was a moment of depressed silence at the mention of the Reaper.

"We've a message for you, Hawk," said Sword. "Beowulf wants to warn you that Venus is planning to have a chat with Jex."

Hawk raised an eyebrow. "Since when is Beowulf on my side against Venus?"

"Since you saved his life, Hawk," said Artemis. "As you've been roaming round the other worlds, acting as bait for the Reaper, you won't be aware there've been a few dramatic shifts in allegiances. Beowulf was critically ill when he entered Game, he'd have been killed by a high-speed defrost, so his opinion of you has changed."

"Beowulf isn't the only one feeling that way," added Sword. "A lot of the family appreciate what you and Jex did to save Celestius. What you're still doing, attempting to trap the Reaper. Sadly, your increasing popularity has angered Venus."

Sword turned his head, looking at something out of my view down the path. "That's unfortunate."

Hawk stood up. "Venus is coming?"

"No," said Sword. "It's Hercules. If you want to try to escape, we can delay him for you."

Hawk nodded, grabbed my hand, and he towed me out of the arbour. We ran off down a narrow path lined with fragrant flowering roses, my speed limited by my long dress and the fact I was helpless with laughter.

CHAPTER THIRTY-FOUR

After we'd taken three random turnings, Hawk stopped by a large pool. A low, stone wall surrounded it, and in the centre a fountain shot jets of water droplets high into the air.

It was a minute or two before I finally managed to stop laughing and speak. "Why did we run away from Hercules? I thought we'd agreed he wasn't a problem any longer."

"I wasn't running away from Hercules," said Hawk. "I was running away from that conversation with Artemis and Sword. They were bound to start talking about the Reaper again, and I don't like lying to my friends."

I perched on the stone wall, and watched the constantly shifting patterns of the fountain. "I like Artemis and Sword."

"Cassandra, Artemis, and Sword are three of my closest friends."

"Cassandra still seems to be on good terms with her first husband, Pendragon."

Hawk sat next to me. "Yes, that marriage was always a friendship more than a passionate affair, so they remained friends after the split. Venus keeps making snide comments about that, but Thor is much too sensible to listen to her."

"Venus again. Why were Sword and Artemis warning you about her?"

"Because she's likely to be as big a problem as Hercules."

"I've seen lots of images of Venus, but I don't know much about her."

"Oh, yes," said Hawk sourly. "There are plenty of images of Venus around, with her famous cascades of blonde hair. Usually images of her surrounded by her adoring fans. Venus likes being adored."

"You clearly don't like her. She doesn't like you either?"

"Venus hates me even more than Hercules does. I failed to adore her enough. In fact, I once turned down her advances."

"You turned down Venus?" I shook my head. "I thought you said that none of the female Founder Players had ever been interested in you."

"Venus wasn't interested in me as a person. It happened the first year I fought in the Battle Arena, and half the family came to watch the final duel. Venus offered me her ribbons as a favour to carry in combat, but I turned them down. I'd been wearing Cassandra's scarf in all my previous duels. It would have been horribly rude to toss it aside for Venus's ribbons."

He shrugged his right shoulder. "Anyway, everyone knew Venus was offering me more than her ribbons. She'd always sneered at me until then, but if I won the champion's crown of the Battle Arena then she'd forget about ghastly Michael and reward me with her attentions for an hour or two."

"You didn't like that idea?"

Hawk shuddered. "Definitely not. If it had been one of the other female Founder Players who have a rapid succession of partners, such as Helen, then it would have been a different situation. Helen's relationships are brief, light-hearted fun for both parties. The problem with Venus is that her favours come with a price tag. I've watched her pressure several of my friends into doing things they deeply regretted."

He paused. "So I turned down Venus's offer. I tried to be polite about it, but she took the rejection as the ultimate public insult. She's hated me ever since. She won't like you either, because she'll see you as unfair new competition on Celestius."

I frowned. "Cassandra said the Sisterhood voted unanimously in favour of making me a Founder Player. If Venus didn't want me coming here, why didn't she vote against it?"

"Venus had no choice but to vote the same way as the rest of the Sisterhood. She's had a lot of conflicts with Sword over the centuries, and the situation came to a head at the last party here in the Grand Ballroom. Venus ambushed Sword in one of the bowers, and managed to kiss him just as Artemis arrived. Fortunately, Artemis wasn't fooled for a moment. She and Sword complained to the Sisterhood, and Venus was confined to her castle for three months. Her sentence has only just ended, so Venus has to play the good girl for a while."

"Oh." I thought that over. "So Sword and Artemis are enemies of Venus, and friends of yours. That's why Beowulf gave them the message for you?"

"Exactly. Beowulf wouldn't want to talk to me directly because there's a bit of history between us. Quite a lot of history in fact. I cut off his head once." Hawk grinned. "I'm afraid the family feuds and allegiances get complicated."

I decided not to ask why Hawk had cut off Beowulf's head. "If it was possible to get a stress headache in Game, I think I'd get one from trying to understand your family politics."

"All you really need to know is that Venus will grab any chance to talk to you tonight, and she'll do her best to turn you against me. Please, Jex, if anything worries you, give me the chance to tell my side of the story. I'll do my best to be honest with you."

I sighed. "I can see this is going to be a really fun party."

A group of men were walking down the path towards us. Romulus and Remus were at the back with their arms round each other, but I didn't recognize the other three.

Hawk stood up and pointed at each man in turn. "Jex, you've already met Romulus and Remus. These are Narcissus, Destin, and Louis."

I stood up as well. "I'm pleased to meet you."

The men murmured greetings, and Louis gave a formal bow that included an exaggerated flourish of one arm.

"Hawk," said Romulus. "We need to warn you that Venus is extremely displeased with you."

"As in even more displeased than usual," said Remus.

"I'd already heard about that," said Hawk. "I don't see why

Venus is so annoyed with me. Given a high-speed defrost would have killed her..."

Louis spoke in a voice with a strong French accent. "At the risk of sounding like Hercules, I have to say you were never good with girls, Hawk."

Hawk gave him an angry look.

Louis raised both hands in surrender. "Don't slaughter me, oh mighty warrior. I just feel that given the current situation, someone should point out a fact you've been failing to notice for four centuries. Ever since you established your reputation as Hawk the Unvanquished, Venus has been more interested in you than in any other man. She's obviously going to be furious about you declaring undying love for another woman. Hopefully not furious enough to risk the anger of the Sisterhood, but you should still watch your step."

I blinked. Nothing Hawk had said about Venus had suggested she was seriously interested in him. I turned to Hawk, and saw he looked equally bewildered.

"But Venus has said so many dreadful things about Michael."

Louis sighed. "That's because she kept making hopeful advances towards you, and you kept ignoring them."

Hawk waved his hands in disbelief. "I didn't ignore any advances. Venus never made any. At least, not until that business at the Battle Arena."

Louis shook his head in a sorrowful fashion. "Ah yes, Venus finally despaired of the subtle approach, and bluntly offered you her favour at the Battle Arena. You didn't gratefully worship at her feet. You publicly rejected her. Now you're worshipping another woman instead. Think about it, Hawk."

He faced me, and gave another elaborate bow. "Enchanting Jex, please be careful. You've chosen an exclusive relationship with Hawk. His allies are now your allies, but his enemies are your enemies too, and the female Founder Players are far more deadly than the male."

He turned and walked away, and the other men followed him.

Hawk stared after them. "Louis can't possibly be right about Venus."

Romulus must have heard that, because he turned his head for a moment, and called back to us over his shoulder. "When it comes to family politics, Louis is *always* right."

I waited until the group of men vanished round the corner before speaking. "I'm beginning to think I'd be safer with the Reaper than your family."

"Don't be silly. I realize that the..." Hawk broke off and groaned. "Oh wonderful, Hercules has tracked us down."

The familiar leather-clad figure walked up to us. Hercules bowed and smiled. "Hawk."

"Hercules." Hawk gave him a polite bow in reply, but their eyes met like duellists in the Battle Arena.

Hercules turned to me. "I can't understand why you're settling for Michael, when there are hundreds of single men on Celestius. You could do so much better than someone who makes a habit of cutting your throat."

"I don't make a habit of cutting Jex's throat!" Hawk snapped at him. "You killed Fleur, but I..."

"Let me deal with this," I interrupted, and gave Hercules my frostiest glare. "Why are you approaching me about this? I thought the rules on Celestius were that you accept a woman's relationship decisions without an argument."

Hercules gave me a wary look. "I have accepted your decision, Jex. I only came to speak to you because of the message Michael sent to me this morning. He claimed the situation with Susanna doesn't worry you, but if you knew the real facts then..."

"That's enough!" I shouted. "Leave right now or I'll make a formal complaint to the Sisterhood about you."

"As you wish." Hercules turned and ambled away, with the smug air of someone who'd already said everything he wanted to say.

"I'll kill him," muttered Hawk. "I'll tear his head off and shove it where..."

"Hawk!"

He turned guiltily towards me.

"I told Cassandra that I was in an exclusive relationship with you. She told all the Founder Players about it. That was supposed to put a stop to the problems with Hercules. Why did you send him a message about me?"

Hawk looked at me with a nervous expression that definitely belonged to Michael. "I wanted to make sure that Hercules understood the situation, so I sent him the news myself."

"You mean that you couldn't resist sending Hercules a gloating message?"

"Well, yes," said Hawk.

"So why were you mentioning Susanna in that message? She's the ex-girlfriend you keep running away from, isn't she? The one Game Techs warn you about?"

"I didn't mention her at all in the first message."

I groaned. "The *first* message? How many messages have you been exchanging with Hercules?"

"I'm not sure," said Hawk evasively. "A few."

I groaned again. "I thought that Hercules was the one keeping this childish feud going by sniping at you, but you're just as bad as he is."

Hawk cringed. "I only intended to send Hercules the one message, but he threatened to tell you the details of what happened with Susanna."

"How does Hercules know about Susanna?"

"I was on Starlight watching a concert years ago. Hercules turned up to annoy me, and then a Game Tech appeared and warned me Susanna was coming, so I left at once. Hercules promptly tracked Susanna down, started dating her, and talked her into telling him every awful detail about the past. He's been holding the secret over my head ever since, waiting for the moment when he could use it to do the most damage, which is obviously now."

He paused. "I suppose I'd better tell you the whole humiliating disaster before Hercules does. It was…"

I held up a hand to stop him. "No! You don't have to tell me anything about it. I know Hercules is just trying to cause trouble between us."

"I want to tell you anyway," said Hawk. "You've threatened to report Hercules to the Sisterhood, so he won't dare to cause more trouble himself, but I can guess his next move. Everyone's going round discussing how angry Venus is, so Hercules will tell her everything about Susanna. Venus is bound to find a way to tell you about it, so it's better if I tell you the story myself."

"If you must." I looked down into the water and saw the pool was full of tiny, multicoloured fish. A berry had fallen into the water from a nearby bush, and a shoal of fish chased it in circles, eagerly nibbling at it.

"I should have known right at the start that Susanna wasn't really interested in a mess like Michael. In fact, I did know it. When she started talking to me, I thought it was too good to be true, but after three weeks I was fool enough to believe she..."

He broke off and took a deep breath. "I'm making a mess of this. I should have started by explaining that my father was a teacher. You know how some teenagers get a crush on a teacher. My father was a handsome man and..."

Hawk's words trailed off, and he frowned. "Your face, Jex. You aren't understanding a word of this, are you?"

"No," I admitted. I'd assumed that the split with Susanna had been something to do with sex. Michael had said he'd never had sex in real life, so I'd added two and two together and been braced to hear the details of a disastrous attempt at seduction, but I was just hopelessly confused now.

Hawk hit the palm of his right hand against his forehead. "Of course you don't understand. I'm four hundred bleeping years out of date. So is Hercules. So is Susanna. So is this whole stupid story."

He let his hand drop and laughed. "These days, kids never physically meet their parents; they just get an occasional call from a shadowy figure in Game. They don't get crushes on their teachers, because their teachers work from within Game using a controlled droid, and anyway kids leave school at ten years old."

I still had absolutely no clue what he was talking about. The fish in the pool had eaten their berry but were still hopefully swimming in circles. I reached up to pick another, tossed it into the water, and they instantly gathered round it.

Hawk shook his head. "I've been worrying about Hercules

telling you, terrified what you'd think about Susanna using me as a way to get to my father, but it has no meaning to you at all. Even if I explained the way society worked back then, explained all about families and schools, you still wouldn't understand the humiliation."

"Probably not," I said. "Can we forget about Susanna now?"

He grinned. "Yes, though maybe I should send a message to Hercules to tell him that..."

"No!" I said. "The childish messages have to stop right now. I can't complain to the Sisterhood about Hercules bothering us if you keep sending him messages."

"Point," said Hawk reluctantly. "I just hate letting him have the last word. He knows exactly how to annoy me. The way he twists things round, like saying that I make a habit of cutting your throat."

"Yes, Hercules knows exactly how to annoy you," I said. "That's precisely why you have to stop responding to him, turn your back, and walk away. If you don't, this feud will go on forever, and eventually Hercules will find a way to spoil things between us, make you lose control and do something that I can never forgive."

I took a deep breath and looked him in the eyes. "Hawk, you need to think about whether you want a childish feud with Hercules or an adult relationship with me, because I'm not sure you can have both."

Hawk looked terrified at my ultimatum. He hastily nodded. "You're right. The feud stops right away. I'll let Hercules have the last word."

If the Michael I'd met in the real world had said those words, I'd have believed him. Michael was insecure and vulnerable and very human. He got scared, but did brave things anyway. He'd run from bullies as a child, but he fought for justice now. He had his immature moments, but he wanted to grow up. I loved him for all those things.

Hawk had a lot of the same qualities as Michael, but with the one key difference that the glittering legend of Game was frozen in time. However much Hawk wanted to stop his feud with

Hercules, however many times he promised me it was over, the feud would go on. The only way for it to end was for Hawk to change, and Game wouldn't let him do that.

I'd been worried about the age gap between me and Hawk, and thought that he was too old for me, but the problem was the other way round. Hawk needed to grow up, but he couldn't. I either had to accept him as he was, or walk away, and walking away would be impossibly hard after the things we'd been through together.

My thoughts were interrupted by the sound of bells ringing. I looked round. "What's that?"

"The bells are calling people to gather at the dancing lawn. We'll watch the fireworks together, and then Cassandra will formally introduce you to the family. A whole queue of men will want to dance with you after that, but I hope you'll save several dances for me."

"You can dance? Don't tell me that Michael was a dancer."

"Of course he wasn't. Cassandra forced me to learn to dance centuries ago, so I wouldn't be such a disaster at parties like this one. We'd better go to the dancing lawn now. I'll introduce you to Marcus as soon as we get there. Best to get the worst bit over with right away."

I sighed, and took his arm. "How bad is Marcus?"

"He can often be extremely charming, but his mood changes rapidly. Don't worry though. I'll be standing guard over you to make sure there isn't an unfortunate event."

I didn't want to ask what Hawk meant by an unfortunate event. We walked back towards the dancing lawn, and found a crowd was gathering. Some were standing in groups and talking, while others sat at the tables. The lone man at the table nearest us looked up. He studied me for a moment, and then went back to shuffling pine cones on the table in front of him. I watched him out of the corner of my eye as Hawk led me past.

"Who is that?" I asked. "I don't recognize him."

"That's Thought." Hawk smiled. "You wouldn't recognize him because I don't think he's ever left Celestius. Thought likes order and patterns. He acts as both judge and jury in all the trials on Celestius, because everyone knows that he won't be swayed by personal likes or dislikes when deciding on guilt or punishments. Now brace yourself for the introduction to Marcus."

We walked towards a man with short dark hair, and clothes that were vaguely Roman in style. He was sitting at a seat by himself, and people seemed to be giving him a wide berth. Thor and Cassandra were standing nearby, chatting to a couple of men. The group all had their eyes fixed on Marcus.

When Thor saw us coming, he raised one finger. Hawk nodded in response to the signal, and leant to whisper a few words in my ear.

"We should keep this very short." His left hand tightened on my arm, he led me up to Marcus, and spoke in more normal tones. "Marcus, this is Jex. You must have heard about her coming to Celestius."

Marcus looked at me first, then his eyes drifted to Hawk standing on one side of me, and to Thor standing barely two paces away. Finally, he looked straight at me again.

"Cassandra told me all about you, Jex. I'm very pleased to meet you."

He seemed perfectly normal, even pleasant. "I'm pleased to meet you too, Marcus," I said.

"It's nice to see a new face for a change. A very lovely one too."

"Thank you."

"Perhaps you could tell me something about yourself," said Marcus. "I lead a very boring life, and I've heard everyone else's stories too many times already."

Hawk stirred restively at my side. "Another time perhaps. I'm afraid we have to move on now. Poor Jex has to be introduced to the whole family this evening."

"That's a shame," said Marcus.

I smiled. "Well, I'm sure we'll get to chat for longer another time."

"I look forward to drinking your blood, Jex." Marcus smiled back at me. His tone of voice was so calm and agreeable that my mind had to replay the words before I could take them in.

"I'm planning to keep my blood," I said.

"Time to go." Hawk took my arm and towed me firmly away, while giving Thor a meaningful look. "Marcus enjoys saying that sort of thing and watching how people react. I think he's testing whether they'd make a good victim or not. It's definitely time to move on, but at least we managed the introduction."

As we walked across the empty centre of the dancing lawn, Hawk was looking thoughtfully around at the people. "We've dealt with Hercules and Marcus, but there are a few more awkward introductions to come. The biggest problem is going to be Venus. She's busily watching us right now."

Hawk pointed across at where a woman with long blonde hair was sitting at a table. He was right. Venus was surrounded by several laughing men, but she was staring at us.

"Over at the far end of the lawn," Hawk continued, "you can see a group of a dozen men. They don't have any especial reason to target either you or me, but I'd still suggest avoiding them as much as possible. That's the group who had the big clash with the Sisterhood in the early days. If they weren't Founder Players, they'd either be on Havoc along with the other trolls, or in Game prison."

I wrinkled my nose. "Everyone here sounds so attractive."

Hawk laughed. "It's really not that bad. I've pointed out all the dangerous ones now except for Chiron. He's permanently confined to his castle, but at some point we'll need to take our turn to go and see him."

"Take our turn?"

"Chiron likes having visitors, so the family try to make sure someone goes to see him every day. We do the same for Marcus when he lets us. As Cassandra told you, Marcus often locks himself away for long periods, not answering calls or accepting any visitors."

I had an odd dizzy moment. I'd scared myself to death thinking that the Reaper might have reached Celestius by taking Hawk's place in the Game. I'd been deeply thankful to be proved wrong. Now I realized my idea could have been half right after all.

CHAPTER THIRTY-FIVE

Hawk's arm was round me, steadying me. He gave me a worried look. "Is something wrong?"

"I just realized the Reaper might be a Founder Player after all."

"I hope you haven't gone back to thinking the Reaper replaced me."

"No, but start from the same logic," I said. "The Reaper could replace a Founder Player who wasn't in Game."

"I don't see where you're going with this. I'm the only Founder Player that's left Game in the last three centuries."

I ignored that. "When the Reaper heard you'd worked out the bomber was a Game Tech, he got worried. He prepared an escape route so if things went badly wrong he could give himself a new identity as a player. He also made himself a deletion weapon. We thought he'd made that to use later on, but what if we were wrong? What if the Reaper made that weapon because he needed it to prepare his escape route?"

Hawk frowned but didn't say anything.

"The Reaper was a Game Tech, so he could enter a castle on Celestius and use his deletion weapon on a Founder Player. He'd choose a victim who regularly locked himself in his castle and didn't respond to calls or visitors, so no one would notice he was missing for weeks or even months."

"You mean Marcus," said Hawk. "The Reaper could have used his deletion weapon to eliminate Marcus from Game, and then hidden the weapon somewhere in the castle before leaving."

"Poor Marcus," I said.

Hawk nodded. "Yes. He wouldn't have stood a chance. Once the real Marcus was gone, the Reaper could set up his escape route to recreate himself in Marcus's place. It would be easy to act the part of someone that unpredictable. The Reaper could make any number of mistakes, and the family would just dismiss it as another of Marcus's odd moments."

He paused. "The question is whether that actually happened. Is that Marcus back there or the Reaper?"

"And if it is the Reaper, then what is he planning for the future? To act the part of Marcus, make a gradual recovery, and be let out of his castle to roam the worlds of Game?"

"The Game Techs would never believe Marcus was sufficiently recovered to be set free," said Hawk. "They understand only too well that people can't change their basic natures within Game."

"And the Reaper would know that." I relaxed. "Marcus is just himself then. The Reaper's escape route was aimed at giving himself a new life as a player. He wouldn't sentence himself to spending eternity locked in Marcus's castle."

"But the Reaper's goal was power," said Hawk. "If his bid to rule Game failed, would he really want a new life as a mere player? Perhaps he'd choose to replace Marcus to give himself the best chance of taking revenge on the Founder Players."

I fought the urge to turn round and look at Marcus. "But if that's what happened, and the Reaper's goal is revenge, then he's got the perfect chance here and now."

"Oh yes," said Hawk, in a grim voice. "You're here. I'm here. The whole family is here. I've got my armour and weapons with me because I don't trust Hercules, but most of us are defenceless. The Reaper's best move will be to wait until it's fully dark and the fireworks start. The noise will cover up any warning screams, so he'll be able to kill a lot of us in the darkness."

I instinctively glanced across to where the sky was blazing red with the setting sun. "We've got that same problem again," I said. "How can we be sure if it's Marcus or not?"

"That's simple," said Hawk. "I'll threaten to kill him. If this is the real Marcus, he'll be unarmed, because he isn't allowed weapons. If this is the Reaper, he'll have the deletion weapon hidden on him. He'll try to use it to kill me permanently. I'll Game kill him instead."

"There has to be a safer way to handle this. We should call Kwame."

Hawk shook his head. "Cassandra, Thor, Pendragon, and Ulysses are with Marcus right now, keeping watch on him. If the Reaper sees a Game Tech appear, he won't wait to ask why. He'll start by killing Cassandra, and then take down as many of the rest of the family as he can."

"Then we should go somewhere out of sight and call Kwame."

"There isn't time for that," said Hawk. "It's already nearly dark."

I glanced at the sky again, and bit my lip. Hawk was right.

"We have to keep everything looking normal until Marcus is alone with me," said Hawk. "You'll start walking back with me, but then stop, pretend you need to adjust your hair or something. I'll carry on to reach Marcus, get rid of the others, and then challenge him. If he reaches for a weapon, I'll be ready. Whatever happens, promise you'll keep safely away from us."

I nodded. "Hawk."

"Yes?"

I couldn't stop him doing this. Cassandra would be the Reaper's first target, and Hawk had loved her as his sister for four hundred years. "Be very careful."

Hawk smiled at me, and I took his arm. We walked at a carefully casual speed across the empty circle of grass, heading back towards Marcus. Cassandra was standing only two paces away from him. Thor was at her side, with his arm round her. Pendragon and Ulysses were a little further away. Many more of the family, far too many more of the family, were standing in scattered groups, or sitting at tables nearby.

Marcus turned to look in our direction. He'd seen us coming towards him. If he was the Reaper, he'd wait to let us get closer before he started his massacre. Of all the Founder Players, we were the two he'd most want to kill.

We were halfway there now. I felt Hawk give a meaningful tug at my arm. It was time for me to do my act.

I faked a stumble, and took my hand from Hawk's arm. "I knew these heels were too high. I'll catch you up in a minute."

I stooped to check my sandals, while Hawk walked on. Thor and Cassandra turned to look at him coming, and he waved his right hand in a casual signal that they should let him talk to Marcus alone.

The situation looked under control. Pendragon and Ulysses were already several paces clear of Marcus. Thor and Cassandra were moving away too.

Then Venus wrecked everything. She must have seen me standing there alone on the dancing lawn, and decided this was a golden opportunity to spill poison into my ear, because she started running towards me. Her route took her straight past Marcus, and he whirled round and grabbed her out-flung arm, yanking her towards him.

Hawk stopped and stood there hesitating, his eyes on them both.

"What are you doing, Marcus?" asked Cassandra. "Please let Venus go."

"But I don't want to let her go," said Marcus.

"Cassandra, stay back!" said Hawk. Other people were coming to see what was happening, and Hawk waved frantically at them. "Everyone, stay back!"

"Let me go, Marcus!" demanded Venus. "Someone make him let me go!"

Thor moved forward, but Hawk shook his head. "Let me deal with Marcus. You get Cassandra out of here."

Thor frowned, but turned to his wife, and tugged her firmly back to join the rest of the watching crowd. I was still standing alone in the centre of the dancing lawn. I'd promised to stay here, and I could do nothing to help Hawk. I'd change that in future, I'd train for hours every day until I became a legendary fighter myself, better than Artemis or any other female player in Game, but right now I was nothing but a liability.

"Why aren't you helping me?" Venus looked at Hawk

accusingly. "Why are you letting Marcus maul me like this? You're doing this out of revenge, aren't you? You brought that dreadful, clueless girl to Celestius out of revenge too. All because I wasn't interested in awful, tongue tied, Michael."

"We can trade insults later if you like," said Hawk. "You can remind everyone about the ghastliness of Michael, and I can talk about Eliza's whining voice and ferret teeth, but right now you'd better shut your mouth."

Venus gasped. Hawk ignored her outraged face and looked at Marcus.

"Let her go, Marcus. It's time you went home now."

"Game command!" shouted Venus. "Request Game Tech assistance."

A female Game Tech appeared, and looked at the scene with startled eyes. A second later, Kwame appeared next to her.

"Make Marcus let me go!" demanded Venus.

"Let me deal with this, Kwame," said Hawk.

At the mention of his name, Kwame gave Hawk a look of surprise that changed into comprehension. "Player Marcus," he said, "please release player Venus."

Marcus didn't respond to him. His eyes were fixed on Hawk. "You know what I am," he said. "You know who I am. You know what I have."

"Yes, I do," said Hawk, "and we both know that Venus is irrelevant to this."

"Yes, she is," said Marcus. "You've no reason to care whether Venus lives or dies."

Venus tried changing her tactics. "Marcus," she cooed. "Why are you holding me so tightly? You don't want to hurt me. We could be friends and..."

She broke off as Marcus twisted her arm, and there was a sickening cracking sound, like a stick breaking. Venus screamed. One loud desperate yell of pain, then Marcus literally threw her at Hawk, and jumped towards me.

I was far away in the centre of the dancing lawn. It was utterly impossible for Marcus to cover that distance in a single jump, but he did it, flying high through the air and landing right next to me. Before I had time to react, he had his left arm round me, and his right hand pressing something into my side.

"I have the right hostage now, Hawk," he said. "I can use my deletion knife to kill your lady love very permanently. Now, let's negotiate."

Venus was lying on the ground now, whimpering and clutching her right arm. Hawk was ignoring her, his eyes fixed on me and Marcus.

"What do you want?" he asked.

"I want Hawk the Unvanquished," said the Reaper. "You walk over here, put your sword on the ground, and surrender to me. I'll kill you, and then let Jex go."

"It seems unlikely you'll actually let her go," said Hawk.

"Of course it's unlikely," said the Reaper, "but it's possible, isn't it? You might manage to buy her life with yours. If you don't try, then you know I'll kill her very permanently."

He laughed in my ear and pulled me closer to him. "You love her, don't you? Always. You're such a romantic, Hawk. Think about what will happen if you don't do what I say. You'd have to live forever with the knowledge that you stood by and watched me murder the woman you loved. You won't do that, will you, Hawk?"

Hawk raised his right hand in the air. "Durendal!" The sword flew out of its sheath and hovered above him. Hawk hesitated for a moment before taking hold of the hilt. "That's how you managed that jump."

"Very bright," said the Reaper. "Yes, I couldn't give myself superhuman speed or strength, but this is a standard feature on a two-handed weapon, projecting the item a given distance in a given direction. It was easy for me to add the same feature to a ring so I could use it on myself."

Hawk lowered his sword and frowned down at it. I kept perfectly still and silent, but I was thinking desperately hard. The Reaper was holding his death knife to my side. If Hawk surrendered to him, then he'd kill us both. The only possible way out of this was for me to die. I had to make the Reaper kill me, so Hawk would be free to fight for his life and the lives of the other Founder Players.

Then I remembered when I'd played the sacrifice victim. There'd been a better answer than the obvious one then, and the same was true now. The only possible way out of this was for me to die, but...

I watched Hawk walk towards us, saw his head bow as he prepared to lay down his weapon, and screamed the words that he would understand but the Reaper wouldn't. "Hawk. What Hercules said. Make it a habit!"

Hawk lifted his head, hesitated for a fraction of a second, and then swung Durendal's blade through the air. The Reaper instinctively dodged, but I held still for the razor sharp edge. There was a flash of pure agony as Hawk cut off my head and I died.

CHAPTER THIRTY-SIX

I seemed to be hanging in midair in total darkness. I could see nothing. I could hear nothing. My neck burned as if it was on fire, the pain spreading through my whole body and reaching an agonizing crescendo before gradually fading away. I still couldn't see or hear anything, and now I couldn't feel anything either.

I was dead. That much was certain, but I didn't know if Hawk had managed to kill me before the Reaper did. If I'd been slain by the great sword, Durendal, then I had died a Game death, and I would resurrect in my castle on Celestius. If the Reaper had killed me with his knife, then this was a final death, and I would never return either to real life or to the Game.

My body would sleep forever in a frozen coffin, with no mind to return to it. I would never ride on a winged horse again, or walk under Ganymede's sky. I'd never see the shining wonders of Starlight, or experience life as one of the merfolk of Coral. I'd never make love to a glittering legend of the Game, or to an insecure kid called Michael.

Even if I survived this, Hawk might not. I'd left the legendary hero to fight a fallen god of Game, left him to use Durendal against a weapon that could delete players from existence. At least Hawk could fight now, instead of surrendering his life in a vain attempt to save mine.

Despite his words and his actions, part of me had never really believed Hawk loved me until now. I knew that Nathan believed it, Hercules believed it, Kwame believed it, but how could I think that Hawk the Unvanquished could truly love a girl from the body stacks? Michael could, yes, but not Hawk.

I didn't doubt it any longer though. He'd proved it when he prepared to lay down Durendal, because he'd been Hawk then, and I knew exactly how Hawk would describe surrendering like that. He'd say it was a bleeping stupid thing to do.

Hawk would have made that utterly pointless sacrifice for me, knowing that it only meant two deaths instead of one. The Reaper would never have let me live. He'd lost any chance of power, and had no way to escape justice, so he'd take as much revenge as he could on his enemies before he was captured.

The blackness slowly brightened, and I saw the grey plain that I'd seen when I entered Game. It could be a good sign, or perhaps it just meant that as my body froze, and my mind left it to enter the Game, I had in some way been close to death.

The plain had been featureless before, and there had been the sound of people whispering. There were whispers now too, but this time I could see things as well. The Kraken's saucer-like eyes watched me from a pool of water, and its beak of a mouth seemed to be trying to say something to me. Nathan walked by, holding a tiny world in his hands, frowning with concentration as he carved continents and oceans into its surface. Hawk stood ahead of me, a giant figure, ten times my size or more.

A figure in Game Tech uniform appeared by my right side. I turned and saw it was Kwame.

"Am I alive?" I asked Kwame.

"That is correct."

Another figure appeared on my left. Another Game Tech, a stranger this time, with diamond insignia on his cheeks.

"Am I dead?" I asked the Reaper.

"That is correct."

Then the plain suddenly vanished, and I was in the great hall of my castle. The real Kwame was standing in front of me, while Hawk sat next to him, slumped on the marble floor, with his head in his hands. Nathan's face watched anxiously from a mirror on the wall.

I stared at them for a second before speaking, unsure if this was another vision or real. This was my big chance to say a heroic and memorable sentence, but being me I came out with something ridiculous.

"What happened to the regulations about a player's home being private?"

"Game Techs are allowed to enter a house without permission when a player's safety is known to be at risk," said Kwame. "I admit that bringing player Hawk with me was unprecedented, but so was the situation."

I laughed.

Hawk slowly lifted his head and looked at me. He took a deep breath, but he didn't move or say anything. I was feeling terribly shaky, so I decided to join him in sitting on the floor.

Nathan was grinning widely now. "We've been pretty worried about you, Jex. It wasn't clear whether the Reaper or Hawk killed you. A Game death automatically sends you into the resurrection process. That's carried out by the Game world transfer system, and at any time that holds millions of people who are moving between Game worlds."

He paused. "We'd no way of knowing which of those millions of constreams was yours, or whether you were in there at all. We just had to wait to see if you reappeared in your castle, and the resurrection process takes far longer than just moving between worlds."

I looked at Hawk. He hadn't said a word yet, and was still white and shocked. "The Reaper?" I asked.

"The Reaper is dead. I took his own weapon and used it on him."

"I was expecting to see passionate hugs at this point," said Nathan pointedly.

Hawk shook his head and spoke in defeated tones. "There's always a price."

I stared at him in bewilderment. "What?"

"When I realized what you were suggesting, Jex, I knew you were right. The only way to save your life and defeat the Reaper was to kill you, but I knew the price. I'd seen this happen with Fleur and Hercules. A player's first Game death is a traumatic experience. Fleur never forgave him."

Now I'd caught up with Hawk's thinking. "Hercules killed Fleur with a stupid practical joke. This was very different. The Reaper was expecting you to attack him. If you'd tried it, he was ready to kill me permanently, but he wasn't expecting you to attack me instead. I'm just glad that Hawk the Unvanquished could move fast enough to kill me before the Reaper got over his surprise."

Hawk didn't say anything. I could tell from the lifeless look in his eyes that I wasn't getting through to him.

"This is like that idea you had before, isn't it?" I asked. "The hero against the gods one, where it always ends badly for the hero. You thought that it would end up with you defeating the Reaper, but dying in real life."

"There's always a price," he repeated.

"No, there isn't. You defeated the Reaper, you didn't die, and I didn't die either."

"You didn't die because I had to give you up instead."

I groaned. "You're not Hercules, I'm not Fleur, and this isn't some... some bleeping Greek tragedy. The Reaper is dead, I'm alive, and I have a lot of plans for things I want to do in Game."

I stretched out a hand towards Hawk, and he touched my fingertips cautiously with his own.

"You two really need to work on those passionate hugs," said Nathan.

I ignored him, keeping my eyes fixed on Hawk. "You've got a part to play in those plans. Don't you want us to walk the beaches of Ganymede, visit Starlight, and go riding together on a winged horse?"

And suddenly Hawk's face was alive again, his expression a mixture of laughter and embarrassment. "Of course I..."

He broke off and turned to Kwame. "Thank you for your help. I'm sure you have a lot of other things to do now."

"That is correct." Kwame took the hint and vanished.

I glanced at the mirror, saw Nathan was still watching us, and coughed pointedly. "We'd like privacy now, Nathan."

"Oh. Right. I'll end the call then." The mirror went black for a second, before changing back to showing a reflection of the room.

Hawk's hand took mine. "What now, Jex?"

"If the Reaper is dead, then there's no need for me to hide away on Celestius any longer. As I recall, we were having a special moment on Ganymede when Nathan interrupted us with a call."

Hawk smiled. "Yes, we were. Game command. Request group Game world transfer to Jex private beach on Ganymede."

There was the blurring sensation of transferring between worlds, and we were no longer sitting on a marble floor but on soft sand. There was a faint, mauve mistiness to the air, and it held the scent of flowers mixed with spices and sea salt.

Hawk and I lay back on the sand, and gazed up at the fiery whirlpools of Jupiter's storms for a few minutes in silence. My father had lived here on Ganymede for over a century, walking its beaches and helping its people. The Reaper had killed him with his bombs, and Hawk and I had killed the Reaper in turn. Now my father's name would be listed on the memorial on Avalon, but I would never go there to see it. For me, my father's memorial would always be Ganymede itself.

Finally, Hawk spoke. "The last time we were on this beach, I'd just kissed you when Nathan called us. Would it be rushing things if I kissed you again?"

My father had told me that you should remember the past but live for the future. "I don't think another kiss would be rushing things at all."

Hawk's face blocked my view of the glorious sky, and I closed my eyes to concentrate on the warmth of his lips meeting mine. Jupiter, in all its splendid majesty, waited patiently for our attention.

CHAPTER THIRTY-SEVEN

Hawk and I stood looking out from the balcony of my castle. Several weeks had passed since the traumatic day when Hawk cut off my head, and the whole population of Game must have watched the replays of the final battle on Celestius a dozen times or more.

Everyone believed that Marcus had truly been the Reaper, and had helped and encouraged Tomath with the bombings out of pure joy at spreading destruction and death. There were a couple of obvious weak points in that story, such as how Tomath had managed to get the deletion weapon to Marcus when he was confined to his castle on Celestius, and why Marcus would help Tomath bomb his own world.

The Game Techs had covered the first point by explaining that they'd had to shut down Celestius to make changes to its server configuration. This had been done while the Founder Players were meeting in the Amphitheatre, but the Game Techs had needed to move Marcus and Chiron to another Game world for an hour or two.

That much was perfectly true, but the Game Techs had added some extra details. They claimed that Marcus had asked to spend that time at his house on Camelot, where he'd lived for a couple of years before being put under house arrest on Celestius. The Game Techs said that they'd agreed to what seemed a reasonable request, not knowing that Marcus and Tomath had been friends on Camelot, and Tomath had used Marcus's old house as a safe place to store his enhanced items and deletion weapon.

The other Founder Players explained the second point themselves. They all found it perfectly believable that Marcus would be attracted by the idea of crashing Celestius and killing a lot of the family, and that he'd find it even more amusing if there was a risk of him dying himself.

It seemed unfair to me that Marcus was made doubly the Reaper's victim, first being killed by him and then being blamed for his actions, but the truth was impossible to explain without admitting the Reaper had been a Game Tech. Hawk said that it wasn't as if Marcus had any friends who'd be hurt by the deception, but that made it seem even sadder to me.

My status on Celestius had changed now. Most of the Founder Players had seen what happened at the party, and they'd all watched the replays countless times. They'd seen the look on my face as I saw death coming and wondered which death it would be. They'd seen Hawk's expression of despair when he cut off my head.

They didn't think of me as an unprecedented newcomer any longer. I'd been a key part of the most dramatic event that had ever happened on Celestius, and that made me part of the family too. I even had my very own family feud with Venus.

Hawk and I still had one thing to sort out though. "Are you sure you want to do this?" I asked. "I'm not forcing you into it. There are times when you're maddeningly childish, but there are times when you're unbelievably heroic. I've decided I can put up with one for the sake of the other."

"I'm not doing this for you," said Hawk. "I'm doing this for myself. I've spent four centuries acting the part of Hawk. Four centuries trying to deal with the issues of Michael. Four centuries locked in a destructive cycle of childish feuds with Hercules."

He shook his head. "For all that time, I knew the only way for me to solve my problems was to go back to the real world and do some growing up, but I couldn't face doing that. Now I've been back to the real world once to meet you and chase the Reaper, the idea of going back again doesn't seem so daunting."

He paused. "I have to go back to the real world, Jex, but you don't have to come with me. I'll only be gone for a year. You could wait here in Game for me to return."

"I'm coming with you. The best way for us to build the equal partnership I want is to spend a year together as two ordinary eighteen-year-olds in the real world."

I gave Hawk a mischievous look. "I can introduce you to all my old friends. If you're lucky, then Falcon may let you act a part in his next re-enactment."

Hawk groaned.

"By the time we're back in Game," I added, "people should have forgotten that stupid name they've given me."

"I'm afraid that's unlikely, Jex the Deathless."

I winced. "I feel that being called Jex the Deathless is asking for trouble."

"I've always felt that being called Hawk the Unvanquished was asking for trouble. I spent several decades objecting to it, but it didn't do any good. I was stuck with it, and I'm afraid you're stuck with your name too. The whole of Game has seen the replays of you surviving what could easily have been two real life deaths."

I gazed up at two winged horses that were circling overhead, sighed, and made myself say the words. "Game command. Request Game Tech assistance."

After a few seconds, a figure in Game Tech uniform appeared.

"Yesterday, Hawk and I requested that our bodies should be defrosted," I said. "Is everything ready for us to..." I broke off in shock. The face of the man wearing the anonymous uniform was a little older and more handsome than in real life, and he had blue Game Tech insignia on his cheeks, but he was still easy to recognize.

"Nath..." I broke off the greeting as I remembered the Game Tech regulations. "I've never seen blue insignia before. Trainee status?"

"That is correct," said Nathan, his face impassive. "Your bodies have been defrosted as requested. Do you wish to leave Game now?"

"I don't exactly wish to leave Game," said Hawk, "but yes, it's time for us to go." He paused to give that characteristic, one-shouldered shrug. "Perhaps Michael will grow up to be a bit like Hawk."

"I think Michael has always been a lot closer to being Hawk than you realized," I said.

"Should it be of use to you," said Nathan, "there is a room with the rent paid until the end of this month, and a job vacancy in the body stacks."

Hawk nodded. "That will be a good starting point."

"Nathan, is there any chance we'll see you when we re-enter Game again?" I asked.

"Whenever you wish assistance in future," he said, "please request a Game Tech, and one of suitable rank will respond."

I understood the message. The Game Techs had bent the rules, let Nathan come this once as a special gesture, but it wouldn't happen again. He was a Game Tech now, and this was goodbye forever.

"I'd give you a hug," I said, "but I understand the reasons for the barrier between the Game Techs and the players. You deserved Celestius too. I hope you're happy with your choice."

For one brief second, Nathan allowed his face to change from the mask-like expression of a Game Tech, to one of pure pride and delight. "That is correct."

There was moisture in my eyes, but I blinked away the tears. It would be entirely wrong to cry when Nathan had achieved his dream. Hawk and I were among the legendary ones, the Founder Players, but Nathan was a Game Tech. He would be a god of the Game, and a far better one than the Reaper. Nathan would create not destroy.

"The mental transition of leaving Game will be easier lying down," said Nathan.

Two flower-strewn couches appeared on the balcony next to us. I lay down on one, and Hawk the Unvanquished lay on the other. I took one last look up at the circling winged horses and closed my eyes.

"I'm ready," I said.

"I'm ready too," said Hawk.

I saw the grey plain again. There was one person standing in the centre of it, a blond-haired man dressed in leather armour. He pointed his finger at me.

"Michael belongs to me not you."

"Michael belongs to himself," I said.

The blond-haired man grew transparent before vanishing completely. Where he'd been standing, the grey dust of the plain was covered with flowers.

Everything went black for a moment after that, and then I heard a familiar voice speaking. "Are you awake yet?"

I opened my eyes to find I was lying on a medical table with two controlled medical droids looking down at me. I turned my head sideways, and saw the black-haired boy lying on the next table. He rolled on his side to face me and smiled.

I smiled back at him. Nathan was a Game Tech. Jex the Deathless was sleeping in her castle on Celestius with Hawk the Unvanquished at her side. I was back in the real world with Michael.

Message From Janet Edwards

Thank you for reading Reaper. This book is set in the Game Future, but I also have book series set in two very different future universes. The Portal Future where the invention of interstellar portals has allowed humanity to colonize hundreds of worlds scattered across distant star systems. The Hive Future where humanity lives in vast hive cities.

Please visit my website, www.janetedwards.com, to see the current list of my books. You can also make sure you don't miss future books by signing up to get an email alert when there's a new release.

    Best wishes from Janet Edwards

Printed in Great Britain
by Amazon

84484911R00202